STAR WARS

SHADOW GAMES

SHADOW GAMES

MICHAEL REAVES AND
MAYA KAATHRYN BOHNHOFF

arrow books

Published by Arrow 2011

2 4 6 8 10 9 7 5 3 1

First published in Great Britain in 2011 by
Arrow
Random House, 20 Vauxhall Bridge Road,
London SW1V 2SA

www.starwars.com
www.randomhouse.co.uk

Addresses for companies within The Random House Group Limited can be found at:
www.randomhouse.co.uk

The Random House Group Limited Reg. No. 954009

A CIP catalogue record for this book is available from the British Library

ISBN 9780099542834

The Random House Group Limited supports The Forest Stewardship Council
(FSC®), the leading international forest certification organisation. Our books
carrying the FSC label are printed on FSC® certified paper. FSC is the only
forest certification scheme endorsed by the leading environmental organisations,
including Greenpeace. Our paper procurement policy can be found at:
www.randomhouse.co.uk/environment

Printed and bound by CPI Group (UK) Ltd, Croydon, CR0 4YY

This one's for Gerry Conway
—MR

For Stan Schmidt,
who bought my first-ever science fiction story
—MKB

ACKNOWLEDGMENTS

I'd like to thank our inestimable editors, David Pomerico and Shelly Shapiro, who herded their cats with patience and good humor. (I especially appreciated David's "out-of-office messages.") Also thanks to Sue and Leland at Lucasfilm, Ltd. for their assistance with research and continuity, to Dan Wallace and Jason Fry for their very helpful resource manual, and to the team of researchers who put together the Star Wars Encyclopedia that now resides on my laptop. Also, kudos to the team of volunteers at Wookieepedia for helping me to find things. And a special shout-out to all the fans who have built beautiful *Star Wars*–related websites as a labor of love. You guys are why we write these books in the first place.

—MKB

THE STAR WARS NOVELS TIMELINE

OLD REPUBLIC
5000–33 YEARS BEFORE
STAR WARS: A New Hope

*Lost Tribe of the Sith**
Precipice
Skyborn
Paragon
Savior
Purgatory
Sentinel

3650 *YEARS BEFORE STAR WARS: A New Hope*

The Old Republic: Deceived
*Lost Tribe of the Sith**
Pantheon
Secrets

Red Harvest

The Old Republic: Fatal Alliance

1032 *YEARS BEFORE STAR WARS: A New Hope*

Knight Errant

Darth Bane: Path of Destruction
Darth Bane: Rule of Two
Darth Bane: Dynasty of Evil

RISE OF THE EMPIRE
33–0 YEARS BEFORE
STAR WARS: A New Hope

Darth Maul: Saboteur*
Cloak of Deception
Darth Maul: Shadow Hunter

32 *YEARS BEFORE STAR WARS: A New Hope*

STAR WARS: EPISODE I
THE PHANTOM MENACE

Rogue Planet
Outbound Flight
The Approaching Storm

22 *YEARS BEFORE STAR WARS: A New Hope*

STAR WARS: EPISODE II
ATTACK OF THE CLONES

22–19 *YEARS BEFORE STAR WARS: A New Hope*

The Clone Wars
The Clone Wars: Wild Space
The Clone Wars: No Prisoners

Clone Wars Gambit
Stealth
Siege

Republic Commando
Hard Contact
Triple Zero
True Colors
Order 66

Shatterpoint
The Cestus Deception
The Hive*
MedStar I: Battle Surgeons
MedStar II: Jedi Healer
Jedi Trial
Yoda: Dark Rendezvous
Labyrinth of Evil

19 *YEARS BEFORE STAR WARS: A New Hope*

STAR WARS: EPISODE III
REVENGE OF THE SITH

Dark Lord: The Rise of Darth Vader
Imperial Commando 501st

Coruscant Nights
Jedi Twilight
Street of Shadows
Patterns of Force

The Han Solo Trilogy
The Paradise Snare
The Hutt Gambit
Rebel Dawn

The Adventures of Lando Calrissian
The Force Unleashed
The Han Solo Adventures
Death Troopers
The Force Unleashed II

*An eBook novella
**Forthcoming

REBELLION
0–5 YEARS AFTER
STAR WARS: A New Hope

Death Star
Shadow Games

0

STAR WARS: EPISODE IV
A NEW HOPE

Tales from the Mos Eisley Cantina
Tales from the Empire
Tales from the New Republic
Allegiance
Choices of One
Galaxies: The Ruins of Dantooine
Splinter of the Mind's Eye

3 *YEARS AFTER STAR WARS: A New Hope*

STAR WARS: EPISODE V
THE EMPIRE STRIKES BACK

Tales of the Bounty Hunters
Shadows of the Empire

4 *YEARS AFTER STAR WARS: A New Hope*

STAR WARS: EPISODE VI
RETURN OF THE JEDI

Tales from Jabba's Palace

The Bounty Hunter Wars
  The Mandalorian Armor
  Slave Ship
  Hard Merchandise

The Truce at Bakura
Luke Skywalker and the Shadows of
Mindor

 NEW REPUBLIC
5–25 YEARS AFTER
STAR WARS: A New Hope

X-Wing
  Rogue Squadron
  Wedge's Gamble
  The Krytos Trap
  The Bacta War
  Wraith Squadron
  Iron Fist
  Solo Command

The Courtship of Princess Leia
A Forest Apart*
Tatooine Ghost

The Thrawn Trilogy
  Heir to the Empire
  Dark Force Rising
  The Last Command

X-Wing: Isard's Revenge

The Jedi Academy Trilogy
  Jedi Search
  Dark Apprentice
  Champions of the Force

I, Jedi
Children of the Jedi
Darksaber
Planet of Twilight
X-Wing: Starfighters of Adumar
The Crystal Star

The Black Fleet Crisis Trilogy
  Before the Storm
  Shield of Lies
  Tyrant's Test

The New Rebellion

The Corellian Trilogy
  Ambush at Corellia
  Assault at Selonia
  Showdown at Centerpoint

The Hand of Thrawn Duology
  Specter of the Past
  Vision of the Future

Fool's Bargain*
Survivor's Quest

*An eBook novella
**Forthcoming

THE STAR WARS NOVELS TIMELINE

DRAMATIS PERSONAE

Arno D'Vox; commander, Bannistar Station (human male)

Arruna Var; Javul Charn's engineer (Twi'lek female)

Bran Finnick; first officer, *Nova's Heart* (human male)

Dash Rendar; smuggler (human male)

Eaden Vrill; smuggler (Nautolan male)

Edge; assassin (Anomid male)

Han Solo; captain, *Millennium Falcon* (human male)

Hityamun "Hitch" Kris; Black Sun Vigo (human male)

Javul Charn; holostar (human female)

Kendara "Spike" Farlion; Javul Charn's road manager (human female)

Leebo; repair droid (masculine droid)

Nik; cargo master's assistant (Sullustan male)

Oto; service droid (masculine droid)

"Red" Rishyk; security chief Bannistar Station (human male)

Serdor Marrak; captain, *Nova's Heart* (Zabrak male)

Tereez Dza'lar; Javul Charn's costumier (Bothan female)

Yanus Melikan; Javul Charn's cargo master (human male)

A long time ago in a galaxy far, far away . . .

ONE

"THIS IS IT, EADEN. THIS IS THE DAY WE ONE-UP SOLO."

Dash Rendar sat back in the pilot's chair of the *Outrider*, feeling an almost palpable sense of satisfaction. It was a good feeling—nearly tingly, in fact. And he expected to relive it every time he bragged about how fast he'd done the Kessel Run. It was, after all, acknowledged to be the ultimate test of a pilot's skill . . . and propensity for risk taking. Every time you ran it, you risked your cargo, your life, and your reputation, but you got your goods where they were going faster than more cautious pilots *and* you could walk into any port with a swagger in your step. The faster your time, the bigger your swagger.

"Hubris," said Eaden Vrill, his dark, liquid gaze on the tactical display. His voice was a low rumble, more suited for underwater communication than atmospheric, and his Basic took some getting used to, with its hard-edged fricatives and sibilants. Dash was used to it; he and the Nautolan had been partners for some time.

"Confidence," Dash retorted, annoyed at being pulled out of his pleasant reverie. "The *Outrider* is twice the ship the *Falcon* is." As far as he was concerned Solo's boat was a scow compared with Dash's heavily modified YT-2400.

Eaden glanced at him. "You confuse pride of possession with a distinct entity. The ship is not you, nor did you build it. Its speed—"

"Is largely the result of *my* expert modifications."

"Beg to differ," the Nautolan replied. "The improvements are almost entirely the result of repairs carried out by LE-BO2D9. The rest is unarguably the result of my superior navigation skills."

Dash glanced at his navigator. "*Now* who's overweening? Hubris, my—"

"You imply that I'm boasting. I'm not—but feel free to correct me if I've misinterpreted your colorful patois. I am concentrating." He hesitated, then added: "We're entering the Pit."

Reason enough to concentrate, Dash knew. He rocked his seat forward, hitting the comm button on the pilot's console as he did. "Hey, Leebo, we're headed into the Pit."

"Imagine my excitement." The reply came back in the sarcastic voice of the repair droid's previous owner, Kood Gareeda—a stand-up comic who toured the Rim perpetually. Dash had seen Gareeda's routine; he was wise to keep moving.

"I guess I'll have to," he said in response.

"Try not to break the ship—again," Leebo added. "And try especially hard not to give me anything to shoot at."

"Do my best." Dash took the steering yoke and turned off the autopilot. "Course?" he prompted Eaden.

The Nautolan navigator locked the course coordinates into the navicomp, and Dash watched them appear as a bright saffron arc on the tactical display. He frowned at the solid yellow line. "Hey, this isn't a leisurely holiday tour."

"You refer to the arc of our course?"

Dash sighed and pointed at the navicomp monitor. "Look at the blasted line. Do you see red?"

Eaden looked. "I see no red."

"That's because the course you set is *safe*."

"And this is a problem because?"

"Because safe isn't gonna better Solo's time."

Eaden Vrill blinked his extraordinarily large maroon

eyes. Two of his fourteen tentacle-like tresses lifted their tips toward Dash. "You wish me to recalculate?"

"What I wish is to beat Solo's alleged record."

"I'm simply being careful. We have an expensive cargo that we have yet to be paid for."

"All the more reason to get it to port *quickly*," Dash said. He gestured at the monitor. "So reset the course, please. We have to skate as close to the Maw as Solo did. Closer, if possible."

Eaden made an almost subsonic rumble of disapproval and ran nimble fingers over the console. The arc of light on the tactical display shot forth again. The curve was more pronounced now, running closer to the Maw, where the color deepened from yellow to orange to a satisfying shade of crimson.

"Keep in mind," Eaden cautioned, "that nothing in the galaxy is static. The orbital trajectories of stars, systems—"

"Are negligible within the context of human and humanoid life spans. If I were a Cephalon, say, it might be something to worry about." Dash took the steering yoke in hand, aimed the *Outrider* along the flaming arc, and punched the hyperdrive.

It was just a microjump to put them in the vicinity. To fly hyper along the edge of the Pit was almost impossible. For one thing, the gravity well could yank you out of hyperspace in a heartbeat even if you'd tinkered with your failsafes—which, of course, Dash had. Then there was the fact that the hard radiation from the nebula that cradled the asteroid field played havoc with instrumentation—adhering to a set sublight course that skirted the fringes of the Pit was about the only way Dash knew he could come through in one piece. Deviation on one side could result in clipping a wandering asteroid; deviation on the other would send the ship into the gravitational pull of the Maw, a cluster of black holes that warped local space. Fly too close to one of those singularities and all kinds of bad things could happen—not the least of which was having one's atoms stretched to an infinite length by the tidal forces that waited to tear everything apart.

He was counting down to the end of the jump when the *Outrider* trembled abruptly, the unexpected vibration passing through Dash's hands and up his arms. He frowned. That wasn't right. He opened his mouth to say something to Eaden when the ship bucked like a fractious tauntaun and dropped out of hyperspace.

"What the—"

"Oh, mother of chaos!" Leebo's bleat came through the com in a wash of static. "Incoming!"

"Incoming *what*?" Dash looked frantically at the tac display—which made no sense. There was no gravity well here—

"Incoming Imperials! There's an Imperial cruiser bearing down on us from astern—*Interceptor*-class!"

Dash swore in three languages—adding several choice moans in Wookieespeak. The Interceptors had gravity generators—four of them—that could suck a smaller ship right out of hyperspace or keep it from fleeing by producing a false gravity well. They'd flown right into a trap—probably set up here at the top of the Kessel run for the express purpose of catching smugglers.

The ship rocked violently to port and Leebo uttered a shrill, metallic squeal.

Before Dash's eyes the tac display finally made sense. *Outrider* had dropped back into realspace close enough to the contents of the Pit that they were practically kissing the asteroid field. If the cruiser's gravity well had hit them a few seconds sooner, they might have hit something big enough to hurt. Bad.

He pushed the thought down and focused on the display. A slowly rotating planetoid the shape of an egg and the size of an old-style generation ship lay several hundred klicks off their port bow. It was moving lazily across the general flow of rocky traffic, rolling on its long axis. In a split second, he'd made his decision. They'd hide behind that and use it to guard their flank while they made their getaway.

He manhandled the steering yoke hard to port and hit the ion drives hard. The *Outrider* leapt toward the egg-shaped planetoid, nosing down slightly in anticipation of dropping beneath the great rock.

When they were close enough that the bulging flanks of the planetoid filled the forward viewport, there was a resonant ping from the proximity sensors and Eaden sat bolt upright. "Target dead ahead!"

"And up!" Leebo screeched through the intercom. A barrage of laser fire erupted from the *Outrider*'s cannon emplacement at the upper horizon of the planetoid. Dash looked up and felt his blood run cold. Over the close horizon of the great gray egg loomed the bow of an Imperial light cruiser, its laser ports glowing red. Leebo's useless salvo had pattered harmlessly against its heavy shielding.

Dash thrust the steering yoke forward. The ship plummeted in response, accelerating as she dived beneath the planetoid. A trail of laserfire from the Imperial ship lit up her wake.

"What are you *doing*?" cried Leebo.

"Proving that size isn't everything!"

Dash continued to accelerate, giving the *Outrider* even more juice as they passed beneath the long axis of the planetoid and began ascending. The cruiser was five times bigger than the *Outrider,* which meant it was, at minimum, at least five times less maneuverable. By the time the captain figured out what Dash was doing and was able to turn the ship or order up a new firing solution, the target would be gone.

He hoped.

The *Outrider* described a perfect semicircle in the void of space, pressor beams providing maneuverability in the vacuum. It sailed around the planetoid upside down relative to the cruiser and whizzed over it toward the Maw.

"I need a quick course adjustment," he told his navigator, then spared a second to glance at the rearview screen. As he had hoped, the Imperial captain had read his move as an attempt to flee and had started to turn his ship in anticipation of pursuit into the Pit. He was still swinging to port as the *Outrider* streaked away in the opposite direction, toward the cluster of black holes.

"I sometimes think," said Eaden, as his webbed fingers played over the instrumentation, "that you are a certifiable madman. I assume you want a course that the Imperials will be loath to follow."

"I want the Imperials to think I've chosen death over dishonor."

The Nautolan gave him a sidewise glance. "You may well have done just that."

"Cute. Range to the rim of the Maw?"

"Two-point-three light-hours and closing."

Dash's gaze swept the tactical display, taking in the diffuse rims of the gravity wells, depicted in the display as broad, glowing bands of faded orange. If they eluded the cruiser, and went to hyperspace at the right moment and dived into the Maw at just the right angle, they could, with more luck than anyone had any right to expect, use their superluminal velocity to skip them along the outer edge of the region like a flat stone across a lake. Theoretically, anyway. *If* the gravitational waves generated by the various collapsed masses didn't muck up their navigation or suck them out of hyperspace again. *If* they could maintain a safe course through the complicated orbital arabesques being performed by the singularities.

If they could get far enough from the Imperial's gravity generators to make the jump in the first place.

Eaden pointed out these various risks with maddening calm, and Leebo chimed in over the comm with even more maddening hysteria. Dash shouted them both down.

"As much as I hate to quote an adversary," he said, "remember what Han says in situations like this?"

"Enlighten me," Eaden replied. It was, Dash thought, hard to believe that an amphibious humanoid could manage so dry a tone.

"Never tell me the odds."

The navicomp beeped, and he punched the ion drives. Hard.

TWO

I LOVE TO WATCH YOUR SHOW, AND WILL ALWAYS COME Back for more. I'll be Coming For about the tenth time to see You At Your Next Concert. —a Die-Hard fan

Javul Charn stared at the holographic message that hovered in the air before her face. On the surface it looked just like all the other fan mail she'd gotten in this packet, but her gut told her it wasn't fan mail at all. It was a warning.

Reading it over for the second time, she used the tip of her finger to select the oddly capitalized words from the text and drag them to a separate line, wondering how it had gotten past Kendara Farlion, her road manager and professional worrywart. Dara was used to seeing quirky holomail, but quirkiness usually had a pattern to it.

This wasn't a pattern.

Javul looked at the finished sentences hovering before her eyes: *Watch Your Back. Coming For You At Your Next Concert. Die-Hard.*

Was that last just a throwaway line or something more? A clue, perhaps?

At your next concert, the message said, but that didn't guarantee that something wouldn't happen before then. Her next concert was a little over a week away on Rodia, and would kick off a tour that would take them all the way to the Core Worlds, ending on Alderaan.

Panic fluttered beneath Javul's breastbone and she felt suddenly, unutterably alone. Beyond the door of the luxurious cabin on her equally luxurious private yacht, the *Nova's Heart*—named after her first holo-album to sell ten billion copies—her entourage and crew went about the hundreds of daily tasks that were integral to producing and maintaining her seemingly endless cycles of live concerts, holocasts, personal appearances, and travel. And yet—here, in her private sanctum, no less—someone had managed to breach the battlements of her life.

A slender arm the color of burnished bronze thrust over her shoulder, its index finger pointing at the curt warning still hanging in the air. "Chaos Hell, JC! What the blazes is *that*?"

Javul only just kept herself from falling out of her chair onto the carpeted deck. "Blast it, Dara! Can't you make some noise when you enter a room? Can't you *ping*?" She killed the message and swung around, catching the crest-fallen expression on the other woman's face.

"Since when do I have to ping to come into your office? And—hey—language? You talk like that in front of a holocam, and your name will be mud in households from here to the Rim."

Javul gestured helplessly. "I'm sorry, but you scared the fr—" She swallowed. "You scared me."

"I'm not surprised. Who sent that?"

"Sent what?" Javul said innocently.

"Too late. I saw it. *Watch your back*? What's up with that? I didn't see *that* in your mail."

"It was part of a longer communication. There were capitalized words that spelled out this—message."

"Warning," Dara said.

Javul worried her lower lip with her teeth, reluctant to admit that she'd come to the same conclusion. "I don't know that *warning* is—"

"Oh, it is. Trust me on this one, JC." Kendara's dark violet eyes were huge. "You have a stalker. What remains to be seen is how serious he, she, or it is."

A stalker. There—the word had been spoken, and made real. *Okay. Deeeep breath.*

"Yeah. Looks like it," she said. "This . . . this isn't the first one of these I've gotten. There was one in the batch of holomail after the previous concert, too. Remember the black fire lilies?"

"Do I? Yeah, I should say I do. You mean, that wasn't a compliment?"

Javul shook her head, remembering the rain of gleaming black, pungently fragrant blooms that had fallen all around her and her entourage as they'd ascended the landing ramp of her yacht after an appearance on Imperial Center. "I think that was a warning, too. He wanted me to know the sort of thing he could arrange."

"He?"

"I'm assuming—the messages are anonymous."

"I see. Then all that stuff about cultural relativity and how the black lilies were especially prized by the Elom as—"

"I made it up. I didn't want you guys to . . . you know."

Kendara put her hands on her hips and glared down at Javul, one bright orange curl falling over her forehead. "Yeah, I know. You didn't want us to know your life was in danger. Which is kinda—what's the word I'm searching for? Oh, yeah—*stupid*. Of course, I'm just your road manager, the head of your entourage. What good's an entourage if you won't let us take care of you?

"I can't believe you'd leave me out of the loop on something like this. I'm not just your road manager. I'm your best friend. I'm the one who's been pulling you out of scrapes since we were teenagers. Do I have to remind you of the lengths to which obsessed individuals will go? Do you *remember* any of our so-called adventures on Tatooine? That Zabrak spacer who thought you'd make the perfect little wifey. That guy who wanted to buy out

Chalmun and set you up as the house chanteuse? The stormtroopers who—"

Javul raised her hands against the volley of words. "You're right. Of course, you're right. I should have said something before. But . . . well, at first I was thinking it was just an overzealous fanboy and then . . . I don't know. I figured if the guy was on Coruscant—I mean, Imperial Center—and we were leaving . . ."

"Yeah, well, apparently he's taking his show on the road, too."

The truth of that statement made Javul's throat tighten. She clasped her hands together in her lap, flexing her fingers to make the rainbow stones inlaid into each nail glitter and flash. "So now you know. What do you think we should do?"

Kendara tilted her head to one side in thought. Then she said, "Two things. One, I'd split us into two travel parties. Second, I'd hire bodyguards."

"Okay on the splitting up—but bodyguards?"

"Yeah. Steely-eyed, laser-toting, massively intimidating bodyguards."

Javul shook her head. "I don't know, Dara. It's already freakishly hard to keep a low profile in this business, and if we contract with a security company, we increase our footprint, our baggage . . . and the number of people who have to have oversight."

"I'm not thinking of hiring from a security firm."

"Then where am I supposed to come by these steely-eyed, laser-toting . . . characters?"

A smile curved Kendara Farlion's lips and her teeth showed, white and even in her face. "I never thought I'd say this, but there are advantages to being from Mos Eisley. I know *exactly* where to look for that kind of character."

THREE

Leebo objected to the idea of jumping to hyperspace at the very edge of the Maw. Vociferously.

"Stop shrieking like a stuck mynock and secure the weapons battery," Dash ordered, while inwardly kicking himself for ever thinking that having a droid whose subroutines included a fear of mortality that bordered on paranoia was in any way a good idea. Especially subroutines so deeply embedded in its firmware that it would require major restructuring to root them out, and would likely leave Leebo the cybernetic equivalent of a ripe purnix.

Still, at times like these it was hard to see that as a downside . . .

To Eaden, Dash said, "Give me a mark at . . ." He checked the tactical. "Point-oh-three."

"A bit close."

"You think? Leebo, prepare countermeasures."

"You want me to jettison some junk, boss?"

"Yeah, but *prepare countermeasures* sounds more professional."

"They are continuing to fire on us," said Eaden.

"Good. In a moment, they're going to think they got lucky."

"Mark," said Eaden dubiously.

Dash adjusted their attitude and increased their speed again. The tactical display tracked the cruiser's last shot. The ship shivered as it glanced off her shields.

"Release countermeasures."

"Junk away."

In the rearview screen, Dash saw the debris field spread across their wake in an arc as gravitational waves and eddies tugged it this way and that. A second later the *Outrider* began to fight him, the yoke pulling at his hands as if she were yearning to be at the heart of one of the singularity fields—which, in a manner of speaking, she was. He gritted his teeth harder and began to count: "One-one-hundred, two-one-hundred, three-one-hundred, four-one—"

"Mark point-oh-three."

Dash yanked back on the yoke and accelerated, yet again, hauling the ship out of her dive into a shallow reverse arc. They were about as close to superluminal speed as they could get without jumping to hyperspace. The Maw pulled at them like an undertow, drawing the little ship toward its crushing depths. The *Outrider* quivered; the quivering became a steady vibration that increased until the vessel shuddered as if caught in the throes of a seizure.

"Our port engine is approaching failure," said Eaden quietly, his dark gaze on the internal sensor display. Unlike the tactical readouts, those were working just fine.

Blast. Why couldn't it have at least been the central drive? That could go belly-up without causing instability, even if they lost some thrust by using just the peripherals. Cursing steadily, Dash wrenched at the yoke, flipping the ship over by ninety degrees and—he hoped—increasing their arc.

"Port drive intermittent."

He could feel that as a series of tiny bumps punctuating the trembling of the ship. There was a moist tickle between his shoulder blades. He was sweating. The realization made him sweat harder. Perspiration stood out on his forehead and began to trickle from his hairline down the sides of his face. He didn't dare spare a hand to whisk it away—and if they didn't pull out of this climb into free space in the next several seconds it wouldn't matter. The drive would fail and they'd go into a spin. But if he cut the drive they'd be sucked into the Maw.

Unless . . .

"Kill the failsafes. We're going to hyperdrive."

"We are too close—"

"I know! *Do* it!"

"We are headed into Wild Space."

"I *know*! *Do it!*"

Eaden cut the hyperdrive's failsafes. Dash activated the drive. Nothing happened.

Dash glared at the Nautolan. "I said kill the failsafes!"

"I *did*."

"Then what the hell is—"

"Clearly, we have sustained damage."

"Great. Go to secondary drive."

Eaden shunted the power to the backup hyperdrive. It ramped up quickly—more quickly than was strictly safe, especially in this situation—but it still felt like a long, miserable year to Dash. He felt his navigator's gaze on him.

"We are in jeopardy of—"

"I *know* what we're in jeopardy of," Dash snarled, his own eyes never leaving the power-up gauge on the console. The second the drive came fully online, he activated it.

The ship seemed to hesitate for an instant—an illusion, but terrifying nonetheless—then the stars blurred comfortingly and they leapt out of realspace and away from the Maw and into the Wild.

"We-e-e-ell," said Leebo's voice through the com. "That was a *lot* of fun. Please tell me we won't be doing it again in the near future. Or, for that matter, the far—"

"Hey! A moment of congratulations is in order, okay?" Dash relaxed back on the steering yoke and took a moment to wipe sweat from his forehead and brush his hair back. "We just foiled an Imperial ambush, escaped certain death and . . ." He checked the chrono. "*Hah! And* cut point-three-three-three parsecs off the Kessel Run."

"Except," said Eaden, "that we are headed *away* from Kessel . . . and Nal Hutta."

Dash made a dismissive gesture. He felt exhilarated and lightheaded. "No problem, we'll drop out of hyperspace as soon as we're out of this bad neighborhood, then set course for Nal Hutta. We'll be ahead of schedule *and* earn enough to get the drive fixed twice over."

Eaden was staring morosely at the control console. "Alas, I think not."

"And why is that?"

As if in response, *Outrider* dropped suddenly and emphatically out of hyperspace, stranding them at the edge of the Wild.

"Because," said Eaden, "our secondary hyperdrive has also expired."

A cursory examination of both drives showed that there was no hope of swiping enough working parts from one to repair the other. In the end, they were left with no choice but to patch up the ion engines and make the nearest port at sublight speed, which would take—

"Thirty-two-point-six Standard hours," Eaden announced after consulting the bridge navicomp. "But there is no repair facility there."

So much for the nearest port. Dash stared, unfocused, at the sparse points of light beyond the viewport. "And Nal Hutta?"

"Forty-four-point-seven."

Dash did some quick calculations. With the Imperials patrolling the well-used smuggling corridors, trying to make Nal Hutta on ion power alone was chancy. It severely limited their ability to escape another trap.

"What'll it take to get to Tatooine?"

"Roughly thirty-six hours. Why Tatooine?"

Why, indeed. Tatooine was the lint-stuffed belly button of the universe, but—

"Because that's where Kerlew is. And Kerlew knows these drives inside out. He's the only mech-tech I trust to mess with *Outrider*'s innards."

"Humans," observed Eaden, "are so sentimental."

"They're soft in the head, is what they are," observed Leebo dryly from his post in engineering. "You realize, of course, that the cargo will have to be shipped on to Nal Hutta on a different freighter, which means we'll have to share the take with another space jockey. I mean, who knows if we're going to have any creds left after that to even get this bucket fi—?"

Dash killed the feed from Leebo's comlink, cutting him off mid-rant. "Well, what are you waiting for?" he asked Eaden. "Set course for Tatooine."

FOUR

THE BAD NEWS WAS THAT THE *OUTRIDER* WAS GOING TO be in spacedock for a while. The worse news was that it was going to cost them. And since they were now going to have to farm out the cargo delivery to another spacer, it might eat up all their profits. Then, of course, there was the difficulty of finding someone in Mos Eisley who was (a) trustworthy, (b) in need of quick credits, and (c) willing to take freight to Nal Hutta in the middle of a particularly nasty bit of business between the Jiliac and Besadii clans—mostly orchestrated by the ever-scheming Jabba.

To that end, Dash and Eaden left the ship berthed in Docking Bay 92 behind Spacers' Row and made their way to Chalmun's Cantina, just off Kerner Plaza. Few actually called the place Chalmun's Cantina. It was simply the Cantina or the Mos Eisley Cantina, with emphasis on *the*. There were other cantinas in Mos Eisley, but of them all, Chalmun's was the largest and the easiest to lose oneself in. This, when one was doing business that was less than legitimate, was a plus. Chalmun's possessed a warren of booths and small back rooms for private conferences. And, of course, a back door and a cellar retreat that led to yet another escape route.

Dash was not in a good mood when he and Eaden stepped down from the cantina's foyer into the noisy main room, but he plastered a false smile on his face and gave the room a once-over, scanning for familiar faces.

He saw quite a few, but only a handful were pilots he'd trust with their cargo. Most of the patrons, in fact, were aging Podracers, recognizable for the most part by their various honorary badges. Which, among other things, entitled them to free drinks.

"Must be a convention in town," Dash muttered. "Eaden, how about you take the left side of the room. I'll take the right. We'll shmooze a little bit—see if anyone's looking for a quick turnaround."

The Nautolan fixed him with an eloquent maroon stare. "I do not . . . what was that word? 'Shmooze.'"

In the many months he'd been working with the Nautolan, Dash had yet to arrive at a definitive list of all the things Eaden considered beneath his dignity. "How do you know you don't do it? Do you even know what it means?"

"Whatever it means, I don't do it. I will ask likely candidates if they are in need of a cargo and are willing to take it to Nal Hutta. That's all."

Dash raked his fingers through his thick hair and sighed. *Probably not a good idea to tell him that's a text-book definition of* shmooze. "Okay, look. Let's at least make sure we're in the same starlane when it comes to what we're looking for."

His partner gave him another impenetrable look. "Free of current commitments and desperate for credits?"

"And trustworthy. Don't forget trustworthy. It's bad enough we're losing the full commission. If whoever we hire to take it to Nal Hutta is dishonest . . ."

Eaden Vrill surveyed the cantina. Then he turned his oversized eyes back to Dash with a blink so exaggerated it used both sets of eyelids, *and* produced an audible *click*—the Nautolan equivalent of an eyebrow raised in irony.

"Smart guy. Just help me find us a freighter. And a *relatively* honest pilot."

Eaden moved off with the languid grace that was common to his species, leaving Dash to peruse the side of the room he had assigned himself. A number of spacers were standing clustered in the areas between tables, others were seated at those tables, and still others had sought the more private booths. It would be rude—and dangerous—to poke his nose into those dark little cubbies, but he could chat up any folks in the common room and let himself be seen by those in the booths.

Strolling, trolling, and meeting as many gazes as would allow that privilege, he had gotten about halfway up that side of the large room when he spied a Sullustan spacer of his acquaintance. The Sullustan, Dwanar Gher, saw him at precisely the same moment and waved him over to his table. Seated there as well were a Toydarian Dash didn't recognize and a human he did—to his considerable chagrin. Her name was Nanika Senoj and they'd had a bit of a thing at one point in time. That had stopped abruptly, for the simple reason that she'd driven him swamp-bat crazy. She was gorgeous, no question about that, with her copper-streaked burgundy hair, milk-pale skin, and big, dark brown eyes. But she also had a competitive nature that was perpetually in hyperdrive. No matter where she was or what she was doing—or who she was with—day or night, awake or asleep, she had to be the *best*.

Seeing her sitting there, smiling at him, chin propped on one fist, he almost excused himself and walked away. That would have been the sane move. But he was a man with a mission. "Hey, Nani. How's the vacuum treating you?"

"Can't complain. Except that it's a bit colder out there without someone to come home to," she said pointedly. Dash saw Gher turn away to hide a smile.

"Bantha poo," he said. "*You* moved on, babe. I heard all about it from Leebo."

"Leebo?" Her eyes widened. "What's a droid doing spreading gossip? I would *never* let my droid get away with that—I don't care who programmed him. And false, malicious gossip at that! I'm telling you, *babe*—"

"Cap it," Dash said. He looked past her at the Sullustan. "Dwanar, what's up?"

The Sullustan's wide mouth turned up in a grin. "My associate here"—he nodded toward the Toydarian, a plump little specimen whose wings Dash doubted could carry him more than ten meters before he dropped dead from exhaustion—"is looking for a pilot of an adventurous bent to take on a particularly lucrative job."

Dash's heart rate spiked momentarily. For a second the tantalizing words *lucrative job* had made him forget his circumstances. He shook his head. "Love to oblige you, Dwanar, but the *Outrider* is out of commission at the moment. In fact, I'm looking for someone to take my cargo the rest of the way to Nal Hutta."

Gher snorted. "I'm trying to steer clear of Huttdom these days. Very unstable situation."

Nani didn't say anything; she merely sipped her drink and watched Dash over the rim of her cup. If looks could maim, he'd be doing his smuggling from inside a bacta tank.

"He can't do it," said the Toydarian waspishly, glaring at Dash. "You're wasting my time, Gher. You promised you'd find me a spacer who would undertake—"

"And I will," said the little Sullustan, matching his earnest tone with a soulful look from his impossibly large eyes. "Have patience, Unko."

"Easy for you to say," growled the other. "You're not losing fifteen hundred credits an hour!"

"Why don't you and Nani take his job?" Dash asked.

"We're otherwise engaged right now. And Unko needs someone who can leave immediately."

"Well, then he's right. Talking to me's a waste of time.

I'm going nowhere." He sketched a salute at the table and turned to continue his promenade, stewing over the implications of Gher's words. If a Toydarian was paying someone to help *find* him a pilot *and* a ship, the pickings must be vanishingly slim.

His stroll netted him exactly nothing. Everyone was either engaged, reluctant to go to the Hutt home system, or demanding too many credits. *Far* too many credits. He reached the back of the room and turned to look at the bar, feeling a bit down. The fact that Eaden hadn't commed him meant the Nautolan was having no better luck.

Might as well go for a drink, then . . . if he could thread his way through the screen of old racer pilots who ringed the central bar trading stories about their glory days.

Kill me if I'm ever so used up that the most exciting thing I can do is drone on and on about past exploits, Dash thought.

He managed to force his way to the bar and was surprised to see that Chal himself was tending today. The Wookiee usually spent his "working" hours behind the scenes in his office while his staff tended bar and waited tables. But he had a fondness for Podracing and Podracers, and the bar was full of the latter. He was listening to a pair of the codgers argue some rule or other, and seemed as happy as Dash had ever seen him.

"Hey, Chal, can I get a drink, or do I have to get me one of those astral badges?"

The Wookiee looked up and, with a bleat of pleasure, reached across the bar to give Dash an affectionate pat on his shoulder that almost dislocated it. *"Whiiinu dasalla?"* Chal moaned in his native tongue. What would you like?

"Corellian ale. And by the way—you know anyone with an empty cargo bay who might be looking for a quick score?" Dash's gaze was still roaming the crowded room.

Chal, setting Dash's ale before him, harned and moaned to the effect that he just might at that. It was a good thing, Dash reflected, that over the years he had picked up enough of the big furry bipeds' language to gather the gist of their statements—mostly, anyway. He could still get tripped up by the inflection. Shyriiwook was a tonal language, which meant intonation contour was vitally important. Depending on the phonology, the same phrase could mean either "You honor me with your presence" or "You smell like a dead dewback."

He understood the Wookiee's statement well enough, accompanied as it was with the jerk of a shaggy head toward the nether regions of the cantina. "Really?" He brightened. "Where?"

In answer Chalmun pointed to a small cubicle on the other side of the bandstand and closest to the rear exit. There was but one table in it and he could see nothing of the individual sitting in it, save for a hand gripping a mug. Several empties already cluttered the tabletop.

"Thanks, Chal." He lifted his ale and, sipping it, headed for the corner booth. He could've sworn he heard a smothered chuckle from behind him, but when he peered back over his shoulder the big guy was busily serving drinks.

Just shy of the doorway he bumped into a Kubaz who was nattering at the band to set up faster and begin playing immediately, if not sooner. Dash staggered back a few steps, amazingly spilling none of his ale. Hence the smile he showed his potential mark when he slipped into the cubicle was genuine.

Genuine or not, it faded just inside the doorway. "Sith spit! *You*."

Han Solo looked up from his drink, his eyes coming into relatively quick focus on Dash's face. "Oh, *nice*. Is that any way to greet an old friend, old friend?"

"Old *friend*? You're kidding me, right? I've heard all

the trash you've been talking about me and my ship up and down the space lanes. I seem to recall that the last time we met, you took a swing at my head."

"Hey, I was a little drunk. Okay?"

Dash considered the number of empty glasses on the tabletop. "Not like now, huh?"

"No, I'm not drunk. Yet. But give me some time and I'll manage."

Frowning, Dash sidled into the booth and sat down. "What's up? And where's Chewie?" An uneasy thought made him sit up straighter. "Nothing's happened to Chewie?"

Han waved a dismissive hand. "Not unless you consider fatherhood something. He's back on Kashyyyk with Malla and their new baby boy."

"Yeah? What'd they name the kid?"

"Lumpawarrump," said Han with some difficulty.

"Lumpa . . . Lumpa—?"

"Yeah, that's usually as far as I get, too."

"So Chewbacca's home with the family and you're hanging out at Chal's drinking yourself under a table?"

Han gave him a fierce look. "I'm relash—re*lax*ing."

"Is that what you humans call it? I had wondered." Eaden Vrill stood in the cubicle doorway, thumbs tucked into his weapons belt.

Han smiled broadly. "Vrill, old buddy! Good to see you. Still hanging around with losers, I see."

"So it would seem." Eaden tilted his head toward Dash. "Luck?"

"None . . . unless . . ." Dash regarded Han speculatively. When Solo was this cocky, it usually meant he'd scored some profits. If that were the case, maybe he could be induced to part with a few. Maybe just enough for Dash to complete repairs on *Outrider* and avoid having to hire another ship.

"Luck with what?" asked Han.

"I don't suppose you could see your way clear to lend me a few credits, old friend."

Han poked a finger into his right ear and wiggled it. "Wait a minute, I can't have heard that right. You're asking me for a favor? No—better yet—you're asking me for money? Oh, *that's* rich."

Dash grabbed hold of his temper with both hands. "Can we be serious for just a moment? The *Outrider* is out of commission and I've got a whole lot of cargo sitting in the hold needing pretty desperately to get to Nal Hutta."

"Huh. What's wrong with the old boat?"

"Blown hyperdrives."

"Both of 'em? How'd you manage that?"

"We ran into Imperials on the Kessel Run. Almost got blasted out of space, then almost ran into a planetoid, then almost got sucked into the Maw. We fried our primary and secondary drives getting out again."

Han sat up straighter and leaned toward Dash across the table. "You're messing with my head." He glanced up at Eaden. "Isn't he? He's joking, right?"

"If only. We nearly perished."

Han leaned back in his seat again, taking a slug of his drink. "I guess you're lucky to be here then, aren't you?"

"Sure. Except that I've got a ship that can't fly and a cargo to get to Nal Hutta with no way to get it there." Dash leaned forward, elbows on the table, trying to look earnest. His mom had always fallen for his earnest look. "I just need enough to get the drive up and running . . ."

"Even at Kerlew's best prices that's gonna come to quite a pile of credits. More than I've got. You think I'd be sittin' here if I had a commishun—com-*miss*-ion?"

Unfortunately, Dash's mom was unique.

"Just a few credits to—"

Eaden made a sound like steam venting, then said, "If I may: We have a cargo. Han has a ship. The purchaser has the credits we need so that *we* can have a ship. Again."

Dash looked at Han. Han looked at Dash. It fried Dash's circuits to have to hire Han Solo, of all the people in the galaxy, to take his load to Nal Hutta, but—

Han's slow smile was crooked. "Sounds like you need me."

Dash came to his feet fast enough to reach orbit. "Forget it! I don't need—" He felt a heavy hand fall on his shoulder.

"Pride rises before disaster falls," said the Nautolan philosophically. Then he addressed Solo. "What percentage would you charge to take a full hold to Nal Hutta . . . and a few items to Nar Shaddaa as well?"

Han considered. "Forty percent."

Now Dash leapt to his feet, fists on the table. "That's piracy!"

"It's business."

"It's space lane robbery! It's—*ow*!" Eaden's fingers had tightened on Dash's shoulder in painful warning.

"Twenty percent," said the Nautolan calmly.

"I should strangle you with your own tentacles," Dash muttered.

"Thirty-five," said Han.

Dash exploded anew. "We almost *died* for that cargo! We dodged Imperial ordnance for that cargo! We flew into the sucking *Maw* for that cargo! In other words, Han, *old friend,* we did all the hard work!"

Han made his eyes as wide and innocent as possible and shrugged eloquently. "All right. All right. Ice it, okay? Always was a sucker for a sob story. Thirty. And I off-load everything on Nar Shaddaa."

"Twenty-five," said Eaden. "And you deliver to Nal Hutta."

"Hey, I could be putting my life on the line going back to Nal Hutta right now. Things are kind of tense there, case you hadn't noticed—what with the assassinations and all. And I hear Jabba's in a bad mood. Something about a dropped spice shipment." Han scraped at a smudge on his glass. "Twenty-seven."

"Done," said Eaden and pushed Dash inexorably back into his seat. Dash slumped, defeated.

Han smiled broadly. "Great. Where's the old *Outrigger* stashed?"

Dash ground his teeth audibly. "It's *Outrider*. The usual place—Bay Ninety-two. How soon can you leave?"

"As soon as you can shift the load."

"As soon as *we* shift it?"

Han slid out of the booth and stood, polishing off his drink. "Sure. If you'd been able to do thirty percent on the cut I'd've been happy to help with the cargo transfer, but I don't have a first mate right now and you do. So if you don't mind, I'll just go and prep the *Falcon*. Your hold's full, is it?"

"Yeah."

"No problem. The *Falcon*'ll take that on with room to spare. See you at the docks in a few, boys." Han sketched a salute at Dash, returned Eaden's attenuated bow, and left, whistling.

Dash watched him go, then tilted his head back to look up at Eaden. "Gotta admire your nerve, Eaden. I'd've caved at thirty."

"Which is why we have our respective roles. I knew he would go lower." He flexed a couple of his head-tresses to emphasize the point.

"I thought you said that empathy trick doesn't always work out of water."

Eaden gave the Nautolan version of a shrug—a lifting of side locks. "What can I say? It was a good hair day."

FIVE

"You're not the least little bit nervous?"

"Nope."

Javul Charn adjusted her weapons belt and checked herself in the mirror of her suite aboard the *Nova's Heart*. The wide belt had several utility pockets containing stun pellets, a length of monofilament, a limited-range confounder, and other "gadgets," as Dara disparagingly referred to them. In addition, a customized DH-17 blaster was holstered on one side and a vibroknife on the other, both riding low across her hips. The synthsilk jumpsuit beneath looked like it had been painted on.

You look bad, she told herself. *You look lean and mean.*

In reality, she was distressingly sure that she looked about as dangerous as a Corellian spukamas, no matter how much she tried to convince herself otherwise. She hoped she sounded more confident than she felt.

Behind her, Kendara looked on in admiration. "You amaze me, boss," she said. "I'm a little uneasy about going into that den of thieves and I probably know half of 'em. What if someone recognizes you?"

"I'll just say how exciting I think it all is," said Javul, putting on a look of wide-eyed innocence. "How daring. How I've just *always* wanted to meet a real pirate."

Dara raised her hand. "Excuse me? May I just take this opportunity to say that I think you're more than a little nuts."

Javul laughed. "I'm *eccentric,* not nuts. All celebrities

are eccentric. I'm just more adventurous than most, I guess." *And scared.* And it wasn't Dara's "den of thieves" that scared her. "Besides," she continued, "you forget my official biography. I was born in the lightless sub-levels of Coruscant. Grew up with predatory gangs shooting up the neighborhood."

"Which is all poodoo. You know, I find it insulting that our PR guy actually thought an Imperial Center Slum was somehow more respectable than Tatooine."

Javul grinned. "Not more respectable. More inspiring. And more dangerous."

Dara snorted. "That's a matter of opinion."

Javul settled a bright teal turban over her gleaming silver hair and said, "Let's go shopping for bodyguards."

The news on the *Outrider* got worse, if that was possible. The engines had not only crispy-fried their various components, but destroyed the housing assembly as well. The cost of total repairs would have taken a healthy bite out of their commission even if they'd managed to retain all of it. Having to pay Han essentially ate up any profits. Worse, the docking fees were more than Dash could afford to squeeze out of his credit account.

Kerlew, a fellow Corellian, was a good guy and was even willing to make a start on the repairs in his spare time, trusting Dash for the payment, but Dash knew that trust would evaporate quickly if he failed to pay his docking fees. They needed some sort of work—pilot and navigator, trade liaisons, *something*.

With that in mind, after seeing Han off for Nal Hutta, Dash and Eaden returned to Chalmun's day after day, making the rounds of other freighter watering holes as well, looking for a ship *sans* crew.

On day three, Dash sauntered into the Cantina to see Dwanar Gher and his lovely associate at their favorite table. He went over to pay a visit.

"What happened to your being otherwise engaged?" he asked Dwanar.

The Sullustan blinked at him—an impressive gesture coming from eyes the size of ash angel eggs. "What do you mean?"

"The last time I saw you, you were entertaining that Toydarian character—what's his name . . ."

"Unko."

"Yeah—Unko. You fed him some line about not being available to run his stuff wherever it needed to go."

Nanika rolled her eyes. "We weren't so much unavailable as disinclined," she said wryly. "He wanted one of us to run some contraband to Imperial Center and we're both persons of interest to the Imperial Security Bureau right now."

"No kidding? How'd you manage that?"

Nanika and Dwanar shared a glance. The woman shrugged.

"We're suspected of having helped remove some wanted criminals from the ISB's clutches."

"Why would you do something like that?"

"Who said we did?" She smiled at him slyly. He knew that look well enough to distrust it.

"Is he still looking for a ship?" Dash asked, an idea beginning to form in his head.

"As far as I know," Nanika said.

"Well, I was thinking that, since the Imperials don't really know me from a mynock's mother, maybe I could take one of your ships and deliver his goods. We'd split the commission, of course—"

Nanika laughed brassily. "Oh, c'mon, Dash. I'm not a noob. There is no way I'd let you pilot my ship into Imperial space. They know me, they know the *Imp*. Dwanar can let you take his boat—"

"No one will be taking my craft anywhere," said the Sullustan. "Most especially not you."

Dash's temper flared. "Look, my reputation as a pilot is—"

"Your reputation as a pilot," Dwanar informed him, "is that you take risks that are stupid even for a Corellian. You're not going to play Kick-the-Rancor with *my* ship."

And that was that. After an hour spent in Chalmun's with no better results, Dash dragged himself to the bar and ordered a Corellian whiskey he couldn't really afford. When he finished the first, he ordered another and was beginning to feel pleasantly morose when he realized the Rodian bartender was speaking to him.

"What?" he looked up glaring. "I'm paid up, goggle-eyes."

"Hey! Attitude, pink-skin. I've done you no grief. I am, in fact, about to do you a favor. You're looking for a commission?"

"Yeah, what of it?"

"Well, a commission is looking for you."

Dash's head cleared at lightspeed. "Where away?"

The Rodian pointed over Dash's shoulder. He turned. It was the same booth he'd found Han Solo in only days ago. He closed his eyes, seized by the impression he'd been here before. The Equani had a word for it—Dash frowned, trying to remember it. Ah, yes: çenō-ka. Maybe he could no longer hold his liquor. Maybe he'd slipped into a temporal loop and was destined to live out the rest of his life in Chalmun's. Okay, then. He bolted the last of his whiskey, thanked the Rodian, and headed for the booth.

His surprise when he stepped into the little cubicle was complete. Two women looked up at him. Two young women. Two very human, very beautiful women. One had short spiky hair that was several different and contradictory shades of orange; the other's hair was concealed beneath a turban of vivid teal.

His smile was automatic. "Ladies!" He sketched a bow. "My friend Kendo at the bar there tells me you're looking for a pilot."

The two women looked at each other, sequined eyebrows lifting.

"No," said the one with the turban. "Actually, we're looking for a bodyguard."

As usual, it took Dash's brain a moment to catch up with the booze. "A bodyguard," he repeated stupidly. "Look, I'm a pilot—and a damn good one, at that. I don't—"

The spiky orange woman said, "And we're willing to pay handsomely for the service. Money is no object."

Those last four words went a long way toward clearing the fumes. Maybe money was no object to them, but right now it was Dash's *only* object. He slid into the booth and studied his prospective employers. Both wore polyprismatic lenses that cycled a rainbow of colors over the irises of their eyes. There was no telling what color they actually were; nor could he read their expressions clearly. Camouflage, instinct told him. These fems were in disguise. Why?

Maybe the answer was in why they felt the need of a bodyguard.

"I'm listening. Let's hear your pitch."

Again the exchange of glances. The spiky one leaned forward, elbows on the table. "Here's the deal. My boss, here, has picked up a stalker. Probably nothing. Just an overzealous fan. But we're not willing to take any chances. We need someone to keep an eye on her." She jerked her head toward the turbaned girl, drawing Dash's attention to her.

"Overzealous fan? Are you somebody I should know?"

"Only if you're breathing," Spike muttered.

"My friend exaggerates," said the other woman, with a smile that managed somehow to be both coquettish and self-deprecating.

"Are you going to tell me who you are?"

"If you take the job, I'll have to, I guess."

Dash couldn't tell if she was being serious or sarcastic. *Fine.* "So what's the situation? Where would this guarding take place?"

"Aboard my yacht, mostly. At our ports of call. Wherever I go. This . . . person . . . has let it be known that he can get pretty close to me and so you'd have to stay pretty close to me, too."

"Darlin', that would *not* be a hardship." He smiled at her.

"*Pretty* close, she said," interrupted Spike. "Not skin-close."

That can change, Dash thought, his smile never wavering. "Normally," he said aloud, "I wouldn't take a job like this—I'm a merchant pilot by trade—but my ship is under repair right now, so I'm at loose ends. Until I can get repairs completed. That's gonna take a while."

"How long?"

"I'm flexible."

"I'll just bet you are," said Spike drily.

"So you can start right away?" asked the other.

"Well, actually, it's not just me. I have a partner. A Nautolan. Who *happens* to be a teräs käsi master." He watched for the reaction from the two women and was gratified by the response. They apparently knew something of the sort of threat the masters of the "steel hand" discipline represented.

"We can definitely use someone with those talents," said the turbaned woman. "And it doesn't hurt that he's Nautolan. There are rumors that a high percentage of them are a little Force-sensitive."

"Well, Eaden claims to be able to read emotions even out of the water, but I think he's just showing off. I also have a droid."

"Of course you do," said Spike. "Every pilot I've ever known has a droid. You'd all be dirt-fliers without 'em."

Matching her aggressive, elbows-on-the-table stance, Dash leaned into her across the table. "I beg your pardon, but I'll have you know that I've successfully completed any number of missions without a droid's assistance. And I've gotta say that Leebo's not much of a space-monkey, but he's good company, so I keep him around."

"Really."

"Yeah. He tells jokes. Not very good ones," Dash admitted, "but still—the amazing thing is not that he tells them badly, but that he tells them at all."

The spiky woman snorted. Very unbecoming in a female, Dash decided. At least in a human female. A Zabrak might think it was sexy, though.

"What do you think, JC?" she asked her boss.

"What's your name?" her boss asked him.

"What's yours . . . JC?" he asked in return.

Turban Girl blinked her lenses off and looked out at him through eyes of pale, luminous silver. He almost swallowed his tongue. With an expression that was suddenly deadly serious, she lowered her voice and said, "Javul Charn."

He sat back in his seat, feeling as if a bantha had just sat on his chest. That name he knew, just as he knew those silver eyes. They'd gazed out at him from so many holoposters and performance vids, he'd lost count. He shifted uncomfortably in his seat, suddenly in complete sympathy with the overzealous fan.

"I'm, uh, I'm Dash. Dash Rendar. I'm a pilot."

"Yeah," said Spike. "So you said."

Eaden Vrill was not entirely pleased with their new job. At least Dash didn't *think* he was. It was hard to tell with teräs käsi adepts—they were so *disciplined*. And a

Nautolan's huge, dark eyes were hard to read anyway. Standing in the docking bay, he and Leebo listened to Dash's glowing description of the job in complete silence.

Eaden was stone-still for a full ten seconds, then said, "What will it pay?"

He nodded when Dash named the figure, then turned on his heel and went up into the ship to pack his kit.

Dash turned to Leebo and said, "Well? You gonna say something? Crack a joke? Take a shot at me?"

"Defensive, aren't we? We needed credits. You got us credits. So you get the credit for getting us the credits." The droid added an uncannily accurate reproduction of a percussive three-note trap skin riff. Dash rolled his eyes. It wasn't the first time he'd heard Leebo accentuate jokes in such a manner, nor the hundredth. *But add a few more zeros and we'll be getting close,* he thought.

Leebo then raised one metal arm, servos whining delicately. "Question."

"What?"

"We're going to be working on this woman's yacht?"

"Yeah."

"What's her name?"

"Her name? I told you her name. Javul Charn. You know—Javul Charn, the holostar?"

Leebo made a sound somewhere between a snort and a clatter. "Not the fem. What would I care about a *girl*? The *ship*, protein-brains. What's the *ship's* name?"

Dash laughed. "I keep forgetting your taste in females is toward the hard and ion-powered. She's the *Nova's Heart*—a SoroSuub PLY-3500."

"Ooh," said Leebo, managing to sound rhapsodic, "I'm in love." He turned and tilted his head toward the *Outrider,* sitting forlornly in the center of the bay. "Don't worry, old girl. I'm sure they'll never let me near the engine room." He returned to the ship himself, then, muttering PLY-3500 specs in a mechanical undertone.

"Twin ion/hyperdrive nacelles . . . programmable transponders . . . state-of-the-art gyrostabilizers . . . be still, my recirculation pump . . ."

Dash sighed. He'd still rather be piloting the *Outrider* than be a paid passenger on some personal luxury yacht, no matter what the specs. And he somehow suspected that, as bodyguards for the rich and famous, he and Eaden would be more passengers than crew. They would, after all, have to go where the big holostar went, eat where she ate, be quartered close to her. He had no experience in the field to base that on, but he intended to be as professional about this as possible. It might be a nothing job, but he was going to take it seriously.

He'd arranged with his new boss (damn, but it was hard to even *think* that word—he doubted he could say it aloud) to transfer an advance payment to his account, had dispersed some to Eaden, and used most of the remaining credits to pay several weeks of rent on the docking bay with just a little left for Kerlew as a good-faith gesture. When all was arranged, Dash, Eaden, and Leebo reported to the spaceport, where a shuttle waited to take them up to the orbiting yacht. Dash thought it a little odd that the *Nova's Heart* didn't dock dirtside, but he supposed that had something to do with Javul Charn's celebrity status. Maybe she was afraid of calling too much attention to herself—or giving her "overzealous fan" a heads-up that she was on Tatooine. That made sense. Dash Rendar understood well the need to keep a low profile. Over the years he had, perforce, become a master of disguise, subterfuge, and just plain hiding. He had every confidence that between Eaden's abilities and his own innate wariness, they'd be as good a set of bodyguards as the lovely fem could wish for.

The PLY-3500 was everything the SoroSuub press campaign said and more. As they were greeted by the ship's steward—an E-3PO protocol droid—and shown to their quarters just forward of the observation deck, Dash noticed quite a few "enhancements" that weren't in the manufacturer's literature. He made a mental note to get the ship's schematics and acquaint himself with the vessel, paying close attention to any nook or cranny in which a stowaway might hide. When he'd brought up the idea that someone might sneak aboard her ship unobserved, the celebrity had denied that such a thing was possible—but she had blanched at the suggestion, her skin becoming, if possible, paler than it already was. He'd scared her, but the fact that she hadn't considered the possibility that Fanboy might be able to get *real* close only showed that she deserved to be scared.

Dash and Eaden were quartered in a suite of rooms at the head of the aft quarterdeck immediately abaft a set of emergency doors. Kendara Farlion's suite was next door to theirs, while Javul Charn's chambers took up the opposite side of the aft quarterdeck, her door cattycorner to Dash and Eaden's.

"Rarefied water," said Eaden philosophically as he surveyed the surface of Tatooine from the expanse of transparisteel that ran the entire outer wall of their quarters. Softly lit by clever indirect lighting, the stunning main chamber featured adjustable coloration and lighting schemes, original work from a dozen well-known artists, and sleek, designer furniture, which included state-of-the-art antigrav form couches upholstered in the finest Corellian leather.

"Yeah, there're definite perks to the position of royal bodyguard—having to room near the royal mark being one of them."

"You'd be wise not to let her hear you call her that," observed Eaden.

"Not to worry, I'll be a good boy."

The Nautolan smiled—a peculiar curling of his wide

mouth. "Highly unlikely. Perhaps you should practice saying, *Yes, boss.*"

A strange, metallic sigh issued from just inside the door to the opulent quarters, making both men turn. Leebo stood behind them, looking somehow bereft; an attitude communicated almost entirely by posture, as of course the droid's facial features were immobile.

"What's wrong with you?" Dash asked him.

"Like you care. So engrossed in your silly sentient squabbles while I stand here doing everything. I mean, really, *you* two may have jobs, but me? I might as well be turned off and used as a clothes rack."

"There's a thought," said Dash. "What do you want me to do?"

Leebo's head came up with a faint squeak. "Introduce me to the ship's engineer. Tell him what a genius I am. That you'd never be able to keep the *Outrider* in trim without me, that—"

"Excuse me," Dash said, interrupting the droid's recitation. "Okay, point one: I'd never be able to keep the *Outrider* in trim without you? I hate to spoil this droid fever-dream you're having, boyo, but I kept the *Outrider* shipshape long before you came on the scene. And point two: may I remind you where the *Outrider* is at this moment? Hardly great advertising for your genius."

"That," said Leebo, drawing himself to his full height, "was not my fault."

"Are you saying it was *mine*?"

"*I* wasn't the one who piloted the ship into an ambush then tried to get out of it by sideswiping a singularity . . . or three."

"Now, that just hurts. Look, you whiny bucket of bolts—"

"Do you realize that you're arguing with a mechanism?" Eaden said.

Eaden's question, mildly asked, brought swift embarrassment. "Yeah, yeah, you're right. I oughta just turn him off."

"Hey!"

"When he might actually be useful?" Eaden asked. "Unwise. At the very least, he's another pair of eyes—metaphorically speaking. And he doesn't need to sleep."

Dash grinned. "Night watch, huh? Good idea." He turned back to Leebo. "Looks like you'll earn your keep after all."

"I'm ecstatic with relief."

The door chimed just then and, to Dash's affirmative, slid open to reveal Kendara Farlion. She'd removed her pinwheel lenses to reveal deep violet eyes that exactly matched her sequined eyebrows. "You know, I can hear you arguing all the way out in the hall. And this ship is pretty well insulated. You sure you can all work together?"

"We're fine," said Dash. "Just fine."

"Glad to hear it. Ready for a tour of the ship?"

"More than ready," Dash said, and followed her from the cabin.

SIX

DASH WAS PREPARED TO BE DISAPPOINTED IN, EVEN DISparaging of, the *Nova's Heart*. It was, after all, not a *working* vessel. It was a yacht, which in Dash's mind translated to toy. But five minutes after the tour began, he was grudgingly willing to admit that the ship was pretty well put together, and ten minutes in he'd decided that *Nova's Heart* was a stunning piece of craftswork. He kept that assessment to himself, however.

Every angle was precise and smooth, every curve delighted the eye, every joint was flush. The interior was a tasteful combination of brushed durasteel and fabrics that emulated the metal's satiny sheen. He'd been aboard Lando Calrissian's *Lady Luck*—a PLY-3000—and had been amused at the way the gambler had hidden the secret muscles of the craft beneath layer upon layer of opulent, even gaudy, luxury appointments. *Nova's Heart* was a different sort of creature. Her trim, muscular, graceful frame was draped only lightly with opulence. She was, in a word, a lady: sleek, feline, and—though not afraid of showing off her strength—unmistakably feminine. Definitely not the transportation equivalent of an odalisque.

Dash gave the quarters and living areas of the ship only the most cursory examination. It was the working decks, engineering, and the bridge that fascinated him. He assumed these also interested Eaden, but really, who knew?

In engineering, Dash slowed the tour to a crawl by checking out every nuance of the ship's drives and systems. This caused Spike to roll her eyes roughly every twenty seconds, but the captain, an imperturbable Zabrak named Serdor Marrak, seemed . . . well, imperturbable. Having the captain and Eaden Vrill standing on each side of him made Dash feel as if he were getting serenity in stereo—an eerie feeling. Spike's prickly impatience was almost a relief.

"Your shield generators are Chempat-6s, I see," Dash observed as he crawled around the gleaming deflector system. "But that resonator coil up there doesn't look stock to me." He pointed upward to where a meter-long, half-meter-wide coil of flat optical-quality transparisteel wound its way around the power conduit to the deflector array.

"It's not," said Marrak placidly. "It's a modified Chem-6. I'd almost call it a 6.5."

"Why do you have to call it anything?" asked Spike, glancing at her chrono. "It's a machine."

"Yeah?" said Dash, ignoring her. "May I ask about the nature of the modifications?"

The captain said, "Javul Charn has sufficient reason to want to run silent and to be . . . difficult to track or trace. We modified the unit along those lines."

Dash looked over sharply from the resonator coil. "A *cloaking* device? You modified this to be a cloaking device?"

The captain shrugged. "More of a smudging device. It kicks in once we're in open space. We've installed maximal confounders; the coils have been torqued and the harmonics realigned so that they distort and blur our communications signature . . . among other things."

"What other things?" asked Eaden, betraying his own interest in the ship's construction.

"We beefed up the ablative capacity of the shields while

we were at it. They're virtually impenetrable to communications signals when we want them to be. They'll also fling off pretty big space debris and, if we ever should find ourselves under attack for some reason, they'll do a fine job of repelling energy weapons fire as well."

Dash frowned, puzzled. "They block communications. Why, exactly?"

"Keeps people from eavesdropping on us," said Spike. "We don't want everybody to know Javul's plans, do we? I can't begin to tell you what a pain it is to get into a port of call and find a literal fleet of overeager fans waiting in orbit. Javul likes to keep a low profile. I think you can appreciate that."

Dash moved to peer out through a long, narrow viewport at the port engine nacelle. "Combined ion/hyperdrive, huh?"

The captain nodded while, behind him, Leebo gave an ecstatic sigh. Dash stifled a grin. "Those modified, too?" he asked.

"A bit. They were rated to just lightspeed. We managed to push them a bit farther than that. My engineer is quite an innovator."

Dash nodded. "I'd like to meet him."

"Her."

"Oh. Droid brain?"

The captain blinked. "Excuse me?"

Dash laughed. "Not your engineer—although I guess she might have a droid brain. Mine does." He jerked a thumb back toward Leebo, who was gazing around like a lovesick Wookiee. "I meant the ship. I have a . . . an acquaintance who installed a full-faculty droid autopilot and system controller in his ship."

"Ah, I see. As it happens my engineer is a Twi'lek named Arruna Var. Our steward has a droid brain, though. So does the ship's doctor."

"It's too bad *you* don't have a droid brain," Spike told

Dash, "we could download all this information right to your cortex. Save a lot of time." She checked her chrono again.

Dash grinned at her. "That is a fantastic idea. In fact, if you could take Leebo, here, and get those schematics downloaded into his neural net, that'd be stellar. Eaden and I can go over them with him later."

She stared at him a moment. "All right, but do you think you could hurry this tour up just a bit? We need to make sure we're secure before we leave Tatooine."

"What did you think I was doing? This *tour*, as you like to call it, is my way of making sure we're secure. If I don't go over every centimeter of this ship, how can I foresee problems?"

She aimed those violet laser cannon eyes at him for a moment more, then ordered Leebo to follow her back to the upper decks.

"Nervous little thing, isn't she?" Dash murmured.

Somehow she heard him. She turned on her heel and marched back to meet him nose-to-nose, eyes narrowed to slits. "Who're you calling *little*, space-monkey? I'm not little. I'm almost as tall as you are."

He glanced down. "You're cheating. You're standing on your toes."

She let herself down to her heels with a bump, pivoted, and marched away again, pulling Leebo into her wake.

"These schematics you mentioned," the droid said as she led him away, "would they happen to be holographic schematics? Three-dimensional schematics?"

"Sure."

Dash, Eaden, and Captain Marrak continued making their way from stem to stern, even going out over the fantail on the observation deck to gaze back at the hull from that extreme point. Dash cocked his head to one side and eyed the lower hull.

"She seems . . . deeper than the average 3500. More girth below the centerline."

"Indeed," said Eaden, tilting his head in the same direction.

The captain joined them in peering down the ship's graceful flank. "Another modification the boss made. Increased stowage. Takes a lot of equipment to stage one of her shows. And a good-sized crew. Of course, we're only part of the picture."

"What do you mean?"

"We recently split the setup between two vessels: the *Nova's Heart* and a freighter—the *Deep Core*. Each carries just enough equipment for her to be able to pull off a creditable performance if something should happen to the other ship or its cargo. Javul hates to let her fans down."

"Has she ever?" Dash asked.

"No, but we had a near disaster about six months ago when one of our containers turned up empty. It was supposed to house a setup for a big cityscape performance framework that she uses. But somehow that got left behind . . . or stolen."

Dash wondered how much the captain knew of more recent developments. "Has Charn told you why we're here?"

"Of course. You're security consultants."

Dash nodded. "So you'll understand why I'm asking you if anything else . . . suspicious or strange—or even dangerous—has happened recently."

Marrak gave him a knowing look. "You mean the sort of thing that might have led to hiring a security consultant?"

"Yeah. That sort of thing."

The Zabrak captain showed the first sign of emotion since Dash had met him. The emotion was unease. "Well, she will have told you about the black lilies . . . yeah, I thought so. So I knew perfectly well that if the person who arranged that little present understood the symbolism . . . let's just say it could be construed as a threat. But before that—about three weeks before that—we had a stowaway. A fan concealed himself in one of the containers and wasn't found until we reached our next port of call. I understand he was in pretty bad shape when they found him. No food, water . . . little oxygen." The Zabrak shuddered, his ritual tattoos horripilating as though momentarily imbued with life.

"Really? Anybody aboard now who'd know more about the incident?"

Marrak shrugged. "Dara would. And of course, the cargo master—Yanus Melikan. Since that incident he's double-checked every container."

"Well, I may just have him triple-check it," Dash said and drew a droll sidewise look from Eaden.

"Would they have informed Javul Charn of this incident?" the Nautolan asked.

Captain Marrak snorted. "Don't know. Farlion will go to great lengths to keep our holostar from being rattled by stuff like that. She can be very protective."

"Really? I hadn't noticed," said Dash wryly. Chances were good Dash was going to find out to exactly what lengths Spike would go to protect her stunning boss.

They worked their way from the observation deck down to the well-deck where Dash, in inspecting the life pods, discovered that the *Nova's Heart* was equipped with a secondary shuttle—a prettier, glossier counterpart to the stubby little planet-hopper they'd arrived in. This shuttle was about eight meters long, held six people and a nav droid, and was sleek as a dart. Its long, tapered hull ended in a deadly-looking point that, slanting down as it did from its backswept stabilizer planes and V-shaped forward viewport, gave the little ship the threatening look of a raptor. He was convinced he was looking at a fighter—not the kind of vehicle you took on a pleasure outing.

"Whoa. That's different. One of Charn's upgrades?"

Marrak shook his head. "It came with the ship. It's a Falleen design."

Dash's insides squirmed. *Falleen.* That explained the faint sense of menace about the thing. Dash had no love for the Falleen—least of all for a particular Falleen, Prince Xizor, with whom his limited contact had been both deadly and disastrous. In Dash's estimation all Falleen were duplicitous and cagey.

He felt suddenly as if Dantari fire ants were crawling across the nape of his neck. He shook the feeling away and studied the Falleen shuttle warily. "Came with the ship, huh? Well, it's definitely not stock—"

"Of course not. It was something the previous owner added, apparently. Maybe he liked to take day trips."

Day trips into danger, maybe. Dash shook himself—damn thing was just a shuttle craft. "I'd like to see the bridge."

"So would I," said Eaden.

The bridge was spectacular. It was a large, open, teardrop-shaped chamber with formfitting seats for the captain and mate, and seats of only slightly less impressive design at three other consoles along the sloping bulkheads. Between the flight console and the viewport was a holographic tactical display that made Dash's mouth water. Lando didn't even have one of those on the *Lady Luck.*

Of course, Dash reminded himself, *Javul probably makes in a day what Lando—or I—make in a year. If it's a good year.*

"*That's* not stock equipment."

The captain smiled. "No, it's not. And let me tell you it is worth the cost in an asteroid field or maneuvering in close quarters."

"Indeed," murmured Eaden, moving toward the flight console as if drawn by a magnet.

"I see communications and security consoles," Dash said, waving at the stations along the port side of the bridge, "but what's that over there?" He gestured to a station just starboard of the copilot's seat.

"Weapons control," said Marrak. "Another artifact of days gone by. The previous owner had laser cannons mounted on the fuselage." He pointed up, then down. "They're still there, but we've never had occasion to use them. It's not polite to shoot at your fans, even when they're really annoying."

"Yeah." Dash's eyes were drawn back to the captain's chair. "Um . . . can I?" He tilted his head toward the flight console.

Marrak's smile deepened. "Be my guest."

When they at last finished their tour, Dash was weary and his head felt as if the ship's specs were leaking from his ears. It would all sort itself out during a good night's sleep, though; that he knew from experience. By the time he woke tomorrow to his first full day of work as Javul Charn's "security consultant," he would have the various decks, rooms, and passageways of the *Nova's Heart* categorized, cataloged, and classified. His mind worked best, Dash liked to say, when he wasn't using it.

He was forced to use it, though, during dinner, at which he and Eaden were introduced to the ship's complement as the "new security officers." This was greeted with some interest by the crew, who exchanged knowing looks with one another. The officers present in the mess included the Twi'lek engineer Arruna Var, Marrak's human first officer, Bran Finnick, and cargo master Yanus Melikan, who was also human, and from Corellia.

Melikan was of great interest to Dash because he, of everyone aboard the *Heart,* had the most intimate knowledge of the ship's lower decks—which would be the most attractive point of entry for someone who wanted to get a bit too close to the lovely Javul Charn. He'd make a point of chatting with the cargo master as soon as possible.

It was not to happen immediately, however. The moment the meal was concluded, the officers scrambled to their posts to prep the ship for departure. Dash's effort to tag along with Melikan was thwarted by Javul Charn's insistence that he brief her immediately on his first impressions of the ship's security issues.

"What do you think?" she asked him when she, Eaden, and Dara had repaired to her quarters.

"I think," he said, "that it would have been a good idea for me to follow your cargo master through his hyperspace flight prep. From what Captain Marrak tells me, the cargo hold may be the weak point in your defenses."

Her brow furrowed. "What did he tell you, exactly?"

Dash glanced at Spike before directing his attention back to Javul. "Well, I may be speaking out of turn, but he mentioned an incident with a fan who hitched a ride in a cargo container."

He'd expected her to be shocked and horrified—or even incredulous. She was none of those things, though she did blush to the roots of her pale hair. The effect was strangely charming. She almost looked like a Zeltron.

"Yes," she murmured. "That was . . . awful."

"It points to some access points that might need to be bolted down."

Spike spoke before her boss could. "I'm sure they have been."

"Can I ask what happened to the fan?"

"It's hardly—" began the road manager.

"He died in a medcenter on Coruscant," said Javul. She looked honestly grieved. "Mel was devastated. He took all the blame on himself. He wanted to quit. Said he'd fallen asleep at the controls." She shook her head. "I couldn't let him do that. He's a good man. The best."

"I assume you won't mind if I ask him some questions about his protocols and procedures." Dash felt more than saw Eaden's burgundy orbs slide into a sidewise look.

Javul shook her head, still looking so forlorn that Dash had a strong impulse to put his arm around her. One look at Spike, however, was enough to nip that impulse in the bud. If only it would deter the stalker.

"Protocols and procedures?" asked Eaden when they'd returned to their own quarters. "When have you ever been on speaking terms with protocols and procedures?"

It was late evening by the ship's chrono and Dash was fuming a bit at having to put his investigation of the hold off until the new day. He shrugged and looked around for Leebo, but the droid was nowhere to be seen. Probably off whispering sweet nothings to the *Heart*'s ion engines. "I was just trying to sound . . . security-officer-ish."

"You were trying to impress a female."

"What'd I just say?"

"What *are* our protocols and procedures going to be, Officer Rendar?"

"I intend to do this job right. Okay, so we may be just glorified nursemaids for a pretty prima donna, but I intend to give this little prima donna the best care I can."

"And how do you wish me to employ my highly talented cortex during our voyage?"

Dash rocked forward in the chair, ignoring the panorama of stars beyond the viewport. "I'd like you to attach yourself to the engineer, Arruna—you might mention what a pretty name that is, by the way—and find out as much about the ship's systems as you can. Specifically, keep your magnificent maroons peeled for systems that might be most easily sabotaged. If someone is really serious about getting to our new boss lady, be-calming her ship might be a component in the plan."

"You think this threat she received is linked to the in-cident with the black lilies."

"I think it would be stupid to assume it wasn't."

Eaden stood and moved toward his room. He paused in the doorway. "I don't know if it's important, but there's an exchange of energy happening between Kendara Far-lion and the captain."

"Exchange of energy? Could you be more specific?"

A couple of tresses bobbed and quivered slightly. "Let us just say they seem very aware of each other."

"Oh, that's helpful. I'm very aware of Spike, too."

"Not, I think, in the same way the captain is," said Eaden as he disappeared into his sleep chamber.

SEVEN

LEEBO DID NOT RETURN UNTIL THE FOLLOWING MORN-
ing. In fact, Dash and Eaden woke to his off-key whistling.

"You're a *droid*," complained Dash as he threw himself into one of the formchairs in the suite's parlor. "How
can you possibly be off key?"

"I am merely paying homage to the sentient who programmed me. He couldn't carry a tune in an antigrav
pod."

"*He* was naturally tone-deaf. You are not naturally anything. You can be perfectly in tune if you want to be."

The droid approximated a shrug, lifting one shoulder
with a whine of servos. "Think of it as an artistic choice."

Dash opened his mouth to retort when Eaden, who had
appeared silently in the door of his sleep chamber, said,
"Dash, once again I'll remind you that you are arguing
with a mechanism. Leebo, where were you all night?"

Dash closed his mouth, his teeth meeting with an audible *click*. If Eaden noticed the sign of human irritation, he
gave no sign of it, but merely waited for Leebo's answer.

"I was in medbay," the droid replied.

Dash and Eaden exchanged glances. "I'm afraid to
ask," said Dash, "but—why?"

"As it happens, I got on quite well with the ship's medic.
She's fascinating. Knows more about the officers and crew
of this ship than anyone alive."

"She?" repeated Dash. "The ship's medic is a sentient?

That's kinda weird, isn't it? Most ships this size would staff a medical droid."

"She *is* a medical droid. A GA-7, as it happens, but with programming that's definitely gender-biased. I said she knew more about the ship's complement than any one *alive*."

"Okay, okay, so it's—"

"She."

Dash rolled his eyes. "*She's* a source of intel. Good to know. On to the big-credit question—do you have the schematics?"

"The med droid's schematics? I should say not. I only just met her, after all."

Dash ground his teeth. "I meant the *ship's* schematics, you circuit-challenged drone! You know, what you were *sent* to get?"

"Oh, *those*." The droid made a dismissive gesture. "Of course I got them. You want to go over them now, I suppose."

"No time like the present."

"True. Unless it's the past or the future."

The schematics were not as impressive as the ship herself. They were the SoroSuub factory specs and reflected none of the post-factory modifications. Nor did they note where modifications had been made.

Dash and Eaden consulted with the engineer over a hot beverage in the officers' mess. Going over a holo-readout of the schematics Leebo projected over the center of their shared table, she indicated several points at which the *Heart* did not match her stats, helpfully amending the record.

"Isn't it unusual that no one's done this before?" Dash asked.

The Twi'lek's blue lips parted in a smile, revealing teeth that were startlingly white in comparison. "Not unusual for someone who procrastinates whenever there's vapor work to do."

"Vapor work?" repeated Eaden as he used a laser pen to graft the updated data about the ablative shielding. The schematics, hanging in the air before the Nautolan's face, shifted to accommodate the new information.

"I love engineering. I hate engineering specs. Well, let me amend that: I could easily get lost in someone else's specifications—great late-night reading—but I hate having to write and edit the annoying things. They just get stuffed into some tin can's rattling brain case—no offense to present company—and forgotten. However, I *love* watching someone else edit them for me." She turned her smile on Eaden, who pretended not to notice, though at least three of his tendrils twitched.

"You said the hull is fortified with an over-coat of bandorium," he remarked blandly. "That's quite an upgrade."

"Normal ablative shielding and jammers are fine for the average hotshot yacht owner," she said, watching Eaden annotate the files in Leebo's memory. "But Javul isn't your average hotshot yacht owner." She shrugged her lekku dismissively. "Besides, I'd bet everyone who buys one of these babies modifies it in some way. I hear they've become pretty popular with smugglers." She gave Dash an oblique look from the sides of her startlingly azure eyes.

"I wouldn't know," he said easily. "Who'd this one belong to before Javul Charn bought it?"

Again, the shrug of lekku. Dash thought a couple of Eaden's tresses curled in response.

"I'm not sure. I've heard rumors, of course."

"Such as?"

"I'm not comfortable peddling rumors. You'll have to ask Dara or Javul."

Dash agreed without rancor. Interviewing the charming holostar was no hardship, after all. He spent a moment more studying the changes Arruna had noted on the schematics, then left her with Eaden and headed for the hold.

He found Yanus Melikan in his office on the main cargo deck going over the manifest. Double-checking, no doubt. The cargo master greeted him with a smile, told Dash to call him Mel, and took him on a tour of the hold.

It was tidy. Obsessively so. Every row of containers was arranged according to size and shape; every aisle was even and straight with no odd pallets or boxes sticking out. Everything was clamped down. Tight.

Which made Dash wonder . . .

"How could anybody stow away in here?" he asked as they meandered down one of Mel's scrupulously neat aisles. "I mean, saying you run a tight ship is an understatement."

The cargo master shook his head. "Near as I can figure, the guy got into the container while it was at the venue. Maybe took advantage of a momentary lull in loading or someone being called away to another task. It would only take someone looking away for a moment to allow time for the guy to slip in and hunker down. Then the container gets buttoned up and it's all over . . . except for the dying." The expression on Mel's long, angular face was grim. "Starvation . . . asphyxiation . . . Hard way to go, if you ask me."

"There an easy way?"

Mel chuckled ruefully and shook his head. "Maybe—maybe not. But you'd know something about that, wouldn't you?"

Dash stopped and swung to face the other man, pretty sure he wasn't going to like the sudden turn the conversation had taken. "What d'you mean?"

"I read about what happened to your brother in the newsies. Hardly seemed fair, what Palpatine did to you and your family afterward. There was talk at the time . . . people saying Stanton got off easy, dying in the wreck. I don't imagine you feel that way about it."

Dash scanned the other man's face but saw no hint of derision. "No. I'm glad Stan wasn't around to be punished by the Empire, though. And I'm glad he didn't have to see what happened to the family or the family business."

"You were at the Academy on Carida then, weren't you?"

"Yeah. It was a long time ago. How'd you know?"

"You're kidding, right? Your family wasn't exactly anonymous, Dash. It was in all the newsies: Native Son Accepted to Academy. Takes some talent to be accepted at Carida. I suspect you're a good pilot."

Dash pulled himself a little straighter. "The best, as it happens."

Mel grimaced. "With your ship under repair, I understand. Tough luck."

Dash nodded, glad to be tacking away from the previous subject. "That's why we were available for this gig. Charn caught us at just the right moment."

Mel nodded and turned to continue down the aisle between stacks of cargo.

Dash moved with him. "So, about your system: Who loads the crates—sentients or droids?"

"Both. After the incident with the stowaway we've made sure there's one droid for every sentient in the cargo crew. New rule is—never leave a container open if you have to go do something else. And never open a container that you're not planning to load or unload immediately."

Dash stopped and rested a hand against the side of a large carboplas container the size of a ship's life pod. Half a dozen people could cram themselves in there if they tried, he knew. "Do you think there's any way that could happen again? I mean that a fan with a deep desire to get close to Charn could distract someone and either sneak in or . . . leave her a nice, deadly little present?"

Melikan gave Dash a positively bone-chilling look from his almost colorless eyes. "That's not fannish adoration. It's sabotage."

"Can't they go hand in hand?"

The cargo master raised a ginger-colored eyebrow. Before he could comment, a klaxon pierced the hold's quiet, making Dash just about jump out of his boots. A calm, female voice followed, expressing every spacer's worst nightmare in dulcet tones: "Hull breach on the aft quarter deck. Venting atmosphere. Hull breach on the aft quarter deck. Venting atmosphere." The klaxon resumed its wailing as the *Nova's Heart* dropped back into realspace.

"Shut that stupid thing off!" Mel bellowed, racing for the turbolift with Dash on his heels.

"Sir?" An owl-eyed young Sullustan crewman and an Otoga 222 series maintenance droid met them just outside the door to the cargo master's office. "Did you mean—?"

"Yes, blast it! Shut the klaxon off and stay *here*."

"But if there's a hull breach—"

"Stay on the comm, Nik. If it's bad, you'll be told to abandon ship. If it's not you'll get the all-clear. In either case, *do not leave this area* unless and until you're ordered off the ship. Do you understand?"

"Yessir!"

"Do you wish me to stay, too, Cargo Master Melikan?" the droid asked politely as Mel and Dash stepped into the turbolift.

"Yes!" roared the cargo master as the door slid shut. "Droids," he added for Dash's benefit. "Gotta spell everything out for them."

Despite the fact that Nik had turned off the klaxon in the hold, it was going full-tilt on the upper decks, nearly deafening the two Corellians as they stepped from the lift onto the forward section of the quarterdeck. They were not the first ones to respond. Arruna Var and her new Nautolan sidekick were some meters up the corridor, as were Leebo and the med droid, Gea.

Arruna, her face covered by a breathing apparatus, was in the process of obtaining atmospheric readings from the aft section of the deck, which had self-sealed automatically after the alarm sounded. As new as he was to the ship, it didn't take Dash more than a moment to recognize his surroundings. His quarters were on the other side of those emergency doors . . . as were Javul Charn's.

He ran.

He reached the group clustered about the emergency doors with Yanus Melikan at his side. He was just in time to see Arruna rip off her breath mask and turn her attention to the doors' controls, which were in a panel set into the port bulkhead. She was reaching for the emergency override.

Dash put out a hand to stop her. "What're you doing?" he shouted above the klaxon. "You want this whole section to vent?"

She shook her head, making her lekku swing. "There's no leak. Ask your droid." She pulled her arm away from him and hit the override. Nothing happened.

"Frang!" she said explosively.

The klaxon cut out just then, and the expletive echoed harshly in the suddenly silent hallway. Mel slid into the corner beside Arruna as she began punching codes into the control pad.

"What's she mean there's no leak?" Dash asked Leebo. "The ship seems to think there is."

"With all due respect, the ship is wrong. There's no difference in pressure on that side of the bulkhead and no sign that the air is going anywhere it doesn't belong."

Dash pointed at the emergency doors. "Is Javul Charn in there?"

"We don't know."

"Well, have you tried to communicate with her?"

"Communications seems to have been affected by the event," said Eaden. "Whatever the event was."

Dash turned to Mel and Arruna, who were still poking at the control panel.

"Any luck?"

Arruna glanced back over her shoulder. "The controls are dead."

Dash nodded. "Leebo, open it."

The droid's head swiveled toward him, optics glowing. "What—you mean by brute force? Like *that's* gonna happen. Do I look like an 11-88 factory droid to you?"

"Move back," Dash said sharply, waving aside Mel and Arruna.

They moved back. He pulled his blaster pistol, aimed, and drilled the control panel right above its transparent faceplate. It flew open with a small explosion of sparks and a fizzle. He holstered his pistol.

"*Now* open it," he told Leebo.

"You didn't say the magic wo—"

Dash's blaster was back in his hand. Leebo finished smoothly, "—but you're under a lot of stress. I understand." As the droid spoke, it moved to the door control and inserted an index finger into the servo mechanism. Nothing happened.

"Huh. That's odd. There appears to be no power reaching this panel at all."

He put a second hand to the controls, completing the circuit, and fed a jolt of energy into it. The servo whined, and the doors began to slide open. They got no more than a half a meter apart when they stopped.

"That's all I got, boss."

"It's enough." Dash slipped through the breach and into the aft section of the quarterdeck. It was dark—the emergency lights had apparently been affected as well—and eerily quiet. The air was devoid of the countless background noises—the muffled clicks of relays, the gentle exhalation of recycled air, the felt-more-than-heard *thrum* of generators—that are a starship's usual ambience. More than just the lights had been shut down in this section. Eaden came through right behind Dash, every tendril on his head on full alert.

All along the corridor the doors were sealed shut. At the far end, Dash could see the blur of light and dark as they hurtled through hyperspace. Leak or no leak, his skin still crawled and his jaw hurt from gritting his teeth. He tried to relax his face. Didn't help much.

He waved Eaden to the starboard side of the corridor while he stepped to port. He sensed Mel and Arruna behind him. "Arruna," he whispered to the Twi'lek, "get up to the engineering station and see if you can figure out what happened to the power back here."

"You got it," she said, and headed back. She sounded relieved. *Sensible,* he thought.

"Mel, how good are you with a blaster?"

"Scale of one to ten? Twelve."

"Good." Dash pulled a second pistol out of the hidden holster inside his jacket and handed it to the cargo master. "Just in case."

Mel examined it somewhat dubiously. "Of course, that's a scale where one is the best . . ."

Dash stopped short and looked at him. The other gave a sheepish shrug. "Sorry. Can't hit a cargo hold wall—from inside."

Dash blew his breath out, and noticed that it fogged the air. Even with the yacht's state-of-the-art insulation, it was getting cold fast. He quickly adjusted Mel's hand on the weapon, ensuring that the man's finger was inside the trigger guard. "Squeeze here; death and destruction comes out here. Right? Good. Leebo, stand by."

"No worries, boss. I was planning on doing just that."

Dash passed the door to his own quarters, moving with intent toward Dara's rooms. Eaden was slightly ahead of him and reached Dara Farlion's door first. He raised several tendrils, tapping their tips lightly across the smooth surface and taking on an attitude of intense listening.

After a moment he withdrew his tendrils and shook his head. "No one in there. At least, no one eager to get out."

"If Spike was home, we'd've heard it all the way from the cargo hold."

"Spike?" repeated Mel.

"Pet name." Dash stepped closer to Javul's door. He didn't need head-tresses to tell him what his ears and fingertips could—someone was behind that door making a very noisy, violent effort *not* to be behind that door.

He signaled Eaden, who crossed the corridor to join him. "I make two voices," he said.

Eaden nodded. "Agreed. It would seem they're both in there. And very much alive—at least as long as life support holds out."

Dash moved to inspect the exterior control panel. Dead.

"Dash." Eaden stood with one hand and a couple of tresses in contact with the door. "They've stopped shouting."

"What?" Dash turned back to the door and pounded on it with his fist. "Javul! Dara! Hey!"

No response. He pounded the door again. "Hey! Javul! Dara! If you can hear me, *bang on the door!*"

Nothing.

"Leebo!"

The droid pushed through the half-open emergency doors and moved down the corridor at less than top speed. "Oh, *yes,* Master. Of course, Master."

Dash gestured at the door. "Can the chatter. I need you to work on this door control."

"My pleasure. But let *me* take care of the faceplate this time. Your methods are so . . . brutish." The droid eyed

Dash's blaster while moving to the control panel and pressing an index finger to the upper left-hand corner of the defunct control plate. There was a tiny *tink!* and the plate popped out. Leebo poked an index finger into the guts of the door control. There was a *zap!* followed by a hum and, with a whisper of sound, the chamber doors slid back—to reveal an empty room. The lurid glow of emergency lights washed into the corridor; here, at least, they worked.

Not that they helped much, as Dash, Eaden, and Mel quickly learned by checking the entire suite.

There was no sign of either Dara Farlion or Javul Charn.

EIGHT

"Okay, fact one," Dash said. "The ship's security system thought it detected a hull breach on this deck and set off an alarm. Fact two: there was no hull breach, which means that either there was a malfunction in the security system, or someone tinkered with it. Fact three: the power was cut to the aft quarterdeck just after the emergency doors slammed shut. Which might have been caused by the aforementioned malfunction . . . or by something else. Fact four: Javul and Dara were locked in this suite by the emergency shutdown. Fact five: they've disappeared."

"Fact six," Leebo added. "We are in *so* much trouble . . ."

"The power was not shut down from either the bridge or engineering," offered Arruna, who'd returned to the quarterdeck as soon as she'd restored the deck's functionality. "It was interrupted at the section hub."

Dash frowned. "Manually?"

"I'll have to check the hub. I was able to push a power-up command through from the bridge to the terminus amidships, but only a physical inspection of the terminus itself will tell us if it was spliced manually or remotely."

"Wait. What are you suggesting?" First Officer Bran Finnick had come down from the bridge with Arruna, while Mel had returned to his cargo bay to run through his own security protocols. "You think someone's stowed away again?"

"Maybe not," Arruna said. "It could've been done remotely, as I said."

"How? We were in hyperspace when this happened. If it was triggered by another vessel, they'd have to have set this up *before* we jumped. Which means they'd have been shadowing us. *Closely.* We'd have detected them."

"Not if they were outfitted like this boat," Dash observed. "Might've been pirates."

"Who got onto the ship and sabotaged it?" asked Finnick dubiously.

"Or somehow got access to its passcodes."

Arruna was shaking her head. "If it had been pirates, they would have forced us out of hyperspace and tried to board us. More likely it was a timed event."

"Or an inside job," Dash mused.

Everyone turned to stare at him. He raised his hands as if to ward off the intensity and incredulity of their looks. "I'm just sayin' . . . anyway, we won't *know* until we've done some more detective work, will we? Meanwhile, I think we need to broaden our search for the missing women."

"Broaden our search?" repeated Finnick. "They were in this room. You heard them."

"Yeah, and now they're *not* in this room. Meaning that somehow they got out."

Finnick snorted in disbelief. "How?"

Dash gazed around the luxurious quarters in which they now stood, trying not to look as if he were mentally scratching his head. This was absurd. There was no place the women could have gone. There were no exterior hatches in the room; they'd searched the closet and peered under every article of furniture that had an under. The two women had vanished as thoroughly as if they'd been vaporized.

Maybe they had . . .

Dash slapped his hands together in a single brisk clap.

"Oh-*kay*, we've checked all the furniture for hiding places; now let's check it for possible exits."

"Exits?" Finnick repeated, and Dash bit back a sarcastic crack about echoes.

"Tables that are on movable plates," he explained. "Wardrobes with false bottoms. Wall shelves that slide or swing and—look, can we just have everybody check for that kind of stuff?"

Finnick snorted again; Dash was getting extremely tired of that particular mode of disagreement. "Spy story nonsense," the first officer muttered. Nevertheless, he started to search, as did Leebo. The droid stopped when Dash added, "Not you, Leebo. I want you to scan for hidden weaponry."

That stopped everything. Dash once again became the cynosure of everyone's gaze. "What are you thinking?" asked the first officer.

"Let's get real," said Dash. "The previous owner of this ship was most likely doing less-than-aboveboard business. The stealth shuttle is sort of a clue, right? That, and the amount of ablative shielding and other safety features that your boss *didn't* have to install because they were already here. At a guess, I'd say *Nova's Heart* belonged to a smuggler—who just might have installed a high-security system in this suite that included defensive weaponry to take out intruders. Maybe something tripped it before or during the emergency and—"

All the color had leached out of Bran Finnick's face. "And it thought Javul and Dara were intruders? No. There was no such system." He looked at Arruna. "Right?"

The Twi'lek looked paler as well. "There's no record of it in the original schematics."

"Doesn't mean it's not there," said Dash. "I don't like the idea any more than you do, but it has to be either validated or invalidated." He turned to the droid. "Leebo, call up the schematics and see if there are any logical places to hide surveillance and defensive equipment."

Leebo uttered a chirp of assent and brought up the schematics' holos without argument. Dash watched for a moment as Eaden, Arruna, and Finnick began pushing and pulling at the cabin's furniture. Then he began a slow tour of the perimeter of the room. It struck him, as he turned from the interior bulkhead between the living room and the bedroom in the small but luxurious suite, that there was something odd about the room, but he could not, for the life of him, put a finger on what it was. As he was trying to figure it out, Leebo's head came up with a snap.

"Huh." The droid turned to face the interior bulkhead on the opposite side of the cabin. "Hey, boss—check this out."

Dash moved to where the droid stood, the quarter-deck schematics projected onto the burnished brown surface of the wall in front of them. "What is it?"

"That area I've so helpfully highlighted in red for you is the original schematic for this row of suites."

"Yeah, so what am I looking at?"

"Boss," Leebo said, in what was, for the droid, a patient tone. "What's *wrong* with this picture?"

Dash peered at the red area and noticed something right away. He also realized why the room had struck him as peculiar.

"This schematic shows these cabins as all being the same size." He swept an index finger down the line of renderings. "But they're not. This one is smaller than our suite. Or at least the front room is smaller, by about half a meter."

"Hurrah—you're teachable," said Leebo.

Dash stepped through the schematic's lines of light and pressed his hands to the wall. "There's something behind here," he said. He moved to the front corner of the quarters as the others left off their poking and prodding and came to see what he was doing.

"The schematics show this wall as being about half a meter farther aft," he said as he continued to run his hands over the surface, searching for unevenness or seams.

"Unless you've got bionic fingers, boss, I'm pretty sure I'm better qualified to find what you're looking for."

"The droid's right," said Finnick. "If all else fails we can burn through the metal."

"I really wish you wouldn't. I just had it refinished."

The entire group turned as one to see Javul Charn standing nonchalantly in the doorway of her suite. Dara and Mel were with her.

Dash just kept from letting loose with a scalding expletive. "Where have you *been*?"

Dara rolled her eyes. "Sounds like my dad."

Mel stepped into the room. "They scared the hell out of me by appearing in the cargo bay, literally out of nowhere."

"Not nowhere," Javul corrected, looking contrite. "We came out of a escape panel that connects—"

Dash pointed at the wall. "Here."

"We didn't know what was happening, Dash," Javul said. "The alarm went off, the power cut out, and we thought there was a hull breach back here. We tried to raise somebody by banging on the door, but then we figured if there really was a hull breach, we might be in pretty bad shape if the doors failed. So we used the escape tube."

"I've already explained to them," Mel said, "that there wasn't a hull breach. It was something else."

"Yeah. Sabotage, apparently," said Dash and was gratified when Javul paled, her flesh looking almost translucent.

"Is there any way to be sure?" she asked.

"I'm going to go check that power terminus, first off,"

said Arruna grimly. "I'd like some company. Someone with a blaster and more than a little experience using it would be nice." Her gaze turned to Eaden, who bowed, then followed her from the room.

"You're sure you're all right?" Finnick asked Javul.

She nodded. "I'm . . . I'm fine. Why don't you secure the ship, run diagnostics on everything, then get us back in hyperspace as soon as you and Arruna and the captain feel it's safe. We don't want to be late for our Rodian engagements."

The ship's systems showed no sign of damage or further sabotage, the hull was fine, and a G2 repair droid was scrambled to fix the broken door panels. Arruna determined that the power outage in the aft quarterdeck had been triggered remotely, and immediately disappeared into a conference with First Mate Finnick to pore over the computer records. If an event had triggered the outage, she reasoned, it would show up somewhere as a surge, a blip, or even, if they were far luckier than they deserved, a clear command sequence.

Meanwhile, Dash and Eaden examined the access tube that led from Javul's suite to the cargo hold—Dash wondering how his easy celebrity-sitting job had suddenly become dangerous.

The tube was pretty slick, actually, equipped with hand- and footholds that would serve a broad variety of sentients (Hutts being an obvious exception), a stand-alone air filtration system (which allowed it to double as a hiding place), and a strip of light-emitting plasteel that required very little energy to burn virtually forever. The ship's a-grav had been shut off within the tube so as not to register as an inexplicable power drain.

"I gotta get me one of these," Dash said as they finished their inspection and emerged into the ship's cargo bay.

"Straight shot from the *Outrider*'s bridge right down to the hold."

"And what would you propose we gut to make room?" asked Eaden mildly. "The dimensions of the *Outrider* won't allow for this sort of . . . excess."

Dash grinned. "We could take it down through your quarters. You keep bragging about how little sleep you need."

"I do not brag," returned Eaden. "It is a statement of simple fact. The teräs käsi discipline allows me to sleep less and more lightly than most diurnal sentients."

Dash was about to offer a sarcastic retort when he looked down the aisle between shipping crates and saw Yanus Melikan striding toward them with a grim expression on his long face.

"Arruna and Bran have found something," he said before Dash could ask. "They want you up on the bridge."

"Approximately one minute and twenty seconds before the alarm sounded, we contacted the Rodian Space Authority for approach protocols," said Finnick. "We sent the standard approach sequence and received the standard acknowledgments. Except that *this* came in, riding a subsidiary carrier wave." He indicated a long string of Rodian characters that scrolled down the flat display of the bridge engineering terminal he, Dash, and Arruna were hovering over.

Arruna leaned in and ran a finger along the sequence of symbols and numbers. "It exchanges the correct protocols, here, then tells the ship's system there's been an event of some sort in the aft section of the quarterdeck, which the ship interpreted as a hull breach. Then it tells the system to shut down power to the affected area."

"It actually targeted a specific area of the ship?" asked Dash.

Arruna tapped the code with a pale blue fingernail. "This command, right here, targets the quarterdeck abaft the beam. Where Javul, her guests, and the officers are housed."

"That's pretty specific."

Arruna's left lekku quivered. "And peculiar. The command sequence doesn't *cause* a disaster—which, theoretically, it could have. It simply *fakes* one. Why?"

"Sending a message?" suggested Dash.

"What message? It's not exactly along the lines of *I'm your biggest fan.*"

"No. It's more along the lines of *I'm your biggest threat.*"

The Twi'lek's lekku twined about each other—a sign, Dash knew, of extreme anxiety. "Again, why?" Arruna asked.

"I don't know, but I have to think someone does."

He excused himself from the bridge and went aft to find Javul Charn. She was on the observation deck with her road manager, but she dismissed Dara as soon as she saw the look on Dash's face.

"Talk to me, Javul," he said when Spike had left the deck. "Tell me everything you know about this over-eager fan of yours."

"I've already done that."

"Okay. Then let me tell you what *I* know about him . . . or her, or it. He isn't just overzealous. He's obsessed. And he's not just a nut. He's *clever.* And he's not just wealthy. He's got resources some small planetary governments don't have."

She paled. It made her eyes look huge in her heart-shaped face. Dash swallowed. *Whoa.* That was some look she had there. Once again he was reminded why fans became obsessed with her.

"What makes you say that?" she asked.

"The black lilies might've taken some credits—buying

and bringing in all the flowers, bribing port officials, setting up the stasis field over your docking slip. But that was a parlor trick compared with this. The signal for the ship to respond to a fake hull breach and shut down power to the quarters was riding the carrier wave from the Rodian controller. It gave all the appropriate handshakes, and it knew where in the ship you lived . . . or at least the guy behind it did."

"What do you want me to say?" she said, her voice unsteady. "I guess I have overzealous fans with too much time and credits on their hands."

"Banthaflop."

She blinked. "What?"

"You have something a lot worse than that and I think you know it."

"What do you think I have?"

"Someone with a *serious* gripe against you. The kind of someone who can and does hold grudges for life—and beyond, if he can possibly manage it." Dash folded his arms. "It's time to come clean, little miss Star Bright. It's not that this guy likes you too much—it's that this guy really *doesn't* like you. And I'm not real happy myself," he added. "I don't like flying backward and blind through an asteroid field, I don't like facing a rancor with one hand tied behind me, and I *don't* like this. At all. So 'fess up. What'd you do—kick someone out of your backup band? Refuse to date some high roller? Trash his pad? Break his heart?"

She stood silently for a long moment, her forehead resting on the transparent canopy of the observation deck, gazing out into space while Dash watched her reflection in the transparisteel surface. Then she said, "Not exactly."

Dash exhaled sharply. "Not exactly what? You didn't exactly trash his pad or you didn't exactly break his heart?"

"*I* didn't do anything." She lifted her head to glance at him before returning her gaze to the stars. "It's like this— there was this Vigo—"

A prickling of primal hatred crawled up Dash's spine. "A Vigo? As in *Black Sun*?"

Javul made a face. "Is there any other kind?"

Dash wanted nothing to do with the notorious and powerful interstellar crime syndicate—even once-removed. He wasn't afraid of Black Sun . . . but he was afraid of his own deeply buried hunger for revenge.

"How soon do we get to Rodia? If you've got bad blood with a Vigo, I'm catching the next transport back to Tatooine."

NINE

Javul eyed Dash narrowly. "You didn't let me finish. This Vigo had a girlfriend—her name was Alai Jance, as I recall. She started out the same way I did—as a small-time singer on the Corellian circuit. She hooked up with this Vigo—I don't remember his name—and her singing career took a turn for the better. Then she dumped the Vigo and dropped out of sight, which probably wasn't her best career move."

"And this has to do with you, how?"

"I'm getting to that," she said patiently, as if she were talking to a one-function service droid. "When I . . . burst onto the scene, I occasionally got mistaken for her. Apparently, we bear a striking resemblance to each other. As a result, I had to do a massive PR campaign establishing that I wasn't a pirate's brat from Nar Shaddaa, my hair wasn't really red, I wasn't just a glorified lounge singer, and I wasn't the same woman who'd stupidly hitched herself to a Black Sun crime boss and was now trying to make a comeback."

"Really."

"Yes, really. I had no idea about any of this until I started getting increasingly strange holomail. And then, the black lilies . . ." She rubbed her hands up and down her arms as if she were suddenly cold.

"So you're suggesting your stalker is somebody who doesn't believe you. Big surprise there." He held up a hand to halt her protest. "Any idea who that might be?"

She shook her head. "A rival maybe. Maybe one of this guy's lieutenants—someone who thinks he might get in good with the boss if he—I don't know—teaches the boss's ex a lesson. Maybe none of the above. I don't know for sure."

"Well, fine then. If it's a rival or a lieutenant, then the thing to do is let this Vigo know about it and let *him* take care of the problem."

She grimaced. "I did mention that she's his *ex*-girl-friend, right? He doesn't really care what happens to her . . . much less to me."

"If he's a fan, he might. I mean, look—you're big business. Chances are good he's already got credits invested in you, right? If he thinks the galaxy is about to lose the considerable talents of Javul Charn because of some rival of his—or worse yet, one of his own guys . . ."

"Trust me," she said. "He won't care. Alai Jance, wher-ever she is right now, is of no concern to her notorious ex." She straightened away from the window and brushed her hands off on her tunic as if wiping the problem away. "Look, we're going to be docking on Rodia soon. I need to be thinking about my performances."

"You're kidding me, right? You're not seriously going to go through with these gigs?"

She shrugged. "I don't have a choice, Dash. I'm under contract. A lot of people are depending on me. I can't let them down."

She turned away from him and disappeared through the sliding doors that gave onto the quarterdeck, her head held high.

The performances on Rodia were in Equator City. No surprise there . . . except that Equator City was a hotbed of Black Sun activity—mostly credit laundering—that centered on the network of casinos operating there. Dash would have thought that, under the circumstances, Javul

Charn would want to steer clear of the Rodian capital. He was surprised she'd brought her tour anywhere on Rodia.

He said as much to her as they took a shuttle to the venue from the ultraprivate landing facilities at the spaceport. The venue—the Holosseum—was a huge structure of transparisteel and durasteel big enough to house three *Nova's Hearts,* the *Outrider,* and the *Millennium Falcon* all at once. It looked, Dash thought, like a giant crystalline egg half buried in the ground, pointy-end up.

"Actually," she told him, "I feel a bit safer here than elsewhere. Whoever's after Alai Jance is apparently afraid of the Vigos headquartered here."

Dash glanced at her sharply. "Vigos headquarter here?"

"One or two—or so I'm told."

"Yeah? By who?"

"By me, as it happens," said Spike.

He looked across the shuttle to where the road manager sat facing him. Beside her, Eaden sat cross-legged on the couch, seemingly half asleep. That's what his lidded eyes said, but his head-tails told a different tale. They were poised in an attitude that Dash thought of as *stealth mode.*

"You? What do *you* know about Black Sun?"

"I was raised on Tatooine. My daddy owned a grog shop until he got bought out by Chalmun."

"The Cantina?"

She shook her head. "Naw. Little place in Kerner Plaza—Chalmun turned it into a café for his wife. Daddy made a pretty pile of credits on the deal, too. Anyway, you hear lots of interesting things in a grog shop."

"Yeah. Did you hear which Vigos are holed up on Rodia?"

"I've heard a few names tossed around."

Blasted spiky fem. "Which names?"

"Guy named Clezo, for one. A Rodian."

"Sounds familiar—little wiry guy with buggy eyes?"

"Yeah, Clezo's pretty short. And *all* Rodians have buggy eyes."

"His are buggier." Dash thought about the implications of this for a moment. Then he asked, "Who's the other one?"

She made a face, thinking. "Not a native. Lemme see . . . oh, a *former* Mandalorian named . . . what was it?" She looked at Javul, who shrugged and shook her head.

"I try not to pay attention to stuff like that," Javul demurred.

Dash kept his mouth shut, because if he opened it the frustrated scream that would result would be audible only to an Ortolan.

Spike snapped her fingers. "Kris. That was it, I think. Rumor had it that he sort of wandered in and out of Rodian space and made Clezo nervous."

"As I recall, just about anything makes Clezo nervous," Dash said.

Javul turned to look at him. "You know a Vigo? And you were concerned because you thought *I* knew one? Isn't that kind of a double standard?"

"I wasn't concerned because I thought you *knew* a Vigo. I was concerned because I thought you'd *crossed* a Vigo. There's a big difference."

"But you know a Vigo."

"Not socially."

Javul laughed and turned to look out the shuttle window as the vehicle pulled up at the front of the giant crystal egg that was the Holosseum. "And that, I suspect, is Dash-Rendar-ese for I-don't-wanna-talk-about-it."

Dash stifled a retort and asked, "Why are we pulling up to the front of the building? Shouldn't we enter through the stage area?"

"The front is more public. Look." She canted her head

toward a barricade behind which a large crowd of devoted fans waved and jumped up and down and did whatever else it was that devoted fans did—all at the tops of their lungs, air sacs, bronchi, or whatever respiratory organs they owned.

"You like being noticed, don't you?"

"I like being *safe*. I figured our zealot wouldn't be likely to try something major in such a public place—and besides, I can't exactly sneak past these guys, can I?"

"Sneak past them? You let them know you were coming."

"No—the adverts did that."

"Down to the day and hour?"

Spike leaned across the space between them. "They've been there all night, laserbrain. Look at the camp gear."

Dash looked. She was right, of course. Most of the people at the front edge of the crowd had vac-paks, canteens, and expandable sleep-cocoons with them. He even saw a couple of little enviro-tents pitched along a grassy sward. These were the hard-core fans, obviously here for the long haul.

They stepped out of the shuttle onto a broad swathe of glittering duracrete. The humidity hit Dash like a soggy mallet. He looked up at the energy dome over the city. It seemed that, no matter how many advances in technology the Rodians acquired, they couldn't quite govern their homeworld's environment. The entire planet seemed like a bog to most humans—a cool, misty bog in the extreme southern and northern climes and a hot, steamy one at the equator.

Dash and Eaden stood flanking Javul Charn, while she waved at the cheering crowds gathered to see her. They were meters away and behind a force barrier, but still, Dash's gaze swept the fringes and beyond, looking for anything that might be a weapon.

"You're too exposed here," he said, taking Javul by

the upper arm. "Let's get inside." He was a little surprised when she didn't resist the suggestion.

It was measurably drier inside the Holosseum, and cooler as well. They made their way into the main hall through a gigantic circular atrium that rose to immense heights, creating the impression of an egg within an egg. Inside, Dash revised his estimate of how many ships the place could hold—he'd been too stingy. The entire broad bottom of the venue was taken up by the stage. The audience would sit in antigrav seats arranged in sections in the curve of the dome. At the moment, those seating sections were sunk into the floor, stacked one atop another so that only the topmost ones were visible. When the audience was admitted, they would file into the seats, filling each section, which would then lift toward the ceiling. Most holo-halls were like this, but Dash had to admit being awfully impressed with the Rodian venue. The only one bigger was the Holodome on Coruscant, and it was of an older design—the audience had to take lifts and mono-jets to fixed seating built into the walls or suspended from high-tensile cabling.

Javul smiled as she stepped up onto the stage. It was made of white, translucent plasteel that glowed like the shell of a Nautolan moon-snail, lit from beneath with soft, ambient light.

"I love performing here. It's like a shrine."

Dash followed her onto the stage, peering suspiciously at the gleaming surface underfoot. "Yeah, right. I feel like I'm about to have a religious experience."

The words were no sooner out of his mouth than a hole appeared in the middle of the stage and irised out as if they stood on the eye of a titanic beast.

"*Drop!*" he shouted, going into a half crouch, blaster already aimed steadily at the hole—out of which appeared the heads and shoulders of Yanus Melikan and his cargo droid.

"Come on," said the cargo master, his pale eyes focused on the business end of Dash's weapon. "Do you have to draw that blasted thing *every* time something surprises you?"

Dash glanced at Javul, who was staring at him, wide-eyed . . . and obviously holding back laughter. Spike didn't bother to hold it back. She burst into a cascade of unfeminine guffaws that grated on his ears. A second later Javul was laughing, too, though much more attractively. She held out a pacifying hand to Dash, who could only glare from the women to Mel and back again.

"I'm—I'm sorry, Dash, but the look on your face . . ."

He holstered his weapon and turned to look behind him as a strangely musical hissing caught his ear. Eaden blinked at him, lips drawn into a straight line.

"You did *not* just laugh at me," Dash told him, pointing an accusing finger.

The Nautolan blinked and said, "As you wish."

"Well, what am I *supposed* to do? A hole opens up in the floor—"

"We have to bring the equipment in from somewhere," said Mel mildly. "In a three-dimensional performance space, that somewhere must be below."

Dash and Eaden explored that "below" as much as possible as the stage gear and holo-emitters were put in place by a mixed stage crew of droids and sentients. It was big and open with few places to hide . . . until flat after antigrav flat moved Javul Charn's equipment into place. Then it became a warren.

"Do you have to travel with all this stuff?" Dash asked the star of the show as she watched her setup grow. "Isn't the whole point of a holoperformance that it's all—you know—holo?"

"That's just it," she said earnestly, leading Dash to discover another *look* that made it hard to remain professional. "Holography has reached such a level that *nothing* is real. I mean, if those people hadn't seen me walk in the front door, they'd have no way of knowing—if I didn't make a point of showing them—that I'm really here and not in some studio in Imperial Center. To enhance that effect, I do some of my acts with real props. Wire frames and gantries and fly-hooks."

"*Fly*-hooks?" He was confused. "You mean skyhooks?"

She pointed up into the gigantic rotunda, which Dash was sure was big enough to have its own weather system. "I fly. I literally fly, Dash. Not virtually, but really. Not antigrav, either. I use an opti-fiber tether." She grinned at his horrified expression, then leaned toward him and added, "It's so thin, it's invisible."

For at least the second or third time that day, Dash was speechless. He'd played catch-as-catch-can with Imperial cruisers, navigated asteroid fields, confronted pirates, bounty hunters, Imperial goons, Black Sun operatives, rancor beasts, and even an Inquisitor, but this . . . For a moment his mind held a horrible image of her dangling, hundreds of meters above a very public stage, suspended by a glowing opti-fiber the thickness of a Gamorrean's nose hair. If someone were to cut that slender lifeline . . .

"Under normal circumstances, Javul, none of this would bother me—well, okay, it would bother me a little. But these aren't normal circumstances. If they were I wouldn't be here."

She put a hand on his arm. "I'm a pro at this, Dash. I've done it hundreds of times. I'm as much in my element up there—" She nodded at the faraway ceiling. "—as you are piloting your ship. Don't you have *anything* you do that most people think is just nuts, but you do it anyway . . . because you *can*?"

He flashed for a moment on the Kessel Run and the maneuver that had gotten him and Eaden into this situation. He hated that what she said almost made sense to him. *Almost.*

"Eaden," he said.

His first mate responded with a grunt.

"You stay here and keep an eye on our little holostar. I'm going to take Leebo and head back to the Rodian flight control office at the spaceport. I want to see if I can scare up any intel on that coded piece of sabotage we picked up. Like for instance who sent it."

Javul made a pouty face. "You're going to miss my rehearsal."

He gave her an icy look. It had been known to terrify younger, less experienced space jockeys. She just laughed.

The Equator City Flight Control Authority was abuzz with activity. Dash's polite request to review the outgoing messages to the *Nova's Heart* got him exactly nowhere. Frustrated, he filed a formal complaint with flight control, stating that the ship had been sent erroneous information. That at least got him some attention.

"What sort of erroneous information?" asked the midlevel Rodian functionary.

"Information that caused the ship to register an imaginary hull breach. Our security systems went berserk and shut off part of the ship. The ship's owner was almost suffocated in her own quarters." A bit of an exaggeration never hurt.

The Rodian flight admin consulted his holo-terminal. "The *Nova's Heart* docked two standard hours ago. Presumably this exchange of false information occurred somewhat earlier?"

"On planetary approach. It was part of the second packet of instructions our navicomp received from your control."

The Rodian shrugged. "A diagnostic would have been run since then. I'm sure the anomaly was cleared up."

"This wasn't an anomaly," said Dash carefully, just managing to quell the urge to drag the bug-eyed imp out of his seat and dig into the guts of the system himself. "It was a very specific and very dangerous instruction set."

The Rodian blinked. "You're suggesting it was deliberate?"

"That's what I'm trying to find out. Now if you'd be so kind as to let me go back over the communications between this facility and the *Nova's Heart*?"

The little toady was shaking his head. "I'm sorry, Captain . . . I didn't catch your name."

"Dash. Dash Rendar."

The functionary pushed and stroked the virtual buttons and pads that floated in the air between them. "Pardon me, *Captain* Rendar, but the commander of the *Nova's Heart* is registered as a Serdor Marrak." He pulled up a flat image of Marrak, not bothering to perform even the small courtesy of spinning the pic toward Dash so that the stats weren't reversed. "A Zabrak. You," he continued, "are not Zabrak. Or, if you are, you should shoot your cosmetic surgeon." He uttered a rude quack intended for a laugh.

"I'm not the ship's captain. Never claimed otherwise. I'm Charn's security officer."

The bug eyes blinked. "Charn? As in Javul Charn?"

Now he was getting somewhere. He smiled. "The very same. She's setting up over at the Holosseum even as we speak. She asked me to come down here and see to this matter. So if I might go over those flight logs?"

"I'm sorry, Rendar, but I can't let you do that."

Dash regarded the admin for a moment, cast a glance at the silent Leebo, then pulled on a jaunty smile. "I can make it worth your while."

"No, you cannot." The Rodian sounded genuinely regretful, but he also sounded firm. "There are regulations to uphold. I cannot grant civilians access to the system. Under any circumstances. You've filed an official complaint. It will take several days to process, but it *will* be dealt with."

"In several days, we'll be moving on to our next stop!"

"That is not my affair. Good day."

Stung by the dismissal, Dash removed himself to the corridor outside the flight control office. Of all the admins that might have been on duty, he had to trip over an honest one. "What are the odds?" he asked himself softly.

"Well, what now, boss?" asked Leebo.

"I suppose we could wait for the next admin shift. Find someone willing to be bought off. Of course, that'll take hours."

"Seven-point-oh-four-four, to be exact," offered the droid. "We don't—"

"—have that kind of time," they finished in unison.

Dash frowned, peering up the corridor, wondering where the communications systems were housed. "If we could find the communications hub, we might be able to slice in and—"

He stopped. Leebo was shaking his head slowly. "There's a reason they call it Comm Central, Boss. It would be too well guarded—not to mention having security protocols up the exhaust pipes."

There was a moment of silence as Dash pondered the situation; then Leebo uttered a tinny sigh. "Do I have to say it?"

"Say what?"

"I've got an idea, boss. Of course, I *always* have an idea."

Dash glared at him. "So spit it out."

"Housekeeping."

"Excuse me?"

"Housekeeping bots and droids have to plug into protocol terminals to receive instructions. The ports are unguarded. Who cares if someone steals the trash compactor schedule? You see, all systems are connected at some level in a facility like this. They have to be, because if it's ever necessary to reboot the entire system or to power it up after a disaster, you can't initialize every system independently; it'd take forever—well, actually, only seventeen-point-nine hours, but still—I'm sorry; did you just make a noise?"

Dash made the noise again. "I get it," he said. "There's built-in redundancy and subsystems that tie the whole mess together. Like housekeeping."

"You *do* get it. Imagine my delight."

"Shut up," said Dash, "and find a terminal."

Even down in the sublevels of the building there weren't many maintenance droids of Leebo's class engaged directly in the housekeeping activities. They were overseers, leaving it to the smaller, simpler service droids to scurry about doing the grunt work—cleaning floors, scooping up trash, sucking up dust. Noting this, Leebo snatched up an MSE-6 cleaning droid, tucked it under one arm, and pretended, quite credibly Dash thought, to be adjusting its communications port.

Such a task required that the droid plug the MSE-6 into one of the many maintenance ports integrated into each doorway along the service corridors. Leebo did this with mechanical panache, uttered the droid equivalent of a "Tsk," then sliced in himself, using the MSE-6 as a conduit.

Dash, watching from where he pretended to be awaiting a lift, froze when a Rodian maintenance supervisor stopped to see what Leebo was doing.

"What's wrong with the MSE unit?" he asked. "If it's broken, just take it down to the shop and have them issue a new one. It'll save time."

"Not necessary, sir," Leebo said. "It seems merely to be misinterpreting its instruction set. I believe I can have it set to rights in moments once I determine the source of the problem. I am currently," he added as the Rodian's gaze took in the fact that he was linked into the system through the maintenance droid, "ascertaining that the fault does not lie in the instruction set itself."

"Oh. Yeah. Sure. Good idea. Carry on, then." The Rodian departed, Dash relaxed, and Leebo continued his tunneling through the port authority's housekeeping system.

Dash's hope that the hallways would remain empty was a forlorn one; when the lift opened for a trio of Sullustan mech-techs, he was forced to enter and ride it up several levels until they got off. Then he rode it down again. In fact, he rode it up and down several times while waiting for Leebo to finish.

He'd returned to the maintenance level for perhaps the fourth time when the doors of the lift opened and Leebo stepped in.

"Mission accomplished."

"You got the records?"

The droid tapped his durasteel skull with a finger. "Got 'em."

"Anything interesting?"

"I didn't have time to analyze them. That maintenance super came back."

Dash glanced down. "You still have a cleaning droid tucked under your arm."

"Yes. I do, don't I? Can I keep it? I've always wanted a pet."

"You're joking."

"Droids don't joke—not really. We just regurgitate learned responses. Fact is, I may have to keep it. I told the maintenance super I was taking it down to the shop after all, but this lift is going up . . . and up and up. He may have noted this."

"So just turn the thing loose when we get out."

"Bad idea. It's got a unique ID. If anyone suspects I

was tampering with it, they could track it down and discover that that's just what I was doing—using its protocols to slice into the system."

"You *can't* have left fingerprints."

"Shows what you know. In connecting to the MSE-6, I left my own indelible mark on the little guy. Unless I completely wipe its core, they might be able to identify me by *my* unique ID."

"So? Wipe its core."

Leebo reacted with a shocked stance. "How rude." He patted the top of the droid's metal casing. "Pretend you didn't hear that, Mousie."

"Mousie?"

"An MSE-6 cleaning droid. Serial number E3E3EEK. *Mousie* seems an appropriate, if unimaginative, name."

"Uh-huh. And you're going to get it out of here how?" The lift doors hissed open, and Dash nodded to the broad, crowded hallway that gave onto the port authority's entry.

"It's rather a warm day, sir," said Leebo blandly. "Allow me to carry your jacket."

TEN

JAVUL WAS NERVOUS. NERVOUS IN A WAY SHE HADN'T
felt since she'd embarked on her career. Before a performance she was always keyed up, always edgy, amped,
eager to be onstage. That came with the territory. But
right now, she was just plain jumpy. "Jinky," as Dara
would say.

And why not? Before she'd acquired her "stalker," the
most she'd had to fear was a missed lyric, a missing prop,
a mechanical glitch. Now . . . now she didn't know what
to expect.

She stood on the stage below the Holosseum dome and
looked up into the vast scaffolding that served as the
framework for her show. Flown in the ether beneath the
crown of the Holosseum were four separate sets. One was
a stylized forest with treetops suggested by vertical masts
of aluminum swathed in synthsilk. "Clouds" of zoosha
fabric—able to be rendered invisible at a command from
the rig master—floated in among the tree limbs.

The second set was a balcony that formed the only solid
surface in a cloud city described in sheets and streamers
and billows of translucent material.

The third and fourth pieces represented the duality of
Coruscant/Imperial Center—the first gleaming and grand,
reaching up toward the distant sun; its alter ego dark and
enigmatic with edges that were cold and hard and unfor-
giving.

These, Javul had designed herself. She didn't openly

proclaim that they represented Coruscant's past and present, of course. That would have been subversive, and Javul Charn stayed as far from subversive in her stage act as possible. But she was not averse to admitting a little nostalgia.

The costumer brought out a pair of wings and began securing them to her back, carefully adjusting them so they wouldn't foul the opti-fiber cable attached to Javul's ultralight harness. They looked like gossamer—slender arcs of the finest metal overlaid with panels of zoosha. A tiny power generator poured colored light into the threads of the fabric and up the length of the tether, cycling through all the colors of the spectrum—even colors visible only to nonhuman eyes. The little power source also generated an emergency antigrav field just in case the opti-fiber were to fail. In the average venue, the field would let Javul down to the stage gently.

The Rodian Holosseum was no average venue, either in size or opulence. It was easily the largest, most luxurious indoor concert hall she'd ever performed in, and that domed ceiling seemed a kilometer away just now.

She took a deep breath, voice-activated the antigrav field, and bobbed up from the floor.

"Make sure of the coshtumes, please," said the wardrobe designer, a Bothan woman named Tereez Dza'lar. "I'd hate to have you acshidentally turn thish into a holo-peep-show."

Javul smiled and murmured, "Act One, Scene Two."

The pale gray one-piece body stocking she wore shimmered out of existence to make way for a diaphanous dress of sky blue with a shower of golden glitter that seemed to migrate over the surface of the fabric. The ragged hem of the skirt floated about her hips and knees. Her hair framed her face in a pale, lustrous gold.

"Good," said Tereez. "Try shomething a bit more opaque."

"Act Two, Scene Three."

The dress dissolved, and was replaced by a regulation Imperial uniform of the type worn by intelligence officers. In drab brown with gleaming rank insignia, it was about as far removed from the insubstantial fey blue gown as it could get.

Tereez laughed out loud—a sound somewhere between a hiss and a purr. "The wings!"

Looking at her projected image in an offstage holo-display, Javul joined in. The Imperial getup clashed horribly with the wings, an irony that was not lost on her. "Wow, now there's a new concept: an Imperial sprite. Think we could build a show around that?"

Tereez shook her head. "I think it would be shuicide to try. The Emperor would never approve. Try the Firsht Act coshtume. The cap was cutting out lasht time."

Javul complied and faced her costumer wearing a green tunic with green leggings and a jaunty green cap with a bright red feather that nearly matched the new color of her hair. This time the costume accommodated the wings by making them seem to disappear. They weren't programmed to do that with the Imperial intel costume because she never wore wings with that during the live show.

"Looksh good. Everything sheems to be functioning perfectly."

Javul looked up at the rigging again, hyperaware of that old show business axiom that the one thing a performer didn't want right before a performance was a perfect rehearsal. She found herself hoping something would go wrong.

"Places please!" she called to the crew. "Let's take the first number, okay?"

Everyone faded from sight . . . except for Eaden Vrill, who stood impassively at the extreme edge of the stage, arms folded over his broad chest, tentacles waving gently about his shoulders.

Dara appeared behind him at the edge of the stage and tapped on his foot. "Sorry, big guy—you can't stand there."

With a last look up into the dome, the Nautolan bodyguard descended from the stage into the shadows between two sections of seating, his head-tresses dancing as if in an eddying wind.

Javul felt a tingle of apprehension. Where was Dash and what had he found out at the spaceport?

"It's trashed," said Finnick. He returned to the spot in the comm readout where the sub rosa message began. There was no clear instruction there, just a string of jumbled garbage that neither Leebo nor the ship's communications computer could make anything of. "I'd guess it was programmed to deteriorate after broadcast."

"But we've still got the substance of it on our end, right?" Dash asked.

"I doubt it." Finnick called up the ship's transceiver records and went to the time index in question.

More garbage.

Dash sat back in his seat next to Finnick on the bridge of the *Nova's Heart*. "Then we're stumped. There's nothing we can determine from this."

"Yeah there is," said Arruna, leaning over Finnick's shoulder to point at the very beginning of the message in the flight control record. "This was keyed in. Probably from the sender's console."

"How can you tell?" Dash asked, frowning.

"If it were sliced in from a remote source, you'd see some artifacts from the tunneling. There'd be, um, slicing and transport code, basically. That is, the code that created a hole in the data stream, then inserted the message. As you can see"—she pointed from the flight control readout to the one from the ship's transceiver—"these two pieces of code, while pure garbage, are identical pieces of pure garbage. They're deteriorating in the same predefined way."

"Yeah. I get it," said Dash. "There was no slicing code in *our* message, so if there was any in the port's exchange, we'd see it as . . . different garbage."

"Exactly."

"But that means that whoever was sitting on the console in flight control deliberately sabotaged us. They're part of the conspiracy." He hated the word, but there it was.

"It might have been a flunky who was just told to enter this code without realizing what it would do," said Finnick, "but yeah, there's a chance it was someone who knew exactly what they were doing."

Dash stood up and moved away from the console. "And they might've been doing it because they *wanted* to do it or because they were *paid* to do it or because they were *ordered* to do it by a superior. And there's no way for us to know which."

"One thing we do know," said the Twi'lek engineer. "Someone with tentacles in the port authority set this up. Which suggests—"

"Someone with almost unlimited resources," said Dash. *Like a Vigo, for example.* He rubbed at the back of his neck. This whole situation was giving him a headache.

Javul flew at the end of her lifeline high up in the dome, adorned in her sprite costume, her wings trailing glitter through the star-spangled ersatz heavens. Music soared around her—the opening strains of the centerpiece of the second act in which the sprite bemoaned the loss of her free-spirited love to the groundlings who could not fly and who therefore sought to keep all others from the sky.

Borne upward on the winds of melody and harmony, she opened her mouth and began to sing:

I see you in your tiny box;
My heart falls and breaks and bleeds.

The opti-fiber line played out and she plummeted right on cue, drawing up mere meters from the floor.

I would come to you.
I would rage for you.
I would free you.

She raised her arms in a graceful dancer's pose and shot skyward again.

But if I come and if I rage and if I seek to free,
Will they not spring the tender trap?
Your pain is only bait . . . for me.

She'd reached the apex of the dome again and let the last note of the verse ring out long and mournfully before swooping into the aerial "steps" of her dance. She worked in a spiral, pushing the circumference of the dance out and out. With the seating in place, it would seem to her watchers that they sat within the forest of Kashyyyk or cloud city on Bespin or the heights and depths of Imperial Center. She would pass so close to them that they could almost reach out and touch her.

She looked down as she soared through the forest of Kashyyyk and saw the holographically projected trunks of the great trees reaching down and down.

Then she saw something else. She saw the aperture in the middle of the stage begin to iris open.

Before she could wonder what Mel was doing moving scenery during rehearsal, she felt a deep thrum, a mechanical rumble. The air trembled and the concert seats—all of them—shot out of their storage pits into the great, open dome.

Javul shrieked and jerked out of her spiral into a back-flip that carried her toward the center of the space. The seats were moving many times faster than intended . . . and all at once. Chaotic air currents struck her, buffeted her, redirecting her flight. She tumbled, saw a bank of seats flying up toward her, and pulled into a somersault. The seat assembly missed her, but clipped her wing, tearing at the fabric and twisting the aluminum struts.

She twisted—out of control for a moment—and reached up to grasp the opti-fiber. It cracked like a whip, then snagged on the corner of the topmost seating unit as it hit the limits of its flight. The unit swung in a crazy arc, dragging Javul with it at the end of her glowing leash . . . directly into the path of another careening bank of seats.

She was out of options. She reached up through the holographic fabric of her costume and twisted the emergency catch on her harness. It released. She plunged downward.

She heard someone else scream then, far below on that seemingly tiny stage. Dara. She heard an answering yowl from Tereez. She activated the antigrav unit in her wings. It caught her in an invisible net of buoyancy, stopping her descent. She was still falling, but in slow motion now. It was okay. She'd make it.

She tried to reposition herself so as to land on the stage rather than falling through the opening iris. No luck. She was in an antigrav bubble. There was no way to swim through the air outside of it. But that was okay, too. The iris was starting to close. She relaxed. She could see Dara and Tereez and Mel and Eaden awaiting her and could make out the shadows of others emerging from the side-lines in a gabble of speculation and shouted orders.

"Open it!" Mel was yelling at someone. "Open it!"

The antigrav generator gave out when she was about twenty-six meters from the stage floor, plunging her once again toward the closing iris. If it closed completely . . .

She was mere centimeters from the collapsing maw when somebody collided with her in midair, grasped her in a set of powerful arms, and turned her head over heels. She heard the iris snap shut and her rescuer utter a gasp of surprise or pain. She landed atop his body and the two slid to a stop.

There was a moment of silence, then a rush of sound—talking, crying . . . swearing. She realized her eyes were squeezed shut and opened them as hands explored her limbs. She looked up into Dash Rendar's ashen face.

"I don't think anything's broken," he said and lifted her away from . . .

She turned and looked down. Eaden Vrill, his face pulled into a tight grimace, sat up, then stood in a movement so fluid she wondered if he had antigrav tech built into his clothing.

"Oh. Oh, Eaden, thank you!" She shuddered as a sudden chill swept through her body. She needed to sit down or her body was going to shake apart.

"Yeah, big guy," Dash said. "Way to guard the princess. That was one amazing leap you performed . . . You okay?"

"I am not okay. I am . . . injured." The Nautolan glanced down at the several head-tresses that were sorting themselves out. One of them was missing about two centimeters of its tip, which had been sliced through as cleanly as if it had been taken off with a vibroblade.

Javul raised her hands to her face and trembled harder. Tears pressed for release. She held them in check with a will. "Oh. Oh, Eaden. I'm so *sorry*."

Dash put his arms around her. "Hey. Hey. He's just doing his job. Besides, it's not that bad. Tell her it's not that bad, Ead."

The Nautolan looked at Javul, his facial expression softening very slightly. "It is not that bad."

Not that bad? It was horrible. She felt her knees going wobbly. "I need to sit down."

In seconds Dara and Tereez were flanking her, leading her away from the scene of her near-death experience.

Behind her she heard Eaden say, in an impossibly deadpan tone: "It's not that bad?"

"It's just one tiny bit of one little tentacle."

"Really? What if someone were to cut off the tip of one of your little fingers. Not much, just the pad, just the part with all the nerves in it. The part you use to feel things."

"Well, yeah," said Dash, "but I'd still have nine fingers left. You got—lemme see . . ."

"Don't. I doubt you can count that high."

Javul giggled. And kept giggling. And wondered if she'd ever stop.

ELEVEN

"THE FIRST FAILURE WAS IN THE HOLOSSEUM AUDIENCE and stage subsystems. Specifically, there was a power surge that *somehow* triggered all the seating mechanisms to fire and then essentially put them into overdrive."

Arruna Var sat cross-legged in a formchair in the main venue control center of the huge stadium. The large, crescent-shaped room—situated high up on the curve of the rotunda—offered a breathtaking view of the hall. Gathered around the engineer were Dash, Eaden, the costumer Tereez, and Yanus Melikan. Leebo, and Mel's service droid, Oto, stood unmoving at the outer fringes of the group. Dara had whisked Javul off to the green room.

"The second failure," Arruna continued, pointing out power linkages in the visual display of the building's vast systems, "was in the iris control for the stage door."

"Was the surge responsible for the iris malfunctioning?" asked Mel.

Arruna shook her head. "Not impossible, but improbable. The two systems are separate at the control level. Yeah, they're ultimately linked through the power grid, *but* the stage door has an independent backup power supply in case of emergency. So if the main grid goes down for some reason, it can be opened to allow for evacuation. It also serves as a power modulation trigger. When hit with a surge of the type the diagnostic recorded, it's supposed to cut itself loose from the system and go to the backup power supply. It appears to have done just that. I think it was instructed to open . . . and close . . . through the control net."

Behind Dash, Leebo uttered the droid equivalent of a grunt. Dash glanced back at him. "You got something?"

"I scanned the stage door controls for genetic residue and fingerprints," said the droid. "Nothing."

"Okay, well, who had access to the controls?"

Mel looked down at his hands, fisted atop the venue control console. "We all did. Every member of the crew did. And, to be fair, so did the maintenance crew for the facility, though they were relegated to second-level support. The primary controls are beneath the stage in the pit, but those can be overridden from here. And that doesn't address the second level of failures—Javul's umbilical and her antigrav unit."

"I was the lasht pershon to touch that," said Tereez, the irises of her great golden eyes narrowing to slits. "If I did shomething to damage the unit—perhapsh when I attached the opti-fiber . . ."

"Whatever happened," said Dash, "this was no accident. So it's unlikely anything you did *unintentionally* caused the shorting out in the antigrav."

Dash didn't miss the fact that Tereez's ears flattened at the word *unintentionally*. Well, too bad if her feelings were hurt. If this was sabotage, everyone was a suspect.

"The timing, also, was too perfect," said Eaden. "But we must remember that Javul Charn, herself, disconnected the umbilical."

"Yes," said Arruna, "but she did it because the cable had fouled the seats, which wouldn't have happened if not for the power surge."

Dash frowned. "But even assuming the seats were sabotaged, whoever triggered that couldn't count on the cable getting caught in them."

"True, but the same surge that launched the seating

arrays also charged the metal framework in the vault. Watch."

Arruna rattled off a command to the diagnostic program she was running to display what had happened in the superstructure of the hall during the incident. The diagnostic showed a simulation of the power flow. The power surge, indicated by a flood of golden light, ran up the spines that supported the "eggshell," into the coupling for the opti-fiber cable, and down into the cable itself. In the sim, the cable gleamed like molten metal, whipping through the air as if its passenger weighed nothing.

"Four separate failures then," said Mel. His voice was tight, the glacial expression in his pale eyes somehow infusing his quiet words with violence. "Four well-timed or improbably coincidental failures."

"Depends on how you do the math," said Dash. "The power surge triggered the seats, and took the stage iris offline. Might it have kicked enough juice through the circuit as it did to short the iris and force it open?" He looked to Arruna, who nodded with a shrug of her lekku.

"Unlikely," she said. "But . . ."

"But possible," he finished. "The power surge also caused the opti-fiber to misbehave, so the only variable the power surge absolutely can't account for is the failure of the antigrav unit."

"Actually, boss," said Leebo, "I think it can. If the power in that opti-cable hit the wing framework with enough of a charge, it might've destabilized the antigrav unit. I know I'm just a hunk of metal, but in my humble opinion the only facet of this fascinating sequence of mechanical events the power surge is unlikely to have caused is the freakishly well-timed closing of the stage iris."

"I think he's right," said Arruna. "The power surge might have caused the iris to open, but once the backup power supply had kicked in it would have to have been closed from the stage control. In fact," she said, paging back to the functional display of the venue's control grid, "it could *only* have been closed from that console, because the stage system was independent at that point."

Dash considered that. "I suppose it's possible that someone saw the iris opening and, not realizing anything else was wrong, tried to close it." He looked up and met Mel's gaze.

The cargo master's eyes narrowed. "An unfortunate sequence of accidents? Do you really think that's what this is?"

"Nope. Not at all. I mean, it *could* be that, but it would be stupid to act as if it were. I'm saying I think whoever planned this was very clever. Maybe even clever enough to count on our reactions to make matters worse. The saboteur knows that once the iris goes offline, he loses control . . ."

Mel raised an eyebrow. "So he uses the power pulse to open the iris and hopes someone in the pit will try to close it? That's a little risky, isn't it?"

"Maybe it's the best he can do. Unless, of course, he's in the pit himself."

Mel's gaze was icy. "What are you insinuating?"

Dash raised his hands. "Not a thing. Not a blasted thing. I'm just saying—whoever closed the iris would've had to do it from the pit, right?"

Mel sat back, apparently deciding not to take umbrage over these insinuations. "Not necessarily. Frankly, it's more likely that it was triggered remotely in some way. For one thing, if that closure was triggered from the console in the pit, whoever did it would have had to clean up after themselves well enough to pass a scan for traces of organic material."

Dash turned to Arruna. "You've looked at the engineering involved in this. What sort of resources would have been necessary to pull this off?"

Arruna met his gaze levelly. "The power surge came from the city grid, Dash. The *city* grid. That's beyond an irked ex-boyfriend. Even a Vigo."

It was also beyond a single member of Javul's troop. Which meant what—a conspiracy?

"Depends on which Vigo, though, doesn't it?" Dash asked. He rose to pace the carpeted floor of the control room, looking down into the hall where the Holosseum maintenance staff—droids and sentients, alike—scurried to secure the rogue seating sections. "An offworld Vigo messing around on another guy's turf would have to be nuts to try something like this. I mean, who'd risk it just to scare an ex-girlfriend?"

"Sentients," said Leebo. "Who can figure 'em?"

"I think the intent was to do more than frighten," said Eaden quietly. "I think this was intended to maim or kill."

Dash let out a gust of breath. "Yeah. That raises the stakes a bit, doesn't it? But it still doesn't make sense. It's overkill—you'll pardon the expression."

"And it would still seem to call for operatives in key places," Eaden observed.

There was a long silence in which Dash could almost feel the several sets of eyeballs behind him exchange wary glances.

Mel broke the silence . . . and changed the subject. "We never asked—what did you find out at the port authority?"

"That someone rascaled the flight control messages to the *Nova's Heart*. And according to Leebo they did it from the communications console in the C and C. So if we've got a lovelorn Vigo on our hands, Eaden's right: he's got operatives in some very key places." Dash turned on his heel and headed for the door. "It's time for me to talk to our boss-lady again. Something's seriously out of whack here."

*   *   *

"I will *not* cancel the show," Javul said doggedly for the third time. "We can work around this. The seats weren't badly damaged, and the maintenance super thinks he can have them fixed by tomorrow night."

"That's not the worst of the problems," argued Dash doggedly, "and you know it. Yeah, sure you've got redundancy built into your system, but how are you going to make sure something doesn't happen to the backup equipment?"

"My crew will check every—"

"Someone on your crew," said Dash, squatting next to her chair in the Holosseum's luxurious green room, "may very well be on this guy's payroll—whoever this guy is."

She looked up at him, silver eyes wide. "No. I don't—"

"*C'mon*, Javul! Look at the facts! Somebody was at that iris control when the power went down and timed the iris closing to your fall. Eaden barely got to you in time. If he wasn't a teräs käsi master, he wouldn't have and you'd have been sliced in two."

"Who? Who do you suspect?"

He rose and started to pace, tugging at his lower lip. "Not Dara. She's had too many other opportunities to do you damage. Unless, of course, your mysterious admirer has only recently gotten to her."

Javul shook her head. "No. Not Dara. I've known her since before I was anybody."

"Yeah, and she was topside when the iris went rogue. Arruna has the most technical knowledge. How well do you know her?"

"She's been my engineer for about two years. Mel brought her on."

"Okay. So she's a maybe. Except she was allegedly aboard the ship running diagnostics when this whole thing happened. I'll have Leebo check that. What about Mel?"

She shook her head. "No. It . . . it just can't be Mel.

He . . . he's pulled me out of more situations than I can count. He's run my backstage since the beginning."

"He's got the technical know-how to pull this off. And he had access. No one would have even questioned him being at the controls."

"It's not Mel," she said stubbornly.

"How can you know that, though?" he insisted, equally stubborn.

"I—just—do." The set of her jaw said she could out-stubborn him any day of the week and knew it.

Something about the way she said it made Dash's hair prickle at the back of his neck. "You know him pretty well, do you?"

"I . . . yes. I do."

He took a deep breath. "Are you . . . close? As in . . . you know . . . friends?"

"Of course we're—" She broke off and looked up at him.

He'd turned to face her. Their gazes locked for a moment and set him pacing again.

"You mean, are we lovers?"

He made a dismissive gesture. "Hey, it's your own business."

"No, we're not lovers. Look, I trust Mel."

"Is there anyone you *don't* trust? What about Tereez? Could she be an operative for whoever's behind this. After all, she said it herself—she was the last one to handle the antigrav unit. How long have you known her?"

Javul sighed. "Not that long. She came on about nine months ago at Cloud City on Bespin. We had an opening for a costumer and she applied. She does beautiful work. She's a real artist."

"On Bespin. That's kind of unusual isn't it? A Bothan costumer on Bespin?"

"She'd been working for an administrator of an urban mining corporation—name of Lando Calrissian—

designing clothes for him, uniforms for his crew and—
What? Don't tell me you know Lando?"

Dash had stopped in mid-stride and done an about-face. "Yeah. Yeah, I do."

Javul smiled. "Small galaxy."

"Why'd she leave him?"

"She hated living on a floating platform. Said it made her feel as if the world was going to drop out from under her feet. Leave her treading air."

As opposed to living in a space yacht? That seemed a thin excuse to Dash, but he didn't comment on it. He could look more deeply into the Bothan's background later. Right now, he had more important matters to address. He moved to stand in front of Javul.

"Okay, look, here's the bottom line: Someone has raised the stakes. The black lilies might have been intended to make you nervous and the fake hull breach to make you respect your saboteur's power, but this last thing—this could have ended with you and possibly others dead or maimed. I'm thinking if a Vigo is involved and he's not a local, he's just overstepped his bounds by messing around in another Vigo's territory. So a word to whichever of the local guys is at the top of the heap should do the trick."

She was shaking her head.

"But," he added, his voice hard, "I'm thinking it's more likely one of the local kingpins. Which leaves us with two prime candidates—Clezo and the Mandalorian, Hitya-mun Kris."

"Hitch," she said quietly.

"What?"

"He goes by Hitch Kris. He's powerful. And he's the one who's after me."

"You mean, he's the one who's after Alai Jance." Dash felt a tickle of suspicion that had been growing since she'd told him the story.

She looked up at him, pinning him to the carpet with that gleaming silver gaze. "I mean, he's after *me*. I was . . . am . . . Alai Jance. And I was also Hitch Kris's bride-to-be."

Oddly, Dash's first impulse was to laugh.

TWELVE

THE GIRL HAD MOXIE, DASH HAD TO ADMIT IT. ENGAGED to marry a Vigo, beginning a career underwritten by a Vigo, and then—poof!—she ends it because of her fiancé's violent tendencies.

"He was into the worst kind of crime," she told him. "Murder, assassination, drugs, kidnappings. I just couldn't handle it."

He wanted to ask whatever had made her think she *could* have handled it, but he didn't. Instead he asked the inevitable: "How'd you meet such a lowlife?"

"I was performing in a club on Coruscant—the Quarek'k, a favorite watering hole run by Neimoidians for all sorts of high-class lowlifes. Black Sun, Imperial, mercenaries—every sentient who considered itself a tycoon came through the place. I can't even imagine how many business deals went down on an average evening. And to be truthful, I didn't want to. I just sang and danced and did little dramatic scenes from different cultural mythologies. I think that was my claim to fame—my little send-ups of everybody's favorite ancestral legend or cultural icon. It's why Hitch noticed me. I was doing this song cycle about the human immigrants on Mandalore and he said it brought tears to his eyes."

Dash choked on the sudden urge to laugh. A mercenary ex-Mandalorian Vigo brought to tears by a nightclub chanteuse. That was rich.

"So you thought he was just a big, cuddly art patron, huh?"

"I suppose I did for about five minutes. Until I saw the crowd he did business with. No, I had an inkling of what Hitch Kris was before I . . . got involved with him." She paused, catching his expression of distaste. "Look, you've made bad choices, haven't you? Don't tell me you haven't. Everybody makes bad, stupid choices. Sometimes we're lucky enough to grow out of them."

"Okay, so what caused you to grow out of Hitch Kris?"

She gave him a searching look, then said: "I thought he'd set me up in a career as a touring entertainer because he loved me. Because he believed I had talent. I came to realize through a series of blunders committed by his operatives that he'd done it because my touring provided him with a way to move certain items around the galaxy without anyone suspecting. His ships were known to the Imperials and to competing Vigos . . . and they were known to the Underlord Prince Xizor. Anything Hitch needed to move that he didn't want those parties to know about, he arranged to have placed on my manifest. I was moving drugs, weapons, biological agents . . . and people. And no one was the wiser. Especially not me."

"And then?" Dash asked.

"And then a diplomat on the Empire's hit list turned up dead in one of my shipping containers. We found him completely by accident. We had a spot of trouble that caused us to have to drop out of hyperspace suddenly and the ship took quite a buffeting. The container was damaged, and in setting it to rights Mel found this poor man. Dead."

"What did you do with the body?"

"We turned it over to the authorities on Coruscant and that was that. The official story was that he was a fan who had stowed away and died of asphyxiation."

"Yeah. That's also the *story* you told me," Dash reminded her. "So what's the truth?"

"The truth is that ambassadors to the Imperial court don't usually stow away in the equipage of some holo-show."

"Was that your first stowaway?" he asked.

"Yes," she said, blanching. "But not our last."

Even after she'd parted company with Kris, and gone off on her own to make a new name for herself—literally—she'd been vigilant because her ex-beau had continued to try to use her tours to move his contraband. Dash didn't press her, but clearly losing his fiancée was the least of the Vigo's vexations. Losing a means of moving his extra-special secret cargoes without drawing suspicion onto himself was probably all he cared about.

This led Dash to wonder about the intent of the unhappy accidents. Was Kris trying to kill his ex, or simply drive her back into his arms? Sure she might've been injured in the fall, but that's what medical droids and bacta tanks were for—both of which were part of Javul Charn's retinue. If he'd sabotaged the ship, he did it in such a way that a trip down the escape hatch saved the day. And Dash was willing to bet that Hityamun Kris knew the inside of the *Nova's Heart* almost as well as her mistress did. *Heart* had clearly been a smuggler's ship at some point in her career—all the extra bells and whistles pointed to that conclusion. And who knew smuggling better than a Black Sun Vigo?

Well, with the possible exception of himself.

No, it made no sense for Kris to maim or kill Javul. If he did, that would be the end of his sweet setup. Which meant that either Kris was acting out of sheer, irrational rage (unlikely), or that the perpetrator was someone who didn't care about him losing his sweet setup—a rival Vigo, maybe, or possibly a lieutenant with his eyes on a higher rung on the Black Sun corporate ladder.

Javul was spunky and cocky, but Dash believed she had no idea what she was really up against. Finding that dead diplomat might have scared her, but it apparently had not taught her to respect the sheer power of Black Sun and its higher-up operatives. He, on the other hand, had all too clear an idea of what Black Sun operatives were capable of.

He considered bailing out at their next port of call. Considered it a hundred times between his revealing conversation with Javul (or Alai) and the night the show opened, but he needed the money and—who was he kidding?—he cared that Javul didn't end up as a smudge on some stage floor. And then there was that other impulse—the one that made him want to give Black Sun a bloody nose . . . or worse.

So instead, he gave the entire crew a blistering speech on awareness, made sure everyone had a communications device, divided all offstage personnel into teams of two, and ordered them to buzz him or Leebo or Eaden if anything—anything at all—looked the least bit out of the ordinary or if they lost sight of their partner. Then he armed himself, assigned himself a territory—anywhere within sight of Javul—and patrolled it all during the performances she insisted on giving.

There were three of these, and Dash ticked them off one by one—uneventful, mostly uneventful (except for a momentarily missing prop), and oh-blast-it-all. For on the third night, with two nerve-stretching performances under their belts—and Dash finally seeing the light at the end of the wormhole—who should show up but Hityamun Kris. The Vigo appeared at the hall with a team of three Mandalorian bodyguards and headed for one of the private skyboxes permanently mounted to the vast inner haunch of the Holosseum.

Dash was curious about Kris. He'd met Mandalorians of several species, but he'd never met one who had left the mercenary clans and set himself up as a master of business, let alone risen to such heights in Black Sun. Kris was, in short, an anomaly.

Dash didn't like anomalies.

He was standing in the below-stage area, half listening to Javul go over some costume notes with Tereez, when her ex swept into the Holosseum as if he owned the place. Actually, chances were good that he *did* own a piece of it. Did that necessarily mean he had something to do with the power fluctuations?

Mel, standing at the stage manager's station, made a hissing sound to catch Javul's attention. He gestured at a nearby security monitor with his head. Dash saw Kris before Javul did, so his gaze was on her face when she lifted her eyes to the display.

"He's coming down," Mel said tersely.

Kris walked right by the lift that would have taken him to the skyboxes and led his retinue toward the restricted-access lift that would bring him down into the broad, carpeted backstage hallway that housed the dressing rooms.

Javul went pale. Her fear of the Mandalorian was apparently sincere. Which made her next move completely unexpected. She handed the bit of fluff she'd been holding to Tereez and started for the hallway.

Dash, caught off guard, had to run to catch up with her. He reached her and grasped her arm. "Where are you going? You want me to run interference?"

She looked up at him. "I'm going to meet him."

"*Meet* him? Are you out of your mind? He's tried to kill you!"

"Maybe. Maybe not."

"*Maybe* not? You've gone mental if you think—"

She sighed and disconnected his hand. "Look, he's not going to shoot me in a public venue. Besides, I don't think he wants to kill me—if he's even the one behind this."

"You could've fooled me. And, having dealt with Black Sun before," Dash said, "I can tell you that if he wants to kill you, witnesses will mean nothing. He'll pull a blaster and burn you where you stand, even if it's in front of the entire Holosseum. A hundred witnesses—a thousand witnesses—mean nothing to his kind, Javul. Not when he can have an entire *planet* swear he was a thousand light-years away when the deed was done."

She put her hand on his arm. "I'm going to go make nice, Dash. You can come guard me, if you like, but stay out of it."

"Whatever." He glanced back over his shoulder and waved at Leebo, who was observing an interaction between Mel's droid and his assistant, Nik. "Leeb, I need you."

"Right there with you," said the droid, "normally. But I'm under orders to stay with my buddy Nik here."

"Yeah, they're my orders. I'm rescinding them."

Oto swiveled his round head toward Leebo. "I can monitor the activities of Nik adequately," he said.

Javul was moving again. "C'mon!" Dash snarled and went after her, leaving the droid to follow or not.

The lift doors opened just as Dash stepped out into the hallway behind Javul. She hesitated only for a moment, then squared her shoulders and went on, meeting Kris as he exited the lift with his bodyguards arrayed about him—one behind and one to either side.

Kris saw Javul the moment he stepped out onto the thick carpet and stopped to watch her come to him. When she was a meter away he raised his eyes to Dash, quirked a blond eyebrow, then returned his gaze to the woman. He smiled.

Dash shivered. Those were without doubt the coldest pair of eyes he'd ever seen. They were the blue of ice— the blue of moonlight on a knife blade. His hair was pale, as well. Not the shimmering silver-white of Javul's, but a shade of brilliant gold that rivaled the sun-washed rocks of Tatooine. They would've made, Dash thought begrudgingly, a beautiful couple . . . except for those eyes. How could she love a guy with eyes like that? It seemed . . . out of character somehow. But like she'd said, sometimes people made bad choices. Sometimes they grew out of them.

Sometimes they weren't allowed to.

Javul stopped in front of Kris, leaving a little more than an arm's length between them. Dash made sure he was closer to her than an arm's length, himself. He heard the muted whine of Leebo's servos as the droid took up a position just over a meter behind him.

The Vigo folded his long-fingered hands over his belt. "What? No kiss for me, Alai—or should I say Javul? I didn't think you had it in you to be so . . . uncharitable."

"I have my reasons to be standoffish. I think even you would agree. Why have you come here?"

Kris spread his big hands. "I love to watch you perform. You know that. And a live performance here in this splendid hall—well, that's more than I could pass up even given our . . . falling-out. And besides, you know what they say about hope." He laid a hand over his heart. "It never dies where love remains."

"Hope?"

Javul turned to look back over her shoulder at Dash and he realized he'd said the word in unison with her. He snapped his mouth shut.

"Who's this?" Kris asked gesturing at Dash with his chin. "New boyfriend? No. Wait. Not your type, is he? Wannabe boyfriend, maybe. Or bodyguard."

His own guards, all but one dressed in full Mandalorian body armor, assessed Dash through narrowed eyes—and dismissed him.

He bristled. "Boyfriend," he said as Javul said, "Bodyguard."

Again, the look from Javul. "This is my security chief, Dash Rendar."

The big, blond head tilted to one side. "Rendar. That's a familiar name. That was the name of the family that owned RenTrans before Prince Xizor acquired it, if I'm not mistaken."

Dash didn't blink.

"Surely, you're not related. I had heard the entire clan was wiped out."

The bodyguard at Kris's back—the one not in armor—leaned forward and murmured something into his boss's ear.

"Ah! Of course. The outcast of the family who insisted on going to the Imperial Academy rather than take up the family business. Lucky move, that. But you're a trained pilot then, aren't you?" He put on a mask of theatrical confusion. "An Academy-trained pilot serving as a bodyguard for a spoiled, pampered holostar? How in the name of Chaos does that happen?"

"Security *chief*," said Dash through clenched teeth. Then he smiled. "A clan-trained warrior in line to be *the* Mandalore serving as a Vigo to a spoiled, pampered pirate like Prince Xizor? How does *that* happen?"

Kris blinked, and the guard to his left took a half step forward. Dash's hand was on the butt of his blaster when Kris put his arm out to stop his goon.

"Please, Dash—may I call you Dash? We have no reason to bandy accusations in this way. I merely came down here to see the show and renew my acquaintance with an old friend."

"You sure you didn't come here to strong-arm your ex-fiancée?"

Now Javul whirled on him. "Dash!" she hissed. She turned back to Kris. "I hope you enjoy the performance, Hitch. For old times' sake. It's the only hope you're going to get from me."

The big Mandalorian sighed dramatically. "After all I've done to prove my devotion to you? I'm hurt."

"I doubt it. But *I* might have been. I'm sure your spies told you about our . . . problems. Starting the day of our arrival."

"Problems?"

Now, if that wasn't a disingenuous furrowing of the brow, Dash was no judge of bad character. "Yeah," he said. "Someone tried to make the *Nova's Heart* think she'd sprung a leak on the way in. She buttoned up tight, sealing Javul and her road manager into the supposedly ruptured area of the quarterdeck. And three days ago, there was a freakish power fluctuation that almost got our lady friend cut in half. If not for the fact that my assistant is a teräs käsi master, she'd likely be dead right now."

Kris's eyes narrowed. Surprise? Disbelief? Sly satisfaction?

None of the above?

"A teräs käsi master?" Kris said. "A martial arts adept and a crack pilot? What a waste of talent. I'd like to make you an offer, Dash. Leave this menagerie and come work for me . . . as a pilot. Bring your assistant with you. I could use someone like that in my own security team. I'll triple what she's paying you."

Dash heard a low mechanical whistle of appreciation behind him—and had the absurd thought of how much more quickly he could repair *Outrider* with that kind of money. He shook himself. "Sorry. I got a job."

"I'll quadruple it."

"No thanks."

The Vigo shrugged. "Your loss, Dash. But if you should change your mind, the lady knows where you can find me. Don't you, my love?"

When she didn't say anything, he took a half step forward and lowered his head toward hers. Dash instantly went on full alert, but the Vigo only murmured, "Don't be stubborn, Alai. You seem to forget what your stubbornness has cost you in the past." He straightened, turned on his heel, and led the way back into the lift.

Dash and Javul stood a moment longer in the hallway, frozen in place. Dash realized suddenly that Javul was trembling. He moved to stand in front of her. For just a moment, her expression was unguarded—and so bleak it made Dash want to chase Hityamun Kris up to his skybox and push his face in. Then her show-must-go-on bearing was back in place.

"My, that went well," she said and started toward the stage door.

Dash caught her arm. He wasn't sure what he meant to say.

She shook her head and pulled her arm free. "Don't," she said. "I just need to get through tonight. Just get through it. Tomorrow evening we'll be back on *Nova's Heart* and out of here."

Dash followed her backstage, wondering what the hell he should do. Leebo made a tiny interrogative noise as he passed the droid.

"What are you staring at?" Dash growled.

"Who me? Not a thing. I was just going back to work."

Dash hesitated just inside the stage door, watching as Javul was swept into the final preparations for her evening's performance—the fitting of her harness and wire, a final safety check of all the bits and pieces of stuff that went with her onstage. He sensed a presence at his side.

"Assistant?" Eaden inquired.

Dash rolled his eyes. "I had to think on my feet, okay? It just came out."

"I prefer *associate* or possibly *partner*. And you should try thinking *with* your brain instead of *on* your feet. It would be vastly more effective. Assuming that your sense of balance is adroit enough to keep you poised on something so small."

Leebo cocked his head. "Not bad for an off-the-cuff."

Dash gave him a glare.

"Shutting up," the droid said.

Dash turned back to Eaden. "Were you listening in on the whole conversation?"

"Yes." Eaden lifted a tendril and uncurled it slowly. "Interesting dynamic, that. She is afraid—no surprise or secret there. Even you must have sensed it. But Kris . . . strong emotions, very muddled. And you . . ."

Dash turned to look at him. "What about me?"

"You turned down quadruple pay."

Nothing in the Nautolan's voice or expression gave Dash any indication of the emotion behind the statement. He hated that—it made him feel . . . off balance.

"Look, I'm sorry, but—"

"I'm not in disagreement with you. I merely find it remarkable."

Dash expelled a gust of air. "Yeah, well . . . so do I."

THIRTEEN

DASH WOKE IN THE MIDDLE OF THE NIGHT WITH HIS brain in hyperdrive. He had dreamed of Javul's fall from the vault of the Holosseum's fake night sky repeatedly. It had given him a dark epiphany: he had heard multiple descriptions of the "incidents" that had preceded the sabotaged rehearsal—had even witnessed one of them firsthand—and he knew, at an instinct-deep level, that this last one was different.

Why was it different? What had changed?

He got up. He got dressed. He got a cup of caf from the beverage bar in the suite's main room and sat, staring out at the landing park beyond his bay of windows.

Whip the gray cells awake. Think, Dash, think. Why would the agenda change?

He went over in his mind again the confrontation between Javul and Hitch backstage—the weird dynamic between the two.

What was wrong with this picture?

He tried to put himself in Kris's place—tried to imagine that she had been his fiancée, that she had gummed up his clandestine operations, then resisted his every effort to scare her and escaped his one effort to do her real harm.

Hell, he'd be spitting mad. On several levels. And if he'd seen her with another guy—a guy who seemed to be "attached" to her in some way—it would've deep-fried his circuits. But old Hitch was as cool and calm as a customer service droid on a HoloNet help node.

And *that* did not make sense. The escalation from scare tactics to all-out, gonzo vengeance bespoke a towering rage. All Hitch Kris seemed to be harboring was a towering and perplexed annoyance. He was methodical, Dash would bet—and patient and implacable—but he was not murderous.

What did that mean?

It means he's a Vigo, said Common Sense. *He's too self-important to lose it over a woman. This is business to him, not revenge. There's a method to his madness—you just have to figure out what the method is.*

Dash set his cup down, snatched up his jacket, and headed out into the corridor. Leebo, stationed by Javul Charn's door, swiveled to look at him.

"Did you know that metal creaks as it cools?" the droid asked.

"Do you know how easily I could pop your head off with a pair of extractor forceps?"

"Boorish threats."

Dash crossed to the droid. "Been any activity out here?"

"I've been standing here for hours listening to metal cool. What do you think?"

Dash moved past the droid to the door. He hesitated only momentarily before punching the call pad. He could hear the ringing tone on the other side of the door—though just barely. He waited.

Nothing.

He hit it again.

More nothing.

He pressed the intercom switch this time and said, loudly, "Javul? It's Dash. We need to talk."

Not a peep from the other side.

A very bad, very dark feeling began to rise up from the pit of Dash's stomach. In all likelihood, there was a mole in the crew . . . and the crew now knew about Javul's escape route.

Cursing, he manually punched in the security override code for the lock. The door slid back, revealing the dimly lit living room.

"Stay out here in the corridor," he told Leebo and stepped into the suite.

"And I wanted *so* badly to risk my life alongside you. But hey—you're the boss."

Dash ignored the droid as he moved deeper into the suite. The lights were on, but dimmed, and he knew before he looked that he wouldn't find her. The bed hadn't been slept in, the suite was empty, and she hadn't gone past her guardian droid. That meant only one thing—it meant Dash Rendar was an idiot for not posting another guard at the far end of Javul's no-longer-secret escape route.

"She's gone," he told Leebo tersely as he left the suite. "Roust Eaden, will you?"

"The last time I rousted Eaden, I ended up embedded in the bulkhead of his quarters."

"This time it'll be different."

"How so?"

"Softer bulkheads. Now move!"

The droid moved off, grumbling, while Dash went next door and pinged Dara Farlion's door . . . repeatedly. She answered within ten pings, her hair twice as spiky as usual, her eyes at half-mast. She was wrapped in a velvety-looking shawl.

"What's up? Sheesh, Dash, you got a death wish? You'd better—"

"Javul is gone."

"*What?*"

"She's gone. Out through the escape hatch—I assume

willingly, though I could be wrong. There was no sign of a struggle, but I suppose someone could've slipped in and drugged her."

Dara's eyes flicked toward Javul's door. "Not with the alarm system . . ."

"Do I need to remind you that someone has been able to get close enough to her to sabotage her props and rigging?"

"What d'you want me to do?"

"Get everybody up and accounted for. I'm going to see if she left any kind of trail."

Eaden was just entering the hallway from their suite as Dash crossed back to Javul's door.

"Leebo explained," the Nautolan said, tying the sash around the waist of his tunic. "Down the hatch?"

"Yeah . . . and Leebo," Dash told the droid, "stick with Spike. She's gonna wake everybody up and make sure they're all here."

Dash and Eaden popped the door on Javul's secret gangway and descended carefully to the cargo hold. Neither saw any indication of a struggle in the narrow passage. The hold was surprisingly eerie without most of its crates and containers, which were currently stored beneath the Holosseum stage, awaiting the morrow's packing. Dash was surprised to find a light on in Mel's office. He was more surprised to see that it was Mel's apprentice cargo master, Nik, burning the midnight photons. The young Sullustan jumped almost his height out of his seat at the computer console when Dash leaned into the office through the open door.

"Where's your boss?"

"Uh . . . sleeping. Like most people."

"Yeah? Why aren't *you* sleeping—like most people?"

"Schoolwork. Mel insists that I keep up my education."

"You're doing schoolwork in the middle of the night after a three-night gig?"

The kid looked guilty. "I . . . sort of procrastinated this week. 'Cause of the gig. Mel says I have to finish this tonight or I don't get to help with tear-down."

Dash shook his head. *Get to help?* Whatever happened to adolescent laziness?

"You been up for a while, kid?"

Nik nodded solemnly.

"You see anybody come through the cargo hold?"

The Sullustan's big dark eyes shifted from Dash to Eaden and back. "Anybody?"

"Charn. Did you see Javul Charn down here tonight?"

The youngster nodded, looking guilty. "Yeah. Yeah, I did. She, um, she went out."

"We *know* she went out. Was she alone?"

The youngster nodded again.

"Did she say where she was going?"

"I didn't talk to her. She just came straight through and headed for the cargo bay hatch."

This was like pulling teeth. "She see you?"

"Yeah. I went out on the catwalk and she saw me and put her finger to her lips and went on out."

"And you didn't think to wake up Mel or report the incident to Dara?"

"No, sir. I mean, it's like Mel always says: *Whatever it was you just saw—you didn't.*"

"Says that often, does he?"

"Often enough."

"Well, I'm sure he doesn't mean when something like this happens. Someone tried to kill our boss three days ago, Nik. Given that, she shouldn't be out roaming around the city, should she?"

Nik had the good grace to look contrite. "No. I suppose not."

"Okay, kid, listen—this is important. What was she wearing?"

"Uh, she was dressed pretty wild. Lot of makeup—that

glowy stuff around her eyes and a jewel in the middle of her forehead. She had this sparkly outfit on that . . ." A blush spread out across his dewlaps and over his large ears. ". . . Well, you could see through parts of it. And she was wearing one of those light-fiber hair things."

"How long ago did she leave?"

Nik shrugged. "Sorry. I was doing homework. Lost track of time."

Dash pulled out his comlink, called Leebo, and told him to let everyone go back to sleep. There'd obviously been no kidnapping. "I don't suppose you saw which way she went when she left the landing park."

Color suffused the Sullustan's ears. "Actually, I did. I watched her all the way down the ramp and across the pad. I mean, I've never seen her dressed like that before. Ever." He swallowed.

Dash scowled at him discouragingly, but he just shrugged.

"I think human girls are pretty. And Javul is one of the prettiest," Nik defended himself.

"Which way did she go?"

"West. Toward Port Town."

West toward Port Town led Dash and Eaden directly into a brightly lit warren of entertainment spots—cafés, music clubs, spice houses, pubs, gambling dens, and places that tried to corner the market by being all of the above. Middle of the night or no, the streets were alive with people of diverse species, drifting back and forth, staggering here and there, even dancing in the street. Equator City nightlife was in full swing.

The two men stopped at the top of the glittering main avenue to consider the sheer magnitude of the task before them. They had no idea when Javul had left the ship, where she was heading, or why. Which meant they were effectively groping in the dark.

"You got your comlink with you?" Dash asked Eaden. The Nautolan nodded.

"Great. You take the right side of the street; I'll take the left. If you see her or see anything that might—"

But Eaden was already gone, slipping into the traffic and somehow managing not to look horribly out of place despite his somber, almost monkish garb. Dash took a deep breath and muttered a prayer to any Corellian deities that might be eavesdropping. If that failed, he hoped maybe the Force might lend a hand if it had no more pressing business. He headed for the first establishment on the left side of the street.

Long after Dash had lost count of the number of doors he'd plowed through into too-bright or too-dim rooms, he came to the broad archway of a place that promised every delight. In fact, that was the name over the door: EVERY DELIGHT. Stepping through the entry, he realized it was a bazaar of sorts—a row of rounded arches along a broad central arcade, each decorated with a skillful painting that indicated what type of delight lay within.

Some of the doorways were bright and some were stygian or filled with shifting, muted light in a rainbow of hues; some blared music and some were silent or carried the sound of breezes or wind-bells or ocean tides. Dash moved slowly past the doorways, wishing he had some keen sixth sense that would light up like a targeting array when he neared his goal. Alas, he had no such sense, but Eaden did—sort of. Dash stepped into a niche that was half filled by a kinetic sculpture of something vaguely humanoid, then pulled out his comlink and called Eaden.

The Nautolan was there in short order, and Dash pointed him in the direction of the row of arches. "You've read Javul before—sort of. Think you could pick her out of a crowd?"

Eaden looked at him skeptically. "My sense is just that—a sense. It is not a scientific instrument."

"Yeah, well—it's all we've got."

The Nautolan shrugged and started a slow walk down the broad, festively decorated gallery, his head-tresses turning this way and that in graceful unison. As they passed each doorway, he murmured a word or two about what he sensed from within.

"Dancing—much mindless celebration. Anger—ah, a gambling den, of course. Chaos—a spice parlor, I suspect . . ."

Toward the end of the bazaar, before a dark archway to the left, Eaden paused and tilted his head, his tresses moving in sinuous harmony. "Something is buried in there that does not belong."

"Worth a look?"

In answer, Eaden moved through the arch, slipping past a clump of patrons clogging the entry. Dash noted their position in case he and Eaden should have to make a hasty exit. The large, long room was dark, lit by tiny table lights and wall sconces that only relieved the gloom within a bare meter radius. It created the effect of hundreds of little pools of illumination around which faces floated in the darkness like disembodied spirits. Occasionally, a hand or its equivalent would flash out into the light to snatch a treat from the array of containers on the table, then dart back into darkness.

There were other, smaller archways along the walls of the big room that hinted at privacy. All were protected by damping fields that served as curtains. You had to pass through the damper to see what was inside. Moving close to one of the fields raised the hair on Dash's head—they were weak electrostatic fields as well, warning the careless wanderer not to enter.

Eaden led Dash straight to the far end of the room,

past little groups of people who talked, drank, smoked scented death sticks—and who seemed to be predatorily intent on one another. Reaching the wall, the Nautolan hesitated, his head tilting first this way then that.

"What is it?"

"Let's try that one." He tipped his head toward the door directly before them. It seemed silent inside, but that was an illusion—each patron could be, and probably was, listening to his, her, or its own personal soundtrack, beamed in tightwave hypersound.

Dash resisted the urge to fidget; the various fields were just strong enough to make him antsy. "But is *she* in there?"

"I don't know. A certain . . . energy is within. Akin to what I felt earlier, when she spoke to Kris."

"Well, then it must be her." Dash took a step toward the doorway, only to be brought up short as a woman in a glittering and very revealing bodysuit stepped out. Pulses of light like little shivers of lightning ran through the fabric of the outfit, imprinting the shape of that body on Dash's retinas. The light fed upward through a shock of electrostatically charged hair into a woven cascade of light-emitting filaments that rotated through all the colors of the visible spectrum.

She bumped into him, looked up with an apology on her lips, then gasped in recognition. "Dash? Eaden?"

"Well," Eaden said, his tentacles weaving a complex pattern in front of her, "she's not amnesiac."

"Good." Dash turned to Javul. "Here I was afraid it had to be amnesia, given that you must've forgotten what almost happened to you the other day or who showed up at your gig tonight."

"Not here," she said, putting a hand on his arm and glancing about.

"We've been looking all over—"

"You found me, okay? Now drop the big, bad bodyguard routine, will you? A girl's gotta slip the leash once in a while. Right?"

"Slip the leash? *Slip the leash?* Lady, I think you've slipped your—"

The darkness in the doorway Javul had just exited rippled and a tall, slender person of indeterminate gender and species stepped out into the room. On second look, his gender was unquestionably male, but his face was so thickly painted with the same glowing makeup that Javul wore and his hair—or were those feathers?—formed such a massive, wild cascade about his head and shoulders that all features were blurred except for a pair of enormous golden eyes.

"You okay, Night Cat?" the person asked. "These guys bothering you?"

"Night Cat? *Night*—oof!"

Eaden stepped adroitly in front of Dash to give his partner time to recover from the elbow he'd just received in the solar plexus. "We're her co-workers."

"Right," Javul said. "I guess it's time for us to get back to the conference hotel. C'mon, boys." She turned on her heel and strode off down the length of the room, her stride snappy and quick, her hips swinging, her hair changing color rapidly. The two men gave her companion a last once-over before following her.

Dash and Eaden caught up with Javul simultaneously as she reached the outer mall. They flanked her in silence, Dash slipping his arm around her—he was *not* going to lose track of her again—and pulling her tightly to his side.

She laughed at him.

"What in the name of all that is patently idiotic were you doing out there after everything that's happened?"

Dash paced behind Javul's chair as she sat at her vanity console and removed her makeup. She turned off the tiny generator that had charged her hair, peeled off prosthetics that made her nose longer and her face wider, and took out lenses that turned her eyes a pale mauve—a pastel version of the bodysuit she'd worn. That had been discarded as well, and she'd wrapped herself in a long, fluffy tunic that ended just above her knees.

"I told you. I was slipping the leash—blowing off steam. And I needed to do that *especially* after everything that's happened. Do you have any idea what it's like to come that close to dying?"

Dash stopped pacing and glared at her in the mirror.

She blinked back at him. "Oh. Of course you do. Sorry."

"What were you doing—spice?"

She shook her head.

"That weird guy? Were you and he—?"

She smiled but shook her head again. Well, that tallied with what Eaden had sensed. Dash found that more of a relief than he was comfortable with.

"Then what, *Night Cat?*"

Javul adopted a look of long-suffering patience. "Everybody uses pseudos in places like that. The guy's was *Rancor's Wrath*. It's just a bar."

"Just a bar with enough dark spots, strobe lights, and hypersound to give an assassin all the cover he could ever ask for."

She lowered her gaze, turned back to her mirror.

He had her on the ropes and knew it. He pressed his advantage. "You didn't think of that, did you? What if whoever made the attempt on your life knows you well enough to know you'd go out to blow off steam? What if they followed you?"

She stopped, frozen in the act of fluffing out her short hair. After a moment of silence, she lowered her hands and turned to face him. Her face was almost albino white. "Do you think someone did? Other than you and Eaden?"

"No. You're still alive."

"Right." She took a deep breath. "Right."

Dash sat down on the foot of her bed. "Javul, listen to me. I've been thinking a lot about this. Before, the stuff that happened—the lilies, the mail, even the fake emergency—none of it was deadly. But this last one— that was potentially fatal."

She nodded. "Yeah. I get that."

"And?"

She shrugged artlessly.

"Blast it, Javul, you're not a child! You may think of this—this crazy behavior as *slipping the leash* but it's likely to get you killed. The *leash* is what keeps you alive."

"Yeah. I get that, too, believe it or not. But here's the problem. Right now, I don't know who I can't trust. I only know who I *can* trust." She looked him square in the eye. "That's a select group. It includes you and Eaden and Leebo."

"Okay. So, what're you going to do?"

She took another deep breath. "I'm going on with my tour, Dash, because I don't have a choice. I'll just have to . . . keep my eyes open, I guess."

"You *guess*."

"Can I sleep now? I'm really, really tired."

She looked it.

He stood. Shook his head. Impotent anger roiled his gut. "You're crazy, lady."

He thought he heard her crying as he left her room.

FOURTEEN

THE NEXT MORNING A CREW CONSISTING MOSTLY OF droids broke down the concert rig and loaded it back into the tour's two vessels. Reloading took until early afternoon. *Deep Core,* being the slower of the pair, was packed up first and sent on her way. *Nova's Heart* left Rodia two hours later bound for Christophsis, where Javul planned to do a special open-air performance using the natural properties of the planet's crystal formations to enhance her holographic and photonic displays.

Arruna recalibrated their communications system to screen for peculiarities in the carrier waves coming out of Rodian space control (and any other source), and Bran Finnick kept a close watch on the live chatter the flight controllers were routing to their helm.

Even with those precautions, Dash was nervous. That whoever was after Javul could dance into Rodian space control and issue spurious orders to incoming vessels implied a level of authority that made his head hurt. He wouldn't relax until they'd engaged the hyperdrive.

Traveling at flank speed, they'd just cleared the Rodian system, when the proximity alarm sounded.

Captain Marrak sat bolt upright in his command chair, his eyes on the main viewport. "Chaos take it!" he shouted. "Evasive maneuvers! *Now!*"

Finnick leapt for his controls and executed a hard roll nintey degrees to starboard.

Through the viewport, Dash saw a small, dart-like

ship stooping toward them at an extreme angle. It was matte gray—almost invisible against the roiling blur of stars—and unmarked.

How the . . . ?

Nova's Heart rolled to starboard again as a series of blue-green charged-particle bolts zapped from beneath the little ship's prow. The *Heart* jumped and shimmied. Klaxons sounded; Captain Marrak checked his instruments and swore in Zabraki.

"We're losing pressure. Looks like the cargo area."

The bridge comm bleeped. It was Mel, confirming their worst fears. "We've had a blowout down here. Outer cargo hatch went, damaged the air lock. Oto was able to get a patch on the door, but we don't dare go anywhere until we can secure it."

"I'm on my way down," said Marrak.

Dash followed him into the lift, and they went down to the cargo hold together. As they exited the lift, the cargo master's Otoga 222 unit was in the process of making fast a hard seal around the edges of the large, clear duraplast bubble he'd affixed as an emergency patch. Mel was checking the seal by dragging a piece of diaphanous fabric over it, looking for flutters and drag on the thin cloth.

"What's the damage?" Marrak asked the moment he was out of the lift.

Mel finished his survey of the patch job and straightened to face the two men. "Not sure, but it looks as if there was some warping and we lost a little hull integrity right around the hatch. What happened?"

"We were attacked," Dash said.

"*Attacked?* By who?"

"Unknown," said Captain Marrak. "It was a small ship, unmarked. How bad is it?"

"Bad enough," said Mel. "I'm not sure we're safe to go into hyperspace. At least not for the long haul."

Dash moved to the bubble patch and peered through it, scanning the inner hatch. A spot about a meter in length seemed to be the only part of the inner hull that was visibly damaged. Looking beyond the clear surface of the patch and through the air lock window, he could see the emptiness of space and the mangled frame of the blown hatch. The worst damage to the outer frame was also about shoulder height on the left side.

The hatch frame was bent outward.

"That was a lucky shot," said Mel. "Gunner must've been a pro."

"He had help," Dash said, turning from his inspection.

Both men stared at him.

"The hatch frame is pushed *out*. That means there was some sort of explosion on the *inside* of the air lock."

Mel's pale eyes narrowed. "Are you sure?"

"Pretty sure. Take a look for yourself."

Mel moved to peer through the plastic bubble for a moment, then shook his head. "He's right, Captain. This is getting uglier by the minute."

"It's worse than ugly if we can't get into hyperspace. We're stranded over Rodia. It would take forever to get to Christophsis on sublight power alone. We could limp back to Rodia."

"We're not going back to Rodia." Dash blurted the words before he could think better of it.

The Zabrak raised one brow.

"That might be exactly what the saboteur intended. Need I remind you of what happened on our first approach to Rodia? You really want to let them take another shot at us?"

"Can we chance going to hyperspace?" the captain asked.

Mel pursed his thin lips. "Well, I'd have to consult with Arruna, but it's possible we can . . . if we don't try too long a jump. I mean, we could probably make it to

Christophsis, but there's no major SoroSuub repair facility there. We could get a few dents hammered out or get some scarring planed and polished, but we'll need to replace both the inner and outer hatches."

The captain nodded. "Then the most logical place to head for would be Edic Bar. The SoroSuub facility there could set this thing to rights better than anybody."

Mel shook his head. "I can almost guarantee we wouldn't make it that far."

Captain Marrak blew out a gust of air. "Exquisite. What about short jumps, though? We can make it to Christophsis, you thought. Fine. We do that. The rest of our jumps are relatively short—"

"Bannistar to Bacrana?" said Dash. "Not my definition of short."

The corner of Mel's mouth twitched. "No, it's not. Besides, cumulative stress is just as bad as prolonged stress in cases like this. The ship essentially has a hole in her side. I'll send a droid out to patch that, of course, but it's still not going to take well to the rigors of hyperspace travel. I'd advise against making more than one jump with her in this condition."

He was right. Captain Marrak acknowledged it with a nod. "I suppose the most logical thing would be to go to Christophsis and keep our appointed schedule. We'll be there for four days. Maybe during our stay we might make better repairs or locate a replacement hatch or find some other solution to the problem."

Mel snorted. "Like what—a whole new ship?"

Marrak's expression said that he wouldn't consider it out of the question. "Time to bring Javul into the conversation."

Javul stared at the tabletop before her as if their options were laid out there for her to sort through. Dash had to admit that none of them looked very good.

Javul agreed. She looked up at the group gathered around the table in the crew's commons, and said, "Tatooine is within reach. We'll go there."

Everyone stared at her. Everyone being Dash, Eaden, Mel, Captain Marrak, Bran Finnick, Arruna Var, and Lady Spike. Well, Eaden didn't so much stare as blink slowly and waggle a couple of head-tresses in Javul's direction, but the general mood was one of disbelief.

"What's on Tatooine?" asked the captain.

"A ready supply of scruffy-looking freighters," said Javul without hesitation.

Dara was nodding. "Sure. I should've thought of that myself. Makes perfect sense."

"No, it doesn't!" objected Finnick. "What we need is a replacement air lock. Yeah, you might be able to get a stopgap one on Tatooine, but that's not really a solution, is it?"

"Hence the term *stop-gap*," said Spike.

"And it's better than no air lock at all," Dash pointed out.

"Hear me out," Javul said, holding up her hands to quiet dissension. "We're not going to make it to Edic Bar. It makes more sense to me to send the *Deep Core* on to Christophsis while we go back to Tatooine, pick up a freighter capable of handling this load, then rejoin *Deep Core*. We could have a new air lock sent from Edic Bar and installed on Tatooine. I'm sure there are repair bays on Tatooine that could handle the job."

"Any number of them," Dash said. "In fact, the guy who's working on *Outrider* for me is one of the best."

"Great. Then maybe he can work on *Nova's Heart*. And while he's at it, he can make sure there aren't any more hidden booby traps aboard."

Dash blinked. He hadn't thought of that, but it made perfect sense.

Captain Marrak said, "All right, yes. That seems reasonable. With the repairs done we can rejoin you on one of the later tour stops. No later than Corellia, I would hope." He rose from the table. "I'll have the helm reverse course immediately."

The rest of the group dispersed, returning to their duties, but when Dash and Eaden rose to leave, Javul put out a hand to stop them. She watched as the commons cleared, then turned to Dash.

"You said this engineer was working on your ship— the *Outrider*. How close is she to being refitted?"

"I'm not certain. That is, I'm not sure how much work Kerlew's done on her. I, uh, wasn't able to pay the full amount he needed to finish the repairs. That's why I'm working for you, if you recall."

"Of course. If I were to pay for the repairs, would the *Outrider* be able to handle the contents of the *Heart*'s hold?"

Dash exchanged glances with Eaden, who gave the Nautolan approximation of a shrug.

"Absolutely. With room to spare."

"Is she fast?"

"The fastest."

"I think you're biased. Let me get a second opinion." She turned to Eaden. "Is she as fast as he thinks?"

"Quite nearly so. There might be one or two as fast." Dash glared at him.

"But none appreciably faster," Eaden concluded.

Javul nodded. "All right, then. When we get back to Tatooine, we'll look into resurrecting your ship. We'll see if the *Outrider* can get us to Christophsis on time."

When Javul left the crew's commons, Dash let out a hoot of laughter and drummed exuberantly on the tabletop. "Did you hear that? Did you *hear* that? We're gonna get the *Outrider* back. And it's not gonna cost us a single millicred."

"You're celebrating?" Eaden asked blandly. "You

realize, of course, that our lady friend's enemies will continue to try to get to her. Are you really happy to have to transport her aboard our own ship?"

Thoughts of the *Outrider* with holes in her hull brought Dash up short. His smile faded. "Anyone ever tell you you're the biggest killjoy in the galaxy?"

Within half an hour of docking on Tatooine, Dash was in Kerlew's facility promising him payment in full for *Outrider*'s retrofit. Kerlew was pleased. Dash was pleased. Everyone was pleased . . . until Kerlew gave his estimate of how long it would take to complete repairs on the hyperdrives.

"A *week*?" Dash gasped.

"More or less."

"I need *less*, Ker. A *lot* less. As much less as you can manage. My client needs to be on Christophsis in four days."

Kerlew gave him a wry look. "It takes a day and a half to get from Tatooine to Christophsis. That would leave me two days to do the repairs. I'm good, but I'm not that good. Besides, I've got other jobs—"

"Put them on hold. She'll pay more if you give *Outrider* priority."

Kerlew was skeptical. "She's got that kind of money?"

"You have no idea. This is big, Ker. And important."

The mechanic looked up at the *Outrider*. She sat in the middle of the bay, her engines completely disassembled. He sighed. "Okay, I'll give it my best shot. But I'll need the credits up front. I'm going to have to buy new power couplings for the starboard and central drives, and you know how Watto is about being paid up front."

"No problem," Dash said.

"Problem," Dash said. "Kerlew wants payment up front."

Javul cocked her head to one side and wrinkled her

nose. She was sitting on the edge of a chair dressed for Mos Eisley in formfitting bush pants, a smuggler's jacket with a multitude of pockets, and a pair of tall black boots all but identical to his own. "I'd pretty much expect that, under the circumstances."

"Really? I mean, you're willing to do that?" Dash frowned. "Wait—what do you mean, under the circumstances? What circumstances?"

"I mean, he doesn't know who I am. I'm sure he's used to people stiffing him for repairs."

"Not me—I've never stiffed Kerlew. I never would. And he knows it."

She held up her hands. "I didn't mean to imply that *you* would. Anyway, it's no problem to pay him up front. I'll do it right now, in fact." She jumped to her feet.

"Actually, it's not that simple. You see, it's like this. Ker's not sure he can have the repairs done in the time frame we need."

She frowned. "How long did he say he needed?"

"About a week."

She sat back down. "That's too long, Dash. We have to keep to our schedule. That means we have to be on Christophsis in four days." She thought for a moment, then said, "Offer him more money. Maybe if he's able to hire more men, afford more resources . . . In the meantime, I'll try to come up with a contingency plan."

Staring at the ceiling of the docking bay, Kerlew ran a hand over his lined face and considered Javul's offer: more money to commit greater resources.

"You know how many months it takes a bantha to foal?"

Dash, leaning against one of the *Outrider*'s landing struts, looked at the older man. "What does that have to do with anything?"

"I'll tell you—roughly eleven."

"So?"

"So, if I have eleven banthas, d'you think I could have a baby bantha in one month?"

Dash gritted his teeth. "No, of course not. But *Outrider* isn't a bantha."

Kerlew sighed. "Look, Dash. It's all about dependencies. Having more credits will get me the power couplings. In fact, I can have them within the hour. But it takes the same amount of time to install those new power couplings whether I've got two mechanics per coupling or four. And when it comes to wiring them into the main bus, only one mech will fit into the conduit tunnel at a time—well, unless they're Sullustan, but a Sullustan's arms aren't long enough to reach the bus panel. Then there are flight tests. You can't hurry those, either. With more money and more resources, I might be able to shave a day off the repair time, but no more."

Dash rubbed his temples. He had the makings of a supernova headache. "Okay. All right. Just do your best."

Kerlew gave him an offended look. "I *always* do my best."

Dash made his way back to the *Heart*'s docking bay, where he found the scaffolding already going up for repairs to the exterior hatch. He took a moment to climb the ramp and take a look at the damage from the outside. It was weird. The scorch marks from the attack ran along the flank of the ship's elegant fuselage and had clearly intersected the missing hatch. But it wasn't deep damage. Not deep enough, he would have said, to have blown the hatch . . . without help from within. Someone had wanted that hatch blown out awfully badly. Someone with inside help.

He went aboard to find things in a general uproar. He found Mel in his office, going over the manifest.

"You get a close look at the damage to the external hatch?" he asked.

The cargo master nodded. "You're right. It exploded outward. The emergency evac system kicked in and blew the cover."

Dash frowned. "Was it triggered by the attack?"

Mel shrugged, his expression wary. "It shouldn't have been." He hesitated, then added, "There are four explosive clamps in the evac system—one at each corner of the portal. They're supposed to fire off simultaneously to blow the hatch in case there's a need to jettison the cargo. One of them was already damaged—someone set a small charge on it. That was the damage you saw to the top left clamp. I suspect that's what triggered the other clamps."

"You told Javul yet?"

"Not yet."

"She needs to know."

But Javul was nowhere to be found and no one had any idea where she'd gone—including Spike, which Dash thought was awfully peculiar.

By the time he'd scoured the ship from stem to stern, he was getting a really bad feeling about the whole situation. Finding that Mel had conscripted Leebo to help evacuate the cargo hold in advance of repairs, Dash went in search of Eaden. He found the Nautolan meditating in their quarters—*meditation* being a rather inexact term, Dash thought, for the surreal position his partner was in when he entered the suite.

Eaden was seated cross-legged . . . fifteen centimeters from the floor. His only support was the arm that extended down within the confines of his crossed legs so that he balanced on the palm of one hand. Dash stopped just inside the door and stared. Then he fidgeted. Then he cleared his throat.

Eaden half opened one maroon eye, then closed it again. While Dash watched, the teräs käsi master uncoiled from his cross-legged position—still supported by that single hand—until his body was stretched out horizontal to the floor. Then he moved sinuously into a full handstand from which he flipped himself upright with the grace of a predator hunting prey.

"What was that?" Dash asked.

"What was what?"

Dash gestured at the spot Eaden had occupied moments before. "That . . . what you did just then. Is that teräs käsi stuff?"

"Teräs käsi . . . stuff?"

"Okay, moves. Were those teräs käsi moves? I mean, I've seen you practice forms before, but—"

"I was meditating in a posture known as Sleeping Krayt, so named for the krayt dragon that is native to this world. I then performed the Leaping Veermok."

"Whoa. Doesn't your arm hurt? I mean, my arm hurts just from watching you."

"My arm does not hurt," Eaden said. "You wanted something?"

"Huh? Oh—yeah." Dash shook himself. "She's disappeared again. Javul. I want to find her before she does something stupid."

"More so than she has already?"

Remembering Javul's excursion on Rodia, Dash had to admit that was a tough act to follow.

"I figure we'll check Chalmun's first," Dash said as they strode along the dusty avenue toward Kerner Plaza. "Since that's where we met her originally, she might've gone there to see if she could come up with a backup plan. If not, someone there might've seen her." Eaden didn't reply, but his head-tentacles, to Dash at least, seemed on high alert. Dash kept looking about as they walked, but he didn't see any sign of Javul on the way to the cantina. Once inside the crowded main room, Dash blinked to banish the lingering glare of the twin suns.

Eaden, who wore his moisture suit with its protective goggles, was not similarly affected. He made his way immediately to the bar and engaged the bartender in a brief conversation. Dash reached him as he turned from the counter.

"She is here," Eaden said. He tilted his head toward the rearmost booth.

Dash let out a whoosh of air. "Thank . . . whatever deity is in charge of protection from lame-brain moves. Let's go."

He led the way to the booth where, not that long ago, they had first met Javul Charn and her spiky sidekick. He was prepping himself for what he would say to her—something about having a death wish maybe, or asking if her contingency plan included getting herself killed. Should he glare at her, or appear nonchalant?

He stepped into the booth's narrow entrance, swiftly deciding on wry condescension. "Is this your idea of coming up with a contingency plan?" he said, then nearly choked. *"You!"*

Han Solo spread his hands in an expressive gesture of bemusement. "Yeah, me." He put a hand to his ear. "What's that you say? 'Thanks, Han, for getting my lousy cargo to Nal Hutta'? No problem, old buddy. I mean, there's a palace insurrection going on there or something—*I* sure wouldn't know—and I don't think Jabba was even onworld. Which meant I had to dump the whole load on the open market on Nar Shaddaa. 'How'd you do, Han?' I did pretty well, thanks. Got more for the load than I expected, given the circumstances. But here I am, all in one piece—thanks for caring—and your share of the credits is already in your account. It's not much, but it's better than what you had when you rolled in."

Dash sputtered for a moment, then looked at Javul. She was attempting, with little success, to hide a grin.

"Yes," she said.

"Yes *what*?"

"This is my idea of coming up with a contingency plan. In fact, you're looking at my contingency plan: Captain Solo is going to take us to Christophsis—and beyond, if necessary."

FIFTEEN

"I QUIT."

Javul and Han stared at Dash. Her expression was incredulous; Han rolled his eyes. Actually *rolled his eyes*.

"You're kidding," said Javul. "Dash, I need you more now than ever."

"Oh, really? And why is that? You've got Old Hotshot here. What do you need with me?"

"Old Hotshot here is going to be piloting the ship. I still need a security chief."

"Yeah," said Solo, with that annoying slow grin. "And I need a copilot and navigator. And Chewie's still on Kashyyyk—won't be back on Tatooine for at least two weeks."

Dash's face suffused with heat. "Me? You want *me* to be your navigator? When Mustafar freezes over."

"Actually, I was thinking of Eaden. I hear he's a pretty good second in command."

"You lame-brained, arrogant son-of-a-spavined-nerf—"

Javul reached up and caught Dash's wrist. "Dash, please. I really do need you. I'm scared, okay? Really and truly scared."

He shook her hand from his arm. "I'll see you back at the ship. We can discuss this later." He glared at Han. "When do you leave?"

"As soon as your crew can get the cargo moved over to the *Falcon*. I'll go to the bay now and open up the passenger quarters. Air 'em out. It's been a while since the old girl had guests."

"Fine," Dash said and left. Behind him he heard Han ask Eaden, "So, you ever pilot a YT-1300? Of course the *Falcon*'s nothing like a stock model."

"I doubt there will be a problem."

Dash had cleared his belongings from his quarters on the *Nova's Heart* by the time Javul returned to the ship. He was going to move them back to the *Outrider,* he told himself. Figure out some way to have Kerlew finish the repairs. Maybe there was enough credit in his account to at least make her spaceworthy. Then some weird little voice in his head started nattering that he really ought to just stuff his ego and haul his body over to the *Falcon*'s berth in Docking Bay 94. Javul was in danger—he knew that more now than ever. There was no way that air lock blew out without inside help. She had to know that, at least, before he left . . .

If he left.

"Don't quit on me, please, Dash," she said when she found him glaring out of his window into the docking bay.

He didn't respond. Just kept glaring out the window.

She sighed heavily. "What'll it take for you to stay?"

He turned to face her, took a step forward—and nearly tripped over the MSE droid that Leebo had claimed as a pet. It was busily vacuuming the carpet.

That was the straw that broke the bantha's back, as far as Dash was concerned. He kicked the tiny cleaning unit across the length of his quarters. Mousie landed on its side, righted itself, and fled a short distance before it cowered between Leebo's legs, the droid having entered just in time to see what had happened. "Hey!" he said indignantly. "Pick on someone your own size!"

"Suits me," said Dash, who had crossed the small

chamber by the time Leebo finished his challenge. Before the droid could react, Dash reached out and flicked Leebo's master control switch to OFF. The droid drooped like a marionette whose strings had been lasered.

Dash, anger momentarily quelled, looked at Javul, who raised an eyebrow at him.

"Leebo's right, you know. You really ought to pick on someone closer to your own size."

"Like you, maybe? Level with me, Javul. What's really going on with your ex?"

"I don't know what you mean."

"This is not just good love gone bad, is it? And it's not just that you kept some of his toys—at least, I assume the *Heart* was his property at one time."

"Actually, no. The *Heart* belonged to someone else with reasons for escape routes and secret hiding places."

"But—?"

She bit her lip. "Okay. All right. I'll . . . it's like this. When I left Hitch he was angry, sure, and threatened and pleaded—mostly threatened—to try to get me back. When I refused, he made a show of cutting off contact with me, but then I discovered he was still hiding his illicit goods in my gear. Like I said: drugs, weapons, illegal tech . . . and people."

"Wait . . . this kept happening *after* you parted company? You told me he *tried* to use your tour but—"

"He succeeded. I told you before: the dead ambassador wasn't the last supposed stowaway we had, nor was he the only sort of cargo Kris snuck onto the *Heart*. We found all sorts of 'items' among our gear. When we found them in time, we left them in the loading bay or 'liberated' them. We didn't always find them in time. He actually managed to get a few people through alive—mostly."

"What sort of people?"

"Some of them were the victims of turf wars between

Hitch and his fellow Vigos; some of them were criminals on the run; some of them were political abductees. And honestly, I'm pretty sure Kris wasn't the only one with access to my ship and cargo."

Chilled, Dash asked, "What makes you say that?"

"The ones that didn't make it. Like that ambassador. I don't think his death was accidental."

The *ones* that didn't make it? "How many bodies are we talking about?" Dash asked.

"Three . . . that we found. All supposedly suffocated." She crossed her arms over her chest as if she were cold.

"So what did you do?"

"What I told you before. I went to the Imperial Security Bureau. They raided my ship, confiscated things and people, and . . ." She hesitated, took a deep breath. "They made some arrests within Black Sun that netted several lieutenants in the central organization and came oh-so-close to Kris himself. My tours have gone off without a hitch ever since."

"Until now," Dash noted. "And I admire how you were able to use that pun with a straight face. So you didn't just embarrass old Hitch and lose him a courier vessel; you almost got him fried."

"I did."

"And you put a hole in Black Sun's operations."

"I did that, too."

"So this is revenge for Kris."

"Of the worst kind, Dash. He's basically giving me two choices: come back into the fold and be a good little soldier—or die. He doesn't just want my ship. He wants me."

"And it's payback for messing with Black Sun, too, isn't it?"

She looked so lost for a moment, he almost put his arms around her. Instead he put his hands on his hips, hoping he looked intimidating. "Admit it, Javul. It's not just Hitch Kris who's after you, is it? It's Black Sun itself. It's Prince Xizor."

She lowered her eyes, folded her arms across her breasts, and nodded.

"Okay. So you've told me what I wanted to know. Now I'll tell you what I know. I know that the cargo hold air lock blew out from the inside."

Her face paled and she sat down on the edge of a table. "The—the emergency jettison system?"

"Mel thinks it was triggered."

She swallowed, peering up at him through her lashes. "By what?"

"The attack may have damaged it, but someone wanted to make sure it blew. Someone aboard the *Nova's Heart*. Looks like someone may have planted a small charge in one of the four outer hatch fail-safe mechanisms. Whether it was blown from inside or triggered by the laserfire doesn't really matter. Either way—"

"Either way someone has access to my ship—either a stowaway or a mole among my crew." She glanced up at him, eyes glittering. "The cargo. If we move it to Han's ship—"

Han already, was it? "I'm one step ahead of you. Mel and Oto are checking every crate as it leaves the hold. And you said it yourself—it's not just Hitch who's had access to the *Nova's Heart*."

"Yeah," she whispered. "I get that."

After a beat, he asked, "Have you thought about who's coming with us on the *Falcon*?"

She hit him with a dazzling smile that was so unexpected, his pulse kicked up a notch. "Us? Does that mean you're still my security chief?"

"Yeah, I'm still your security chief. Who's coming along for the ride?"

"Mel, Nik, Dara, you, Eaden, and Leebo. Mel will

bring Oto and a few of the cargo droids, of course. Everyone else can go with *Nova's Heart*."

He looked at her with growing admiration. She really had thought this through. She had the crew she needed and a decent chance of leaving the mole behind on her own ship. He wondered if there was any chance of figuring out who that mole was before the *Heart* was spaceworthy.

"I'm going to go help Mel and Oto," he said. "I'll bring Leebo along." He reactivated the droid.

Leebo straightened up, optics brightening. "Had enough?" he asked.

"Come on," Dash said, and strode from the room.

Leebo clambered to his feet, servos whining. "Humans," he said to Javul, "fight dirty." He followed Dash, the MSE unit scuttling along behind him.

They lifted from Tatooine as soon as the gear was stowed safely. Mel grumbled about the unfamiliar dimensions and arrangement of the *Falcon*'s holds and, after checking every centimeter of each compartment with Dash and Nik at his side, he went off to talk to Javul, who was settling into her quarters on the lower deck.

With Eaden up in the cockpit with Han, and Leebo at a computer terminal "getting acquainted" with the ship and her various modifications, Dash found himself alone with Oto. It was as good a time as any to probe, he figured.

"So tell me, Oto, how long have you been touring with Charn?"

"Three standard years, sir," said the droid, ticking off items on the manifest Mel had put him in charge of.

"And before that?"

"I have been attached to Mistress Charn's service since she purchased *Nova's Heart*."

"Yeah? What about your boss, Melikan. He always been with the tour?"

"No, sir. Yanus Melikan was previously with another vessel."

"Yeah? Merchant or Imperial?"

"Merchant, sir."

He'd have to check that out. "What about Nik?"

The droid made a faint clicking sound that in Leebo, Dash would have read as a sigh. "What about Nik, sir?"

"Where'd you pick him up?"

"He joined the crew about a year ago. Cargo Master Melikan took him on."

Dash thought about that. "He seems kind of young for an apprentice. Still in school—doesn't he have any parents?"

"I believe he is an orphan. I have no further knowledge of the young man."

"I—uh—found him doing his homework really late one night in Mel's office. He do that often?"

"Quite often." Oto's flat mechanical voice somehow conveyed disdain. "He is likely to procrastinate."

"Mel likes him, though."

The droid didn't answer.

"Mel seems like a good guy. Steady, reliable, predictable. Is he?"

Oto made the clicking sound again. "I am unable to determine if he is a good guy. However, I would say that he *is* steady and reliable."

"Not predictable?" Dash jumped on the omission. "Does he do . . . unexpected things sometimes?"

"He occasionally makes requests for which I do not see a rationale."

"Yeah? Such as . . ."

The droid looked at him blankly.

Blasted mechanicals. Sometimes you had to lead them

by their tin noses. "Nik once told me that Melikan tells him not to notice things. Does he ever tell you not to notice things?"

"He occasionally requests that I do not take note of certain comings and goings."

"Like when Javul leaves the ship in disguise?"

The droid's optics blinked. "I would not have noticed, sir."

No, he wouldn't have, having received a direct order not to. "What else might you not have noticed?"

Click. "If I have not noticed something, sir, how would I know what it was that I have not noticed?"

With the beginnings of a headache, Dash wandered to the crew's quarters, turning the conversation over in his head. Yanus Melikan was in the picture-perfect position to wreak all sorts of havoc on the ship. Could it possibly be coincidence that several of the episodes had involved the hold or its contents? Mel had an apprentice who was young and loyal and a droid who was—well, a droid— and he was close to Javul.

Dash stopped on that thought, spinning it on various mental axes as he went to the galley and poured himself a cup of caf. He sipped it, wrinkling his nose. Wretched brew. No more than he'd expect of Solo's bucket of bolts. He took the caf to the single table in the middle of the common area and sat down. Blowing steam off the top of the cup, he tried to work out the logistics of Mel's guilt or innocence in the string of sabotage.

The cargo master was in an almost unassailable position when it came to Javul. She trusted him and he protected her peculiar "comings and goings"—perhaps for his own purposes?

And here, both logic and logistics broke down. Mel was *close* to Javul. So close that if he was working for someone who wanted her dead, she'd be dead. What did that mean? Did it mean that Mel was guilty only of being very protective of his employer, or did it mean that he was the mole but whoever was pulling his strings didn't really want Javul dead? They just wanted it to *look* like they wanted her dead.

"Why would they want it to look like they wanted her dead?" he murmured.

"Herding the nerfs, I would imagine."

Dash shook hot caf from his hand and glared at Eaden, who leaned in the hatchway of the crew's commons observing him. "*Never* sneak up on a guy like that. You could get yourself shot."

"How so? You didn't even sense my presence."

"I was thinking."

"You were also talking to yourself. Neither bodes well for your sanity."

"Stow it. What do you mean by *herding the nerfs*?"

Eaden shrugged and moved to the beverage server to pour himself a cup of some weird-smelling tea. "Just what has been suggested before: that it is not Javul Charn's death that is desired, but the modification of her behavior."

"That'd be true if we were just talking about a jealous boyfriend, but we're not. She admitted to me that it's a lot more serious than that." He leaned across the table toward his friend. "She's in hot lava with all of Black Sun. Apparently her attempts to get shed of Kris caused her to go to the ISB and, in turn, brought down several of Xizor's Vigos. You know how much Xizor hates the Imperials."

"With as good a reason as you have for hating Black Sun."

It was a quiet remark, delivered in a gentle voice, but it struck Dash all the way to the core. He would not feel this. He would not let his own entanglement with Black Sun make him crazy. He'd controlled the impulse to strike out at Hitch Kris just for breathing the same air;

he'd intended to control the impulse to take on Prince
Xizor, but . . .

"It's not the same thing. My family was no threat to
anyone. We were just . . . in Xizor's way."

"*His* family was no threat to the Empire. They just
happened to be too close to Vader's ill-fated bioweap-
ons lab. You might say his family died of hubris and
stupidity."

"Yeah? And what would you say mine died of? Greed?"

Eaden was silent for a moment, then said: "You think
Xizor is involved with our current situation?"

"I can *smell* him on this, Eaden. Look, what if it's like
this—what if there are two parties involved here? Two
motives?"

"Involved in the sabotage?"

"Yeah. Because it doesn't make sense to me any other
way. You're right—it seems as if someone is trying to
herd the nerf back into line. But some of these incidents
could have caused real harm. What if there are two different agendas at work here? What if Kris wants Javul
back, but someone else wants her dead? What if there
are *two* saboteurs?"

Eaden considered that, his prehensile tresses eerily still.
"If that someone is Prince Xizor," he said, "then you may
find yourself in his way again."

"I wasn't in his way before," Dash growled. "I was collateral damage. He was after RenTrans. I just got taken
down by shrapnel. He doesn't give a womp rat's ass about
me personally."

Which, odd as it seemed to him at the moment, galled.
It would have been somehow comforting to be able to
say that he was a personal enemy of Prince Xizor—that
the Black Sun Underlord hated him. In reality, the Falleen didn't even know that he existed, much less care.
The Rendars had served their purpose. His brother's
ship had been sabotaged and used to destroy Imperial

property, which in turn had ruined the family and put their business on the auction block for Xizor to scoop up. Just a day in the life of a Vigo.

"Perhaps we should walk away from this, Dash," said Eaden. "If Javul Charn is going to come into direct conflict with Prince Xizor, it might be best if you were not in her immediate vicinity to become collateral damage yet again."

Walk away? The thought sat heavily in his gut for a moment until he rooted it out. "I don't walk away, Eaden. Especially when someone else is counting on me to stay in the game."

"This is not a game."

Dash glanced up at the Nautolan sharply. "You pickin' up something? Y'know . . ." He made a circular motion indicating the ether.

Eaden frowned. Or at least his face did something as close to a frown as a Nautolan face could perform. "I am . . . uneasy," he admitted.

"Why?"

"Uncertain. There is a pattern to events I have not yet recognized, but do not like."

"Uncertain," repeated Dash. "I'm really beginning to hate that word. I'm uncertain myself—uncertain about who's doing what to whom." He filled Eaden in then, on his thoughts about Mel's possible involvement. "I mean, think of it: He's in a perfect position to plant explosives, sneak things into containers, allow access to the ship. *But* he clearly can't be the one who wants Javul dead or she'd already be that way. In fact, he may be protecting her after a fashion—maybe even on Kris's behalf. Who knows?"

"A tangled scenario. And our most recent sabotage?"

"I don't know. It could have been catastrophic, I suppose. But then Mel's the one who told me that."

"What would be his motive for such sabotage?"

Dash leaned back in his chair and stared at the bulkhead above him. "Well, let's catalog the effects it had on the tour. We had to either repair the ship or hire a new one; we've had to lose most of the crew, which may mean Javul is more vulnerable—or less, depending; we went to Tatooine."

The Nautolan cocked his head. "Why Tatooine?"

"That's what I'm trying to figure out."

"You're not entertaining the idea that Han Solo—"

"No. Han can be a jerk at times, but he's honorable. He wouldn't deal with Black Sun. Not even if you tied him to the *Falcon*'s plasma vent and threatened to take off."

"Then . . ."

"Isn't it obvious? If we'd gone directly to Christophsis, we'd have stayed with the other ship and the entourage. This way, Javul gets cut out from the rest of the nerfs. This way, we're on our own."

SIXTEEN

DASH WAS NERVOUS. NO, NOT NERVOUS—HE NEVER GOT nervous, he told himself. He was on edge. Waiting.

He hated waiting. He was really and truly bad at it, and right now it was all he could do. Mostly, his waiting took the form of wandering the ship, poking his nose everywhere, and staying close to Javul. The latter was no big hardship, but it did put him in the crossfire between Han Solo—who was trying to make time with the lovely holostar—and Spike, who was running interference against both of them. Thank the stars Han was usually engaged in the cockpit.

Dash felt lucky to finally get Javul alone at roughly the midpoint of their voyage to Christophsis. Han had created a little guest lounge in a storage compartment between his quarters and the cabin Javul shared with Spike. Dash found Javul there, frowningly studying a datapad . . . or maybe just reading a book or watching a vid. She shut the little machine off when he entered the room and smiled up at him.

"How's my shadow?" she asked brightly.

He stopped just short of sitting down at the small makeshift table Han had fashioned out of a cylindrical container and an emergency hatch cover and stared at her. "Your shadow?"

"You haven't talked to me much, but I know you're there. Following, watching—"

"You make it sound creepy."

"No, it's nice. Makes me feel safe. It's been a long time since I've felt safe."

You're not safe, he wanted to tell her. *You may have brought the mole with us.* Should he tell her that? He used the act of pulling over a chair to sit in to cover his deliberations.

I should tell her.

No, I shouldn't. It would just scare her needlessly.

Yes, I should. I don't want her to relax too much, become complacent.

"Well, are you gonna tell me?" she asked when he'd gotten himself settled.

He glanced at her sharply. Her eyes were mischievous. "What?"

"That little argument you were just having with yourself. You gonna tell me what it was about?"

Was he that transparent?

"It was about how much to tell you."

She raised an eyebrow. "About . . ."

"When we did this—split up the tour—I'm pretty sure you were thinking that maybe we'd left the spy behind. Am I right?"

She made a wry face and bit her lip. "Yeah. The thought had crossed my mind."

"I'm not sure we've done that. And I'm not sure the attack on the *Nova's Heart* wasn't purposeful."

She looked at him oddly. "Of course it was purposeful. Someone wanted to damage the ship."

"Or someone wanted to drive you back to Tatooine and/or separate you from the rest of your entourage."

"Who?"

He hesitated. This wasn't going to be pleasant. "How well do you know Yanus Melikan?"

She stared at him, her eyes wide. After a long moment of silence, she laughed. Normally, the happy trill would have mesmerized him. Now it grated.

"Mel? You think I should distrust Mel? Why?"

"Because he's been the one person in a position to figure in just about every one of your little incidents—most especially this last one. He's the master of that hold," he added as she screwed up her face in denial. "He knows everything that goes in and everything that comes out. And he routinely tells Nik and Oto not to notice things."

"You mean my little field trips? He only does what I've asked him to do so that I have some privacy."

"Are you sure?"

Before she could answer, Han Solo stepped through the hatch into the chamber, a crooked grin on his face.

"Am I interrupting anything?" he asked, glancing between the two seated at the table.

"Would you care if you were?" asked Dash in return.

Han grinned unrepentantly. "Nope."

"Shouldn't you be up in the cockpit steering this crate, *Captain* Solo?"

"Shouldn't you be checking shipping crates or something . . . *Security Chief* Rendar?"

"I've checked them, thanks."

Han shook his head, moving farther into the room. "Oh, but you can never be sure about these things, Dash, old buddy. I mean, you can't be watching all the holds all the time."

"I've got a maintenance droid posted at every entrance."

"Droids? Man, you'll be up a wormhole without a hyperdrive if your saboteur knows how to fool a droid. Which doesn't exactly take a degree in Neural-Net Psych One-Oh-One."

He had a point. A good point. One Dash hadn't even considered.

"It's about time for my rounds anyway." He rose and gestured at his chair. "All yours, Han, old buddy."

Han smiled and took the chair.

"Dash?"

He turned back at the sound of Javul's voice.

"I'm sure," she said.

He hesitated a moment, trying to remember where they'd left their conversation when Han had strolled in. He'd asked if she was sure she could trust Mel. In the moment their eyes had met, he thought he'd read doubt in hers.

"I'm gonna go check the holds again anyway," he said.

He checked in with Leebo and Oto first—asked them to examine the droids he'd posted outside the various holds, dividing the duty between the two of them.

"And what exactly is it I'm supposed to be checking for?" asked Leebo. "Oto's got an uplink to all of them and they haven't so much as peeped."

"Find out if they recorded any peculiar comings and goings."

"Peculiar comings and goings? Oh, now there's a real clear description. What d'you think, Oto? You think the droids will understand what we mean by *peculiar comings and goings*?"

"I am uncertain how to respond to that, LE-BO2D9. I have no internal description of what constitutes *peculiar comings and goings*."

Leebo swiveled his head toward Dash. "There, you see? Clear as mud. Care to try again?"

Dash blinked at the droid. Tried to remember that it really wasn't being a smart-mouth—it was the programmed personality. This was just a request for more information; Leebo's way of saying *Please specify*. He took a deep breath.

"Inquire as to whether the droids have observed anyone—and I do mean *anyone*—entering the holds or tampering with the containers, or with the droids themselves, in any way."

Leebo tilted his head sideways. "There, now. Was that so hard?" He started to turn away.

"Wait." Dash tapped him on one metal shoulder. "Ask if anyone even *approached* them. I mean, there's a chance maybe someone messed with the droids' memory. Did something to the containers then wiped their record of it."

Oto made a hostile-sounding clicking noise. "Such reprogramming would require that Cargo Master Melikan was the aforementioned someone. Likewise, if they were instructed not to notice something, the cargo master would have had to deliver the instruction."

"Ask," Dash insisted. "That's an order. I want to know if anyone so much as breathed on those droids."

"Breathed on them, sir? Do you wish me to inquire—"

"It's a figure of speech. Just ask if anyone attempted to enter the cargo holds. Or, in fact, did enter. Or approached the droids. Got that?"

"Yeah, we got it," said Leebo, sounding annoyed. "We're not a couple of food service units here, you know."

"I was trying to be precise. The last thing I need is for someone to plant a bomb in one of the cargo bays and not find out about it until it goes off because I failed to ask the right question."

He left the two droids to their task—Oto blessedly silent and Leebo lauding the virtues of "sensible programmed persons." He made a quick tour of the ship, ascertaining where everyone was. Mel was asleep in the quarters he shared with Nik—a makeshift berth in a corner of the forward hold; Nik was doing his schoolwork; Spike was up in the cockpit pestering Eaden—and of course he knew exactly where Han and Javul were.

That done, he started on the holds, beginning with the main hold on the port side. He determined that Leebo had been here already asking a series of questions. No one else had come except, of course, himself. He went into the hold anyway and prowled around the containers, looking for anything that seemed amiss. He found nothing. The droid he'd stationed in the loading bay between the forward and number two holds gave the same report, as did the one in hold number three.

Dash wondered if it was even worth his while to go into the number three hold. He sighed and checked his chrono. If he'd done his time estimation right, they'd be coming out of hyperspace fairly soon to make a course adjustment. He should have just enough time to do a quick walk-through.

He slipped into the hold and closed the hatch behind him. Everything looked completely normal. The number three hold—actually the freight cargo chamber, located immediately behind the *Falcon*'s huge electromagnetic mandibles—was a pretty good-sized space. He made his way through it carefully, peeking into crevices between containers, rapping on the individual boxes, checking the floor, the ceiling, the blinking access panels. He stifled a yawn.

Who would do this kind of work full-time?

He wasn't sure whether he should be in awe of Mel or feel sorry for him.

He was just going to check the environmental control panel by the cargo bay door when the ship shuddered. He felt a moment of vertigo as it dropped out of hyperspace. That was pretty much as he expected. What he didn't expect was that the cargo bay grav-plate stopped working at precisely the same moment. Dash's feet left the deck and the suddenly airborne contents of the bay were in frantic motion. Dash tumbled among them, out of control.

He was no stranger to zero-g. He'd trained in zero-gravity at the Academy and had experienced any number of weightless situations on EVAs. But on none of those occasions had he had to dodge large, inimical objects.

The only fortunate aspect of the situation was that he was headed toward the control panel by the door. He reached it too quickly, colliding painfully with the bulkhead and rebounding into the path of a large cylindrical container. He flailed, thrust out his hands, and pushed away from it, sending it toward the ceiling in a slow spin.

Good news: he rebounded again.

Bad news: he rebounded toward the deck.

He bounced on his hands and knees, struggled to pull his feet under him, to gain some altitude before the grav-plate snapped back on . . . with all that *stuff* careening around overhead. The toes of his boots slid on the textured metal of the decking, just barely allowing him enough purchase to push off toward the hatch again. Unfortunately, he also thrust himself upward, which put him directly beneath the cylinder he'd banked off a moment before.

It was rotating lazily, its metal fittings glinting in the now dim light of the bay. But—wonder of wonders—it was rotating in just the right direction. Dash lowered his head and let it catch the back of his jacket. It gave him an ungentle shove forward and down. He sailed toward the control panel, this time having the time and presence of mind to put out his hands to grasp the hatch frame and buffer the collision. His right hand met the bulkhead, palm flat, fingers splayed. He allowed his arm to bend, using his left hand to grab the hatch frame. He was secure . . . for the moment. Hopefully, a moment was all he needed.

He found the grav controls and started to manipulate them, then stopped in confusion. According to the read-out on the panel, the plate was still engaged and set to standard Corellian gravity. He grasped the slider anyway and started to pull it downward to increase the gravity. Some sense stopped him. If he turned the gravity up and it kicked back in, some of those crates could do serious damage to the ship . . . and to him. He glanced up at the clutter of smaller crates that were collecting above him. He pushed the slider full up to zero-g, then started to bring it slowly back down—to absolutely no effect.

Oh, fine then.

He hit the hatch control. The brightly lit indicators that showed it to be operational lied; the hatch stayed closed.

Dash took a deep breath, took his right hand off the panel, and reached slowly for his comlink. The ship braked suddenly and made a sharp starboard turn. This was when he learned the local inertial field dampers were off as well; all the floating junk in the cargo bay collided high on the port wall of the hold.

The ship dipped and ducked again, this time to port. The containers, hanging in zero-g, stayed put until the starboard bulkhead moved to connect with them. They flew outward from that more violent impact. A loose glow rod someone had left somewhere they shouldn't have hurtled past Dash's head and careened off the inner bulkhead.

He brought the comlink to his mouth and thumbed it on.

"Eaden—Dash. You got gravity out there?"

There was a long enough silence that Dash began to fear that there was something screwy elsewhere in the ship as well; then Eaden's voice came back to him sounding slightly puzzled: "What do you mean—*out there*?"

"In the cockpit. In the rest of the ship! Is there gravity where you are?"

"Yes. There is not gravity where you are?"

"No. I'm in the number three hold. The plate's gone down and the hatch won't open. There are some very large objects floating around over my head, Eaden, and I'd really like them not to suddenly come plummeting down."

The ship juked again and those very large objects reacted. Dash gave a yelp of pure, cold fear and shouted, "I need *out,* Ead! I need out *now*!"

He heard a hurried discussion, recognizing Han's voice—raised in annoyance or excitement—then Eaden came back on.

"We're going to brake, Dash. As gently as possible, considering that we are in rather tight quarters. We are approaching an asteroid field."

"Cancel that," said Han in the background. "I'm gonna land on that big guy over there. Give the hold a bit of gravity."

"I don't *want* gravity!" shrieked Dash, his eyes going to the cylinder now moving inexorably toward him. "I want *out*!"

"Relax," said Han. "I know what I'm doing."

"What?" yelled Dash. "*What* are you doing? Eaden? What's he—"

"He is maneuvering, Dash. I'm on my way to you."

"But what—?"

The ship performed some sort of fluttering maneuver, and the stuff in the cargo bay banked off several bulkheads at once. A second later it all bobbed downward under the effect of a small gravity field. With every ounce of strength in his left arm, Dash yanked himself sideways into the hatch access, spinning so that his back was to the door. It was only half a meter deep, but it was all the cover the hold offered.

He'd just barely hauled himself into the meager alcove when the ship stopped moving, the grav-plate came back on, and the containers slammed to the floor with a sound like the shot of a laser cannon. The cylindrical container—a good two meters in length and as wide as Dash was tall—had bounced off the floor and was rolling toward him, one end angling into the hatchway where he stood. He pressed himself back against the hatch.

"Eaden!"

The hatch behind him opened, spilling him onto the deck beyond, then slapped shut again—an act punctuated by a bone-jarring thud of the container rolling against it. Dash lay on the deck panting, his heart rocketing around in his chest.

Eaden offered him a hand up. "What happened?"

"The chamber gravity failed when we dropped out of hyperspace. And if your next question is if I think this was an accident, the answer is *no*." He turned, then, on the solitary cargo droid he'd left posted to guard the hold. "Did you allow anyone else access to this hold?" he demanded.

"Negative," the droid responded curtly.

"Negative," Dash repeated, adrenaline pushing his temper higher. "Look, you bucket of mismatched bolts—"

Eaden's hand came down on his shoulder. "As I have previously noted, verbally bludgeoning a droid is a futile gesture. I suggest we check the other cargo bays."

Dash nodded. They made their way forward to cargo bay number two and opened the hatch. Every container was in its place. The main hold and belowdecks compartments were similarly untouched.

Dash turned from the orderly stacks of equipment to meet Eaden's gaze. "Well, this is special."

The Nautolan blinked slowly. "You have a talent for understatement."

SEVENTEEN

With the *Millennium Falcon* parked on the pocked surface of a large asteroid, Dash gathered everyone in the crew's commons. Except for Leebo, everyone looked grim. The sudden loss of gravity in the cargo bay seemed clearly to be sabotage. The questions now were: when had it been done, how, and by whom?

Leebo was able to answer the second question through the simple expedient of uplinking with the *Falcon*'s system and tracking down the anomaly. It was indeed in the artificial gravity system, but not at the control panel in the affected cargo bay. It was in a circuitry box in the engineering station off the main hold, which meant . . .

"Anybody could have messed with it," muttered Dash.

"Anybody, of necessity, being one of us." The quiet observation came from Mel.

Dash turned to look at the group gathered around the table in the crew's commons. Mel, Nik, Javul, and Spike. Eaden leaned against the aft bunks looking inscrutable, his tresses subtly sniffing the air. Leebo stood next to him. Han lounged in the doorway, mostly watching Javul.

"Either that or we've got a stowaway," said Spike.

"I can't say that's impossible, but it's highly improbable," argued Mel. "We checked the contents of every single container before we put it aboard."

"I suppose someone could have snuck aboard while we were doing preflight prep," said Dash. "Run up the landing ramp as it was being raised or climbed up one of the landing struts."

"Is that likely?" asked Javul.

Han made a rude noise and straightened from the doorway. "It's impossible. There's no way anybody could sneak aboard this ship without me knowing it."

Dash found himself wishing ardently that that was a big fat exaggeration and that they *did* have a stowaway, because the alternative was thoroughly unpleasant to contemplate. He scanned their faces again—Spike, Mel, Nik. He didn't know either the Farlion woman or Melikan nearly as well as Javul did—or *thought* she did. And Mel's access to the equipment and his look-the-other-way policies made him an especially likely suspect. But if Mel was working for Hitch Kris, then logically he was only responsible for what was annoying and inconvenient, not what was potentially fatal.

Until now.

And this last nastiness had been aimed at Dash, not Javul Charn.

Dash felt a little niggle of something like pride at the thought. Apparently, someone felt he was getting too close to discovering them and had decided to take him out of the picture. One of the people in this room was probably disappointed right now. He just needed to figure out which one.

Nik? He balked at suspecting the Sullustan. He was just a kid. Still, even a kid could be coerced or coaxed into doing heinous things if the incentives were right.

Leebo uttered a soft bleep. "Pardon me for interrupting and all that, but this particular sabotage didn't require the saboteur to stay on board. The grav-plate and the panel controls were impeded by an itty-bitty damper in the hold's power bus where it was routed through the engineering terminal. The damper was set to detect state changes in the hyperdrive, so it kicked in when we dropped out of hyperspace and let only the minimum of power through."

Dash nodded. "To keep from triggering the system alarms."

"That's what I'm thinking," said Leebo. "But here's the deal, boss—if that trap was set up before we even left Tatooine, then it's not much of a trap, is it? How would the saboteur know anyone would be in the hold at the moment we dropped out of hyperspace?"

Dash shot the droid a narrow look. "I thought you were arguing for a hit-and-run saboteur. If the plate was meant to go belly-up while I was in the hold, then you're saying it couldn't have been preset."

"I know this will be a blow to your colossal ego," the droid retorted, "but what I'm saying is that maybe *you* weren't the target."

"Why else would someone want the containers in that particular hold to go flying and none of the others?"

"Good question. I suppose it could've been a coincidence."

"I *so* don't believe in coincidence." Dash turned to Mel. "What's in that chamber? What sort of equipment?"

The cargo master answered without pausing to think about it. "The largest pieces of the framework, the anti-grav generators—primary and backup—the big holographic arrays . . ."

"Could the intent have been to damage them?"

Mel shrugged. "I suppose. But if any of it sustained damage—which we'd find before we used any of it again—then we'd either pull in the backup units from *Deep Core,* restructure the performance so as to not require that equipment, or cancel."

Dash met the other man's eyes in a long, challenging look. "You mean *you'd* find the damage. *You'd* tell us whether it was dire or not. Kind of like you told us what happened in the *Heart*'s hold during that stealth fighter attack. Or like you were the one who indirectly routed us back to Tatooine by saying we'd never make Edic Bar."

Mel didn't rise to the bait, but Spike did.

"Oh, for the love of—" she sputtered. "You're completely *mad*, you know that? I mean, you might as well suspect *me*."

"Who says I don't?"

Javul shook her head. "I will not believe—"

Mel put his hand on her arm. "No, Javul. Dash is right to suspect me. Quite honestly, if I'd been doing my job right . . . most of this stuff shouldn't have happened. I should have caught it. If I were in your shoes, Dash, I'd suspect me, too. But Dara can't be a suspect—she's been with Javul since the beginning."

"Since *before* the beginning," corrected Spike coldly. The glare she gave Dash would have soldered a lesser man to the deck.

Javul, meanwhile, had turned her pale gaze on Yanus Melikan, the two of them trading a long, significant look that Dash couldn't begin to decipher. It ended when Mel dropped his gaze with a slight shake of his head. What did that mean? And what was Dash to make of that sudden wrinkling of Javul's brow?

Whatever it meant, he still had insufficient evidence to accuse anyone—even the cargo master—of the sabotage. He turned back to Leebo.

"So you think the sabotage was in place before we left and the damper was set to fire when we dropped out of hyperspace."

"Or went back *into* hyperspace. State change, remember? That much I can say for sure. What I can't tell you is if there was a second trigger. Say, someone entering the cargo bay . . . or someone triggering the impedance remotely."

"So there's no way to know if the sabotage was aimed at a person or at the equipment," said Dash.

"Well, I guess we won't know that unless whoever it was is on board and tries again," said Han. Then the expression on his face did a flip-flop that Dash would have found comical under other circumstances. "Wait— state change? We have to go *back* into hyperspace. What if there's another one of those power dampers some-where in the system? Or something worse?"

Leebo swiveled his head toward Han. "That would be bad."

Han moved to stand face-to-faceplate with the droid. "Could you detect it?"

"Maybe. Probably, now that I know what to look for."

Han pointed a finger at the spot between Leebo's op-tics. "Then get down to the engineering console and start going through the systems. I'm gonna get us off this rock as soon as I can—which means you'd better have the systems completely checked out before we reach the far edge of this field."

"Why don't you ask me to teleport us to Christophsis while you're at it?"

Han was starting to visibly seethe. "You got a problem, tin man?"

"Yeah, skin job, I got a problem. It will take us ap-proximately three hours and forty-two minutes to cross this asteroid field, allowing for orbital fluctuations. Which is insufficient time to do more than a spot check of the ship's systems."

"Then split the duty with the other droid—what's-his-name, Oto? You should be able to do it in half the time."

"Your grasp of higher mathematics is stunning, Cap-tain Solo," Leebo said. "I'm sure Oto will appreciate your vote of confidence."

Leebo left to retrieve Oto from the number three hold, managing to look stiffer than was normal for a droid. Han gave Javul a deferential and insipid bow, then went to the cockpit.

Dash, who'd watched the interchange with amusement, pulled his mind back to the matter at hand. "Javul, what would happen if your equipment was so badly damaged that you couldn't perform on Christophsis?"

"Like Mel said: Worst case, we'd have to cancel. Best case, we'd go with a scaled-down performance. Either way, we'd have to replace or repair the equipment."

"Which would throw you off schedule."

"Yeah. Yeah, it would." She was looking at her hands folded on the table—smoothing the gleaming, light-emitting fingernails she affected.

"Is that a big deal?"

"Are you kidding?" asked Spike. "We'd lose millions of credits. Ticket refunds, pay-or-play for venues we didn't use, possibly having to rent them again for a makeup performance—if that was even possible. There's no telling how the promoters and shareholders in the enterprise might react. Plus, it would be a public relations disaster."

"Oh, c'mon," Dash objected. "I'm sure you could spin it so that Javul's adoring public would just be glad she was alive. Stealth attacks on your ship, equipment tampering, black lilies—even I can see value in that sort of publicity."

"We have to keep to our schedule," Javul said adamantly. "If we don't—the saboteur wins."

There was a measured silence, broken when Eaden said, "It appears we can't even be certain of the motive or motives for this continued sabotage, let alone the perpetrator. Is the saboteur among us, or hiding aboard somewhere—or, having done his work, has he simply gone on his way?"

If only, Dash thought, *it could be that simple.*

"I saw you sniffing around over there," he told the Nautolan later. "You get anything from the room?"

"Just a sense that almost everyone in it was concealing something."

"Almost? Who's *not* concealing something?"

"Han Solo. His attraction to Javul Charn is palpable."

"Great. That makes me feel *so* much better."

EIGHTEEN

THEY REACHED CHRISTOPHSIS WITHOUT FURTHER INCI-
dent. Leebo and Oto found no more dampers or other
surprises in the *Millennium Falcon*'s systems. Did that
mean, Dash wondered, that the saboteur had been left
behind on Tatooine—or that the saboteur merely wanted
them to *think* that?

He'd asked everyone aboard—one by one—if they'd
observed any other members of the *Nova's Heart* crew
near the *Falcon*'s berth on Tatooine before they lifted off.
The results were inconclusive. Arruna had been there—
Dash had seen that—but he'd swear she'd done nothing
but fraternize with Eaden. And Dara had acknowledged
that Captain Marrak had "been around." But being
"around" and getting access to the secondary engineering
terminal were two different things.

Christophsis was one of Dash's favorite ports of call,
despite the fact that it was an Imperial mining hub. He
liked the scenery. The entire surface of the planet was
covered with huge crystals upon, within, and around
which the major cities were built. He also liked the un-
derground. He'd smuggled cargoes of raw crystals and
ore out of Crystal City in the *Outrider* more than once.
The thought made him wistful for his ship. He was beginning to wonder if he'd ever fly the old girl again.

Javul's concert was set in an amphitheater in the capital
city of Chaleydonia, otherwise known as Crystal City.
There they reunited with the rest of the tour—something

that made Dash's stomach feel as if it were trying to eat itself from the inside out. He assigned Leebo and Oto to keep an eye on things, and oversaw Leebo's reprogramming of the cargo droids to be especially aware of the actions of any sentients within range of their optics and aural units. He even ordered them to keep their olfactory detectors at maximum, and to report anything that smelled funny.

The venue was a wonderland, Dash had to admit. The entire amphitheater was constructed out of the native crystal—including the encircling fence of spires. Lit by Javul's light show and used as a backdrop for her holograms, those spires shimmered and pulsed, reaching toward the sky and seeming, sometimes, to connect with space itself. The sense of being planetbound evaporated, leaving the audience gasping as Javul floated, flew, and walked among stars and planets, a creature of light and mist.

The performances among the soaring blue crystals were exhilarating, mesmerizing, awe inspiring—and blessedly uneventful. Dash didn't know if that was because of the precautions he'd taken, and he didn't care. At the end of three nights, Javul was still alive. Nothing had blown up, nothing had fallen apart, and no one had been caught where they didn't belong. Nothing, in short, had gone wrong.

Dash wasn't nearly as relieved as he'd hoped to be. It could just be part of the pattern—the pattern Eaden saw but couldn't define. It could mean that one or both of their saboteurs were trying to lull them into a false sense of security. Or it could mean that they were waiting until Dash and his trusted agents were looking the other way. Or it could mean they were trying to dream up a scheme that wouldn't point a finger right at them. Or . . .

Dash was fairly certain that, after a few more days of stress at this level, his brain would go nova.

The last hypothesis made the most sense, but it also raised a number of uncomfortable questions, not the least of which was: if there were two independent and different parties involved in the sabotage, why would they both lay off at the same time?

While Javul danced and sang and acted and flew her way through her performances, Dash sat down with Eaden and went through every incident they knew about. They fell into two categories—remote attacks (or at least attacks that *seemed* to be remote) like the one in Rodian space, and attacks that had to have come from inside, like the failure of Javul's harness on Rodia. Dash had hoped that the potentially lethal attacks would fall to one side of the scale or the other, but his hope was in vain.

They loaded the ships to leave Christophsis immediately after the final performance. Dash wanted to take no chances by lingering. Falleen was their next stop, though Dash had tried with every tool at his disposal to get Javul to cancel the performance scheduled to take place in the planetary capital—named, with the characteristic hubris of the species, Falleen Throne.

As Han oversaw the cargo crew's reloading of the *Millennium Falcon*, Dash decided to take one more shot at convincing his boss to cancel this leg of the tour. He headed for Javul's dressing room within the opulent venue's backstage complex. Approaching it, he heard raised voices—Javul's and a man's. He didn't recognize the male voice at first, but didn't think it was a member of the crew. He slowed his pace, made his steps on the crystalline floor slower, softer. Just short of the half-open portal, he stopped.

". . . what you're doing," the male voice said.

"What I do is none of your affair anymore," said Javul, in a tone that said they'd been over this point at least once already.

"I beg to differ. Anything that affects the security and economy of Black Sun is my affair."

Kris. Had to be. Dash fought the urge to barge into the room and send the Vigo packing, but he'd probably just get himself killed. He suspected he'd learn more—and live longer—if he continued to eavesdrop.

"Anything that affects your own economy, you mean. Come on, Hitch. This thing between you and me has never been about Black Sun. It was your own sub rosa dealings you were protecting. The only time you've cared for anything beyond that was when Xizor leaned on you."

"Mm. And he *leaned* on me, as you put it, because of you. He wanted you dead, you know. I only barely talked him out of taking out a contract on you by assuring him I could control you better."

Javul's laugh was a full-throated trill of apparent delight. "You can't control me at all."

"Can't I?" The tone was sly, suggestive. There was a moment of profound silence during which Dash wished he could suddenly be granted X-ray vision. He moved a little closer to the half-open portal, in an agony of suspense.

"I assume," Javul said at last, "that you're talking about your little sneak attacks and sabotage."

"They've had their effect."

"But not the effect you wanted, I'd guess."

"And what effect is that?"

"I'm still alive. That's got to be a huge disappointment."

When Kris spoke again, his voice was subtly changed. Darker somehow, and with an undercurrent of strong emotion. "No, Alai, never that. I would *never* want you dead. As little as you believe it, I still love you. Still have hope of getting you back. Yes, it's slender, but it's hope nonetheless. Yet it's futile if you make yourself the target of forces I can't control."

Dash heard Javul move restively. He crept forward a bit farther and saw her take a seat on the edge of her long, low vanity console. He could just see Kris's right side. The big Mandalorian stood with his back to the door, his right hand clenched into a tight fist. So much for the calm, cool underworld Vigo. This guy obviously had some serious impulse control issues.

"I got a full report on what happened before your performance on Rodia. You were very nearly killed."

"And you're trying to tell me that wasn't your intent?"

Kris took a step toward her, his fist still at his side, but working now, clenching and unclenching like the beat of the Vigo's heart—if he had one. "I told you, Alai. That wasn't *me*. Wasn't *my* work. Wasn't *my* intent. The power outage, yes, that was me. And yes, I meant to frighten you. But what it triggered—and the failure of your anti-grav harness—no, that was *not* supposed to happen. I swear to you by any power you wish to invoke that I was not responsible for that."

"Any power, Hitch? All right. *Your* power. It's the only thing you care about. The only thing you respect."

"Not the only thing. But if that's what it takes, yes, I swear by everything I hold—everything I am and hope to become—that I have done nothing to harm you."

"The failure we experienced coming into Rodia? That wasn't you?"

Kris moved again, another step closer. "What failure?"

Ask him about the hit we took that put us back on Tatooine, Dash thought. *That should be interesting.*

Javul didn't ask. Instead she rose, shook her head, and moved out of Dash's line of sight. "Not important," she said. "What is important is that you understand I'm not coming back. Not to you, and not to your . . . organization."

"If you don't, I can't protect you."

"I don't need your protection. I just need you to butt out."

"Is it that lump of brainless muscle you've hired as your security chief? That Rendar character? Is he why you think you don't need me? Don't want me?"

Javul emitted a huge sigh. "I hate to sound prosaic and trite, but this isn't about you."

"Is it about *him*?"

Yeah, Dash thought, straining to hear. *Is it about me?*

"No, it . . . Fine. If it pleases you to think so, then, yes. It's about Dash. I trust him. I don't trust you. Now I have a tour to rejoin. We need to be on Falleen in six days."

"Alai, *no*." The words were quiet, but delivered with force. "Falleen is the *last* place in the galaxy you need to be."

"Tell that to my underwriters, Hitch. I have commitments to keep. I've had this contract to perform in Falleen Throne for over a year."

"Falleen is dangerous to your health, Alai. You can't go there."

"Are you suggesting that Prince Xizor is lying in wait for me?"

"It wouldn't surprise me, considering what you did to his organization. You crippled his hold on the Corellian Trade Spine."

Dash exhaled slowly. Crippled his hold on the Trade Spine? That had significantly more impact than ratting out a few Vigos. How many layers of half-truths was the real Javul Charn/Alai Jance hiding behind?

"Prince Xizor is on Imperial Center," she said.

"Where he is physically is irrelevant and you know it," Kris replied. "You can't go to Falleen."

"Are you going to stop me?"

There was an undercurrent of nervousness to Javul's voice that Dash found unsettling.

"I'll do whatever it takes to keep you from . . . doing something stupid." Hitch Kris moved again, this time directly toward Javul.

"Don't touch me!" she snarled, and Dash stepped quickly into the chamber.

"Hey, baby, the rest of the crew is waiting on you," he said, then froze in mock surprise at beholding Hitch Kris in gripping Javul's arm. "Problems?"

"Only one, and it was just leaving," said Javul. She pulled away from Kris and moved to pick up her gig bag.

Glowering, the Mandalorian grabbed her again. "You are *not* going to Falleen."

"I am. Now let go of my arm."

"No. You're coming with me. Back to Rodia."

"You got a problem with Basic?" Dash drew his blaster and pointed it at Kris's midsection. "Let her go."

The Vigo spoke to Dash, but kept his gaze on Javul. "If you care at all what happens to her—"

"What—like *you* do? Real convincing way to show your regard, sabotage."

Kris let go of Javul's arm, started to step behind her, then spun back to face Dash, a small blaster suddenly in his hand. Dash, despicable as he found the man, had to admire his moves—Kris's hand had been concealed behind Javul only a split second, yet he'd managed to pull a blaster on Dash during that time. Dash snorted. "What's this—a Mandalorian stand-off?"

Kris shook his head, his gaze flickering to the doorway. "More like a Mandalorian ambush."

Javul's gaze followed, her face paling, panic surging in her eyes. "No, Hitch!"

A frisson of awareness tickled the back of Dash's neck. He knew, without turning, that there was someone standing behind him. He turned his head slightly, staring not back over his shoulder, but beyond Javul's, to the polished surface of a large, ornamental urn. Yep, there they were.

Two huge goons in body armor, framed in the doorway. Though the urn's surface was too warped to make a good mirror, he had no trouble recognizing the species— a Trandoshan and a Shistavanen. Both had blasters, big DL-44s, aimed at his back. An itch sprouted between Dash's shoulder blades and he felt suddenly naked.

"Okay," he said to Kris. "It seems you have the drop on me. So I'm going to ask you—one civilized man to another—to let her go."

Kris smiled. It was a nasty smile. "And I'm going to tell you—one civilized man to another—that I won't. I can't. Now put down your weapon, or—"

"Put down yours, or your bullyboys are cooked meat."

Dash had never expected to be glad to hear that particular voice. He glanced at the urn again. Han Solo stood in the corridor just outside the dressing room, a blaster rifle—a modified DC-15A, capable of punching a hole through both the reptiloid's and the lupinoid's armor— in his hands. Eaden and Mel stood flanking Han, both armed.

Han grinned. "I like to think of this as a Corellian squeeze play. Guns placed slowly and carefully on the floor, gentlebeings. Barrels aimed toward the wall, if you please."

Kris, his big jaw flexing in silent fury, nodded and put his weapon down. His bodyguards followed suit.

"Javul, sweetheart," said Han, "why don't you pick up Kris's blaster and come on out into the hallway."

Glancing from Kris to Dash and back again, Javul disengaged from her ex-beau, picked up his blaster, and moved to Dash, who encircled her with a protective arm and backed them both between Kris's guards and out the door, pausing only to kick the fallen weapons out into the corridor, where Eaden scooped them up.

"Get her to the ship," Han said quietly as they drew level with him. "Kris," he continued in a louder tone, "I want you and your buddies over on the other side of the room, if you don't mind."

Dash kept Javul moving as Han saw Kris and his thugs move to the far side of the dressing room, then punched the door shut.

Han caught up with them as they reached the outer doors and flanked Javul during their swift trip to the venue's landing pad, where the *Millennium Falcon* awaited them. The *Deep Core* had already lifted off.

"Not that I'm objecting—I'm perfectly fine with somebody else saving the day for a change—but to what do we owe the show of force?" Dash asked Han as they hustled Javul up the landing ramp.

"Kind of hard to hide those big, armor-plated thugs he hauls around with him," Han replied. "Plus, Shistavenens and Trandoshans aren't the most fragrant of species at the best of times, and when they're pumped up, anticipating mayhem . . ." Han waved a hand in front of his face. "Wooee! Worse'n a Wookiee on a rainy day. So we knew they were there, and lookin' to be bad. When they slipped inside the stage door all of a sudden, we got suspicious."

"Thanks," Dash said. "Had the situation under control, but—"

"You're joking, right? You barely had your bladder under control. Not that I blame you." Han paused inside the air lock and met Dash's eyes. "Don't mention it." His look turned serious. "Really. Don't. Not to anybody who knows me."

"What? You don't wanna be a hero—the guy who rescued Javul Charn from the big bad Vigo?"

"Nope. Bad for my image." He hit the hatch controls, withdrawing the ramp.

Eaden and Mel had gone to their stations: Javul stood in the main corridor, waiting, her arms crossed over her chest. Her narrowed gaze settled on Han. " 'Sweetheart'?"

"Hey." Han raised his hands in mock surrender. "Just making sure old Hitch didn't get the idea that you've been pining away for him."

She turned her gaze to Dash. " 'Baby'?"

"I was just following your lead. Figured if he thought you were involved with another man he might not be so sure you were . . . uh . . ."

"Pining," Han supplied.

"Look, I don't approve of Kris's methods," Dash admitted, "but I can't argue with his conclusions. You shouldn't go anywhere near Falleen and you know it. If you were smart—" Her eyes narrowed further, and he hastily amended, "—smarter, you'd have Han take a detour and go straight to Bannistar Station."

Han glanced between the two. "Why? Why shouldn't she go to Falleen? Hitch's power center is on Rodia."

Javul sent Dash a questioning look. Should they let Han in on the deeper ramifications of going to Prince Xizor's homeworld?

Dash shrugged. "You know that old saying: What you don't know can't hurt you?"

Han nodded.

"Well, it's total poodoo. What you don't know *can* hurt you, but knowing about it won't hurt you any less. And it's a lot more . . ."

"Complicated," finished Javul.

"Complicated?" echoed Han. "How complicated?"

As they moved toward the cockpit, Javul explained how complicated—sort of.

"I didn't just dump Hitch. I . . . inconvenienced his boss."

Han paled. "His boss . . . Xizor?" He paused at the cockpit hatch to shake his head at Dash. "How did you get us into this sort of banthaflop?"

"Me? I didn't get *us* into anything."

"Well, it's sure not *my* fault."

Han disappeared into the cockpit. Dash considered following him to continue the argument, but decided he'd be better off concentrating on convincing Javul to cancel her performance on Falleen. With that in mind, he turned—only to find that she had disappeared. Cursing under his breath, he went looking for her.

NINETEEN

JAVUL WAS NOT IN ANY OF THE FIRST THREE PLACES Dash looked for her and, by the time he found her staring into space through the portal of the starboard docking ring, he was convinced she was avoiding him.

"You got any more secrets you want to let me in on?"

She didn't even turn her head to look at him. "No."

He paused a beat, then made his way down the short corridor to where she leaned against the air lock's inner hatch. "I'm supposed to take that for an answer?"

"Sorry. It's the only answer I've got at the moment."

"Your boyfriend seems to think you've got a death wish."

She shrugged. "*Ex*-boyfriend. And do you care what he thinks?"

"Why are you hellbent on going to Falleen?"

"I told you. We have a contract. We're legally obligated to go to Falleen."

"Big deal. That's what lawyers are for. I'm sure you've got lawyers."

"I do. But I also have scruples. And—just as important—I have fans. Fans I have no intention of disappointing. Besides, I'm not about to let Hitch Kris or anyone else keep me from doing what I love."

"Uh-huh. Tell me, just what does Hitch think you plan to do once you get there?"

"What?" She turned to look at him.

"When I walked in on your conversation, he was

saying something about what you were doing. Then he strongly hinted that you were about to do something monumentally stupid."

"Yeah. Go to Falleen. He thought it was a direct affront to Prince Xizor. I think it's business. Which the prince understands better than anyone."

"The prince whose dealings in the Corellian Trade Spine you crippled?"

Her gaze flickered to his face. "You heard that, did you?"

"Yeah. And a lot of other stuff I didn't like, but that sort of stood out."

She shrugged again. Abruptly, Dash was angrier than he could remember being in quite a while. He grabbed her by the shoulders and shook her, as much to his astonishment as to hers.

"Javul, stop *lying* to me! You've done nothing but lie to me since the beginning! First it's an overzealous fan, then it's a case of mistaken identity, then it's a jealous boyfriend, then it's an insulted Vigo, then it's a pissed-off Underlord, and now it's a crippled trade run—Prince Xizor's crippled trade run, no less! What's next? Who *else* have you insulted, jilted, or otherwise bollixed up?"

Those eyes. Those pale, luminous eyes were laughing at him again. "You're so cute when you go into a fit of high dudgeon—"

"Don't. Stop trivializing this situation." Dash realized he'd reached his limit with her evasions. He did the only thing he could do, considering that quitting was out of the question. He kissed her.

She did not fight him off or scratch his eyes out or slap him silly. She kissed him back. Not passionately, but deeply. When he raised his head at last, she was watching him, but no longer laughing.

"Poor Dash," she said, her voice soft and annoyingly sweet. "Have I bollixed you up?"

"No, but you're pissing me off. What did Kris mean about you crippling Xizor's operation?"

She lowered her lashes, and he could see the thoughts organizing themselves behind the screen. "Is kissing how you express anger?" she asked. "Wow. I'd hate to find out what happens to women you really like."

He glared at her. "Answer the question. What did you do to Xizor that makes your appearance in Falleen Throne tantamount to the acting-out of a death wish?"

"I turned over a very important cargo. I got several lieutenants and a couple of Vigos in the Corellian Spine captured and imprisoned. And I turned over as much information as I had to the Imperials—which was significant. It included the names of ships and captains, timetables, potential cargoes, methods of operation . . . and Black Sun recognition codes. I told the Imperials how they could recognize a Black Sun operation and how they could interfere with it."

Dash let go of her and sagged against the bulkhead. "So . . . Xizor not only had to replace his people . . ."

"He had to redesign his entire operation along the Spine and come up with a new code cipher."

"Whoa." It was all he could think of to say.

Javul looked at him wryly. "What—you gonna kiss me again?"

"I may worship at your feet. I'd give my weight in glitterstim to have caused Xizor that much trouble."

She nodded slowly, her eyes on his face. "That's right. You need some payback, too, don't you?"

"I need . . ." He trailed off. What did he need? Justice? Redress? What he really needed was his family back. That wasn't going to happen. The only slender thread of hope he'd ever had was that they hadn't found Stanton's body in the wreckage of the *Doriella's Mystress*. Which probably meant nothing except that he hadn't yet squeezed the last bit of childish naïveté out of his soul.

"I don't need anything from Xizor. As Eaden pointed out to me, the universe hasn't exactly been kind to him, either."

"The universe didn't kill your brother and ruin your family, Dash. A being did. A Falleen. Xizor."

"Uh-huh. A being who has every reason to want you and me both permanently out of his way. A being whose people are experts at the kind of sabotage that brought down *Doriella's Mystress* and crippled *Nova's Heart*."

"Are you afraid of him?"

He knew she wasn't appealing to his male vanity. She was asking the question in all honesty. "I'd be a fool not to be. He's a very powerful being. Even Vader thinks twice before crossing him, I've heard."

She smiled crookedly. "Ah, there's a *but* at the end of that sentence."

Dash sighed. "Okay. *But,* if I had an opportunity to pay him back for the grief he's caused my family, I suppose I'd do it. Is that what you're offering me?"

She shook her head. "I've no intention of tweaking Xizor while we're on Falleen, if that's what you're asking."

"*While* we're on Falleen. What are you *not* telling me?"

"Nothing that's going to make a bit of difference to you in the long run."

He looked down at the floor. *Where's your sense of self-preservation, Rendar? You should cut your losses and run like space slugs were nipping at your tail.*

Too late for that, he reckoned. For better or for worse, they were on their way to Falleen.

Funny, he thought, *how when people use that phrase, it nearly always turns out to be for worse . . .*

Dash could have predicted just about anything to happen, except what did, which was—

Nothing.

Hitch Kris did not pursue them. Xizor was not lying in wait at the spaceport when they hit the permacrete. They unloaded the ships onto huge cargo transports and followed them to the venue where the road crew set up. There was no sabotage, no Black Sun minions, no Mandalorian goons. It was enough to set Dash's teeth on edge. He found himself almost wanting Xizor to do something.

The equipment was thoroughly checked under Dash's careful oversight as it left the ship. There had been some very minor damage to the contents of the big cylindrical crate that had almost erased him from the space–time continuum, and a backup bit of set framework had to be subbed in from *Deep Core*'s load. Dash checked that over, too. The *Falcon* was buttoned up tight as a snarebox and put under the watchful care of Oto and two R2 units that Javul purchased from a small-time dealer she'd picked at random.

The first performance went so smoothly it was kind of scary, and if Xizor had snuck home from Imperial Center to catch the show, there was no sign of him—unless he was one of the thousands of anonymous Falleen fans sitting raptly in the audience, changing color with every bit of pathos or comedy.

That was something Dash had never seen before—the collective manipulation of an entire auditorium filled with Falleen. The flow of emotions—manifested in the Falleen as effusions of pheromones and changes in skin color—seemed to wash across the audience in waves, eddying, feeding on itself, and washing back again. Dash watched them the way he recalled watching tide pools at Gold Beach on Corellia: gray-green to aqua to sun-washed golds and sunset reds. It was mesmerizing.

He stood backstage and watched the audience watching

the holostar as she glittered and gleamed—now life-sized, now many times larger than life; first mortal, then a sprite, then a goddess. He wondered what it would be like to be a non-Falleen caught up in that heady stew of pheromones. Judging from the facial expressions of the handful of humans he could see when the lights changed, it was a lot like getting swacked on spiced ale with an eyeblaster chaser.

The show ended, to thunderous applause. Javul did two encores. The crowds departed while Dash kept their darling safely locked away in her dressing room, under guard. They retired to the *Millennium Falcon* after that, where they were greeted with news from Tatooine. Captain Marrak advised them that *Nova's Heart* was nearing the end of her forced sabbatical. He expected to lift off in the next several days and hopefully would reconnoiter with them two stops down the line at Bacrana.

Dash breathed no easier. They had two more performances on Falleen before they lifted for a single concert at Bannistar Station. That was good. It meant a fast turnaround.

Dash prayed that they'd actually make it to Bannistar and decided that if Falleen was not destined to be their graveyard, he would hit the first cantina on Bannistar Station and get royally drunk.

For now, he watched everything and everyone until his head hurt.

By the end of the third performance, however, with no problems that he could see, Dash was finally feeling almost easy. Until the thought came to him, unbidden, that the best way to get rid of a pesky presence like Javul Charn would be to arrange for her ship to quietly explode after leaving Falleen space. Whoever was after her had already shown himself prepared to send attack ships out to back up any onboard sabotage.

"Tonight," he told Oto and Leebo on the last night of the Falleen engagement, "we're going to crawl over every centimeter of that ship and every circuit in her system to make sure no one's planted anything nasty in our absence. Agreed?"

"As you wish," said Oto.

Leebo feigned boredom of his chats with Han Solo's vessel. "She's a vain little thing, you know. Thinks she's the galaxy's gift to the Maw cluster. Solo's filled her CPU with complete codswallop."

"Cods-what?" said Dash.

Leebo's optics blinked. "Huh. Funny. I don't have a definition for that in my data bank. It's just sort of there without explanation. Something Kood Gareeda popped in. I think it means she's full of poodoo."

"What a surprise."

Two hours after midnight, local time, *Deep Core* lifted off. The *Millennium Falcon* lingered while Dash, Eaden, Han, and Leebo split up and spread out to secure the ship. Han and Leebo went over the ship's vital systems, while Dash and Eaden worked with Mel, Nik, and Oto on the cargo bays.

Dash had finished with the last of Han's secret compartments and was pulling the floor grating in the main corridor back into place when he caught movement out of the corner of his eye. Someone had just flitted across the corridor near the crew's quarters.

He rose and followed.

He reached the short corridor that led to the docking ring air lock just in time to see the inner hatch slide shut and the usage indicator for the external doors come on. Someone was leaving the ship!

Dash moved swiftly down through the access corridor to the inner hatch, opened it, and slipped through into the unpressurized air lock. Peering from the outer hatch, he saw her: Javul. At least he thought it was Javul. She was wearing a long black wig and was dressed in a flowing golden robe that billowed around her legs, seeming to shed stardust as she moved.

Cursing, Dash opened a comlink to Eaden. "Javul's run off again. You and Han get ready to cast off. I'm going after her."

He barely heard Eaden's quiet acknowledgment. He was already in motion, following the golden figure along the catwalk that led from Bay 6, then down the long, multilevel terminal to the spaceport's main concourse.

Javul was in a hurry. She fled down the corridor to a turbolift at the confluence of their docking terminal and the main concourse. Dash paused long enough to watch the lift display her descent—twenty-two levels to street level.

Dash followed, choosing a lift on the opposite side of the terminal's broad corridor. He stepped out in the lee of a huge supporting pillar and peeked around it into the concourse. This early in the morning, it was hardly a hub of activity, though there were a few sentients about. Most of the traffic in the cavernous, state-of-the-art building at this hour was made up of maintenance and cargo droids. Dash ignored them all, keeping his eyes trained on the fleeting figure making her way toward the front of the building.

She glanced around as if suspecting she might be followed, then exited to the street. Dash hung back until she was through the doors, fearing she might see his reflection in the transparisteel windows. The doors opened onto a broad avenue that looked as if it were made of gleaming black rock. Javul did not hail a taxi. Instead she darted across the avenue and into a plaza surrounded by softly lit buildings and bordered by well-manicured shrubs and trees.

Dash waited a beat, then hurried after her. She ducked into the shadows of the nearest building, moving from one pool of soft light to another as she navigated the façade. Dash strove to stay a constant distance behind her and was taken aback when, suddenly, the golden billow of fabric entered a shadow between two buildings and stopped.

He had taken four or five long steps before he realized this and pulled up short, his heart hammering in his chest, his eyes on the golden robe. Five seconds passed without movement. Puzzled, he crept forward, keeping to the shadows cast by the ornate shrubs in a planter to his left. The patch of gold still did not move. In fact, it was *too* still.

He emerged from the shadows and slipped up behind the figure, putting out his hand. It met empty fabric. The robe was hanging on the branch of a tall conifer that marked the boundary between two buildings. Even as he clutched at it, it dropped from the tree branch to the glittering permacrete beneath his feet.

He swept the robe up and glanced feverishly around. Where had she gone?

Deep breath, Rendar. Focus.

The plaza was empty. She might be hiding behind one of the cut stone planters, but he doubted it. She wouldn't have used the robe to buy time for hiding. She was clearly headed somewhere with intent. He moved forward again, along the front of the building to his right. The elaborately carved heads of fantastic animals jutted at intervals from the wall, each with a lamp in its maw. The light was dim but warm—golden. Between the animals were strange symbols and occasionally a niche that housed a figurine . . . or rather, an icon.

It was a Wayfarer's Temple complex, he realized. A series of shrines and chapels from a variety of worlds and religious and philosophical traditions set up so that travelers of a meditative or pious bent could offer devotions at the shrine of their choice. Why had Javul come here? They'd never discussed religious beliefs, so he had no idea if she might have gone to a particular shrine. He wasn't even entirely sure what planet she called home, so if she worshiped planetary deities, he was out of luck.

He reached the door of the building. It was made of wood and heavily carved. Though it was closed, light peeped from beneath it. Dash turned the quaint door handle and leaned against the door. It glided open on well-lubed hinges—no squeaks to upset the meditations of the faithful. The place was empty, but a huge piece of statuary dominated the front of the long room. Dash blinked. The deity—if that's what the hideous thing was—looked like what might happen if you took Eaden Vrill, enlarged him, and gave him a beard of prehensile tresses in addition to the ones on his head.

Dash looked away from the figure and listened. The room was silent. He withdrew and moved on, past one of the austere shrines devoted to The Silent—an enigmatic order that operated under a perpetual vow of silence and somehow radiated meditative waves of healing as well. She could only have entered there if she'd taken vows of silence. He didn't bother to peek inside the shuttered entrance. His imagination balked at the thought of Javul Charn taking a vow of silence.

Three empty sanctuaries later, he reached the rear of the plaza and turned left to move along the row of chapels there. The first one to his right was a study in simplicity and clean lines. Not austere, but balanced, with curvilinear ornamentation. It was small, too, almost lost amid the larger, more opulent shrines. The scent of incense wafted from it. It struck Dash's senses like an all-encompassing memory: wood fires, rainy nights, spices, the warmth of a sun, the comfort of a soft word, sleep, waking in the arms of . . .

He shook himself and moved to the door of the little chapel. The entry was covered only by strands of silver beads that seemed to glow softly in the light from the plaza and from within the chapel. At the far end of the dimly lit room was a simple dais above which a holographic representation of the galaxy turned slowly. Behind and above that on the rear wall was a large oval that seemed to mirror the shape of the galaxy. It contained a geometric pattern of black and white.

Dash recognized the symbol. It was the sigil of the Equilibrates—believers in Cosmic Balance, a religion-*cum*-philosophy whose main tenet was that for every action in one place an equal and opposite reaction occurred somewhere else. So one person's fortune was another's misfortune and vice versa.

Somehow he had trouble imagining Javul Charn as a devotee. By that theology, what must her massive success have done to some poor shmuck half a galaxy away? He knew Javul well enough by now to suspect that question would nag at her. But maybe the universe was kinder than that; maybe it parceled the bad luck out among millions in some sort of intergalactic insurance policy.

Peering through the silvery rain of beads, Dash could see that the chapel was occupied. Someone dressed entirely in black knelt at the dais. Dash hesitated. He couldn't tell if that was Javul. She'd been wearing black boots beneath the golden robe, he'd noticed, but other than that he had no clue about her current mode of dress. He started to enter the chapel and stopped as a second figure appeared from the shadows just to the left of the dais.

This person was dressed from head to toe in a hooded robe that seemed to soak up any light that touched it. An Equilibrate monk or priest, Dash guessed. It moved to stand before the kneeling devotee and bent its head toward her, murmuring something Dash couldn't make out. Nor could he hear the answer given by the kneeling figure, but the voice was female.

He pushed through the silver strands and slid into the shadows of a pillar inside the doorway just as the penitent figure rose, revealing a cascade of gleaming black hair and a very female form.

Dash swallowed. Javul.

And who else?

"What do you seek, my daughter?" The voice was androgynous—rich, deep, and somehow reminiscent of the incense that continued to eddy in the semi-darkness of the chapel.

"I seek the balance," Javul answered. "The balance of heart and body. The balance of core and flesh. The balance of line and curve. I seek the passage of the night on its way to dawn."

"This is a hidden way, revealed to few." The priest—if that's what this was—made a gesture with both hands. They were gray-green, long-fingered, elegant.

Dash's heart stuttered. A Falleen. He drew his blaster.

Javul faced the taller figure and made some gesture in return that Dash couldn't see. The Falleen bowed its head, then reached into the folds of its robe.

Heart thudding, Dash trained his weapon on the Falleen priest, his finger on the trigger—

The elegant hand came free of the robe.

There was no weapon in it. Only something small enough to fit in the palm—a data wafer, maybe.

Dash sagged with relief against the pillar. He couldn't see what happened to the small object, but he suspected the Falleen had passed it to Javul.

The Falleen raised its head and hesitated before it lifted a hand and pressed its thumb to Javul's forehead. "I pray you have left nothing behind," the priest said, then turned, retreating to the shadows once more.

Dash was so intent on watching the Falleen that he

didn't realize Javul had moved until she was halfway up the aisle. He pulled farther back behind his shielding pillar.

She swept past the pillar, but stopped just inside the cascade of silver beads. "You gonna walk me back to the ship or what?" She didn't even turn her head. She just glanced in his direction, then stepped out into the half-light of the plaza.

He slipped out after her, caught up with her in three strides, and tossed the golden robe over her shoulder.

"Thanks." She slipped the robe on and strode out into the plaza.

He bit his tongue. There were too many things he wanted to say. To ask. But he knew if he opened his mouth right now, nothing coherent would come out—and it would come out in anger. He was furious with her. Terrified for her. And curious beyond his ability to express it.

They walked in silence back down the length of the plaza. As they crossed the avenue to the spaceport terminal, Javul said, "Are you going to ask?"

He found words. "Hitch is right about you. You do have a death wish."

"No. I don't. Trust me." She stopped to face him. "That was my priest."

Dash blinked in surprise. "You're an Equilibrate?"

"I believe in Cosmic Balance, yes."

"Huh," Dash said, and shook his head. "I never would've thought it."

"Why not?"

"Your success. I mean, you gotta figure that with all you have, there are a whole lot of have-nots out there that you're responsible for, right?"

"I'm not responsible for them, Dash, any more than you're responsible for . . . ugly men."

"What?" He glanced sideways at her, saw the curl of her mouth. "Was that a compliment?"

"Yes, it was."

He let himself be flattered for a second or two, then said, "Don't try to distract me, Javul. Why did you go there? We were getting ready to dust this dirtball. Your life is very likely in serious danger here and you know it. What kind of vacuum-brained stunt was that to pull?"

"I needed some balance, Dash. Is that so hard to understand? I needed . . . guidance. A benediction. A path."

"And is that what the priest gave you on that data wafer?"

"I lost my copy of the *Fulcrum*. The priest had one for me."

The *Fulcrum* was the holy text of the Cosmic Balance. A perfectly reasonable, smooth answer—and yet . . .

Something was still off center.

They crossed the concourse and entered the lift that would speed them to Level 22 of the huge terminal.

Dash counted to ten, then asked, "What's really on the wafer, Javul?"

She had no chance to answer. The lift doors slid open. Outside, in the corridor leading to the *Millennium Falcon*'s berth, was a tall Anomid dressed in some sort of formfitting metalloid body armor. The lower half of his face was concealed by the typical vocalizer mask his species—which had no vocal cords—wore to enable communication with other species. But it was what he carried in one six-fingered hand that caught Dash's immediate attention: a Kerestian darkstick—its long, sharp-tipped blade curved like the talon of some mythical beast. Nor was that the end of his weaponry. A repulsor razor-thrower and a Wookiee ryyk blade dangled from his belt, and a force pike and a Morgukai cortosis staff were crossed on his back, their handgrips extending up behind his head.

Dash took in all this in a heartbeat, which was all the time he had to shove Javul back into the lift and yell,

"Emergency close!" as he dived in behind her. As the door slid shut, he saw the glint in the Anomid's orange eyes, saw the arc of the Kerestian weapon as the assassin whipped it toward them, heard it strike the door.

The tip punched through the five-centimeter-thick durasteel as if it were paper, driving a good part of its length into the lift, level with Dash's eyes.

TWENTY

"Level One!"

The lift plunged, severing the darkstick's thick hilt. The blade dropped to the floor at Dash's feet, reddish, viscous liquid oozing from the tip.

"Wh-who was that?" Javul was huddled in a corner of the lift.

Dash reached down to haul her to her feet, avoiding the dripping tip of the darkstick. "I have no idea. I thought maybe you did."

"Me? How would I know?" She was terrified—finally, when it might be too late. Her breath was coming in sharp gasps, and all the blood had leached from her face. She was shaking.

Dash pulled her to his side, trying to think fast and well. If they went all the way to the first floor, made their way toward the *Falcon*'s berth, chose a way up at random . . .

He pulled out his comlink and hailed Eaden.

"Eaden?"

"Do you have Javul?"

"Yeah, but something almost got *us* just now. We're in a turbolift heading down to Level One. There's an assassin after us, Ead. An Anomid. Armed to the teeth—if Anomids even have teeth. We're in trouble here. We need backup. We'll get to Level One before he does, but—"

Han's voice broke in. "No, not Level One. Go all the way down to the sublevel and head this way. Don't come up to the docking level, 'cause for sure that's where he'll be, right? We'll have to find this guy and take him out."

"Right. Yeah. Sublevel." He punched the lift button. Made sense. They'd have to get to the *Falcon*'s docking bay eventually, so the assassin need do no more than go wait there for them, unless . . . "Han, listen—are there any empty docking bays below or above you?"

"What? Uh, yeah. There's an empty bay about three levels down. A Bothan freighter just pulled out."

"What's that—Level Nineteen?" Without waiting for an answer, he continued, "Take the *Falcon* down there and soft-dock. Send someone out to cover us. We'll be coming in hot."

"That's highly irregular, you know. You're gonna get me in deep banthaflop with the port authority."

"*Han—*"

"Kidding! I'm on it."

At the sublevel landing, Dash held the lift door, then turned to Javul. "You have a weapon on you?"

"Yes."

Probably some feckless little hold-out blaster. "Get it out."

He was boggled when she reached beneath her robe and drew a BlasTech Deathhammer 17 from her sash. "Where did you get that?"

"Mel got it for me, if it matters."

He drew his own primary weapon—a much smaller BlasTech DL-22—which seemed suddenly inadequate. *Helluva time for blaster envy,* he thought. Aloud, he said, "We're going to switch lifts, just in case. All right? Here we go. Ready?"

She nodded.

Dash keyed the door open, and they slipped out into the half-light of the empty corridor. Well, almost empty— a small maintenance droid polished the floor in front of one of the other turbolift cars.

Windfall.

Dash picked up the small droid, shoved it into the nearest turbolift, and punched Level 22. Then he hustled Javul into a car across the corridor and keyed it to go to Level 19.

He stared at the ceiling of the lift, taking a series of deep, lung-filling breaths. Beside him, Javul also seemed to be gathering herself.

"As soon as that droid comes out of the lift up there—" Dash started to say.

"Yeah, I know."

The door of the lift slid open and the two bolted out into the corridor, their boots making the durasteel flooring ring with each step. Bay 6 was third on the right-hand side of the terminal—a distance of over one hundred meters. Dash had to believe they could cover that before their Anomid friend realized he'd been deked. It would take only a glance at the lift control panels for him to see that a second lift had gone up to Level 19.

They pelted down the terminal as if a pack of rabid boarwolves were after them. Dash suspected that the Anomid assassin was much, much deadlier. As they approached Bay 4, Dash saw Eaden and Han step out into the corridor from Bay 6 about fifty meters ahead of them. The two took up flanking positions on each side of the corridor and began moving toward the head of the terminal.

Mel appeared in the lee of the docking port, a blaster rifle in his hands. Dash knew an instant of cold panic at the thought that Yanus Melikan might be their saboteur— might be working *with* whoever it was that was no doubt pursuing them. But Mel simply took up a defensive position in the alcove, his rifle ready.

Han was waving his arm, gesturing for them to hurry. His gaze was focused on the turbolifts now many meters behind. Then suddenly he was running toward them, his blaster raised, eyes focused on something—or some*one*—behind them.

Dash felt a riptide of cold, nasty adrenaline wash down his back.

"Fire!" Han yelled. He dropped to one knee and loosed a barrage of blaster bolts past the fleeing couple.

On the opposite side of the corridor, Eaden followed suit.

Dash heard the bolts sizzle past his ears, and could whiff the sharp scent of oxygen atoms being torn apart into reactive ozone. Out of the corner of his eye he saw Javul glance back over her shoulder. She immediately began to struggle out of her billowing robe. *What was she doing?* He reached over and tried to pull the robe from her hands, but she resisted.

"Just run!" she urged.

He felt rather than saw something whiz between them—something flat, about the size of his head. Only when it flipped over in the air several meters in front of them and began a return trip did he realize that it was the throwing razor he'd last seen on the assassin's belt. The weapon—which he'd thought only Rodian bounty hunters used—had a jagged triangular blade and a homing beacon that gave it a decidedly nasty boomerang effect. It could get you coming or going . . . or both.

Dash put on the brakes, skidding on the durasteel surface beneath his boots. He raised his blaster, fired at the razor . . . and missed. The thing was flying toward him, aimed right at his chest. He flung himself to one side, knowing he was too late. Javul shrieked and a ripple of gold passed before Dash's face. He felt a solid weight connect with his rib cage. He hit the floor, momentarily winded.

He regained his feet to see the gold robe Javul had been

wearing seemingly flee back down the corridor toward the lifts under its own power. As he watched, Javul—running backward—fired her blaster at it. Tangled in the flow of fabric, the razor flipped several times, then hit the deck with a clatter and lay still. Javul turned and bolted toward Bay 6, now only meters away.

A hand gripped Dash's shoulder. "Run or shoot, take your pick." As if to illustrate, Han raised his heavy blaster and fired a series of shots down the corridor.

Dash looked up, seeking his target. The assassin had just left the shelter of the Bay 2 docking port and was making his way toward them along the wall. One hand was extended in front of him, palm out. The other was reaching for another of the weapons on his belt. Neither the particle beam from Han's blaster nor the energy bolts from Eaden's seemed to have much effect on the Anomid, save to slow him down. As Dash watched, he saw another energy bolt, fired by either Eaden or Mel, hit an invisible *something* a few centimeters in front of the Anomid's outstretched palm.

"Personal shield!" shouted Dash over the sound of blaster volleys.

"No, really?" Han glanced over at Eaden. "Gimme more cover."

The Nautolan nodded.

"What're you going to do?" Dash asked as Eaden increased the frequency of his shots.

Han grinned. "Watch and learn . . . but cover me while you're doing it."

Dash obliged, fanning his shots as Han dropped to his belly, aiming his blaster along the floor. He could see that the Anomid had a new weapon mounted on the back of his right hand. A flex-tube ran from it down his index finger. It was a dart spitter.

Han fired.

The beam skirted the lower range of the palm shield,

connected with the assassin's left shin guard just above the ankle, and punched his leg out from under him. He hit the floor—yet even as he did, he was pointing his right finger at them and unleashing a barrage of death.

Dash became one with the deck, willing himself to be flat enough to avoid the darts. When they stopped coming, he hauled Han to his feet and ran. Eaden was already in motion, scuttling sideways down the corridor. And now Mel and Javul—who'd reached the relative safety of the docking port—laid down a barrage of fire that might have an effect.

As Dash rounded the corner into the docking ring, he glanced back up the terminal at the fallen Anomid. He'd been hit several more times, and the armor along his back was smoking in places. Blood the color of sunset's last gasp oozed from the shin guard Han's careful shot had pierced.

The momentary sense of victory and safety Dash felt was crushed by his last sight of the assassin. He'd raised his pale lavender head from the floor and, just for a second, Dash felt the venom of his gaze. The message conveyed was clear:

This is not over.

TWENTY-ONE

DASH HAD NOT QUITE GOTTEN HIS OWN INNER TURMOIL put to rest before he became aware that his perpetually calm and rational associate was extremely agitated. Maybe it was the quivering of his tresses or the rapid blinking of the nictitating membrane over his dark eyes. Whatever it was, it set off Dash's alarms. When they were safely in hyperspace and all had collapsed in the passenger lounge to debrief, he watched his partner with care.

Han had left Leebo in the cockpit to keep an eye on the autopilot and had come back to join the others. On Mel's orders, Nik had gone up to the cockpit as well, with a vague suggestion that he "learn piloting."

Han opened their consultations with a reasonable question: "What the hell was *that* all about?"

When nobody answered, he turned to Dash. "Come on, Dash. Did you have any idea something like this was gonna happen? I mean, how badly does this Hitch guy want her dead?" He jerked a thumb at Javul.

"I don't know," Dash said. "After I'd met him, I didn't think Hitch wanted her dead at all. This was . . . a big surprise."

"You got that right," said Han. "I mean, Anomids have a pretty pacifistic culture. I don't think I've ever even heard of an Anomid assassin or mercenary. Maybe he's some sort of bounty hunter." He slanted a glance at Javul. "You been out breaking the law while you've been breaking hearts?"

"I'm not a criminal," she replied. "As far I know, there's no bounty on my head. As far as I know," she repeated, and turned an appealing gaze to Dash.

How much of that was true and how much a lie? She'd been telling half-truths since he'd met her. On the other hand, what could be worse than disrupting a Black Sun trade corridor?

He shrugged. "Y'got me. I don't know who or what—"

"Edge." The single word came from Eaden Vrill, who stood with his back to one corner of the cramped compartment.

"Beg pardon?" said Spike, who had taken possession of Javul's hand when she'd first sat down and hadn't let go of it.

Several of Eaden's tresses did an enigmatic little dance. "The assassin is called Edge. He has a preference for bladed weaponry and likes to wound his targets, then move in and finish them at close quarters. He . . . also likes to take trophies."

"And you know this how?" asked Dash.

"I have met Edge before. He . . . he assassinated the head of my order."

Suddenly all eyes were on the Nautolan, a situation that he obviously found disturbing.

"Your teräs käsi order?" asked Dash.

Eaden nodded. "I am . . . was . . . a member of a religious order called Säläi Käsi: Hidden Hand. All were at least minimally Force-sensitive. Some time ago—when the Empire implemented Order 66, wiping out the Jedi—the Hidden Hand was targeted as well because of our potential to wield the Force. They systematically hunted us down and exterminated us, one by one, until only three initiates and our master, Neaed Fisto, remained."

"Fisto?" repeated Dash. "Any relation to *General* Fisto?"

Kit Fisto, Jedi Master, was famous (or infamous,

depending on your point of view) for his marshaling of Republic forces during the Clone Wars. He'd later served on the Jedi Council until its destruction by the Emperor. Who knew he'd had relatives back on the Nautolan homeworld?

Eaden nodded. "A brother of his mother. An uncle, I believe you would say. The Force was, perhaps, as strong in my master as it was in Kit Fisto. Neaed was an impressive being and so much a mentor to my family that my mother chose to name me after him."

Nautolans weren't known for seeking the limelight, Dash knew; in fact, they were, as a culture, so self-conscious that honoring a newborn by directly naming it after a famous or heroic character was considered gauche. The closest they would come was to make an anagram of the famous name, and even that was skirting the boundaries of propriety.

"This Edge character murdered him?" Han asked, dropping onto a small container that had been repurposed as a stool.

"Yes. I was present in the clan house of our order when Edge came for my master. Neaed Fisto sacrificed himself that I and the other initiates might escape."

Dash could only guess at the depth of feeling behind the simple words. Eaden was unmatched in the art of hiding his emotions when he wanted to.

"But if this guy was trying to wipe out your whole order," said Han, "then wasn't he after you, too? I mean, who was he trying to kill just now—you or Javul?"

Eaden's tresses swayed this way and that. "Until today, I believe Edge thought me to be dead. After Neaed was killed, the three surviving members of the order—myself, my sister Eawen, and my cousin Nautif—determined that we must disappear. So we scattered and took up separate lives. We wait for an opportunity to rebuild the order and to aid, if possible, in the overthrow of the Empire."

Han snorted. "Oh, great. That's what I get for renting out my ship—not one, but *two* people with a price on their heads." He turned on Dash. "This is why I try to stay away from you, Rendar. You're always getting yourself into seven different kinds of trouble. Your girlfriend has a crazy ex-boyfriend and your partner's got an Empire target on his back. There something you want to tell me about that droid I've got piloting the *Falcon*? What's he done that I should know about? He booby-trapped? Rigged to explode?"

"Worse. His jokes are all duds," Dash said. "Javul, look, I'd swear Hitch Kris was sincerely trying to keep you alive. Am I wrong?"

"No, you're right about Hitch. I don't think he'd do this."

"What about Xizor?"

"If I had to choose between the two," said Javul slowly, "I'd say Xizor was a much more likely prospect."

Dash looked up at Eaden, who stood statue-still against the bulkhead. He couldn't even imagine how the Nautolan must have felt to have such a specter from his past rise up out of the ether. "Wait a minute. You said your order was targeted at the same time Palpatine implemented the order to wipe out the Jedi—are you telling me this assassin works for the *Empire*?"

"I don't know who he works for now, but I am certain he was an Imperial hireling then."

"Okay," said Han, rising from his makeshift stool, "that tears it. I'm dropping you all off at Bannistar Station and going back to Tatooine."

Javul speared him with her electric gaze. "I'll double your fee if you take us to Bacrana. We'll meet the *Nova's Heart* there and you can leave."

Han put both fists on the table and glared down into Javul's lovely face. "Bacrana? I don't think so, sweetheart. I'm due to rendezvous with Chewie in a Tatooine week. Bacrana is no longer in my flight plan."

"We have to leave Bannistar on time, Han," said Javul. "We *have* to. If you leave us in the lurch there, our chances of finding passage to Bacrana aren't good and you know it." There was tension in every line of her face.

"Because of your contracts?"

She nodded.

"Which are more important than your lives?"

She said nothing.

"What's this *really* about, Javul?"

When she didn't answer, Dash glanced at Mel, who'd been silent as a rock throughout. His face, too, was tense, watchful.

Spike was glowering. "What—a bunch of outraged investors, stockholders, and advertising agencies isn't enough for you?"

"Maybe." *And maybe not.*

"We have to keep to our schedule," Mel said quietly.

"Sorry. That's not my problem," Han said, and left the room.

Dash went after him. He caught up with him in the starboard passageway amidships.

"Don't abandon Javul on Bannistar, Han. Look, *I'll* pilot the *Falcon* to Bacrana and you can just sit tight on the station and take a little R and R."

"*You* pilot the *Falcon*? Gimme a break. You're a good pilot, Dash, but you're not me."

"If anything happens to her, you can trust Javul to pay for it. In fact, if anything happens to her, you can have *Outrider*."

Han had been trying to move around Dash, who had been blocking his attempts. Now he stopped moving and stared at the other man, openmouthed. "You are seriously deranged. I feel sorry for you, Dash, I really do. Letting a woman get under your skin like that. I'll tell you one thing—that's *never* gonna happen to me."

"No, I'm sure it won't. You're too hardheaded. But you're wrong about me. I haven't let her get under my skin. I just want her to keep hers. And right now the best way to do that is to get her back with her tour."

"Liar. I've been paying attention. I figured part of the reason she hired me was so she could get *away* from her tour. Didn't you say there might be a mole in her entourage? You want to get back with her tour like a rancor wants to be vegetarian. No, Dash. You think you can save her, but you can't. Trust me on this one." Han put a hand on Dash's shoulder. "I'm warning you, buddy. You're in this over your head. Whatever she's into, it's dangerous, and bigger than we can grasp, I promise you. You should get out—and, as a matter of fact, so should we all."

Han continued on to the cockpit, leaving Dash to marshal his chaotic thoughts before he returned to the passenger lounge. Eaden was on his way out. The Nautolan stopped him.

"Do not think you have left Edge behind. If he lives, he will not give up. He will know her itinerary. You will most certainly meet him again on Bannistar Station."

Dash held the enigmatic maroon gaze for several breaths before he finally looked away. "I'll bear that in mind," he mumbled and reentered the lounge.

Only Javul was there, still sitting at the table where he'd left her.

"Eaden said—" he began.

"I heard."

He sat down opposite her at the little table and took her hands in his. "Javul, I'm gonna make you an offer I hope you won't refuse. Quit whatever it is you're doing.

Change your name again. Come with me. We'll take *Outrider* and go where even Edge won't be able to find you."

Javul gave him the saddest smile he thought he'd ever seen and shook her head. "You have no idea how tempting that is, Dash—but I can't."

He looked down at their clasped hands, took a deep breath, and let it out. "You picked up something in that shrine and I suspect that it's got something to do with why you're being followed and harassed and sabotaged and targeted for murder. You've gone into business for yourself, haven't you? That's why Black Sun is after you, isn't it?"

"You . . . could say that."

Wrong. That answer was too cautious. He'd shot wide of the truth again. He knew it as surely as he knew that Edge was going to catch up with them eventually. He raised his eyes to hers again, capturing her gaze. "Edge was an Imperial assassin when he killed Eaden's mentor. He still is an Imperial assassin, isn't he?"

She didn't answer, and he could see the thoughts turning in her head as she weighed them.

"Come on, Javul. The whole truth this time. If I'm going to help you—protect you—I need to know what I'm up against. *Really.* Otherwise, I'm too likely to make the wrong assumptions, suspect the wrong people, and be looking the wrong way the next time we get blindsided by one of your fanboys."

"Tell him."

Dash jumped and spun, reaching for his blaster.

Yanus Melikan stood in the compartment doorway, arms crossed over his chest, his pale gaze on Javul.

"Are you sure?" she asked.

"No. Not at all. In fact, I think it's a huge risk. But Dash has a point. As long as he's here, he can't protect you if he doesn't know what to protect you from."

Dash felt a nervous itch between his shoulder blades.

"Tell you what, Mel—why don't you have a seat?" He pointed at the seat next to Javul.

Mel smiled crookedly. "You mean where you can see me?" He crossed to the table and sat down, giving Javul a wry look.

She squared her shoulders and met Dash's eyes. "Okay, Dash—here it is. The unvarnished truth. I'm not in business for myself and I'm not moving illicit goods under the cover of my tours. I'm moving something a good deal more important than that. I . . . *we* . . ."—she nodded at Mel—"are moving cargo and information critical to the success of the Rebel Alliance."

Dash felt as if he'd just been shoved out an air lock. "And Hitch Kris . . ."

"My relationship with Hitch—and the career he jump-started—was a cover for our activities. It gave us a certain level of protection and the means of moving information—and resources—with impunity. It also gave us an immense information network—an eye on developments within Black Sun and the Empire. There are Rebellion operatives and informants on every world, and my tours give us access to them."

A few more pieces fell into place in Dash's head. "Your little 'excursions'?"

Javul nodded. "When Hitch was using my entourage for smuggling his own goods and operatives, he put our whole network in danger. As soon as I realized it, I had no choice but to part company with him."

"He almost found us out," said Mel quietly. "And I think he suspects what Javul is really engaged in and is at a loss to know what to do about it. Black Sun has an uneasy relationship with the Empire."

Dash nodded. "Okay . . . so his little sabotage efforts were aimed at getting you to stop?"

"At first, I think they were just aimed at getting me to come back under his influence," Javul said. "But when he came backstage on Christophsis . . . I'm pretty sure he'd figured out that I wasn't just being stubborn. And he realized someone else was in the game."

"Someone who wants your show permanently shut down."

She nodded.

"The Emperor."

"Possibly. Or possibly someone else who suspects what we're doing and doesn't like it. Xizor maybe."

Dash shook his head. "Xizor is no friend to the Empire."

"He's less of a friend to me. In fact, he's supposed to believe I'm an Imperial informant against Black Sun."

"So, when you ratted out Hitch and Xizor, it was to make the Imperials think you were a good little citizen?"

"Exactly. Plus, it shut down Black Sun smuggling in the same trade corridor we were using. Nor did it hurt to have Xizor suspect I had high-level Imperial connections."

"Then," said Dash, "we may have an Imperial spy among us."

"Or did have," said Mel. "I'm not sure that we didn't leave them behind on Tatooine. The cargo bay problem, as Leebo pointed out, could've been set up while we were docked and triggered automatically."

"I guess that attack on the *Nova's Heart* was a lucky break, then, huh?"

Dash caught the look that passed between Mel and Javul.

"Not exactly luck," said Mel.

Dash leaned back in his seat. "You're kidding me. You *staged* that?"

"We staged it," Javul agreed. "I arranged for it our last night on Rodia, in fact. You remember Rancor's Wrath, I'm sure." There was a spark of wry humor in her eyes. "We needed to get back to Tatooine and get a different ship. We needed to be able to leave the crew with the *Heart* because, frankly, I didn't know who I couldn't trust. I only knew who I *could* trust." She glanced aside at Mel.

"Not to be a party-killer or anything," said Dash, "but are you sure about this guy?"

Javul's smile was brief and bright. "Captain Dash Rendar, meet Commander Yanus Melikan, Rebel Alliance, Corellian Guard."

Well, that turned a bunch of Dash's pet theories on their heads. "Oh. Commander, huh?"

Mel inclined his head.

"Okay. Great. I'm up to my eyeballs in a Rebel plot. I really, *really* don't want to be up to *any* part of my anatomy in a Rebel plot. I just want to earn enough credits to fix up my ship and mind my own business and . . ."

He caught himself in the lie. He wanted more than that. His brush with Edge had made him realize, in some place beneath conscious thought, that he wanted to right the wrong that had been done to his family—and to all the other innocent people who'd gotten caught in the crossfire between the Black Sun underlord and the Empire. It galled him that Xizor had used his brother to extract his pound of flesh from the Empire, and had used the Empire to wrest control of RenTrans from his family. It galled him further that Eaden, too, had lost a large part of his life to the Palpatine's lust for power.

He let none of this show in his face. He put none of it into words. Instead he said, "But I guess I'm in too deep not to see this through. Fine, then. What is it we're protecting or moving or whatever it is we're doing?"

Javul flicked a glance at the doorway. Mel rose and went to check the passage for eavesdroppers. He shook his head, but remained standing in the access.

Javul leaned close to Dash across the table and lowered her voice. "At this moment, there is a set of plans on the move that can seriously undermine the Empire's military strategy. We don't know where they are or who's actually handling them. They could be in my hands right now . . . or they could be someplace halfway across the galaxy. None of us knows. Which means that the Empire doesn't know, either."

"You're a decoy."

"I don't know. I might not be the decoy. I might be the real deal."

Dash nodded, noting—as if from a distance—that his sense of self-preservation seemed to have curled up and gone to sleep. Or perhaps it was merely stunned into silence.

"What's the mission?" he asked.

"We're to pick up a container on Bannistar Station. Presumably it contains replacement parts for my holographic rig. We don't know what's really in it. We're to deliver it to our liaison on Alderaan."

"What about the data wafer?"

"Identification codes for the compartment containing the cargo, and new orders."

"After Bannistar Station," said Mel, "we can't continue with our scheduled itinerary. It's too dangerous. We're to pick up the package and go straight to Alderaan."

Straight to Alderaan. Great. All they had to do was avoid being assassinated by Edge, stopped by a Black Sun saboteur, or simply blown out of the skies by an Imperial cruiser.

None of that concerned Dash Rendar so much, though, as how they were going to convince Han Solo to take them to Alderaan.

"Rebel Alliance? *Rebel Alliance?*" Han rocked back in his cockpit chair and stared at Dash, who sat in the co-pilot's seat. He looked almost ill. "You're kidding me. What is this—the cause of the day?"

"It's not like that and you know it. She's completely committed to this mission."

"Mission." Han shook his head. "*Never* trust a woman who's committed to a mission." He sat forward, put his elbows on the console and his head in his hands. After a couple of moments he looked up. "Okay, here's what we'll do. We'll drop this bunch on Bannistar Station and head back to Tatooine."

"You don't understand. I don't want us *out*, Han, I want you *in*. We need to get Javul to Bannistar. While they're getting the show set up, we can get the package from storage and get it aboard the *Falcon*—"

Han raised both hands to stem the flow of words. "Whoa, whoa! You're saying you want *me* to help you get this thing aboard my ship? You want me to smuggle Rebellion stuff under the Emperor's nose?"

"You're a smuggler, Han. It's what you do."

"Yeah, but not for the Rebel Alliance. That's crazy, and I ain't crazy . . . yet. Do you have any idea what would happen if we got caught doing this?"

"Yeah, I do, as a matter of fact. That's why I suggested you could just stay behind on Bannistar."

"The *Falcon* doesn't go anywhere I don't. That clear?"

"So you'll do it?"

Han stood up suddenly, banging his head on the cowling over the flight console. "Ow! *No*, I won't do it! Are you nuts? This is suicide! You may be willing to put your life on the line for this girl, but I'm not."

Dash rose, too, meeting Han nose-to-nose. "This isn't about the girl. Can't you wrap your fat head around that?"

"Oh, really?" Han sat back down. "Then tell me what it *is* about?"

That stopped Dash in his tracks. What *was* it about? He realized he hadn't articulated that fully, even to himself. He clawed ideas out of the air and tried to clothe them in words.

"It's about . . . having your life run by forces outside your control."

"What?"

"Look at me, at Eaden, at Javul—look at *you*."

"What's wrong with me?"

"Not *you* exactly, but what your life is. You're pushed around by forces you can't control—Jabba, the Empire—"

"Hey, *nobody* pushes Han Solo around—"

"Oh, shut up! Why were you in a position to take my cargo to Nar Shaddaa?"

Han blinked. "Well, I . . ."

"You were scrounging for work because Jabba's soured on you. He's caught up in stuff that's bigger than he is, too. Clan politics, Imperial politics, whatever. I'm where I am—living on the fringes—because a Black Sun Vigo effectively wiped out my family. And he did that, in part, because the Empire wiped out *his* family. Javul's where she is because the Empire is running all our lives, whether we like it or not. We have to watch who we associate with, where we go, what we say, and who we say it to. And now I just found out that Eaden's had *his* life jerked around by the same forces. So maybe I am, y'know, a little impressed with the woman, but mostly I think I just want to feel like I'm not playing dead. Like I'm not just keeping my head down and whistling in the dark and pretending that everything's stellar when it's *not*. Javul has found a way to push—no, to *fight* back. I think that's worth my time and effort."

Han was nodding, almost as if he'd been listening. "Yeah, but is it worth your life? 'Cause, with all due respect, that's exactly what your Rebel girlfriend is asking you to put on the line."

Dash considered that. "Yeah. I think maybe it is."

Han snorted. "C'mon . . . whatever this thing is that Javul might be transporting—how can it possibly make a difference? So they get information or something. Big deal. So what's new?"

"Cascade effect," said Dash. "Someone does something. And that proves to someone else that something can be done. So *they* do something and that proves to a few more people that something can be done, and *they* do something. Up until now, the Empire has had the cascade effect on their side: they take out the Jedi, and Eaden's order gets cascaded out of existence; they take out Xizor's family and that cascades into *my* family. Maybe if we help Javul, we can turn the cascade the other way."

Han's face was suddenly shuttered. "Yeah? I know more about the cascade effect than I care to. But I also know that the Rebel Alliance is poison. It's not something I want to get involved with."

"Okay, fine. Don't get involved."

Both men turned at the sound of Javul Charn's voice. She stood in the hatchway.

"Just get us to Bannistar and take us from there to Alderaan. We were originally supposed to perform on Alderaan and leave the container behind where our liaison could impound it as missing property. All very proper. We can't afford to do that now, obviously. Our itinerary is too well known."

"You could send *Deep Core* instead," suggested Dash. "I mean, you may have already thought of that . . ."

"I hadn't. Thanks. It's a good suggestion. Make things look as normal as possible."

"That's all just great as far as it goes," said Han, "but like you said—they know your itinerary. Who's to say you won't get to Bannistar and find a welcoming committee waiting for you?"

"There may be some trouble on Bannistar," Javul granted him, "but I have to believe the fuel on that station is going to make anyone think twice about blowing things up or getting trigger-happy. I'm a courier. I'm not that important in the cosmic scheme of things."

Dash wasn't ready to accept that at face value. He suspected she might be a good deal more important than she was letting on.

Han leaned back in his command chair. "Too risky," he said curtly.

Dash glared at him, opened his mouth to retort. Javul put a hand on his shoulder and shook her head. "How much do you want?" she asked Han.

"You don't have enough money, lady. I'll help you get your package and I'll get you away from Bannistar Station, but I'm *not* going to risk my ship or my life to take you to the Core Worlds. That would be suicide—and while I might not be very bright, I'm not suicidal. You'll have to find some other space jockey to complete your operation."

"I'll double—"

Han was shaking his head. "Let me be real specific: a diamond the size of a neutron star's core wouldn't be big enough."

"All right. Fine. Let me know when we're in the Bannistar neighborhood. I have a message I need to send. I'll have to set up a rendezvous with the *Nova's Heart*." She paused as she turned to go and looked down at Dash, frustration glittering in her eyes. "What about you, Dash? Are you going to pull out before we get to Alderaan?"

"I'm in," he said, his gaze on Han. "All the way in."

Han just shook his head.

TWENTY-TWO

HUNDREDS OF METERS ABOVE THE SURFACE OF A PLANetoid too insignificant to merit a name of its own, huge clusters of fuel tanks floated, tethered to a refinery complex often hidden beneath a roil of clouds. The refinery was serviced mostly by droids. Any sentients in their right minds lived in the habitat rings and towers embedded in the hearts of the tank clusters like seeds in highly volatile fruit. The largest of the clusters—the Command and Control facility—was where the *Millennium Falcon* was headed.

Javul Charn had called in a request for a docking portal herself, explaining that an accident had befallen her ship and she had resorted to hiring this Corellian freighter. The duty officer in the C&C was surprised almost to stammering to find himself face-to-digitized-face with the beautiful holostar. Dash could relate.

"Mistress Charn, this is—this is—this is *such* a pleasant surprise. I mean, it's not a surprise that you're *here* but we weren't expecting—I mean, we were expecting the *Nova's Heart* and we'd set aside a docking port . . . that is . . ."

Javul laughed pleasantly. "Yes, well, the *Millennium Falcon* is a somewhat different configuration, isn't she? I hope you have a dock we can use. Something as close to the hub facility as possible . . ."

"Oh—oh, of course! Um, do you need to be near your other vessel—the *Deep Core*? If so—"

"No. Not necessary. I only need personnel from the *Deep Core,* not equipment."

"Oh, okay. Well, let me check for a free dock. You're a YT-1300 . . . I mean"—he laughed nervously—"your *ship* is a—" He cleared his throat and repeated, "I'll check for a free dock."

The man—a human male—was gone for only a moment before returning to give their navigational array the coordinates for the dock. Han read them over then disengaged the auto-dock feature, clearly intending to pilot the ship in himself.

"What are you doing?" Javul asked. "Doesn't this thing have an auto-dock?"

Dash grinned. "Han has a bit of a phobia about allowing a computer to steer the *Falcon* to dock."

"Yeah," said Han. "Especially in a situation where we may have to make a hasty departure. If I've steered her in myself, I know how to steer her out again without hitting one of these giant space mines or fouling a tether."

"And if you've got your auto-dock engaged, the port AI can lock you down," added Dash. "Which means you may find yourself unable to beat a hasty retreat."

"Makes sense. I'm going to go assemble the troops." She swung out of the cockpit.

Dash turned to Han. "You need me to do something?"

"This ain't brain surgery, Dash."

It wasn't brain surgery, but it was a more complex procedure than Dash or Han had expected. They entered the tanker field and made their way along a series of marker buoys to a docking port at the largest cluster of tanks. There were six of them, in fact, arranged in a ring and linked together by catwalks. A number of small freighters and a single Imperial corvette were docked at various posts around the circumference of the tanks.

Han shook his head as he nudged the *Falcon* into position. "I don't like this. Did you see that corvette on the other side of the command module? If we go back out the way we came in, we'll have to go right past it. Plus the flight path was a maze. If we have to get out of here in a hurry—"

"Well, then I guess we'd better hope we don't have to," Dash said, eyeing the nearest fuel tank. Its huge, oblate body loomed over the freighter, dwarfing her.

"I am *not* looking forward to this," Han grumbled.

Dash rose and clapped him on the shoulder. "Look at it this way—you'll get to see a free Javul Charn concert."

Scaled down—that's how Javul had described her performance on Bannistar Station. To Dash it was even more complicated and grandiose in its own way than her outdoor concert on Christophsis. The larger framework elements and piece scenery that were in *Deep Core's* capacious hold would remain unused; Javul's plan was to give her performance in the free space between several clusters of tanks, making good use of the low gravity to fly the piece scenery and augment her antigrav harness. The tanks and their network of walkways would become her staging area.

Great, Dash thought, *more complicated stuff to go wrong.*

"That doesn't seem very practical." This opinion came from an unlikely source—Javul's devoted road manager, who also turned out to be a Rebel operative. "I mean, look," Spike said, as their party traversed the catwalk from their docking port on the far side of the tanks to the central tower where Command and Control was located. "These sets of tanks are connected to the refineries down there, not to one another. Which means they're bobbing around like Dantooine swamp bunnies. They'd need to be moored to one another somehow, wouldn't they?"

"Yeah, but they're made for that. See?" Javul gestured

upward toward the bulging flanks of the tank closest to them.

Looking up, Dash found himself peering at the bottom of another catwalk. It ran along the tank's broad beam and extended past it to an encircling perimeter walkway. Even from here he could see the scaffolding and hydraulic systems that would allow the catwalk overhead to be extended out past the perimeter. He realized the walkway beneath their feet had the same means of extension.

"They're made to be reconfigurable," Javul said. "They'd have to be. So, I'll just propose that maybe we can reconfigure them for the performance. Link some of the habitable areas together and to the main tower."

Dash glanced at her sharply. This was not about a performance. "Okay. Why do you really want them moved?"

"So that there's a path to that storage facility over there."

Over there was a cluster of four fuel tanks with a cargo storage ring that floated serenely about two klicks away. The designation 4B was painted on each of the tanks in characters three times the height of a man.

"Ah. The mysterious container," said Han.

"Wouldn't it be better to ask for a docking port at that cluster?" asked Dash.

"And what reason would we give for that?" Javul returned. "Everything else we need is over here in the control center. Food, lodging, staging areas—all of it. I don't know about you, but I'd like to raise as little suspicion as possible. A request that can be chalked up to the inflated ego of a celebrity might be annoying, but it's not likely to raise suspicion."

"Yeah, well how do you propose to sweet-talk the station commander into reconfiguring his tanks?"

She threw him a brilliant smile over one shoulder. "Approximately the same way I sweet-talked you."

Behind him, Han let out a bark of laughter. "Boy, does she have your number."

"You should talk. You're right here with the rest of us."

"Yeah, because I'm being well paid, not because I let myself be sweet-talked into this craziness."

"Well, since we ended up in the same place, I guess it doesn't matter why, does it?"

They made their way among the huge tanks into the center of the cluster where a tower many hundreds of stories tall anchored the grouping. The air was quiet this high up, but they could hear the ghost voice of the wind eddying around the fuel line and its laminanium tether. Dash realized that the catwalk on which they stood was vibrating in those same winds.

"I've always wondered how they kept these things in the air," murmured Han as they approached the entrance to the tower.

Dash moved to the front of the group, slipping in front of Javul to activate the door controls. They opened before he could touch the panel, revealing a tall, broad-shouldered man with close-cut graying black hair and ice-blue eyes. He was dressed in an Imperial uniform . . . sort of. At least the jacket was from an Imperial uniform and it carried the code cylinders of a command-level officer, but it hung open to reveal a decidedly nonregulation shirt of some silvery material. He wore a blaster strapped to his belt and a smug smile on his lips.

He looked right past Dash to Javul, and the look in his steely eyes made every male instinct in Dash's back-brain go on full alert.

"Javul Charn, I presume. Welcome aboard Bannistar Station. I'm Commander D'Vox."

Javul stepped around Dash and held her hand out to the station commander. "Commander D'Vox, what a pleasant surprise. I hardly expected this high-level a welcome."

He smiled—an expression that was at once pleasant and creepy—and took Javul's hand. Which he actually *kissed*.

Dash heard a snort of derision from Han and echoed it mentally. He comforted himself that Javul would probably have little trouble wrapping the commander around her every whim.

D'Vox seemed smitten already. "I could hardly let anyone of your celebrity status arrive without my personal welcome, Mistress Charn."

"Please, Commander, call me Javul."

"And you should call me Arno," he said, bowing over her hand again. "Let me show you to your quarters—then, I think, a tour of the facility is in order."

Dash glanced at Javul's face, wondering if she was praying to the Cosmic Balance that the commander didn't put his lips on her hand again. He didn't. Instead, he tucked it through his arm and led her into the lift. The rest of the party followed, exchanging wry and uneasy glances. Dash resolved to stay as close to Javul as humanly possible.

Javul insisted that her security chief accompany her on the tour of the ship. Dash, in turn, insisted that his partner accompany them on the tour. Leebo was also gainfully employed—surreptitiously "chatting" with the station's AI systems about such things as the number of Imperial ships docked here, when they'd arrived, and when they were expected to depart. Ostensibly, he was gauging the size of their audience. In reality, he was looking for anomalies—ships rushed to the station or that had no itinerary registered with the C&C, unusual troop deployments, anything else that suggested they'd been found out.

Dash was hoping that the Empire's love of layers and layers of secrecy—which bred paranoia, lousy communication, and hidden agendas—would have kept D'Vox out of the loop. He was obviously not a stickler for protocol and regulations, if his personal dress was any indication. That, in and of itself, might make his superiors wary of trusting him with sensitive information.

Spike, Mel, and Nik were getting their own tour of the part of the facilities that directly impacted the show, while Oto scrambled the cargo droids to begin unloading the *Millennium Falcon*. Han had disappeared, and Dash was fairly certain he had gone off to locate the station's nearest entertainment sector.

D'Vox wasn't pleased that his guest required the services of her security team, but his only comment as he walked off with Javul on his arm was: "You're perfectly safe with me, Javul. You really don't need the extra brawn. I think I've got plenty." He actually flexed his biceps as he spoke.

As if she heard Dash's eyes rolling, Javul shot him a backward glance over her shoulder. She made a face at him. He laughed out loud, which drew him a not-so-pleasant look from D'Vox.

"Uh, sorry. Eaden just told me a joke."

"Really?" D'Vox said. "When did he do that? I didn't hear him say anything."

"Yesterday." He shrugged. "I just now got it."

The tour was instructive. Dash got a good sense of the overall layout of the control module, which he knew was reprised on a smaller scale in the other clusters of tanks. The immense vertical tower held crew and guest quarters, amenities and command centers. The tanks were linked to it by a framework of platforms, catwalks, and scaffolding that encircled the tower and radiated out from it in all directions. And, as Javul had theorized, the catwalks and scaffolding could be extended to link the tanks and hab modules together in different configurations. The question now was: Did Javul Charn possess the charms to convince Arno D'Vox to reconfigure it for her?

After a brief look at the C&C—and a chance to admire the view from the bridge at the very top of the structure—they moved to the communal habitat areas, strolling along a relatively broad promenade lined with shops, restaurants, entertainment venues, and drinking establishments. Javul and D'Vox were in front chatting; Dash and Eaden, watchful, brought up the rear. D'Vox had just said something that caused Javul to laugh with feigned delight when a man wearing a uniform in even more disreputable condition than D'Vox's strode up to the commander and blocked his path.

"We need to talk," the man said to D'Vox, then gave Javul a scalding once-over through glittering dark eyes.

Dash and Eaden hurried their steps by mutual and silent agreement. The newcomer was almost as tall as D'Vox, but not nearly as well honed physically. He was big-boned, but not particularly muscular. He had a wild thatch of reddish brown hair, an unkempt beard, and a crazy gleam in his brown eyes. The way he looked at Javul made Dash's hands twitch toward his blaster.

"You might have noticed," said D'Vox, "that I'm engaged right now in showing our guest the station."

"This can't wait." The newcomer's gaze shifted from D'Vox to Dash and Eaden. His lip curled.

D'Vox sighed as if his patience were being tested to the utmost. "This is my security chief, Red Rishyk. You'll have to forgive him. He's singularly devoted to duty. Rishyk, this is—"

"Yeah, I know who she is," Rishyk growled. "We need to talk."

D'Vox turned to Javul. "I'll only be a moment. Why don't you wait for me in the cantina here?" He nodded toward a cheerfully decorated establishment just across the promenade, from which strains of relatively innocuous music rolled.

"Sure," said Javul and led the way across the promenade, walking with a bouncy dancer's gait that made her hips sway and her hair ripple like silver fire. Dash and Eaden followed.

The cantina was crowded and had very tiny tables intended for one or two people—three in a pinch. Dash decided they were in a pinch. He snagged an extra stool and pulled it up to the table Javul had appropriated. She'd obviously chosen it for its location—it sat at the terrace rail, overlooking the promenade and allowing them to watch if not hear the dialogue between D'Vox and his chief of security. It did not look like a happy conversation.

All the muscles in Dash's back tightened. He hoped that Javul and her entourage were not the subject matter. He glanced at Eaden, who wasn't looking at the two Imperials, but was definitely "sniffing" at them with a couple of carelessly dangling tentacles.

"Anything?"

"No more than you've probably divined yourself. Rishyk is excited and angry about something. Though I suspect if I were to ask, Commander D'Vox would tell me that was his natural state."

"You can't tell what he's angry about? Or what kind of anger it is?"

Javul made a face. "What *kind* of anger? There's more than one?"

"Yeah. Is he mad because he just found out you're a Rebel sympathizer or because someone put a buzz-bomb in his locker?" He turned his attention back to Eaden. "Any clues?"

"If we were all immersed in liquid, I might be able to tell you about the quality of his anger and excitement, but as it is . . ." He shrugged. "I am a Nautolan out of water."

Javul threw back her head and laughed. Eaden made a funny hissing sound that Dash couldn't interpret.

"What's funny?" D'Vox was approaching the terrace railing from the promenade; Rishyk was nowhere to be seen.

"It was nothing. Eaden just made a joke," said Javul.

D'Vox raised his eyes to scan the room behind them. "Quite the comedian, isn't he? I see an empty table over there that you two could take," he told Dash. "There's really not room for four at this one."

Dash met the other man's gaze in a clash of wills. He held it until he felt Javul's hand on his forearm.

"Dash, you and Eaden deserve a break. I'm sure I'm perfectly safe with Arno. This is his station, after all."

No, Dash thought as he and Eaden moved to a table from which they could only barely see D'Vox and Javul, it *wasn't* his station. It was the Empire's station. But he'd be willing to bet Arno D'Vox sometimes had trouble remembering that.

TWENTY-THREE

"WHAT DO YOU MEAN YOU'RE HAVING DINNER WITH D'VOX?" Dash stared at Javul with the same expression of disbelief his face always seemed to wear in her presence.

"You need a translation? I'm going to take a meal with the station commander."

"Alone?"

She smiled and pulled a blue shimmer-wig on over her own pale hair, peering at herself in the vanity glass of the plush quarters D'Vox had assigned her. "Well, he sure didn't invite my security chief. Or anyone else. Besides, I need you and yours to figure out the best way to get our property off the station."

Dash sat down on the foot of the oversized bed. "Wait. You didn't have that figured out?"

"We did, but I'm doubtful that plan's still safe. I think it's going to have to change."

"What was the plan?"

In answer, Javul palmed the pendant she was wearing, opened it, and extracted a data wafer—presumably the same one she'd retrieved at the shrine of the Equilibrates. She held it up between thumb and forefinger. "This gives the exact location and identifying features of the container and the access codes required to get to it."

"In Module 4B," Dash guessed.

"Yes. Storage compartment nineteen, currently facing away from the control module. The *Nova's Heart* was assigned a berth at that module, which would have made picking up the container fairly easy. We'd stow some of our gear there and when we left we'd take the container with us. Now that won't work. I need you and Mel and Eaden to come up with an alternative. Immediately, if not sooner." She handed him the data wafer, which he pocketed.

"So how big is this thing?"

"It's about two meters high by a meter wide by one and a half meters long. Full specs are on the data wafer."

"Except for what's in it, I'll bet."

"Except for that. At any rate, it's small enough to move along even the narrowest catwalks."

"If you can get D'Vox to move the modules."

"Yes—if . . ." She turned back to the mirror to give herself an assessing look.

Dash thought she looked amazing. Hair rippling in opalescent shades of blue from azure to aqua, a bodysuit and flowing diaphanous robe to match. Her eyes, unaffected by special lenses, were a blue-tinged silver—twin moons.

He warned himself sternly to keep his head on straight. "Let me ask you something—did D'Vox seem different when he came back from his conversation with his security honcho?"

She shook her head. "No. Though I have to admit I had the same scare—that maybe Rishyk was contacted by Imperial High Command. But I somehow doubt it."

"Why? This is an Imperial fuel dump, after all."

"Yes, but it's fringy. We chose this location for the pickup because of D'Vox's reputation as a renegade. He's not a by-the-regs kind of guy."

"So I've noticed." Dash shook his head. "Man, that Rishyk looks more like a pirate than most of the pirates I know."

"D'Vox isn't much cleaner," said Javul, "and I'm not talking about his personal hygiene. According to Mel's intelligence associates, he'll look the other way on just about anything for enough credits."

"So if worse comes to worst . . ."

She shrugged. "We offer a bribe. I'd like to avoid that, though."

"Why? You've got the credits, right?"

"Oh, I've got the credits. Better than that, I've got aurodium ingots. But if we have to pay D'Vox not to notice us, it means he's *noticed* us. That's just one more person who's too close to the truth. It makes him a conscious factor in the success or failure of the mission. Someone else could pay him more to become both conscious and active. It's better if we can just slide in under his sensors."

"Right. Hugely popular holostar, big stage show— nothing to see here."

She grinned at him. "I just dazzle 'em with my footwork. Or baffle them with banthaflop."

Dash's stomach knotted. "Make an excuse to have me with you tonight. Say there were attempts on your life—a crazy stalker. I mean, it's true."

She sobered quickly. "I can't, Dash. You know I can't. I need him to relax all that prickly suspicious male stuff he does when you're hovering."

"I do *not* hover."

"You hover. And I'm grateful that you hover, but not tonight. Tonight you need to figure out a way to get to the package. Besides, I'll have my comlink. If anything happens, I'll call you."

He had an idea. "Hey, I know. What if you double date? Take Mel and Spike with you."

She cocked her head and made a face. "Spike?"

Dash rolled his eyes. "Oh, man, did I say that out loud? I meant Dara."

"*Spike?*" Javul repeated.

Her laughter followed him from the room.

* * *

Javul wasn't surprised to find that Arno D'Vox had chosen to take dinner in a very private dining room at the nadir of the station's primary module. In fact, the restaurant was called The Nadir, and D'Vox's private dining room had a breathtaking view of the planetoid below. This evening it was especially stunning—the rays of the wan star turned the thin atmosphere ruddy gold and painted the clouds around and beneath the station in myriad glorious hues. She could almost forget that down there, sunken into the misty twilight of Bannistar's world, was a clutter of ugly refinery facilities. From here they were magical, twinkling with fey lights.

"Yes, even this grimy place has its beauty," D'Vox said, as if reading her thoughts.

She looked up at him from her view of the planetoid and clouds and endless sky and accepted the seat he offered. The table sat at the edge of a hanging balcony of sorts suspended over an upside-down transparisteel dome.

"It really is beautiful," she told him and indulged in a little apparent mind reading of her own. "And yes, I'm surprised. When you told me where we were going to have dinner, I'll admit I was a little . . . skeptical."

He sat down opposite her. "I've arranged for a variety of dishes to be brought out. I want to impress you, naturally, with my little domain."

"Not so little," she said, smiling. "You have an emperor's view of the world. Or maybe even a god's view."

"How appropriate"—his gaze locked suggestively with hers—"since right now I'm looking at a goddess."

Wow . . . that's one of the corniest lines I've ever heard. "Ooh, and silver-tongued, too."

Their first course arrived at that moment, brought by a trio of protocol droids. The droids were three different models, and Javul suspected D'Vox had "recruited" them from Imperial diplomatic missions.

The food was, indeed, impressive. Well plated and fragrant, it had nothing of the flat taste of hydroponically grown food, and reminded Javul forcefully of how long it had been since she had eaten anything besides ship's rations and auto-galley output.

"So," her host said when the droids had withdrawn, "what brings you to Bannistar. I mean, whatever possessed you to book a performance here?"

"My tour coordinator said he owed one to the crew of Bannistar Station and that the population was underserved. I'm doing an interview here, too, tomorrow. Live. We usually have huge venues," she added. "There's hardly room here for half our rigging."

"I'm disappointed."

"I'm sorry, but you don't have an indoor space big enough."

"What about an outdoor space?"

She smiled, pleased he'd set himself up. That meant she didn't have to do it. He'd think the whole thing was his idea.

"Well . . . I did do an outdoor concert on Christophsis . . ."

"There any way you could do one here?"

"Hmm. I'll have to think about that. You know, this is excellent soup. What is it again—mynock?"

They found Han, at last, in a dimly lit, noisy cantina with discordant music that blared from every direction. To Dash it felt as if he were swimming in sound waves.

He crossed to the bar—where Han was deep in discussion with a female Wookiee and a much shorter male Advozse—and tapped the other pilot on the shoulder.

"What?" Han turned, blinking in surprise when he saw Eaden, Mel, Nik, and Leebo strung out behind Dash in a wobbly queue. He grimaced. "Do you guys mind? I'm trying to do some business here."

The Advozse made a chortling sound and scratched at the base of the short, thick horn that crowned his hairless head. "Who your friends be?"

Dash ignored him. "We need to have a little conference about the package we're supposed to pick up."

"Maybe later. Right now I'm trying to make this trip worth my while."

Dash flushed with sudden annoyance. "Javul's not making it worth your while already?"

Han sighed. "All right, look. Lemme conclude my negotiations here and I'll be right with you. Go . . . sit down over there." He waved his hand toward a table in a particularly stygian corner. "Oh, and try not to look like a cadet review, okay?"

Fuming, Dash, turned to go. Han tapped him. "You couldn't have left the kid on the ship?"

"The kid," whispered Dash, "is part of our cover, remember? We're *your* crew, *Captain* Solo."

"Oh . . . yeah." Han didn't seem overly happy to be reminded of the fact. "Well, you going or what?"

Dash led the others to the corner and ordered a round of drinks. He insulted Nik by offering him fruit juice.

"Rearrange the modules?" Arno D'Vox didn't bat an eyelash.

"I realize it's a lot to ask. But it's the only way I can think of to give you the full Javul Charn experience."

"I can think of other ways."

"I'll bet you can." She gave him the full assault of her silver eyes. She wasn't vain, but she knew the effect they could have on a man's viscera. She'd had any number of men tell her all about it.

His smiled deepened. "To be perfectly honest, it's really not that difficult to rearrange the modules. How many would you need to have in formation?"

She thought of the way the modules were currently

arranged. The one she needed was closest to the control module, but better safe than sorry. She could've done with three, but . . . "Four? Is that too much to ask?"

"For you, not at all." D'Vox laid his napkin on the table and stood. "In fact, let's go up to my office and I can show you what I can do."

Yeah, that's what I'm afraid of.

She went reluctantly, praying to the Cosmos that Red Rishyk would interrupt their stroll. He didn't, and some minutes later Arno D'Vox was ushering her into his office—a private office, attached to his suite of rooms. It looked more like a lounge than an office, in fact. There was a desk with holoconsole, a bar, and a seating area that faced a curving transparisteel window.

Oh, joy.

He surprised her, though, by actually leading her to the holodisplay where he called up a schematic of the station. In mere seconds an image of the station's tactical aspects was laid out, depicting the entire grouping of tank clusters. Module 4B was tethered lower and to the east by a couple of klicks; other modules floated to the south, southwest, and north farther away, but at about the same altitude as the control module.

"How do you move them?" Javul asked, only half feigning her interest. The huge structures were an amazement to her. "For that matter, how do you keep them up?"

D'Vox laughed, showing even white teeth. "It's a combination of the planetoid's relatively low gravity and thick atmosphere combined with antigravity and booster technology. Moving them is a matter of moving the other end of the tether and navigating the module to its new location."

Javul widened her eyes. "Sounds complicated."

"Not really. Huge modified construction droids handle the ground work on the tethers in sync with our navigational systems." He paused to study the situation for a

moment, then said: "What if we move these three units—"
He tapped each holographic image with the tip of a finger. They each lit with a soft green halo. "Here, here, and here?" He dragged them into place one at a time. "Will that do?"

Javul stared at the reconfiguration. Or rather, she stared at Module 4B, still floating alone in its place two klicks to the east. "Oh . . . yes, it should be perfect, but wouldn't it make more sense to move that one? I mean, it's closer, isn't it?"

He didn't seem to think her question odd. "Closer, yes, but it contains fewer habitat units and the superstructure doesn't have as much viewing space. Besides which, you'll note that it's sitting lower than the other modules."

"Uh-huh . . ."

"It's the cargo load . . . and the fact that its tanks have just been refilled."

"Oh, so moving that one would be more difficult, I guess."

"Very much so."

Great. She wondered feverishly how she might contact Dash and let him know that Station Commander D'Vox had just changed up the logistical landscape. Aloud, she said: "Well, this looks perfect to me, Arno. How do you make it happen?"

"I have but to give the command. The whole move should be complete within two hours."

"You don't have to ask permission or inform the appropriate authorities?"

"I'm the commander of this facility, Javul. I *am* the appropriate authority. I don't ask permission—I give it." Suiting action to words, he thumbed on his comlink. "This is D'Vox. Give me the C and C duty officer."

"Lieutenant Ashel here, sir."

"I have new coordinates for module configuration

that I'll be sending down. Check them for any logistical issues and implement after issuing standard warnings."

"Sir? This isn't a scheduled maneuver—"

"Yes, I know. It's a special request." He looked aside at Javul. "A *very* special request."

"Yessir. I'll start proceedings upon receipt of the new coordinates."

"They're on their way." He cut the connection and smiled at Javul.

She smiled back. "Thank you, Arno. I will try not to disappoint."

He shifted closer, looming over her and making her feel small and vulnerable. "I don't think you could disappoint."

Her smile was coquettish. "Such a flatterer."

He was wearing some sort of smoky-smelling cologne that made her feel light-headed. A pheromonic concoction, she was willing to bet.

She took a small step backward. "Does your office have a refresher? I need to . . . tidy up." *And figure out how to get away from you.*

He gestured toward a doorway to his left and Javul escaped through it. Once locked inside the smaller chamber, she did a quick visual scan for surveillance cams. She saw none—which didn't mean they weren't there—but she did notice that there was a connecting door to the suite D'Vox had given her. The urge to bolt through it was stronger than she cared to admit. Suppressing it, she got out her comlink and palmed it as she made a pretense of washing her hands and primping.

After half an hour waiting for Han to finish "negotiating," Dash was fed up. He didn't realize how fed up until Leebo leaned toward him and stage-whispered: "Hey, boss, I had no idea humans were steam-powered."

"What?"

"There's steam coming out of your ears."

Nik sniggered. Mel merely smiled into his drink.

"If Han's behavior bothers you so much," said Eaden reasonably, "why don't you go ask him to expedite his negotiations?"

Dash shoved his tankard of Corellian spiced ale—his *second* tankard of Corellian spiced ale—away from him, half consumed. "Y'know what? I'm gonna do just that."

He got up and crossed to the bar. It was perfectly clear that the negotiation phase of the proceedings was over and they were entering the social phase. Han was telling jokes.

"A Wookiee and an Ewok walk into a cantina, see—"

Dash tapped him on the shoulder. "I've heard this one. The punch line is 'I was talking to the Wookiee.'"

The Wookiee threw back her head and made a sound like metal bending. The Advozse scratched the base of his sagittal horn and said, "What? What? I don't get it."

"We need to move this along," Dash told Han. "We have other business to transact."

"Hey, if it doesn't pay, it's not business."

"She's already paying you, nerf-for-brains."

"I'm just doing a little on the side. You got a problem with that?"

"I do if it—" His comlink pinged. "I'll be right back. Don't go anywhere."

Dash moved to the end of the cantina's long, gleaming black bar and opened the link.

Javul emerged from the refresher to find that D'Vox had poured drinks. She regarded the glass of amber liquid he handed her skeptically. "What's this?"

"It's called ambrostine. It's sweet and rich—like you."

Ambrostine. Yeah—sweet, rich, and potent. She'd heard all about the stuff from Dara. It reduced inhibitions to zero—something Javul knew she couldn't afford. Beyond whatever personally repugnant situation she might find herself in, it was what she might say about her connection with the Rebellion that frightened her the most.

She took the glass gingerly, stalling. Any moment now (she hoped) Dash would comm her and tell her there was a problem with the holo-emitter setup and that she needed to weigh in on it. And right now, too, or they'd be behind schedule and would never mount a performance by the following evening.

She smiled at D'Vox; he'd just proposed a salute to something. "To our . . ." she began.

"Mutual admiration," he finished.

She put the glass to her lips and sipped. The ambrostine was like fiery honey. She held it on her tongue as long as she could, pretending to savor it, before swallowing the tiny mouthful. It burned all the way down—not unpleasantly. Not at all.

"Come sit down," he said and put a hand to her arm to draw her to the plush divan that afforded a view of space from between two of the module's fuel tanks.

Blast Dash Rendar! Where is he?

She took a step toward the divan and was chilled to discover that the ambrostine was already making her feel light-headed. Or was it his karking pheromone-laden cologne? She moved with slow, calculated grace, trailing D'Vox and making him turn back to watch her walk. The expression in his eyes might have been welcome at another time—in other eyes. At this moment, in *his* eyes, it was terrifying.

She sat. He sat.

His door chime rang.

Javul started. Had Dash decided to appear in person to cart her away? She hoped not. As capable as he was in some ways, she doubted that his skills ran to acting. In fact, one of the things she most liked about him was the way he felt his emotions all the way out to his skin.

D'Vox stood, swearing, and rounded the divan to face the door. "Come!"

The door opened, but it wasn't Dash who entered. It was Security Chief Rishyk. His face—not all that pleasant to look at in any situation—was screwed into a scowl of epic proportions.

"Did you give the order to move the blasted rigs into a square?" he asked before D'Vox could ask why he'd come.

"Of course I gave the order. Who else would give it?"

"D'you realize how many fuel ports that cuts off? Are you aware that you've got three Imperial tankers queued up in low orbit, waiting to refuel?"

From her perch on the couch, Javul could see the back of D'Vox's neck flush a deep, angry red. "Refueling is my responsibility, not yours. This has nothing to do with security."

"The hell it doesn't! You get those Imperial captains in an uproar and they'll want to investigate us up one side and down the other."

Javul stood suddenly and turned to face the two men. "I should . . ." The look she got from Rishyk made her stomach twist. ". . . leave you to your conversation," she finished, then moved swiftly to the door, wishing she didn't have go past Rishyk to get there.

"Javul, stay," said D'Vox, putting out a hand to stop her. "This will only take a moment."

"The hell it will!" snarled Rishyk. "Does *she* have something to do with this asinine maneuver?"

"What if she does? I'm commander of this facility, Security Chief Rishyk. I suggest you try not to forget that."

Javul made it to the door and paused a beat to offer a parting shot. "Let me know if you're not going to be able to make that change." She glanced at Rishyk, looking him swiftly up and down. "I'll understand if you can't."

She dodged out the door then, hoping she'd said just

enough to ensure that D'Vox would go ahead with the reconfiguration out of sheer ego. It was no longer important to the retrieval of the container, but they might be able to use the opportunity to move the *Millennium Falcon* to a new dock.

Out in the corridor, Javul quickly rounded the corner, dashed into her suite, and collapsed against the wall. Her comlink beeped.

"You're a little late," she told Dash.

"What? What do you mean, I'm a little late? You don't mean—" The cantina seemed suddenly stiflingly hot.

"I mean I had to take another opportunity to leave. I suspect that D'Vox and Rishyk are circling each other like a couple of rancors in bloodlust right now, arguing over the reconfiguration."

That was a relief. "Rishyk thinks it's a bad idea, does he?"

"Ha. You could say that. He came in snarling and snapping like a boarwolf. I think D'Vox is going to go for it, though—his male ego's got its back up. And I hope it will give us an excuse to move the *Falcon*."

"And if it doesn't?"

He could hear the smile in her voice. "I'm counting on you, Captain Rendar."

An idea struck him between the eyes. "Yeah, well, I'm counting on Han."

He signed off and returned to where Han was still trading jokes with the Wookiee and her partner.

". . . So he says to the Baragwin, 'Hey! Why the long face?' "

This time it was the Advozse who laughed so hard he nearly choked on his drink. Dash helped the alien by pounding on his back for a few seconds, then asked, "So Captain, what's going down with this deal? Where're we going to make the drop?"

Han looked at him. "What drop?"

"In case you haven't noticed, Captain, there are Imperials all over the place. It would be in our customer's interests to be discreet."

The Wookiee said something, to which Han replied, "Of course I'm discreet. I'm *always* discreet." To Dash he said, "What'd you have in mind?"

TWENTY-FOUR

WHETHER D'VOX WON HIS SNARLING MATCH WITH Rishyk or pulled rank on him, the result was that the four great clusters of fuel tanks were pulled carefully toward one another. Mel and Nik moved to oversee the setup of the holographic equipment and piece scenery. Han and his "crew," meanwhile, prepared to pilot the *Millennium Falcon* over to Module 4B, where they had instructed their customers to reserve a section of storage compartment 19 for their "delivery."

"You don't have to move the ship," D'Vox told Dash when he announced their plans. "It's perfectly safe where it is."

"Yeah, well, Captain Solo is—shall we say—a little paranoid about his ship's well-being. Besides we've got some cargo to off-load."

"Really?" D'Vox's eyes betrayed sudden curiosity. "As part of the show?"

"No, no. As part of a business deal. As it happens, Captain Solo was transporting some goods for a couple of your regulars here—Captain Kyobuk and her buddy, Sars Tarquhar."

"Ah, I see."

Dash sincerely hoped the commander did *not* see. "Yeah. So we're just gonna take the *Falcon* on over to their storage facility and unload the goods."

D'Vox seemed not to care, and Dash didn't think it was an act. Even if the commander had been warned by the Imperials to keep an eye on them or stop them from doing whatever it was they were doing, he'd surely try to cut a deal—demanding something from them in order to be persuaded to look the other way. That he hadn't was a good sign.

As the huge modules rotated into position for the performance, the *Millennium Falcon* left her dock at the main hub module and moved down to Module 4B, compartment 19. The storage unit had already been opened by Captain Kyobuk, who met them at the air lock.

They made a big deal out of unloading the rather large container of goods Han had sold the Wookiee merchant. Han and Leebo moved it to the front of the bay, toward the inner portal. Dash was relieved in the extreme when the good captain insisted that she and her associate open the crate then and there to inspect the contents. With the Wookiee and the Advozse focused entirely on Han's floor show and demo, Dash, Eaden, and Leebo set about locating their target container.

They found it in a recess near the external hatch, easily accessible and completely inoffensive in appearance. It was as tall as Dash and twice as wide and deep—large enough, he thought, to hold two people. Three, if they were Sullustan. As they moved it quietly onto the ship, Dash wondered if the "cargo" was live.

"Blasted thing's heavy," Dash complained as they settled it into one of the secret compartments beneath the *Falcon*'s decking. "What's it got in it?"

"You're asking me?" Leebo replied. "Do I have X-ray vision now? Huh. I should pay more attention. When did you install that mod?"

"It was a rhetorical question. You two get this buttoned up. I'm going to check on Han's progress."

Han was just bumping foreheads with Sars Tarquhar— the traditional seal of a gentleman's agreement among the Advozse—when Dash emerged from the ship. Tarquhar, evidently well pleased with their purchase, gave Han a particularly enthusiastic head-butt.

Deal done, Han accompanied Dash back onto the *Falcon*, checking the credit balance on his account card. His forehead, Dash noted, was red and showing the beginnings of a bruise. Dash grinned. Han, being human, didn't possess the Advozse sagittal horn. He was going to have one heck of a headache.

They waited in the ship, watching the conclusion of the dance of the titans as the control module and her three ponderous sister units were locked safely together. Then they returned to their original docking port beneath Module 1A.

Dash breathed a sigh of relief. Another obstacle out of the way. He wondered if he could convince Javul to forget the performance and leave now. He wondered if they were under surveillance. He wondered if D'Vox knew the Empire wanted them. He wondered a huge amount of things, none of them particularly happy. He finally decided to stop wondering and help Mel with the setup.

The newly linked tank modules formed a square. Each had its tanks rotated toward the outside of the formation to allow people in the towers a clear view of the performance area. Additional platforms had been run out within the massive new cluster's hollow core to provide outdoor space for those who wanted an unobstructed view. In the towers, galleries of seats had been set up in conference rooms, recreational facilities, and restaurants, while enterprising entrepreneurs whose private quarters had the luxury of windows converted these into intimate viewing salons. And, of course, there was a holocom feed that would pipe the entertainment to inner rooms.

Mel and Nik oversaw the positioning of holo-emitters and flying set pieces while Oto and his team of droids carried out their placement and calibration. Hoping to help speed things up, Dash brought Leebo over to assist.

"You are rated to handle these calibrations?" the Otoga unit asked Leebo blandly.

"Hey, you tin pot," Leebo responded, "I can calibrate anything you can give me the specs for."

Oto considered the statement. "You are also a tin pot, LE-BO2D9."

Leebo made a queer rattling sound, prompting Dash to step in. "Just give him the specs for the next emitter, Oto. You can fix it if he messes it up."

"Messes it up?" repeated Leebo. "Highly unlikely."

The Otoga 222 reached out a digit to Leebo's data-port. There was a split second of complete silence from both droids, then Oto said, "Those are the specs for the next two emitters. See if you can set them properly."

As if respecting Dash's sense of diplomacy, Leebo didn't respond with some scathing commentary on the other droid's genesis. Instead, he just cocked his head curiously and headed for the next emitter in the array.

Dash shook his head and went about his own business—walking the galleries looking for possible dangers. He saw nothing. This did not, however, set his mind at ease.

"You still get pre-show jitters?" Dash asked Javul later that evening as she awaited her cue to go "onstage."

"Yeah. Now more than ever."

They stood in a comfortable lounge that D'Vox had set aside as a backstage area. Here gathered the needful members of the stage crew—Dara Farlion and her go-fers, the props people, Tereez Dza'lar and her team of under-costumers. They had everything laid out or hung in order of use to either side of the wide doorway that opened onto the private catwalk-*cum*-balcony just outside the lounge where Mel had set up his control console. From there, he could monitor the myriad pieces of the physical apparatus, from the holo-emitters to the piece scenery.

The centerpiece of that was a gleaming spiral staircase of transparisteel, six stories tall, that was suspended in the center of the quad formed by the tank modules. It was a fantastic thing—gleaming, lacy, and transparent— that looked as if it were made of water and ice crystals. From it, Javul would perform the bulk of her concert— acting, singing, dancing . . . and flying.

Dash stared at it now and shook his head. "Yeah, that thing alone would give me the vapors."

"You mean the Helix? That doesn't make me nervous in the least. It's . . . you know. The other thing."

"The item?"

"Yeah, that. Every second between now and the end of the tour, every kilometer between here and the end of the line—seems an eternity. A forever road."

Dash sincerely wished she hadn't said *end of the line*.

"Too late to pack it in and—?"

"Yeah. Way too late." She turned to look at him, her eyes—outfitted with dazzling lenses that contained a set of state-of-the-art miniaturized holo-emitters—seemed to turn like wheels. "We have to do this thing, Dash. Just like always. Just like normal. I go on, I dance and sing and act out stories, then we pack up and on we go."

Except that only the *Deep Core* would go to the next venue on Bacrana. The *Millennium Falcon* would go directly to Alderaan. He prayed the Imperials—if they were watching closely—would follow the *Deep Core*. But if there were Imperial agents watching their every move, he still hadn't seen them. Leebo had found no record of them in the station communications logs—not even in D'Vox's and Rishyk's private ones. Which meant exactly nothing, Dash supposed, except that they weren't in on any Imperial plotting.

Perhaps it was because of all this nonstalking by the

Empire that Dash had made sure Han and the *Falcon* were ready to take off at a moment's notice. The *Falcon* sat with her docking field on loose-lock, meaning that her magnetic clamps were dialed down. The soft dock would break instantaneously if Han made a run for it. It was an old smuggler's trick.

At which point they'd learn whether the station had been upgraded with tractor beams . . .

"Time," said Spike, arriving behind Dash and Javul and making Dash jump.

Javul turned her most brilliant smile on him. "Wish me smooth spacing."

He tried to exorcise the bad feeling in his gut, couldn't, gave up and kissed her instead. "Smooth spacing."

He watched her go out onto the balcony from which she'd sail to the crystalline Helix in full view of the thousands who had gathered in galleries and on catwalks to watch her perform. He watched as she stood, momentarily silhouetted against the play of colorful lights sweeping up and down the four looming towers.

When he'd kissed her, he'd felt her fear. It trembled on her lips, quivered in her breathing. It wasn't his manly charms that had made her shake, he knew. Tonight, Javul Charn had more than stage fright.

Dash took a deep breath and looked around for Eaden. The Nautolan was standing at Mel's shoulder, watching him begin the start-up sequence for the artificial intelligence that ran the performance. Dash moved to stand next to them as Javul stepped off the balcony seemingly into midair, her antigrav harness activating.

In that moment that her feet went from solid metal to thin air, Dash's gut twisted spasmodically, then relaxed. The harness was good. The harness was fine . . . for now.

He let out a sigh as she began her opening song, a whimsically wistful number about a lonely moisture farmer. Her bright, clear soprano seemed to come from everywhere at once: *"I've got no real life. I live on Tatooine . . ."*

The crowd packed onto the external catwalks and balconies recognized the popular song and roared their approval.

Dash put a hand over his stomach, reflecting that of all the experiences he'd had in his life, this was the first one that had made him wonder if he was developing an ulcer. He heard Mel chuckle and looked over to see that the other man was grinning at him wryly. "You, too, huh?" he said, patting his own stomach.

"I guess she just has that effect on everybody."

"Only everybody who cares about her. So thanks," Mel added, "for caring about her."

Dash shrugged. "All in a day's work. And now, if I'm going to be useful to the diva, Eaden and I had better get out there and keep our eye on things. D'you need Leebo for anything? If not, I'll put him to work, too."

"Hey, he's your droid. You can have him. As a matter of fact, you can have Oto as well. That way you can have a man—or a droid—on each module."

"We could use more," Dash observed.

"Sorry, we don't have more . . . at least not that we can trust."

Amid the swirl of light and sound, Dash and Eaden collected the two droids and made their way out through the force shield Rishyk had grumblingly erected around the holostar's backstage area at D'Vox's order. Once beyond the barrier, Dash made sure his team had the passcode Rishyk had provided (with equal reluctance) that granted them access to the restricted security walkways running along the fronts of the public platforms. Thus prepared, they ascended via grav-lift to the topmost platform and then split up.

"I'll take the primary module," Dash decided. "Eaden, take 2A; Leebo 5C; Oto 3C. We'll each move from the highest level to the lowest then back up again. Got it?"

"Affirmative," said Oto.

"Got it, boss," said Leebo. "I keep an eye out for baleful Anomids. How hard can that be?"

Dash held Eaden back until the two droids had headed off for their respective assignments. "So, is this a good hair day or a bad hair day?" he asked, hoping the Nautolan would tell him he was comfortable in this festival atmosphere. Alas, it was not to be.

"I am not at my best with so many sentients focusing so much attention in such a small area."

"So your . . . Force thingamagummie is broken, then."

"It is not a 'Force thingamagummie,' Dash. It is a sensitivity to the Force and to other individual energies—nothing more, nothing less. It is not broken. It is, however, a bit overwhelmed. This makes it more difficult to sort through the input."

"Well, happy sorting, then. Let me know if you feel any murderous rages from anybody except Rishyk, okay?"

"I doubt that the individuals we'll be watching are likely to have murderous rages. They're more the cold and implacable type."

Dash looked at his friend sharply. Had he just made an offhand comment? The Nautolan's expression had not changed. It was as impenetrable as always.

"Great, then keep a tentacle out for cold and implacable as well."

"I shall." Eaden inclined his head then moved gracefully away down the catwalk to his assigned module.

Dash's promenade along the audience platforms was slow and methodical. The viewing galleries were about ten meters wide, allowing for quite a few viewers to gather. He wended his way along the foremost edge, us-

ing the narrow security catwalk just below the main platform only to maneuver around knots of tightly clustered
celebrants. The security walk allowed access to its semi-
enclosed space at regular intervals, fortunately. Unfortunately, when he was forced to use it, someone would
inevitably try to squeeze in after him. An apologetic smile
and a flash of the ID Javul had furnished him, which pro-
claimed him officially her security chief, was enough to
avoid argument.

He covered the top level and paused to signal Eaden
before descending to the next. The Nautolan was fairly
easy to spot among Javul's mesmerized audience. For one
thing, he was moving purposefully through the crowd.
For another, his height and the distinctive shape of his
pale head made him a standout. He reached the lift pad
at the extreme end of the platform and paused to make
eye contact with Dash across the many meters of space
between them.

Eaden gave a slight shake of his head. Dash did likewise. Then he descended to the next level, pulling out his
comlink as he went. He checked in with Leebo and Oto,
got negative reports from both of them, and started across
the broad gallery. He glanced out at the "stage" area as
he went. A gigantic Javul looked back at him from the
center of the module, singing a mournful song about lost
love. The crowd had quieted, hanging on every note. This
had distinct benefits for Dash and company as they
wended their way through the swarm of sentients.

Dash reached the halfway point along the front of
Module 1A and worked his way to the rail. Javul had
begun to dance in the air, using the crystal Helix as a
prop. He checked the module to his left and could just
make out Leebo moving through the audience, his head
swiveling this way and that. He looked to the right—Oto
had gone down to the security catwalk and was working
his way along it. Dash looked across the quad and picked

Eaden out of the crowd, just emerging from behind Javul's holoimage.

As he watched, the Nautolan stopped moving and lifted his head, his tresses in subtle motion.

A frisson of tension scuttled between Dash's shoulder blades.

Eaden's gaze swept to his left . . . and he froze.

Dash tried to follow his line of sight, peering at the crowd gathered along the second platform that fronted Module 3C. At the far end of the catwalk, the shaft cowling of the grav-lift threw a thick shadow against the bulkhead of the module. Someone stood in that shadow—a stark contrast to all of those pressing forward to the edge of the rail, seeking the reflected and refracted light of Javul Charn's holographically projected self.

Eaden unfroze and began to move purposefully toward Module 3C. At almost the same moment, Javul's dance ended and her audience responded with a roar of approval and a paroxysm of jubilant movement. Dash was almost toppled over the platform rail and onto the roof grille of the security catwalk. He regained his footing on a surge of raw, cold adrenaline and began shoving his way toward the right end of the platform. He was met with instant resistance.

"Hey, you fraggin' lunatic!" snarled a Zabrak he tried to squeeze past. "I'm trying to watch the show!"

"Security," said Dash. "I need to get through."

"Security, my horns. I'll give you security—!"

Dash ducked out from under the Zabrak's swinging arm and scurried several yards bent double, before coming upright again. He sought the bar of shadow on the next module over. It was empty. Whoever had been standing there, whoever Eaden had seen, was gone.

Dash pushed forward, but the music had changed: a deep, sonorous note overlaid with a persistent and persuasive drumbeat had the crowd swaying in ragged unison. The holographic Javul had gone into another sinuous dance, seeming to bend herself around the Helix.

Dash pushed his way to the rail, seeking an access to the security catwalk. He lifted his gaze to the far platform and saw Eaden plunging along it, bodily lifting resistant members of the audience out of his way. His gaze was fixed on Module 3C. Dash hesitated, desperate to see what the Nautolan was looking at. This time, he saw it—a huge Anomid moving through the crowd and toward the rail. He was approaching Oto's position on the security walk below.

Dash pulled out his comlink and called the droid. "Oto! It's Edge! Above you on the platform!"

The droid's movement slowed. "Above me, sir?"

"Yes, blast it! Yes! Directly above you!" Dash reached an access to his own security walk and fed in the passcode.

"Thank you, sir."

Over on 3C, Oto had stopped and reached up to open the access panel to his own walkway.

"Wait, Oto!" Dash shouted. "*Wait!*"

The access panel opened just as Edge reached it. Without the least hesitation, the Anomid dropped down onto the catwalk next to the droid. Oto backed up a step, releasing the access panel. It slammed shut. He stood, frozen in apparent mechanical confusion, as Edge drew a large-bore dart shooter from his belt and aimed at the holographic Javul as if he could see the real woman at the heart of the projection.

Dash swung himself over the gallery railing and onto the gridded covering of the security walk, drawing his blaster as he went. His boots clattered and slid on the durasteel surface as he touched down. He teetered and gasped in the cool night air—there was nothing between him and the clouds below. There was no time to aim; he fired wildly at the Anomid, feeling an instant's gratitude for the lack of recoil. Firing a slugthrower might have sent him backward over the walk's edge.

The bolt went wide, but it distracted the assassin— made him hesitate before he fired his dart. It flew . . . and disappeared into the hologram.

A second later the projected Javul's face contorted in fear. Her dance cut off in midmotion, and she screamed. Her shrill of terror, amplified through the elaborate stage system, flayed every nerve in Dash's body. He scuttled along the top of the security catwalk, forcibly shutting out the sudden unrest of the crowd. Was this part of the performance? they would wonder. Was this one of her dramatic selections, or was something wrong?

Mel would know immediately, of course, that something was wrong, but Dash had no idea what he'd do in response. Nor was there any time to communicate. He and Eaden had to proceed as if there were no backup. Even now, they were converging on the spot where the Anomid assassin stood. Dash, his DL-22 in both hands, was running, ignoring the hundreds of meters of empty, mist-shrouded space below, insensible to anything but that big, deadly Anomid. The end of the catwalk seemed an interminable distance away.

Edge tilted his masked face toward Dash, his strange orange eyes gleaming. For a split second, Dash was sure he was going to turn a weapon on him. But he didn't. Instead he sketched a taunting salute, then threw one leg over the railing of the security walk.

What the hell was he doing?

It was only as he drew nearer the end of his own catwalk that Dash realized that a cable of thin, laminasteel filament now connected the assassin to the goddess-sized Javul—or, rather, to the structure she stood on. The dart hadn't been intended to kill, only to provide him a means to get closer to his target. To get within striking distance. Because he liked to kill at close range.

Shouting like a berserker, Dash pounded the last few meters to the end of the catwalk, his boots ringing the steel cage like a tuneless bell. Edge swung the other leg over the railing.

Blast! He would never make it in time.

Eaden, uttering a freakish sound that would have put the fear of the Force into a bull wampa, flew out of nowhere to land gracefully atop the 3C security walk, no more than a meter from Edge. The assassin barely flinched, but it was enough to allow the teräs käsi master to dive, catch the edge of the catwalk roof, and swing his long legs in a swift arc that ended in Edge's midsection. The Anomid was bowled backward over the rail. His dart gun—a heavy Velocity-7—rattled to the catwalk floor, half dangling by the cable he'd run out to the crystal Helix.

Dash dared a glance in that direction and saw that the holographic Javul was intent on something—her eyes were fixed on it, her movements suggested she was making her way toward it. Dash figured it must be the dart. But why? Why didn't she just use her antigrav harness to get herself to safety?

He brought his attention back to where Eaden was now facing off against Edge. He stumbled to a halt and raised his pistol, praying for a clear shot.

The Anomid reached over his back and drew the Morgukai cortosis staff; its business end lit up like a torch as he swung it at the Nautolan . . . who simply wasn't there when the staff reached the target. Eaden had leapt to the rail again and into something like the Sleeping Krayt position Dash had seen him perform in meditation. But there was nothing sleepy or meditative about this. With his forearm serving as a pivot, the adept swept torso and legs about, catching his opponent beneath the jaw and flinging him against the rear of the catwalk.

Edge went down. Eaden landed softly next to him and

kicked the cortosis staff aside. The assassin responded by grasping at the Nautolan's legs, but again there was nothing there to grasp—Eaden had flipped himself backward, coming to his feet next to the dart gun. He reached for the weapon, but Edge was already up and coming at him, his clawlike Kerestian darkstick in hand.

Unable to get a clear shot at the assassin, Dash rushed forward again, calculating the distance he'd have to clear to reach the other catwalk.

Eaden crouched.

In the time it took Dash to reach the end of the roof grating, Eaden had leapt straight up, grasped the grillwork above his head, and punched both feet into the Anomid's masked face. The thirty-centimeter-long poison-tipped claw swept harmlessly beneath him. He dropped to the catwalk, grasped Edge's wrist, and twisted.

There was a grinding sound that Dash could hear even over the crowd noise and the sound of his own passage—then the Anomid grunted and dropped the darkstick. Eaden scooped it up and tossed it behind him.

Dash reached the end of his metal road and launched himself toward the other catwalk. In the blur of flight, he saw Edge reach for another weapon with his free hand. Eaden anticipated him and blocked the movement with a forearm, then performed a move that Dash, sighting his landing spot, did not see but heard well enough.

There was the solid sound of a well-placed kick, the rattle of something hitting the metal floor of the walk. As Dash landed, the Anomid assassin was rolling to a stop several meters from where he'd started out. He rose, casting a glance at Oto, who was standing, stone-still, against the rear of the catwalk bare centimeters away. The droid began to inch his way toward Eaden's end of the catwalk. Edge shadowed him.

Puzzled, Dash swung himself from the roof into the catwalk, alighting about two meters behind Eaden. The

Nautolan said nothing, but gestured at the dart shooter hanging over the railing.

Yeah, if he could eliminate that avenue of escape . . .

He moved toward the dart shooter, intending to disengage the cable. He'd just picked it up when several things happened at once: Edge charged, Eaden leapt to meet him, and Oto scrambled around behind the Nautolan to get out of the way. The two warriors met in a tremendous collision, both flung backward by the encounter. Edge caught his balance against the catwalk railing; Eaden staggered back into Oto, then fell heavily to the steel decking.

He landed on his back, but instead of flipping back to his feet as Dash had seen him do with great grace any number of times, he gasped and writhed, his body contorting in a horrific seizure.

Dash hurled the dart shooter over the railing, then dropped to his knees at Eaden's side. Reaching beneath the fallen Nautolan, his hand met the hard, cold hilt of the darkstick, slick with Eaden's blood. Dash felt as if all the warmth had been sucked from his body. He looked up at Oto.

"Help him, you kriffing tin pot!"

The words had no more than left his lips when he caught movement from the corner of his eye. He glanced up to see Edge standing farther down the catwalk with a second dart shooter in his hand. Dash reached for his pistol, but the Anomid paid him no heed. He swung himself up and over the railing and fired a second dart into the holographic image of Javul Charn. The cable played out.

Dash aimed and fired, but the assassin was gone, swinging through the air at the end of his laminasteel tether. As Dash watched, he disappeared into the hologram.

Oto hadn't moved.

"I said *help him*," Dash repeated. Gritting his teeth, he pulled the darkstick's claw-like blade from Eaden's back, knowing that it was too late. He looked down into his friend's face as the droid finally responded. Eaden's eyes were deep, dark pools of agony.

"Javul . . . ," Eaden mouthed.

"Yes, but you . . ."

He shook his head feebly. "Leave me."

"I can't—"

Eaden heaved himself onto one elbow and used the other arm to shove Dash backward.

"Go!"

Dash hesitated, glancing at Oto, now down on his spindly metal knees. The droid seemed indecisive. "I'm not programmed as a medical droid."

Eaden raised a hand to Dash's arm. "Dead . . . already." His voice was barely a whisper.

"I'm . . . I'm sorry," Dash whispered. But Eaden could no longer hear him.

He left Eaden in Oto's metal arms and scrambled to the railing. The holographic Javul loomed above him, her body twisted in a defensive posture, her eyes wide and bright with terror.

Why hasn't she fled to safety?

Maybe her harness had failed, stranding her on the Helix. Even as the thought crossed his mind, the holographic image winked out, leaving only the terrifying reality: out in the center of the module, the great crystal spiral had begun to swing from its suspension guy wire, propelled by the force of Edge's leap. The assassin clung to one of the lower treads of the Helix, crawling to more solid footing. Above him by seven or eight meters, Javul was already climbing toward the top of the piece. But when she got there, there would be no place for her to go.

Dash swore. He'd thrown the first grapple over. No doubt it was dangling somewhere below, but he couldn't see it. The distance between him and the Helix was ever-changing. He swung up onto the rail. The Helix was on its outward arc now, but if he waited until it neared the end of its inward journey, he might make it.

No, he *would* make it. He would.

He had to.

He shut everything out of his mind except that glittering mass of fake crystal. The roar and scream of the crowd, the scent of their fear, the vibrations their panic sent through the framework beneath him—all faded as he focused his entire being on that swinging spiral stair. It reached the end of its outward trip and swung back. Dash was vaguely aware of Javul making her way slowly toward the top of the structure, of Edge moving up from below. Dash's muscles tensed, and pinpricks of light danced before his eyes.

He was aware only of the gleaming pendulum as it flashed toward him. Then it was beneath him, slowing . . .

He jumped.

His feet hit first, landing him on the narrow inner lip of a translucent tread. He flung himself forward, face-first, grasping at the smooth surface with desperate fingers.

Fortunately the transparisteel wasn't as slick as it looked. He grabbed the center post of the spiral with both hands and hauled himself upright. The force of his landing had lent more momentum to the swing of the Helix—Dash felt the wind rushing past him as he strove to orient himself. He was between Javul and Edge on the structure, closer to the assassin than to his target.

He braced himself against the stair and drew his blaster, peering down through the transparent struts and lacy treads, trying to see what the Anomid was doing. He had a weapon in his hand—Dash couldn't tell what it was. Something small. It wasn't until Edge leaned back and cocked one thick arm that Dash realized it was one of those throwing razors.

He pointed his blaster down and fired.

The crystal Helix may have looked delicate and lacy,

but it was not. It deflected the energy bolt and showered his adversary with molten bits of transparisteel, causing him to flinch momentarily. Edge made no reaction when he looked up and saw Dash crouched above him, and Dash realized he had only managed to postpone the inevitable for a few seconds. Once the spatter of molten steel had ceased, Edge cocked his arm again and threw the razor.

TWENTY-FIVE

DASH WATCHED THE RODIAN THROWING RAZOR FLASH past his position on the swinging staircase—followed the shallow curve of its arc upward. Above him, Javul continued to climb. She hadn't seen it. In a moment, however—if he didn't do something—she would definitely feel it.

Dash raised his blaster again and shouted, "Javul! Under the steps!"

She glanced down at him, saw the gun in his hand and ducked beneath the treads above her.

Dash peered up at the razor. It was slowing, reaching the top of its arc about four meters above Javul's head. He eyeballed the arc, led the thing with his pistol. No big deal. Easier than shooting snake bats on Naboo's swampy moon. With the bats, you had to guess where they were going to be in a split second, and then you—

Dash fired. The razor exploded in a shower of sparks, shooting shrapnel in all directions. Dash felt something sting his cheek and scorch a trail along his neck. His right eye burned and watered. He ignored the pain and turned his attention back to Edge.

He drew in a hiss of breath. The assassin had used his enemy's focus on the razor to get closer—at least three meters closer. As Dash watched, blinking, the assassin pulled another razor from his belt.

The spiral was near the center point of its arc. Dash thrust his blaster grip between his teeth and scrambled

upward. He got about two meters higher when the tilt of
the structure became too much to manage. As he grasped
the tread above him, hooking his foot around the center
post to keep from falling, Edge threw the second razor.

This time Javul saw it coming and tucked herself tightly
beneath the treads above her. She was tearing at her
jacket with one hand. Dash prayed that meant she had a
weapon, but he was disappointed. Instead, she pulled the
jacket off and wadded it up. Was she going to try the same
trick she'd pulled with the robe? No way it would work.

Dash glanced back at Edge. The masked humanoid
was on the move again, drawing closer with every lunge
of his long, pale body.

Blast!

Dash took quick and shaky aim and fired down at the
Anomid, stopping his upward progress. But the razor . . .

He glanced up—cursing his right eye, which was all but
blind now—to see Javul fling both jacket and antigrav
harness away from her. He tried to focus, realizing that the
lack of depth perception was going to be his downfall. The
razor adjusted course subtly to track the jacket. It acquired
the target and sliced into it, missing Javul by mere centimeters and carrying her shredded gear back to its master.
Just as the razor reached Edge and he put out his hand
to retrieve it, Dash leaned out from the Helix and fired
another blaster volley. It struck the treads very near the
assassin's masked head and sheared off a bit of slag.

Edge jerked his arm up to cover his eyes—and the razor bit him. It caught him in the right shoulder, spraying
blood onto the bright crystalline surfaces. Then it plummeted, uncaught, to the planetoid's surface far below.
The watching crowd roared.

Dash expelled a gust of pent-up breath.

Someone fired a blaster from the sidelines. The bolt of
energy hit the swinging structure just above Edge's head
with the inevitable results.

Dash wanted to cheer.

There was another bolt, this one closer. Dash took aim again, himself . . . just as the stage lights went out, plunging the performance quad into darkness.

"Oh, that's not good," Dash muttered.

He fired anyway. The bolt momentarily lit up the crystal stair, allowing him to see that Edge was in motion again, climbing inexorably toward them. And, as if that weren't bad enough, people continued to fire from the catwalks. Only now they couldn't see what they were shooting at. In fact, when he looked up to see if he could find Javul, he could swear someone was firing at the guy wire that secured the spiral.

He had more pressing concerns—he realized he could see Javul very well, indeed, despite his weeping eye. Her hair and lenses were glowing—emitting a rainbow of light and making her far too obvious a target. As if realizing this, she tore off the wig and dropped it, but the lenses were problematic. They gave Edge something to aim for and he was coming straight up the pike—Dash could see him as a moving body of darkness illuminated slightly by the lights from the station and silhouetted dully against the roil of the planetoid's poisonous atmosphere. His continued silence, despite his wounds and effort, added to the overall eeriness.

Dash swore and fired again. And again. An answering bolt from the sidelines nearly parted his hair. "Hey! I'm the good guy!" he shouted, as if anyone had a chance of hearing him.

He tried to holster his weapon, but the swinging staircase bucked suddenly as if it had hit something. In the darkness, clinging to the thing for support, he missed the holster. The blaster fell away, disappearing as soon as it left his hand. He leapt upward, grasping the treads above him and hauling himself toward Javul as fast as he could go. What he'd do when he got there was anybody's guess, but her gleaming eyes beckoned to him.

He reached her, got an arm around her, tried to shield her with his body.

"Close your eyes," he told her, "and listen."

She did.

"They've got to be trying to get us off this blasted thing," he murmured in her ear. "And we're not defenseless yet. I've still got this." He pulled his hold-out blaster—a compact Q2—and pressed it momentarily against Javul's hand so she'd know what it was.

She nodded. "Where is he?" she whispered, her voice almost lost in the flow of wind around the Helix's convolutions.

"About three meters below us." He wished he could have her open her eyes and project some light from the holo-emitters in her lenses, so he could see exactly where. But that was a bad idea, of course.

Unlesss . . .

He glanced up at her face. In the dim light of the station it was tense and drawn. "Javul, listen. Tilt your head down about two centimeters. Right there. When I say *open,* open your eyes and project something, then close them again immediately, okay?"

"I'm disconnected from the control board. I don't have anything to project."

"Doesn't have to be anything specific. Just light." He didn't tell her he couldn't see well enough from his right eye to make out more than light, shapes, and movement.

She made a soft sound of assent.

He looked down at the assassin's silhouette, drawing inexorably closer. "Come on, you ugly son-of-a-tairn," he told Edge. "Come *on*!"

Two meters below them, the Anomid drew a vibroblade. Dash could see the blade's edge as a haloed blur, feel the prickle of energy in the air.

The hold-out blaster would do no good until the assassin reached the spot on which Javul had trained her eyes. Until then he would be shielded by the curve of the stairs.

Dash found himself counting seconds as he swung, half blind, through the air. The Helix bucked again. What was that? Dash couldn't let himself be distracted. He had to time this just right.

The Anomid rounded the curve of the spiral one meter below.

"Now!" Dash shouted.

Javul opened her eyes and directed their holographic blaze directly at the spot where Edge clung. She was a bit off, so that the light caught the Anomid at about shoulder level, but she quickly adjusted so that she was looking directly into his eyes and he into hers.

Dash fired. The bolt from the Q2 hit the Anomid's body armor and was deflected, though not without inflicting a bit of damage. He fired again. A clean hit to the same spot.

Edge loomed just below them now. Clinging to the Helix with his legs, he reared back, now with a vibroblade in each hand. Javul opened her eyes again and, for a breath, the assassin was caught in the blaze of her regard before the knives descended.

Dash had one charge left in the Q2. He aimed, willing his hand to be steady—

As he squeezed the trigger, the assassin swept upward with one long arm, lunging as he did. He caught the muzzle of the hold-out blaster with the vibroblade's tip and knocked it away, his blade continuing downward to slice through the calf of Dash's boot and into his flesh. Dash roared in pain and jerked his legs upward.

The masked face loomed over him, eyes blazing. Edge raised both vibroblades and—

The ululating sound that cut through the air was one

Dash had expected never to hear again. For a split second he thought Edge was making it. But then the Anomid was broadsided by another large body. Dash recognized the mass of tresses and the huge, seemingly lidless eyes of a Nautolan.

"*Never* turn your back on an enemy," Eaden rasped as his arm came around the assassin's neck. "Especially a dead one." Then the momentum of his attack broke Edge's hold, and carried both men off the crystal Helix and into the darkness below.

Javul closed her eyes, her body going limp beneath Dash's. They swung back and forth in the dark for several more moments before the Helix trembled yet again, then tilted crazily, finally coming to a stop on an off-kilter diagonal, its lower end at last tethered by a grapple.

"It's over," murmured Javul.

Dash barely heard her. His one good eye was trying to find the spot in the moonlit gray cloud-tops below where Eaden Vrill and the assassin had fallen. He hoped that his friend had died before he hit the ground.

TWENTY-SIX

"THAT WAS A PAID ASSASSIN. WHICH ONE OF YOU HAS A price on his or her head?"

In the backstage lounge, Arno D'Vox held court, his security chief at his side and a couple of armed guards flanking the door that Dash was eyeing nervously. Dash and Javul, injuries patched—including a temporary one on his right eye—and nerves minimally restored, sat side by side on a padded bench along an inner wall. Yanus Melikan stood near the balcony doors staring out at the devastation. He'd sent everyone else to safety. The *Deep Core* was gone—spirited away during the fracas, Bacrana-bound.

Arno D'Vox and his security chief were both grim with rage—D'Vox probably more so because Rishyk had warned him against honoring Javul's request to moor the tank modules together. Their indignation was righteous to some degree. Their crew's attempts to lash down the crystal Helix had resulted in damage to several of the station's platforms, and the façades of all the units showed scorch marks from errant blasterfire.

D'Vox repeated his question.

Dash and Javul exchanged glances, then Dash mumbled, "Ask her."

D'Vox moved to tower over Javul. Rishyk continued to glower at Dash as if he was counting the seconds until he could tear him apart. Dash hardly cared what Security Chief Rishyk was counting. He was holding in a roil of violent emotions, none of which he wanted to examine more closely. Rage, loss, fear . . . if D'Vox and Rishyk got it into their heads to hold Javul, her mission was over.

And Eaden would have died for nothing but revenge.

Nothing but revenge.

There'd been a time—maybe five minutes ago—when Dash would've thought revenge was a fine reason to die. Hadn't he occasionally contemplated revenge on Xizor and Black Sun? In the final analysis, hadn't that played into his decision to take this job with Javul's tour? Hadn't he liked the idea that he'd heroically protect her from Black Sun's mistaken identification? And when that had turned out to be no mistake at all, hadn't he welcomed the opportunity to get back at a Black Sun Vigo? Hadn't he been downright tickled when he discovered that she'd hurt Xizor's operation in the quadrant?

Dash might easily have died seeking revenge. Instead, Eaden—stoic, rational Eaden—had done it. And if his Nautolan friend were standing in front of him right now, what would Dash say to him?

He shook his head. That ship had spaced. The only person he could counsel about revenge now was himself, and his counsel would be: Revenge is a zero-sum game. *Everybody* loses.

He glanced over at Javul, watched her meet D'Vox's intimidation eye-to-eye. He could tell himself that Eaden had died to save her, but deep down inside he knew that Javul's involvement had only given Eaden permission to live for a few minutes before he died. That, and to take Edge down with him.

"Well, Javul," said D'Vox, his voice a threatening growl, "I'm asking. Can you explain to me why you had a Grade A assassin after your pretty head?"

She looked him right in the eye and said, "Prince Xizor."

Dash turned to stare at her. What the hell was she doing?

D'Vox straightened, his face going blank for a second. "What's Xizor got to do with any of this?"

"You asked why the guy was after me. I'm telling you." Dash wriggled uncomfortably. "Javul . . ."

Rishyk raised his blaster and aimed it at Dash's head. "Shut up and let her talk."

"It's like this: I was engaged to marry one of Xizor's Vigos. A guy named Hitch Kris. Maybe you've heard of him."

"Yeah, I've heard of him," said D'Vox. "What's this got to do with—"

"I'm getting to that, okay? I was engaged to this Vigo and I broke it off. He tried to get me back and he . . . did some dumb things to mess up my tours, like smuggling—"

"What're you doing?" Dash asked sharply. "Don't bring Black Sun into this."

Rishyk stepped past D'Vox and backhanded Dash across the face with his pistol hand, toppling him off the couch and onto the floor. "I said: *shut up!*"

Great, now *both* his cheeks hurt. And now Javul was glaring at him, too, gripping the edge of the sofa until her knuckles were white.

"Black Sun is *already* in it, Dash. Xizor is in it. Up to his neck." She raised her eyes to D'Vox again, while Dash wiped blood from a split lip. "They were running contraband in my ship. Turning me into a mule for their secret business. I decided I was tired of being the only one who wasn't benefiting from the situation. So, I decided to . . . take things into my own hands."

Dash gaped at her. *What?*

He got it when D'Vox's eyes widened, showing a combination of unease and respect. "You stole from Black Sun?"

"Let's just say I took a cut. Xizor didn't like it. He made

Hitch pay out of his own deep pockets. Which, well . . ."
She smiled. "Let's just say Hitch wasn't too happy with
me, either."

"Which one hired Edge?" growled Rishyk. He spoke
to Javul, but his eyes were still on Dash, as if he was just
waiting for the other man to do something stupid that
he could punish him for.

"We don't know," Dash mumbled. "All we know is
that when their attempt to kill her on Rodia failed, they
got sore and blew up the venue she was performing in."

Okay, a bit of a stretch, but it had the desired effect.
Both D'Vox and Rishyk took a semi-step back from Javul
as if they suddenly didn't want to be quite so close to her.

"We came here because we thought it was safer," added
Javul. "We figured with the Imperial presence here, they
wouldn't try anything. I guess we were wrong."

"So," said D'Vox after a moment of thought, "if we
turn you over to Xizor, everyone is happy, right? Well,
except you two, of course."

Dash nearly groaned aloud. That was not the desired
effect. He glanced at Mel, who had turned from his view
of the balcony to listen. Mel gave Javul a look and
reached up to scratch the back of his neck.

"In case you hadn't noticed," Javul said quietly, "Xizor
is not asking to have me turned over to him. He's trying
to kill me and he doesn't much care who comes along for
the ride. His agents are probably somewhere on the station already. They'll know that Edge failed, of course . . ."

Rishyk growled like a dog and made a frustrated gesture. "Let's get them off the station, D'Vox, before Black
Sun takes their failure out on us."

That's more like it.

D'Vox was shaking his head. "No, we can make sun-
shine out of this, I'm sure of it. We just need to let Xizor
and Kris know that we've got their pretty little playmate.
I have to hand it to you, though, girl. You've got some

amazing gall to pull this sort of thing off in such a public way."

She smiled at him, but Dash could see the fear in her eyes. "Thank you. But I've also got an amazing amount of credits to my name. Enough to make you very forgetful about everything that's happened."

D'Vox was shaking his head again, which caused Rishyk to get right up in his face—literally standing nose-to-nose with him.

"Blast you, D'Vox! What are you playing at? You're commander of an Imperial fracking fuel dump on the backside of nowhere. You do *not* want to get directly involved with Black Sun. Turning a blind eye to their business here is one thing, but doing business *with* them is suicide. I say we take the credits she's offering and get them off the station."

"And *I* say—" D'Vox began, but they never heard what he was going to say because at that moment the chamber doors hissed open.

The two guards, who'd been focusing their entire attention on the argument, were taken completely unawares when Dara and Nik appeared, both armed with a blaster in each hand. To the kid's credit, his hands didn't even shake. He held his blasters steadily on the party in the room while Spike ran the show.

"Everyone just drop your weapons, okay?"

Rishyk's blaster muzzle wavered slightly.

"Oh, I wouldn't do that if I were you," said a voice from the other side of the room. "I just had the firing mechanism on this old piece of mine fixed and I'm not quite comfortable with the new trigger action yet." Han Solo stood in the balcony doorway. His "old piece" was aimed at Rishyk's midsection. "Pulls a bit easier than I'm used to."

The DL-44 "accidentally" went off, drilling a smoking hole in the bulkhead right beside Rishyk, who flinched.

"Okay," Han continued, "it pulls a *lot* easier. Sorry; I'll try'n make sure it doesn't happen again."

Mel was armed now as well, with a hold-out blaster that had appeared magically out of the collar of his jacket. Spike relieved the guards, D'Vox, and Rishyk of their weapons, then marched them into the refresher. She closed the doors, fused the controls with a blast from her pistol, then herded Javul and Dash toward the balcony.

"We've got all kinds of chatter on Imperial bands," she told Javul. "Something's shaking and we can't afford to get caught up in it."

As Dash limped across the threshold and stepped out into the night, he saw that Han had brought the *Millennium Falcon* right up the central core of the station's re-arranged modules. She hovered at balcony height, her hatch wide open and spilling welcoming light across the duracrete surface. They were aboard within thirty seconds. Han relieved Leebo of the pilot's seat and dropped them down out of the station core. They hurtled into hyperspace the moment they were clear of the planet's gravity well.

"Can I have a word?" Dash stood in the hatchway of the *Millennium Falcon*'s "guest" quarters, his eyes watchfully on the two women who sat, cross-legged, on the bunks facing each other.

If he'd come across them in another setting, under other circumstances, he'd have said they looked like a couple of girlfriends—one consoling the other after a tragic breakup. It was hard to believe that less than half an hour ago Javul had been literally a knife's edge away from death.

Spike made a crooked grimace and pointed at Javul. "A word with her, you mean?"

He nodded.

The obviously weary road manager rose from her bunk

and moved past him out the door. "Don't freak her out any more than she is already," she warned him. "And don't take too long. We both need to sleep."

He nodded, slipping into the room to sit next to Javul on her bunk. "Hey," she said. He thought her eyes were wary, haunted.

"You okay?" he asked. "I mean, really okay? That was . . . tough . . . out there."

"Me? Are *you*? I mean, you . . ." She put her hand over his where it rested on his thigh. "I'm so sorry. About Eaden. He was . . . he was . . ." A tear ran down her cheek. She tried to wipe it away and missed.

Dash reached up reflexively and brushed it aside with his thumb. "I'm . . . I'll be all right. In a while. I've lost friends before. It . . ." He laughed humorlessly and shook his head.

"You were going to say it gets easier, weren't you? But it doesn't."

She sounded so sure of that, he turned his head to look at her. "Who did you lose?"

"My mother and father. When I was fourteen. We were living on Nar Shaddaa at the time."

He frowned. "I thought you were born and raised on Coruscant." Light dawned. "Cover story."

She nodded. "My younger brother, Ayx, and I went to Tatooine to live with Dara's family. Our fathers were close friends. Served together in the Republic space corps."

"Let me guess—the Imperials had something to do with it."

She nodded again. "The Imperials always have something to do with it."

"Yeah. Seems like they're at the bottom of everything dark and scary." It struck him suddenly that even Prince Xizor thought the Empire was dark and scary. He wondered if the prince was reminded of his own loss every time he had a brush with Vader or Palpatine. "What happened?" he asked.

She shrugged. "The Empire didn't want to risk an uprising. All those well-trained ex-soldiers and ex-pilots were a threat. Even if they were just farmers and merchants and musicians now, maybe someday, under the right circumstances, they could be incited to fight again. So . . ." Again, the eloquent shrug. "They got rid of them. Mom and Dad were musicians. They toured the Mid and Outer Rim. Hutt space, sometimes. Trying to keep a low profile. Wasn't low enough; Imperials staged a raid on the venue they were playing on Bothawui. When the shooting stopped, Mom and Dad and three members of their band were dead."

"I'm sorry."

"Me, too. But they knew what they were doing was dangerous. Ayx and I both understood they were doing it for us."

He peered into her face. "You're saying they were in the resistance."

"The rambling life of a musician makes a great cover for running information." She grimaced. "Mel didn't exactly recruit me. When I was old enough, I went looking for him."

"And your brother?"

"He's working with a cell on Alderaan. I was hoping I'd get to see him. If we'd been able to stick to our original plan, that might've worked out." Javul stifled a yawn. "Is your family . . . I mean, I know you lost your brother, Stanton."

"My parents are still alive . . . after a fashion. I haven't seen them for years. I'm not even sure where they are. Losing Stanton and the business at the same time . . . changed them. Changed all of us."

He felt Javul's weight against his shoulder and shifted to put his arm around her. He looked down, expecting to find the large silver eyes trained on him, filled with compassion, maybe something more—

And then her eyes slowly closed, her head became a deadweight against his arm. He sighed and lowered her gently to the bed. She didn't wake. Dash kissed her forehead, hesitated a moment, then set a kiss on her lips for good measure.

Out in the corridor, he headed immediately for the cockpit. He had to talk Han into getting them at least as far as Corellia. They'd be able to get another ship there, he was sure of it.

He found Han in the pilot's seat, hands on the steering yoke, staring moodily out into the void. He dropped into the copilot's station and succumbed to inertia.

"You can't sleep there," Han said.

The edge in the other man's voice made Dash sit up and study him. He looked grim. And who could blame him?

"Look." Dash sighed. "I know you're itching to off-load us at the earliest opportunity. You'll be rid of us as soon as we can rendezvous with the *Nova's Heart*. I wish I could tell you when that will be exactly, but I'm not in Javul's inner circle. Captain Marrak will call us when—"

"You trying to be insulting, Rendar? Why would you want the *Nova's Heart* when you've got the *Millennium Falcon*?"

"What?"

"I'm taking you to Alderaan."

Dash sat forward in the copilot's seat and studied the side of Han's face. "Why? Before, you couldn't get rid of us fast enough. What changed?"

Han was silent for a moment, then turned to look at him, his gaze impenetrable. "Y'know what I've been thinking about, sitting up here alone?"

"No."

"That empty copilot's chair." He nodded toward the seat Dash now held. "I've been thinking about how I'd feel if it was permanently empty—if it'd been Chewie out there tonight."

Dash nodded, meeting Han's eyes dead-on. No more needed to be said.

Han turned back to the view through the forward viewport. "I picked up some subspace chatter from Bannistar. They haven't retrieved the bodies yet. They think they fell into a loch on the outskirts of a refinery complex."

Dash took a deep breath. "I hope they never do find them. Edge doesn't deserve a ritual burial and Eaden . . . Eaden's at home in the water."

Several moments of silence elapsed before Han said: "That was the good news. The bad news is they've scrambled two Imperial corvettes and a Dreadnought from Bannistar to chase us down. The even worse news is there's a Star Destroyer en route from Byblos."

"Squeeze play, huh?"

Han's grin was wicked. "Not if we're not there to be squeezed. Besides, from what I can tell, they're heading for Bacrana. Of course, they'll realize we're not with the *Deep Core* at some point, but by then I hope we'll be off their star charts. After all, we could be going to any number of places." He swept Dash with a wry gaze, then added, "You look like a rancor's leftovers, Dash. Why don't you go get some chow and some sleep? I'll get us to Alderaan."

Dash *was* tired. Soul-weary, mind-numb, bone-tired. He nodded and dragged himself out of the seat.

Leebo met him as he stepped into the corridor behind the cockpit. "Where you going, boss?"

"To sleep, Leebo. I'm going to sleep. It's this thing organics do."

"I need you to take a bit of a detour first."

Dash sagged against a bulkhead. "Can it wait?"

"Not really."

"All right, but make it quick, okay? I'm about to fall asleep on my feet."

"Thanks, boss. I got something in the forward hold I think you should see."

Leebo led the way. There, amid the jumble of containers, stood Mel's Otoga 222 unit, unmoving and seemingly dormant. After a moment of inspection, Dash realized he'd been fitted with a restraining bolt.

"What's wrong with Oto?"

"That's a matter of opinion, but offhand I'd say somebody seriously tinkered with his programming."

"What do you mean—tinkered with his programming?"

"Well, boss, for one thing, while you and the lady were having your wild ride on the Helix, he was trying to shoot through your lifeline."

TWENTY-SEVEN

DASH WAS FULLY AWAKE BY THE TIME MEL RESPONDED to his hail and came forward to the cargo hold. If it pumped up Dash's adrenal gland, Leebo's revelation was enough to knock the cargo master's props out from under him. He sat down hard on his makeshift bunk, staring at his droid.

"*Oto? Oto* was shooting at the Helix tether?"

Leebo nodded, servos humming softly.

"Why? Why would he do that?"

"Maybe the same reason he picked my brain when he gave me the specs for the holo-emitters."

"Explain," said Mel.

"When we got back from getting your container, Dash had me help Oto set up the holo-emitters for the show. When Oto passed me the specs, he picked my brain—literally. He tapped my memory core to see what I'd been doing. Kind of rattled me. I mean, how *rude*."

Dash remembered the moment. "I thought it was kind of weird that you didn't jump all over him for returning that tin pot insult."

"You caught that, huh? Yeah. On top of sucking my brain, he cracked a joke. Not a terribly funny one—and not that he meant to—but still . . . that's *my* territory. Anyway, I thought it was kind of suspicious, so I kept one eye on him while I was keeping the other on the crowd. I was sure he was bad news when he let the assassin into the security walk." He looked at Dash. "Frankly, I was surprised you didn't blast him to metal shavings right then and there."

Dash felt blank. "I just thought he was going to try to . . ."

"To what—shoot the guy? He couldn't shoot the guy. For one thing, he wasn't armed. For another, his programming isn't *that* twisted. He was giving the assassin better access to his target."

Dash recalled the scene: him telling the droid Edge was right above him on the platform; the droid thanking him politely and turning to open the catwalk; his sudden reluctance to act. Dash had assumed he was merely out of his element. "Whoa, wait, hold up," he said. "You're saying that *Oto* is the saboteur?"

Mel was shaking his head. "That's not possible. Whoever did all of that put Javul—and everyone else—in harm's way time and again. You said it yourself, he's still programmed not to harm sentients."

"Not *directly*," corrected Leebo. "And he didn't. Not once."

"You're right," murmured Dash, mentally running back through the series of incidents—the rain of lilies, the enabling of the false hull breach, the sabotaging of the irising stage door on Rodia, the setup of the gravity failure in the cargo bay. "None of it was direct. He didn't pull the trigger, he just supplied the ammunition."

"Yeah," Leebo agreed. "Or left the door wide open."

Mel rose and moved to stare at the Otoga 222. "All right. Let's say he did do all of it. How do you account for the seemingly dual agenda—one to discourage, one to harm?"

"I'm clueless," Leebo admitted. "Why don't we ask him?"

Mel, looking grimmer than Dash had ever seen him,

checked the restraining bolt, reached for the master re-activation toggle—then stopped and checked the bolt again. Only then did he reactivate the droid.

The large hemispherical optics lit up. Dash had the impression of someone caught napping. Oto's servos whined, his digits clacked, he looked from one of his interrogators to the other. "May I be of assistance?"

"You can," said Mel. "You can tell us who you're working for."

"I am working for you, Cargo Master Melikan. And, of course, for Javul Charn."

"No. I mean who programmed you to sabotage Javul's tour?"

"You would have to be more specific, sir. To which particular sabotage do you refer?"

Mel's eyes widened. He sent Dash an incredulous glance.

Dash nodded. Suddenly everything made sense. Well, most of it. Or at least *some* of it . . . "Oto, if I under-stand you, you were programmed by different parties with different agendas."

"Yes, sir. That is correct."

"All right—who's who? Start with this: somebody wanted you to frighten Javul to get her to behave in a particular way, right?"

"Correct. Vigo Hityamun Kris wished Mistress Charn to cease working—as he first suspected—to unseat Prince Xizor. He felt she was placing herself in harm's way. And he wanted her to return to his sphere of influence. I was required to perform such sabotage as would effect this result either by inducing fear or by throwing the tour off schedule such that she could not complete it."

"By, for example, sabotaging the gravity grid in the cargo hold?"

"Yes, sir. That is a very good example."

"But someone else wanted her stopped permanently."

"You are again correct, sir. An Imperial agent programmed me to spy on Mistress Charn and to gather evidence that she was a Rebel operative. And since such evidence existed, they wished me to enable their efforts to stop her. To capture her, if possible, at a point that would cause the most widespread damage to the Rebellion."

Mel paled visibly. "Such as when we deliver the package."

"That would be most reasonable to assume."

Dash blew out a gust of air. "That must have been some programming job to get around your safety protocols. How did they—?"

"I wasn't finished, Security Chief Rendar. There is one more party involved."

"What? Who?"

"Prince Xizor. He, too, had me programmed to enable his efforts to stop Mistress Charn. It is Prince Xizor who wishes her dead."

Dash's jaw dropped. "You're joking."

"No, sir. I am not programmed for humor."

"You can say that again," muttered Leebo.

"I am not programmed for humor," repeated Oto obediently.

Dash raised his hands to stop Leebo from further comment. "How was all this accomplished, Oto?" he asked. "How could they get to you?"

"Hityamun Kris originally had me reprogrammed during my scheduled maintenance prior to the second half of our last tour."

"But how did he get his programmer access to you?" Mel asked. "I've known our Otoga specialist for almost a decade. I would have sworn he was completely trustworthy."

"Yes, sir. But he was unaware that anyone else had been allowed to tamper with my subroutines."

"Who *was* aware, Oto?" Mel asked. "Who brought the Vigo's programmer in?"

"First Mate Finnick, sir."

Mel swore. Loudly. Violently. "Bran? Gods of Chaos! How the hell did they get to him?"

"I don't know, sir."

"Is he an active agent?" asked Mel. "Has he been aiding you in your sabotage?"

"I don't know if he's an active agent, sir. He has not communicated with me or aided me in my programmed assignments. He merely facilitated my reprogramming."

"How did Xizor get into the act?" Dash asked the droid.

"*Into the act,* sir? I was unaware of any theatrical aspect to—"

"How did he gain access to you?"

"The programmer was aware of Prince Xizor's interest in Javul Charn. He made the underlord aware that he had compromised my programming. The prince then used the subroutines he installed to piggyback his own suggestions for my activity. Mostly this involved what he called *upping the ante*. I would do what Hityamun Kris required of me and a bit more. And I would give Xizor's operatives access to our effects."

"And the Empire?"

"The Imperial Security Bureau connected with me through the *Nova's Heart,* sir. Via subspace messages. Of course, the previous programming alterations made their task easier."

Mel grew even more pale. "The signal from Rodian space control to the ship's AI."

"Yes, sir. That was one of their avenues of access."

"Wait," said Dash. "You said the Empire didn't want Javul dead. *Xizor* wanted her dead." More revenge.

"Yes, sir. That was my assessment based on my instruction set."

"Then Edge was hired by Xizor?"

Oto tilted his ovoid head, his optics flashing. "I . . . am uncertain, Chief Rendar. There has been a great deal of . . . meddling with my software. But it does stand to reason."

Dash and Mel exchanged glances.

Dash said, "I wonder if Xizor knows he failed."

"Of course he knows, sir," said Oto reasonably. "That was part of my instructions as well, from both Xizor and the ISB. And I am to transmit our location as soon as we drop out of hyperspace."

Dash, Mel, and Leebo all moved at once. Leebo got there first and flipped Oto's OFF switch, sending the droid back into dormancy.

Mel looked at Dash. "Bran knows we're rendezvousing with the *Nova's Heart*. Somehow we've got to get a message to Captain Marrak—let him know he's got a spy on board—without tipping off Bran."

"Excuse me," said Leebo, "but isn't Finnick also communications officer?"

"Yes. Yes he is."

"Well, that complicates things a mite."

Dash was thoughtful, his mind working swiftly through the connections, expectations, and agendas of all the parties involved. "Maybe. Or maybe it simplifies them . . . for us."

TWENTY-EIGHT

WHEN DASH AND MEL GATHERED EVERYONE IN THE cargo hold and described the convoluted set of connections that all led back to the Otoga droid, Han laughed outright.

"So we've got a Black Sun underlord and a bunch of Imperials just waiting for Oto's invitation to a party? Does that about sum it up?"

"I fail to see the humor in the situation," said Spike. "If Leebo hadn't been so observant . . ."

"What d'you mean you don't see the humor? Can't you just imagine what would happen if a Black Sun frigate and an Imperial Dreadnought popped out of hyperspace in the same spot? I'd *pay* to see that."

"You may not have to," said Dash.

Spike turned to stare at him. "You deactivated the droid, right? He can't send the signal if he's deactivated."

"Yeah. But I think we should let him send it."

Han met Dash's gaze and grinned. "Are you thinking what I'm thinking?"

"We drop out of hyperspace with Oto deactivated and send Captain Marrak a message about his mole," Dash said.

"Then we reactivate the droid and let him send his signal."

Dash nodded. "Then we jump to lightspeed again and go—"

"To coordinates we'll share only with Captain Marrak," finished Javul.

Han frowned. "Why? I told you—I'll take you all the way to Alderaan."

"We may need someone to run interference for us. Draw the dogs off. Serdor's good at that."

"How're you going to get a message to the captain without Finnick intercepting it?" asked Dash.

"All the cells of the Rebel Alliance have a shared code," Mel answered. "We can use that to let him know about the spy in his crew."

"Won't Finnick know the code?"

"Bran Finnick isn't part of our cell," said Javul. "Not everyone on the crew is, even though I thought we'd vetted everyone pretty well. Finnick was Republic. No sign of any connection to Black Sun. Apparently, Hitch got to him somehow."

Dash snorted. "I bet I can guess how."

Javul shook her head, walking a slow circle around the dormant Oto. "I don't get it. Oto's been compromised since sometime last year. He's been leaving our flank open to attack at every turn and hiding his activities. Yet he just opened up to you and told you everything. Why didn't he tell us before?"

"If you knew anything about programming," Leebo said, "you wouldn't have to ask."

Javul arched a perfect eyebrow and waited.

"It's simple. Nobody asked him a direct question."

Mel laughed mirthlessly. "And why would you? Who'd suspect a droid of playing three ends against the middle?"

They overshot Bacrana, holding to a course that swung them to Galactic East toward Cyrillia. Between Cyrillia and Rhommamool they dropped from hyperspace to send a coded message to the *Nova's Heart*. The message was: *We're departing from our charted course under restrictive conditions. Material acquired. Will contact you.*

Dash, sitting next to Javul at the subspace communications console in the forward circuitry bay, watched her send the coded characters. "I don't get it. Where's the hidden message?"

"It's called a URC," said Javul, "which is a sort of an acronym for 'you are compromised.' Literally a three-word sequence that begins with *U, R,* and *C*."

"So how do they know Finnick is the source of the compromise?"

"The first word after the URC." Javul nodded at the screen.

"Uh . . . *material*." He shrugged. Then, "Oh! *Mate*. Is that it? You want Marrak to see *mate* within *material*?"

"Exactly. Now the question is: what will he do about it? He may elect to leave Finnick in place and just alert the other operatives in the group or he may decide to stow him in the cargo hold."

"What do you think he'll do?"

"I'd almost be willing to bet that he'll leave him in place. Finnick may have just been paid to perform a simple task—or he may be an active agent regardless of the fact that Oto wasn't aware of him as such. Hitch might be expecting to hear from him."

The message sent, they jumped back into hyperspace, heading even farther from their charted course toward the Circarpous system.

"Why there?" Dash asked Han as they prepared for the next stage of their plan.

"Because it's a busy system. It gets a lot of traffic *and* it'll set us up for a fast run through a pretty sparsely populated region that's off the beaten path . . . plus it gives us a straight shot to Alderaan."

Javul poked her head into the cockpit. "Leebo's ready to bring Oto back online on your mark, Han."

Dash rose from the copilot's seat. "I'd better go back then, just in case the tin can's got some more surprises in store for us."

"Suit yourself," Han said.

In the hold, Dash, Javul, Leebo, and Mel waited tensely for the *Millennium Falcon* to drop to sublight speed. They felt it before Han sent down the message from the cockpit, but they waited for his signal. Then, with Dash and Mel holding blasters on the Otoga unit, Leebo reactivated him, but not without the extra security of a direct connection to his dataport. It was Leebo's opinion that they should make absolutely sure he didn't send some sort of additional information or a distress call.

Oto booted up, looked around, and asked Leebo, "We have reentered realspace, have we not?"

"Reality is a matter of opinion," said Leebo philosophically. "But we're no longer in hyperspace, if that's what you're asking."

"That was my query," replied Oto. He was still for a moment, his optic half orbs dimming then brightening. Then he asked, "May I be of assistance?"

"You've sent our coordinates?"

"Yes, Chief Rendar, I have."

"Then you've done your job, Oto. Take a nap." Dash nodded at Leebo.

"I do not need a n—" Oto went silent again, his optics going dark as Leebo withdrew his interfacing digit from the other droid's dataport.

"Well? Was there any additional messaging going on there?"

Leebo shook his head, but he was tapping a metal finger against his faceplate. "No . . . he just sent the comm, but . . ."

"But what? He's a ticking time bomb? He called Darth Vader directly? What?"

"Relax," the droid said. "It was no big deal. Just a sort of odd background noise."

Mel looked at the droid sharply. "Background noise? What sort of background noise?"

As if in answer to the question, the *Millennium Falcon*'s emergency klaxon sounded, prompting a shriek from Javul. All three humans in the bay pressed their hands over their ears.

Adding to the cacophony, Han's voice blasted from the intercom: "Dash! Up here! Now! We have a problem."

Dash bolted for the cockpit, gritting his teeth against the grating blare of the horn and the ache of his wounded leg. He threw himself through the hatch and into the copilot's seat just as Han shut off the klaxon.

"What's going on? Why aren't we—?"

His eye caught on Han's "problem," then. A huge, black-hulled yacht easily three times the size of the *Millennium Falcon* hung over them like the threat of imminent doom. It had no markings on it. Glancing at the communications board, Dash could see it had not identified itself.

He swallowed. "Where'd *that* come from?"

"It just appeared there. Or just about. Dropped out of hyperspace practically on top of us."

Dash's mouth was as dry as the Jundland Wastes. "Black Sun."

Han glanced sideways at him. "Y'think?"

"Can we throw this thing in reverse and get out of here?"

"You see that weapons port, there? The one that's aimed right at me? Hi, fellas." He raised his hand and waggled his fingers at it.

Dash took a deep breath. "It's probably Xizor."

"If it's Xizor, why are we still alive? And how'd he find us so fast? Our little droid buddy just sent our position."

"Oh, son-of-a-bantha." Javul had slipped into the cockpit and into the jump seat without either man being aware. "Oh, you perverse, stubborn, *boneheaded* son-of-a-bantha! Where's the comm?"

Han made a half gesture at the communications board in front of him. Javul reached between Dash and Han, shoving both aside, and activated it.

"Hailing Black Sun vessel. This is Javul Charn. What are you doing?"

Han's eyes were wide as he met Dash's over the curve of Javul's back. *What's* she *doing?* he mouthed.

There was a moment of dead silence, then a male voice said, "I might ask you the same thing."

"Who, me? I'm just waiting around to get skewered by Prince Xizor and half a dozen Imperial vessels. You?"

"I'm tracking you—"

"Javul," began Dash, "maybe you should—"

She bulled through both of them. "Hitch, listen to me: if we do not jump away from here in short order, a lot of really bad things are going to happen."

"What are you talking about?"

"I don't have time. Do you intend to fire on us?"

"I might."

She cut the connection and sat back in the jump seat. "He's bluffing. Get us out of here."

"Yes, ma'am." Han didn't wait for her to repeat the order. He fired the thrusters, sending the ship back and down, then pivoted and shot away toward the Circarpous system.

"How did he know?" demanded Dash. "How did he know where we were going to be? Oto just sent coordinates and—" Dash broke off, remembering what Leebo had said about the funny background noise.

Han was watching him. "Bad feeling?"

"Very bad." Dash took off for the forward cargo bay.

Mel was still there with Leebo and the dormant Otoga droid. Nik had joined them and sat on his makeshift bunk, looking scared.

"What's happened?" Mel asked.

Dash held up a hand. "In a minute. Leebo, the background noise you were picking up from Oto—could it be some sort of homing beacon?"

The droid seemed almost to blink. "Uh-oh."

"Can it be sending while it's shut down? Please tell me it can't be sending while it's shut down."

"It can't be sending while it's shut down . . . although . . ."

"I don't wanna hear—aw . . . Although *what*?"

"You just said you didn't want to hear—"

"Forget what I just said."

"Although it's theoretically possible that someone fitted Oto with an independent transponder."

"How would you tell?"

In answer, Leebo moved to stand face-to-face with the other droid. He poked his data transfer digit into the dataport behind Oto's left optical array. After a moment he swiveled his head to look at Dash. "It's still transmitting."

Dash drew his blaster.

Mel stood, waving him back. "Don't. Not unless we absolutely have to. He's worth a lot to us whole, if for no other reason than that we can study how he was compromised. He may also have intelligence on both Black Sun and Imperial operations."

Dash hated complications. He re-holstered his blaster and pointed at the cargo droid. "Find it, Leebo. Take that mechanical traitor apart piece by piece if you have to, but *find that transponder*."

"Will do, boss," Leeo said. "What do you want me to do with it when I find it? Toss it out an air lock?"

"Not yet."

"Where were you going to rendezvous with the *Nova's Heart*?" Dash swung back into the cockpit to find Javul still sitting tensely in the jump seat.

Han called up a tactical display of the region on his console and poked a finger into the Circarpous system. "Somewhere in here—close to Mimban."

Mimban was the local name for Circarpous V—a system ideal for their rendezvous because of its sheer size and complexity. Circarpous Major was an O sequence star, which meant that it had a large habitable zone. Traffic of all sorts—mining platforms, ore carriers, freighters, passenger vessels, and pleasure craft—buzzed through the system making "noise." And noise, Han said, was exactly what they needed.

"But we can't pop in there if we've got a tracking beacon on us," he observed. "Has the tin man solved that little problem yet?"

Dash headed for the forward cargo hold, but didn't make it that far. He found Leebo in the forward engineering bay just off the main hold, practically bumping heads with Mel and Nik as they examined something sitting between them on the circuitry console. Dara Farlion sat on the padded bench that ran around the holo-display, trying—and failing—to concentrate on the three-dimensional schematic puzzle.

Dash had scarcely entered the area when Leebo turned and put a small, irregularly shaped object into his hand. "Here y'go, boss."

The transponder. He blinked at it. "Deactivated?"

"Oh, no, I thought I'd just crank up the gain and let all of Black Sun and the entire Imperial Navy know where we are."

"You know, I'd cheerfully punch you in the nose if you had a nose and I could do it without breaking my hand. You didn't destroy it, though, right? We can turn it back on?"

"Yeah, but why you'd want to is beyond me."

"That," Dash said, "is why I'm the captain and you're the funny tin sidekick."

TWENTY-NINE

THEY DROPPED OUT OF HYPERSPACE WELL BELOW THE plane of the system's ecliptic, and emerged in Mimban's gravity shadow on the dark side of her largest moon, just a tiny blip among hundreds of other tiny blips. Han locked the ship in selenocentric orbit and ordered everybody to battle stations.

"I'm tired of getting caught with my pants undone—at least by nasty-tempered, oversized Anomids with attitude problems," he told them. "So I want Dash in the—"

"I'm in the cockpit with you. I'll take the forward lasers."

"Just what I was gonna say. Leebo, handle countermeasures."

The droid saluted smartly. "Handling countermeasures. Copy, sir."

"Good. Dara, can you take care of the main weapons battery?"

"You bet. Cut my teeth on laser cannons."

"I can believe that." Leebo said aloud what Dash was only thinking. Spike ignored the droid and headed for the gunnery tower amidships.

"Mel, keel battery."

Mel glanced at Javul, then nodded assent. "Nik, why don't you come with me? Probably time you learn something besides shifting cargo."

The young Sullustan was on his feet in a flash, his huge, dark eyes sparkling. "Yessir!"

"What about me?" asked Javul.

"I need someone here in engineering . . . just in case we sustain damage. And to keep an eye on *that*." He nodded toward the dormant Oto, who stood in a corner of the hold where Leebo and Mel had stowed him after his hasty reassembly.

They'd been at their various stations for perhaps an hour when the communications panel beeped. Han sent a shipwide heads-up, then answered the hail. It was *Nova's Heart*. Javul connected with the bridge of her ship from engineering. "I've got this," she said, and the cockpit communications feed went silent.

Han stared at the console, his mouth open in disbelief. "She just overrode the bridge. She's got my control codes. How did she get my control codes?"

Dash wasn't all that surprised. "She's clever that way," he said.

"Well, what do I do?"

That deserved—and got—a full-throated laugh. "You're asking *me*? Let's review," Dash said, counting points on his fingers: "I'm the guy who thought he was providing token protection from an overzealous, stalking fanboy. Only it's not a fanboy, it's a Black Sun Vigo, after my client due to a case of mistaken identity. Oh, wait, no—not so mistaken after all. I'm really protecting her from an extremely mad jilted Vigo fiancé. But no, it's *not* an extremely mad Vigo ex-fiancé, it's the Black Sun *Underlord* himself I'm protecting her from, and he doesn't just want her back, he wants her *dead*. Except that it's not Prince Xizor who's got her in his crosshairs, it's the *Empire*, which means Palpatine, Vader, and who knows who else? But wait—there's more! Because it's not just an obsessed fanboy, or a jilted Vigo, or a pissed-off underlord, or the Imperial high muck-a-mucks who're after her, it's—wait for it—*all of the above*."

Han was staring at him. "Was it really . . . I mean, did she really . . ."

"Yeah. She really."

"All that and you haven't bailed on her?"

Dash glowered at him. "I suppose you would've."

"Blasted straight, I would've."

"Uh-huh. Yet here you sit with her secret whatever-it-is in your hold, no longer in charge of your own bridge control codes, while she uses your comm to chat with her confederates, and Black Sun and the Empire close in for the kill. Did I miss anything?"

Han didn't respond. He just turned and stared at his sensor display. "Well, at least it really is the *Nova's Heart*."

"Han, at this point I wouldn't be surprised to find out the entire crew of that black yacht are Jedi and that the Empire's sent Darth Vader himself after us."

Han's face drained of blood. "Tell me you're joking."

Dash sighed and rubbed at his patched right eye, watching as Javul's yacht drew up along their flank from the stern. "Yeah, I'm joking. Everybody knows there aren't any more Jedi."

"Dash?" Javul's voice came to them from the console.

"Here."

"I need that transponder Leebo took out of the other droid. Can you bring it back to engineering?"

"May I ask why?"

"We're going to use the *Nova's Heart* as a decoy."

"And that," said Han as Dash exited the cockpit, "is the first thing I've understood in the last week."

Dash reached the engineering bay to find not just Javul, but Mel, Nik, and Spike as well. As an added bonus surprise, the container they'd snatched from Bannistar Station had been moved from concealment to the center of the main hold.

"What are you doing?" Dash asked.

Javul held out her hand to him. "Do you have it? The transponder?"

Dash hesitated.

"Trust me," she said.

Why not? He was too tired not to. He dug the transponder out of his jacket pocket and handed it to her.

She smiled at him. "It's almost too bad the eye patch will come off soon. It makes you look rakish and piratical."

"Yeah, and plays havoc with my depth perception. What are you doing?" he repeated. "What's with the container?"

"The container and this transponder are going over to the *Nova's Heart*."

"Okay. The transponder I understand, but why the container?"

"We've got a big fat target painted on our hull right now," she answered. "The *Nova's Heart* has been out of sight and out of mind for a while."

"Not sure I agree with your line of reasoning, but it's your show."

Javul nodded. "Yeah, right now, it is. Thanks, Dash."

"What for?"

She smiled gently at him; even a man with only one good eye could read plenty into it. "For trusting me, even though I've given you every reason not to."

He felt the gentle bump as the yacht made a soft connection with the *Millennium Falcon*'s port-side docking ring. Mel moved to cycle the air lock. A moment later the hatch opened and Captain Marrak appeared in the pass-through between the two vessels.

Javul flipped the transponder to Spike, who grinned and strode with it through the access tunnel to meet the yacht's Zabrak captain. She handed him the transponder, then kissed him enthusiastically enough to raise Dash's temperature.

Mel and Nik, meanwhile, were maneuvering the container into the cargo pass-through. Behind Javul a light flashed on the sensor panel. As Dash reached for the comm, the ship trembled.

He grabbed the back of the engineering station's chair to steady himself. "Oh, that can't be good."

Javul's eyes were wide with sudden alarm and, from the cockpit, Han was shouting, "Rendar! Get up here! Now!"

He got up there.

The approaching ship was stealth black, so light-sucking fuliginous that it registered on Dash's wonky perception as a hole in space. It was coming at them at an oblique angle, from around the curve of another of Mimban's moons.

"Hitch Kris again," said Dash. "I'll get Javul to talk him down."

"Well, she'd better be on her toes, 'cause he just fired a shot across our bow."

And there was no one in the laser turret to fire back, Dash realized. But if Javul could dissuade Kris from being a pain in the rear, there'd be no need. As if the Vigo had read his mind, the big black yacht fired another blast of high-energy particles at the smaller vessel, rocking it sharply.

"He's really mad, Dash. Get Javul!"

Javul stuck her head into the cockpit. "I'm here. What's hap—" She stopped, staring through the viewport.

"Would you please tell your fiancé to stop shooting at us?" asked Han.

"That's not my fiancé."

"Okay, *ex*-fiancé."

Javul was already backing out of the cockpit. "No.

That's not my ex-fiancé, either." She ran down the passageway, shouting now. "That's Xizor!"

Han hit the intercom to the main hold. "People, we are leaving—*now*!"

Javul's voice came back through the intercom. "You can't! We're still locked with *Nova's Heart*. We're going to have to fight back."

Han's hand flew over the controls. "Then we'll fight back from behind the moon."

"We can't move—"

"You do your job—I'll do mine! Get someone to the laser turret, get that container off-loaded, and cycle the locks. I'll take care of the rest."

Han opened a link to the bridge of the *Nova's Heart*.

"What're we doing?" Dara asked as Javul turned from the communications panel.

The container was half in and half out of the passthrough, and a couple of the *Heart's* crew peered at them from the other side of the connected air locks.

"Change of plans. We're under attack."

"I heard," said Mel. "I'm going up to the laser turret. You stay," he told Nik and sprinted for the turret access tube.

As Javul moved to help Dara with the container, the ships shuddered and a low thrum shivered through the joined hulls. Cold adrenaline shot through her. The sublight engines had come online. They were moving.

"Hurry!" she shouted and reached for the container.

Moving in tandem, the two small ships ducked beneath the moon and into a sharp curve that put the bulk of Mimban's satellite between them and the Black Sun Underlord—though it brought them closer to the surface than was probably safe. Worse, Dash thought, if Xizor was able to bring his big yacht through the screen of mining traffic and slide between them and the planet, they'd be effectively trapped.

"I hope you know what you're doing," he told Han.

"Trust me."

"I do. It's Xizor I don't trust. He might just blow up this moon to get at her. Where is he?"

Han checked the sensors. "Coming over the lunar north pole. Dead ahead."

He was sweating. Dash hadn't ever seen Han sweat before.

"Arm missiles," Han told him.

Dash armed the missiles and started sweating himself.

As the bow of Xizor's yacht peeked over the curve of the moon, the ship's comm came to life. Dash jumped as Prince Xizor's dark, silken voice addressed them.

"I know you're in one of those two little tin cans, Alai Jance. Which is why I intend to blow them both to dust. I admit, though, that I don't know what you're up to and my curiosity is piqued. Enough that I may—*may*, I say—make an attempt to capture you. I suspect you may be of some strategic value. So understand, Alai, that your continued existence depends on your next action. If you're tempted to fire on me, think twice."

Dash, his hand hovering over the missile launch button, was more than tempted. The man who had blown his family apart was *right there,* right above him, silhouetted against the ambient glow of the system's sun and planets. Two missiles fired at just the right interval and at the right angle could punch a momentary hole in Xizor's shields at their weakest point and take out their shield generator. A second barrage might disable their ventral laser cannon, leaving the keel unprotected. And if he did it in the next five seconds, before Xizor's ventral gun battery had cleared the moon, he might just be able to blow the prince to whatever afterlife the Falleen believed in.

He brushed the tips of his fingers over the button, hand trembling with the desire to push it.

What was keeping Javul? How much time did they need to push the container over and button up the two air locks?

"Steady," breathed Han, as if he could read Dash's thoughts.

Javul's voice shattered the tension. "We're clear! We're clear!"

"Hold on!" Han shouted. He flipped the ship over, pivoting on its beam, and shot beneath the moon. *Nova's Heart* mirrored their movements, then wheeled over the south pole of the moon and shot off in another direction.

The *Millennium Falcon* sailed toward the heart of the system, into an area of high traffic between Circarpous IV and V. Dash understood the strategy. Even Prince Xizor would be reluctant to take a chance on the sort of collateral damage that might result if he attacked in such a crowded corridor.

But suddenly Prince Xizor was the least of their worries. The freighters, ore carriers, and passenger ships that usually dominated the intersystem space lanes were scattering in the face of two Imperial cruisers and a Star Destroyer— the latter of which was just pulling out of the lee of Circarpous Major.

Han let out a whoop and hauled back on the steering yoke. The ship shot straight up, ninety degrees relative to the system plane, picking up speed . . . and leaving Xizor and the Imperials on a collision course.

Dash hit the intercom and shouted, "Countermeasures, Leebo! Drop countermeasures!"

But the Star Destroyer had already gotten off a shot. It struck their aft shields just off center and threw the *Millennium Falcon* into a wild half turn. The second shot caught the cloud of trash Leebo had jettisoned, but they were so close to the ship that it bucked again.

If she'd been alone in the area, the *Falcon* would have been able to move at will, but even here there were enough other ships to make maneuvering hazardous. And unlike Black Sun, the Imperials obviously wouldn't think twice about shooting up the locals. The *Falcon* had only one advantage—size. They could move much faster in this crowded space than the Star Destroyer, but the cruisers were much smaller and much more agile. They were already reacting to the *Falcon's* radical course change and giving chase.

As they dodged a string of three ore carriers, Javul came forward and fell into the jump seat behind Han.

"The gunnery crew still in place?" Han asked.

"Mel's up in the dorsal turret. But I sent Dara and Nik over to *Nova's Heart*. We're a skeleton crew now."

"Are you kidding? It's usually just me and Chewie. I still feel over-occupied."

Another shot just cleared their sensor array. The cruisers were gaining on them.

"Can't we jump to hyperspace?" Javul asked, her eyes fixed on the tactical display.

"Not yet," Han muttered. "Still too close to the star's gravity well." He glanced sideways at Dash. "You're gonna have to take the belly turret."

"I have a better idea—let me steer and you can go and shoot at the Empire."

"Yeah, like that's ever gonna happen. You pilot the *Falcon*? In your dreams. Go take the gun."

Dash licked his lips. "I . . . can't, Han. I can't aim. Even without the patch, I still can't see clearly out of my right eye. Not well enough to target."

Han's expression was opaque. "Okay, you've got the con, but don't do anything I would."

Dash put his hands on the copilot's yoke, and Han climbed out of the pilot's chair and headed for the hatch. He paused to point a finger at Javul. "Keep an eye on him. Don't let him do anything dangerous. Or stupid."

"Right."

Dash did something both dangerous and stupid almost immediately. He turned the *Millennium Falcon* over again and aimed her bow directly at Circarpous Major. If he was at a disadvantage visually, flying into the sun, so should be their pursuers. Not only would their visual acuity be cut by the glare, but it would also muck up their sensor arrays. At times the older, simpler instruments were the best; a brand-new, right-out-of-the-shipyards Star Destroyer couldn't have anything as antediluvian as a simple radar array.

Advantage: *Falcon*.

The problem was, of course, that the sun's gravitational pull and magnetic fields played havoc with the *Millennium Falcon*'s systems as well. The one-eyed pilot was going to have to eyeball the right moment to veer off. Ironic.

Javul slid into the pilot's seat. She was silent, her gaze on the viewport, which had darkened automatically to screen out the sun's radiation. Dash somehow knew the silence was trust, not fear. It made him tighten his grip on the steering yoke.

His concentration was broken when the Imperials hailed them. "Unidentified craft, this is Commander Corsa of the Imperial cruiser *Valiant*. You will heave to and be boarded, or we will destroy you. Do you understand?"

"Oh, I understand just fine, thanks," Dash murmured, keeping his focus on the looming star.

"I didn't catch that, Captain," Commander Corsa said. "Say again."

"Catch *this*, Corsa! Fire at will!" Han's voice shouted over the intercom, followed by the distinctive sound of a barrage of laserfire.

Javul, peering through the viewport dead ahead, suddenly went stiff and pointed. "What's that?"

That was a black hole in the sun. A vaguely ship-shaped hole. It was moving toward them rapidly—clearly not a fleeing freighter. Dash's heart hammered and his throat went suddenly dry. If that was Xizor, his intention was clear—to blow them out of the sky and . . . and what? If that was the plan, it was suicide. He'd be flying right into the path of an Imperial formation. Did Xizor really want Javul dead that badly?

The oncoming vessel hailed them. "Alai Jance."

Javul shot a startled look at Dash. "Hitch!" She mouthed and leaned forward in her seat. "Here."

"You really want to go through with this?"

"I have to, Hitch. You know I do."

There was a moment's pause, then the Vigo said, "All right. Just now the Imperial's sensors can't read me. I'm in your shadow. On my mark, dive minus ninety degrees. Understood?"

"Understood," Dash said, perspiration trickling down the sides of his face. The eye patch itched. He pulled it off and tossed it.

The sun had filled the *Falcon*'s viewport, and now the vessel barreling toward them was an expanding black mass in the midst of that fiery backdrop. A blurry black mass.

"Mark!"

Dash leaned into the steering yoke, and the *Millennium Falcon* dived straight "down" and into the stew of traffic in the Circarpous system's temperate zone. He dodged other vessels, spinning, spiraling ever-downward through the core of the system and out the other side. This time there seemed to be no pursuit. Free of the system's gravity fields, beyond a far-flung circling shell of asteroids and comets, Dash turned the *Falcon*'s bow toward Alderaan and prepared for the jump to hyperspace.

Just before they jumped, Hitch Kris contacted them once more.

"Congratulations, Alai. You've shaken the tail . . . for now. The Imperials split up to chase other targets, and my boss"—he laid subtle stress on the word—"has galloped off after the *Nova's Heart*."

"And you, Hitch?" she asked softly.

For a few moments, there was nothing but the faint hiss and crackle of the carrier wave. Then Hitch's voice said, "I'm done, baby. You're into something that's way beyond my pay grade. Good luck."

"You, too . . . that is, I assume you're one of the targets the Imperials are chasing."

He laughed. "Don't worry about me, Alai. I may have lost you, but I still have resources neither the Empire nor Underlord Xizor know about. Smooth spacing."

"Smooth spacing," she answered.

Dash turned to look at her. Was that wistfulness in her expression? Did she still harbor some fondness for her Vigo ex? He engaged the hyperdrive, watched the stars blur, then closed his eyes.

Han interrupted his semi-coma by appearing and demanding his command back. Dash was happy to comply. His leg ached, his shoulders were throbbing, and his right eye felt like there was sand in it.

He and Javul made their way aft to the crew's commons where she sat him down, got out a medkit, and forced him to let her work on his eye for the fourth or fifth time. She flushed it out with a medicated solution that stopped the stinging, then applied some ointment. He sagged in the chair, wanting desperately to sleep. His mind wandered, wondering about the relationship between Javul Charn and Hityamun Kris.

His mind hit a snag. His eyes flew open.

"What?" She was watching him through the steam from a hot cup of caf.

"Hitch said that Xizor was chasing *Nova's Heart*."

"Yes."

"Why? The transponder was Hitch's and he's not chasing anybody anymore."

"Xizor isn't chasing the transponder. He's chasing Oto. We reactivated him, gave him some new instructions, and put him on *Nova's Heart*. That's why it took us so long to disengage the air locks." She smiled at his dazed expression. "Why don't you get some sleep? Make that eye feel better."

He was asleep before he could muster the energy to answer.

THIRTY

DASH WOKE TEN HOURS LATER WITH THE SURE KNOWL-
edge that they were still in hyperspace. He was disoriented for a moment, because he was lying in his bunk,
not hunched over the table in the crew's commons or
curled up on the floor beneath it. He tried to imagine
Han being enlisted to help move him here and failed. He
turned his head and realized two things simultaneously:
that his right eye was significantly better and that Han
was the occupant of the nearest bunk.

Who was piloting the ship?

The question brought Dash to his feet and out into the
corridor. He made his way to the cockpit, where he found
Leebo ensconced in the pilot's chair, with Mel sitting beside him. The cargo master glanced up as he slid into to
the jump seat.

"He left *you* in charge?" Dash asked the droid.

"Yeah, and I didn't even have to pretend to have a bum
eye."

"I wasn't pretending. It hurt. I couldn't see out of it,
okay?"

"So you say."

Mel chuckled. "Where did you get him?" He nodded at
Leebo.

"Guy traded him to me for passage off Rodia. A comedian."

"Ah. It all becomes much too clear."

"Yeah. Oh, and Leebo, I'll thank you to remember

who programmed you to pilot a spacecraft. If it weren't for me, you'd be hanging out in the hold twiddling your little tin thumbs."

"My thumbs are neither little nor tin. They are a laminanium–quadranium alloy with an overplating of terenthium."

Mel gave Dash a sidewise look.

"Yeah, annoyance makes him pedantic. I didn't program that. Not sure who did."

"That was my previous employer," Leebo informed them.

"Owner," Dash couldn't help correcting.

"Now who's being pedantic? He was a great comedian," the droid added in an aside to Mel.

"Who's changed professions," Dash added, "because he managed to insult the Rodians' head honcho, Navik the Red."

"Ah. Hence the necessity of getting passage off Rodia."

"Artificial intelligence, it seems," the droid said, "is no match for natural stupidity."

The two men sat in companionable silence for a moment, then Mel said, "So, you have quite a history with Prince Xizor."

Okay, that was a crash turn onto a new subject. Still, Dash saw no reason to be coy. "Yeah. Yeah, you could say that."

"That must have made this tour of duty a bit . . . difficult."

"Hey, I'm a big boy. I can handle it."

"Pardon me for saying so, Dash, but that sounds an awful lot like bluster to me."

Dash opened his mouth to retort, then met the older man's eyes. There was no judgment in them, only honest compassion. He took a deep breath and let it out. "Okay. You got me. The truth is . . . the truth is that when Xizor's ship was bearing down on us, I really wanted to fire those missiles. There was a split second when I didn't care about Javul's mission or Han's ship or my life. All I could think of was that if I fired at exactly the right moment, one missile might hole his shields and the next might punch through."

"*If* you got off the second shot before they unloaded on us."

"Yeah. Big *if*."

"What stopped you?"

Dash flushed and was glad the cockpit was dimly enough lit that Mel might not notice it. "I'd like to say that it was the sure and sudden knowledge that if I didn't fire at exactly the right moment, Xizor *would* unload on us and kill everybody aboard, not just me. But to be honest, I didn't have to make that choice. Han stopped me. Made me hesitate. The next second *Nova's Heart* was clear and we were gone. I never had to make the choice."

"Do you wish you had?"

Dash nodded. "Yeah, I do. I'd kind of like to know what I would've done."

Mel looked right into him. "You know what you would've done. You wouldn't have let personal revenge trump duty . . . You'd be a good man for the Rebellion, Dash. We need people who can set aside their personal goals the way you have."

Dash shook his head. "Naw. Not me. I'm too much of a lone wolf to take orders the way you guys have to. This whole Rebellion thing is outside my comfort zone. Too many ways to end up dead."

"Dash, the Rebellion is outside *everyone's* comfort zone. Mine, Dara's, Javul's. Nobody wants to have to be here. But look at the alternative—lying down and letting the Empire suck more and more life out of all of us. There was a time people living on Rim worlds could just ignore what was happening at the Galactic Core. That time is long past. The Empire has reached out to the very fringes of the galaxy and is squeezing the life right out of it. Have you been to Corellia lately? They've got our homeworld locked down so tightly, people can barely move or draw breath without the Security Bureau showing up on their doorstep."

Dash didn't know what to say. He could feel Mel's words pecking at him, could feel the penetration of his gaze.

He changed the subject. "Let me ask you something. *Nova's Heart* has the container and is, I assume, heading for Alderaan eventually. But *Nova's Heart* is also broadcasting a signal that's drawing off at least some Imperial forces and giving Prince Xizor a come-hither. Why both? And why are you and Javul still here aboard the *Millennium Falcon*?"

"Javul and I need to report to our liaison on Alderaan."

"Your boss, huh?"

"Our boss."

"That's it?"

Mel shrugged.

"You put Nik aboard the *Nova's Heart*. Y'know what that tells me? That tells me that he's safer there than he'd be here." Dash leaned back, lacing his fingers behind his head. "It tells me that we still have the container. Don't we?"

Mel didn't answer. He glanced over Dash's shoulder. "Good morning, Captain Solo. I'm guessing you're going to want your seat back. Come on, Leebo. I've got some exceptionally high-grade joint oil that I think you're gonna love."

Mel slipped out of the copilot's seat and shifted past Han, laying his hand briefly on Dash's shoulder. "You're a very smart man, Captain Rendar. I think you'd be a credit to the Rebel Alliance."

Han stood in the accessway for a moment, staring after the Rebel commander. "What was that? Was he trying to recruit you?"

"I guess." Dash really didn't want to talk about it.

Han slid into his pilot's seat and checked the readouts before swiveling to look at Dash. "Seriously. He was trying to get you join the Rebellion?"

Dash shrugged. "Yeah. Fool's errand."

"Fool's errand. I'll say. Man, they must be scraping the bottom of the barrel."

"Oh, really? They ask you to join?"

Han blinked at him, not catching the implied insult. "Sure . . . sure, of course they did. I turned 'em down. Flat. I mean, who needs the added risk, right? Your lady friend is crazy—you know that, don't you? Her and all her crew." He described a circle around his right ear with his index finger.

"Yeah," agreed Dash.

The trip to Alderaan was uneventful enough to make everyone relax. And that, all by itself, made Dash nervous. Surely by now the *Deep Core* would have been discovered to be an innocent cargo vessel "crewed" mostly by droids. The *Nova's Heart* would have certainly deactivated Oto and jettisoned the transponder. That meant Xizor and the Imperials knew they'd been deked and were seeking a heavily modified YT-1300 last contacted in the Circarpous system.

Dash Rendar found himself in the unlikely position of wishing someone would just attack and get it over with. He said as much to Han as the two of them sipped hot caf in the cockpit.

Han looked at him as if he were out of his mind. "Bite your tongue. We have to refuel on Commenor. If there's an Imperial Star Destroyer waiting for us there, I'm gonna blame you."

"Do we have to refuel on Commenor? Can't we just plow on through to Alderaan?"

"We could try, but we might end up dropping out of hyperspace short of the goal. I'd rather not chance it."

"I thought this old crate had extended range. *Outrider* could make it from Bannistar to Alderaan on one fuel pack."

Han glared at him. "This *old crate* has been hauling more crew and more cargo than usual. And she's been jumping in and out normal space like a madman was at the helm."

"Got that right. When do we get to Commenor?"

Han checked the chrono. "Oh-three-hundred hours, give or take."

"Should we put Leebo in one of the weapons turrets? Maybe have Mel in another one?"

Han choked on his caf. "Dash, you're even more paranoid than I am, and that's saying a lot."

"C'mon, Han, what could it hurt? Better safe than sorry."

Han shrugged. "Hey, if you wanna crew up the weapons, I got no reason to argue with you. As long as you're not going to ask to pilot again."

Dash had been thinking about it, but his eye was better now and focused well enough for him to target accurately. "I'll take gunnery. Give us about a ten-minute heads-up."

Roughly ten minutes before they were to drop out of hyperspace, Han's voice sounded the heads-up for their arrival in the Commenor system: "This announcement brought to you by Dash Rendar, mother hen and professional worrier. All hands to battle stations! All hands to battle stations! We are approaching impending doom!"

Dash climbed into the dorsal gun battery, wishing that

Han wouldn't be quite so cocky. It was his observation that when you yawned in the face of the universe, it felt compelled to do something rude to wake you up.

Javul sat next to Han in the copilot's seat as the *Millennium Falcon* decanted and then soared into the Commenor system on a heading toward the fourth planet, where, Han assured her, they'd find fuel and friends.

"I do lots of business on Commenor," he said. "There are very few inner worlds as unimpressed with the Empire as these guys. Our chances of finding an Imperial presence here are astronomically small."

Javul looked up at the curved flank of a gas giant as the *Falcon* sailed serenely by. "How do they keep the Empire at bay?"

"Ironically, by being very important to the Emperor. Commenor is a gateway colony. Believe it or not, more trade passes through here than through Corellia. I think the Emperor knows that if they lean on Commenor too heavily, they'll lose that gateway. I mean, imagine what would happen on Coruscant and some of the other Core Worlds if basic resources were suddenly cut off. Food, fuel, other necessities."

Javul nodded. "Coruscant can't produce much of its own food."

"Exactly. So, the Empire goes out of its way not to arouse Commenorian umbrage. It's too key a port."

Javul saw, ahead of them, a large planet surrounded by vessels. She pointed. "Is that the hub world?"

"Yeah. There's activity on some of the other planets, but Commenor is the heart of it all. Pretty fun place, too, I might add."

Javul smiled wryly. "I've had enough fun on this trip, thanks."

"No, I mean *real* fun." He turned his head to look at

her appreciatively. "In fact, if we could afford the time, I'd love to show you some of the nightlife in Chasin City."

Javul laughed. "*You* want to show me the nightlife? I thought you thought I was a crazy lady."

"I *do* think you're a crazy lady. But you're a pretty crazy lady, not to mention a famous one. Saying I've gone out with Javul Charn would give me some serious creds in the circles I travel. You know what I mean?"

"Oh, I know exactly what you mean. I do. But we can't afford the time."

"Yeah, I figured not."

Javul didn't answer; no sense telling him that if she went anywhere with anybody for fun, it would be Dash she wanted on her arm. Maybe because they'd been through so much together. Maybe because he'd saved her life. Maybe because he'd stuck with her even in the face of her duplicity. Or maybe because she liked what happened when he kissed her.

She settled back in the copilot's seat and watched Commenor draw closer, the ships and satellite stations around it coming into sharper focus. She wasn't exactly conscious of when she started to feel uneasy. There was just something *wrong* about the silhouette of a ship coming toward them from out of the Commenor sun, something jarringly familiar about the configuration of another moving slowly out from behind a moon . . .

She sat up, put her hand on Han's forearm. "Han . . ."

He turned toward her, a smile curving his mouth, but the look on her face wiped it away. "What is it?"

"To starboard at about thirty degrees." She recognized it now and the recognition brought a chill. "Imperial Dreadnought."

"Do you think they know—"

In answer to Han's quandary, the Imperial hailed them.

"Rebel freighter, this is Commander Zarin of the Imperial Dreadnought *Avenger*. You will stop and be boarded."

"*Rebel* freighter? I'm no Rebel anything!" Han hit the intercom. "Hold on, everybody, we're outta here!"

They dived—down and to port, twisting, turning toward the moon.

"But there's a—"

"I see it!" Han said, his eyes on the Imperial corvette that was even now pulling out from behind Commenor's large natural satellite. He put on speed, looped beneath the moon, and came up under the corvette's keel. Then they were sweeping in a long S-curve around Commenor.

"TIE fighters in pursuit!" Dash called down from the gunnery.

"Fire at will," Han told him and then concentrated on getting them out of the system so they could return to hyperspace. He aimed them ninety degrees from their course, heading toward the Inner Rim.

They could hear the slash of the laser cannon as Dash and Mel fired at the swarm of attack ships behind them.

"Leebo!" Han hailed the droid.

"Yeah, I know—countermeasures. I'm on it."

They swept out of the system with Leebo's spread of countermeasures littering their back trail. Javul watched the tactical display as the TIE fighters and the corvette's missiles collided with the live ordnance amid the debris, then flared and died. The corvette blew through the debris field without hesitation, picking up speed as it pursued them.

"This is gonna be close!" Han shouted. "More countermeasures on my mark!"

He jerked the steering yoke hard over to port, yelled "Mark!" and fired the hyperspace engines. They flipped over, their wake lighting up brilliantly for the split second before they leapt out of realspace.

Leaning back in his chair, Han turned to Javul. "You're a religious type, aren't you?"

"I . . . have my beliefs."

"Then pray that they think we leapt toward the Rim."

"Han," said Dash's voice from the intercom. "She's been praying since she got on this bucket."

THIRTY-ONE

DASH DIDN'T DOUBT THAT JAVUL CONTINUED TO PRAY. Having gone without refueling, but with some additional crash maneuvers, the *Millennium Falcon* wasn't in the ideal state to complete her journey to Alderaan. Han was sweating again, but he wasn't going to admit it. He wasn't above grousing about the fact that they probably wouldn't make it all the way to Alderaan and would have to limp in under ion power.

"Could take days, you know," Han complained, "during which we will be completely vulnerable to attack."

Luckily, they were only moments from the perimeter of Alderaanian space when the hyperdrive used up the last of its reserves. That put them hours, rather than days, out. Mel went back up to the dorsal laser cannon; Dash and Javul hunkered down with Han in the cockpit. They had no more than entered the system when they were hailed.

"Unidentified freighter, this is Alderaan Space Control. Please provide ID."

Han swore. "What's up with that? I fly into Alderaan time after time with almost no trouble and *this* time they ask for ID?"

"That's because you're not broadcasting your ID, Han," Dash reminded him. "You haven't been broadcasting ID since we left Bannistar."

"Well, I don't feel too good about starting now."

Javul leaned in from the jump seat to activate the comm. "Alderaan Space Control, this is Javul Charn. This vessel is now part of my entourage."

There was a long moment of silence, then the controller came back with a cautious, "Javul Charn, would you please transmit your personal identification code?"

She slid farther down between the pilot's and copilot's seats and typed a series of characters on the communications keypad.

"Checking your ID, please wait—oh, I'm informed you may establish orbit around Alderaan at your earliest convenience."

"At your earliest convenience," muttered Han. "I'll bet that's not what he was informed."

They were in orbit before Alderaan control established contact with them again. This time the agent was a female—probably the superior of whoever had hailed them before.

"Charn," she said in a rich contralto, "may I ask what happened to your tour? We weren't expecting you for two weeks and with different vessels."

"We had an equipment failure en route and had to hire another vessel and captain to carry my crew and cargo. We also had a bit of trouble on Bannistar that prompted a change of schedule."

"I hope everything is all right. You said an equipment failure—you haven't lost any technology or personnel, have you?"

"No, but we have had to separate our remaining vessels."

"Are you aware that the ship you're on is wanted for unspecified infractions against the Empire?"

"Now, wait a minute!" said Han. "All we did—"

Javul silenced him with a look. "Very much aware, Control."

"In fact, the ship is suspected of smuggling."

Javul gave Han a sidewise glance. "Yes, well . . . our captain does have an entrepreneurial streak."

"Guy's gotta make a living," muttered Han.

"Sounds like a real scoundrel," said the controller wryly.

Dash glanced down at the tactical display. "Uh-oh. We've got company . . ."

Han followed his gaze. "What? Oh, come *on*. Who's that?"

"Um, Control," said Javul. "We seem to have an escort."

"Yes, you do. And you will follow the lead ship in that escort all the way in or the vessel behind you will take exception to your actions. We're getting a docking facility ready. When you enter atmosphere, we'll activate a homing beacon. At that time, you will relinquish control of your vessel to our autopilot."

Dash looked at Javul, a cold, hard knot in the pit of his stomach. "Javul . . ."

"Do as she says."

"You're sure?"

Javul shrugged. "What're the alternatives, really?"

"We can cut and run," suggested Han. "Melikan's still up in the turret."

"Cut and run using what for fuel?" asked Javul. "Besides, those aren't Imperial ships, Han. They're Alderaan Port Authority vessels. These are the friendlies."

"Yeah," muttered Dash, "real friendly. Friendly with those Imperials, I'll bet." He nodded to port, where two Imperial cruisers peeked menacingly around the planet's equator. They were making no moves toward the *Millennium Falcon*, though.

The descent was uneventful, though nerve racking as far as Dash was concerned. The only thing that set his mind at ease was that Javul did not seem so much nervous as determined. He saw less and less the touring diva and more and more the Rebel operative.

The autopilot took control as they entered atmosphere and drew them to the planetary capital, Aldera—more specifically to the main docking facility in a secure part of the spaceport. That made both Dash and Han a bit squeamish.

By the time they were approaching their landing bay, Mel had made his way to the cockpit, as well. The *Millennium Falcon* slowed. All four humans watched in silence as a warren of docking pads and service facilities passed beneath them.

As they approached a cluster of hemispherical buildings, Mel turned a solemn gaze on the two Corellians. "I want you both to know," he said, "Al—I mean Javul—was perfectly serious when she suggested you'd be an asset to the Rebel Alliance. To say you've been invaluable to us would be a tremendous understatement. We simply wouldn't have survived this far without you—either of you."

"I'll second that," said Javul. "Seriously, Dash, Han, the offer still stands—"

Han was already shaking his head. "Sorry, sister. Dash'll tell you—I don't do causes. I'm the only cause I . . ." He hesitated. "I'm used to being responsible for me and nobody else. I'm not at my best when other people are depending on me."

Mel fixed him with a laser gaze that Dash knew from experience cut right to the soul. "Your friend Chewbacca doesn't depend on you? Can't trust you to be at his back? I find that hard to believe, Captain Solo."

Han just shook his head and returned his gaze to the view from the cockpit.

"What about you, Dash?" Javul said softly. "Are you ready to sign on? It seems to me you already have."

Suddenly Dash felt as if he and Javul were the only two people in the cockpit. He looked into those intense silver eyes and knew he was being drawn in—reeled in, maybe. He had the unworthy thought that Javul Charn was one heckuva Rebellion recruitment tool. He shook off the thought, but the chill remained.

"I can't argue with the ends, Javul," he said finally, "but I . . . I'm a freelancer. I'm the boss on the *Outrider*. You understand? I'm not real good at taking orders from on high."

She looked sincerely aggrieved. But was there anything personal in it, or was it just the disappointment of losing an asset for the "cause"? He wished he could ask, but with Han sitting there, watching him out of the corner of his eye . . .

"I'm sorry you feel that way," Javul said. "For a lot of reasons. But think about it—both of you—" She turned her head to take in Han. "The Empire is tightening its hold on our lives—*all* our lives—day by day. You function freely now—if you can call it that—so maybe you think this isn't your fight. You're wrong. It is your fight. It's *our* fight. All of us. If you wait to act until the Empire reaches out for you, personally, you will have waited too long."

"I can't," Dash said, and felt a deep and sincere regret. "I'm just not made for this sort of work. I'm my own man. I make my own rules. Fly my own course. It's safer that way—for everyone concerned."

Mel smiled and shook his head. "You really believe that, do you?"

"C'mon, Mel. You've seen me operate. I'm just bad at taking orders. And *he's* even worse." He jabbed a thumb at Han. "We might look like assets, but in the end we'd be liabilities. We'd go rogue at some point. Screw something up. I wouldn't want that."

The control beeped just then, and Dash looked out

through the forward viewport to see that one of the docking domes had opened up below them. They were descending toward it.

"Charn," said the woman from the control center, "prepare your crew for landing. You should be on the ground in approximately two minutes. Standard procedure."

Javul pressed the TRANSMIT button on the console. "Affirmative." She turned back to Dash. "I guess we'd better get ready to debark."

"What's to get ready?" Han grumbled. "They're running the show. All we have to do is show up at the air lock. What's gonna happen to our cargo?"

"I don't know," Javul answered. "This wasn't what was supposed to happen."

Han blinked. "You mean you're making this up as you go along?"

She smiled, dazzlingly. "Pretty much."

The ship settled gently into her berth in the landing bay and the dome slid shut, closing her in. Han, looking up through the forward viewport, shook his head.

"I don't like this. This feels bad." He climbed out of the pilot's chair and headed aft.

Mel followed him. Javul didn't. She turned to Dash as he rose from his jump seat.

"You won't reconsider?"

"Who's asking—the Rebel operative or the woman?"

"One and the same, Dash. The Rebellion isn't something I do. It's something I am." She took a deep breath, let it out. "But if you're asking if I, personally, would like you to stay on for my own selfish reasons . . . the answer is yes. My motives aren't entirely defined by what the Alliance needs. And that worries me a little. Sometimes I think it's a bad idea to form attachments here, now, under these circumstances. And other times I think . . ."

"That life's all about attachments?" he finished.

She nodded. "That those attachments to people we care about are essential to the fight . . . and make the fight essential."

She kissed him this time, and he thought about attachments and things worth fighting for. He'd fought for her during this tour again and again. He'd almost died a few times. Eaden *had* died fighting for both of them and for his dead master. Dash knew, on some level beneath the clamor of his hormones and heartbeat, that there was a truth of some sort in what Eaden had done.

In a blinding flash of insight, as their lips parted and Javul pulled away, he thought he knew part of that truth: Eaden hadn't died to avenge his master's murder. He had died to save the lives of the two remaining members of his order—his sister and his cousin.

Watching Javul walk away from him toward the main cargo hold, Dash almost called her back to tell her he'd throw in with her—with *them,* with the Rebels. But something stopped him. He tried to tell himself it was common sense.

There was an escort awaiting them when they left the ship—half a dozen soldiers armed with blaster rifles. The crew of the *Millennium Falcon* were quickly disarmed and led to a holding area. Leebo, who had exited the ship with them, was ordered back aboard. The human members of the group were marched into a small, spare room and left. They'd been there only moments when another set of guards appeared to take Mel and Javul away for questioning.

The look Javul gave him as she left the room made him squirm. *We're on Alderaan,* he reminded himself. *They're civilized people. They won't do anything nasty.*

"Those soldiers," murmured Han. "Did you notice?"

"Notice what?" Dash brought his mind forcibly back from his unwelcome thoughts.

"They weren't regular army. They were some sort of elite corps."

That was alarming. "What sort of elite corps?"

"Not sure. Didn't recognize the uniform. There was an insignia on the collar. Gold. Sort of an upside-down triangle."

Dash shook his head. "Meaning what?"

"Meaning they could have been Royal Guards—House of Organa."

"Is that good or bad?"

Han gave him a strange look. "You tell me. Who's your girlfriend's liaison on Alderaan?"

"I don't know."

"I guess she doesn't trust you that much after all." Han grinned.

Dash felt a flare of anger under his breastbone, but tamped it down. "It makes sense that she wouldn't tell me. That way if I ended up in enemy hands—"

"Like now, for example."

"Maybe like now. The point is, I couldn't give up critical information, put that person's life in danger. If I were—you know—interrogated or something."

Han seemed darkly amused. " 'Or something'? You mean like tortured?"

But as it turned out, they were neither interrogated nor tortured. Instead, after roughly an hour in the holding area, the doors slid back and they were marched back to the docking bay with an invitation to leave. Quickly, quietly, and anonymously.

"Why wouldn't they at least question us?" Han asked as the landing bay doors slid shut with an emphatic *thud,* as if to underscore the "invitation" to get lost.

"Maybe because we're not members of the Rebel Alliance," Dash said.

"You mean you think they believed Javul when she told them we were just unlucky mercs?"

"Yeah. Something like that." The impulse to throw himself at the durasteel doors and demand that Javul be sent out was strong, but not strong enough to overthrow his rationality . . . or his dignity. Instead of making such a token display, he turned on his heel and went back to the ship.

The main cargo hold was empty. Every piece of Javul's equipment had been removed. Han stood and stared at the empty compartment for a moment.

"Blast! I wonder what else they took."

He and Dash moved methodically from hold to hold. Sure enough, every scrap of Javul Charn's presence had been removed from the *Falcon*. Even her personal effects were gone.

Anxious, Han hurried to the secret compartments beneath the decking in the starboard passageways. He knelt to activate the hydraulic mechanism on the aftmost deck plate. Apparently it rose too slowly for his taste; he poked his head beneath the rising hatch cover to check the contents, then sat back with a sigh of relief. The cargo he'd picked up on Bannistar was intact.

"Good news. They didn't find this stuff."

"No, they found it, they just didn't care," Dash amended. He was looking down into the forward compartment. "The container is gone."

"The container? You mean the one we lifted from Bannistar? Sure it's gone. They stowed it aboard the *Nova's Heart*."

"No, they didn't. They moved the droid and reengaged his signaling devices. They put the container back. We had it all the time. They took it."

"*Who* took it?"

"They knew where to look," Dash murmured half to himself. "That means she must've told them." He hoped that meant she'd *wanted* them to know where it was. He closed the deck plate that covered the now-empty compartment. It glided shut with a solid *thump* and a click from the locking mechanism.

Han straightened. "Let's get out of here."

Dash didn't move. "Yeah. I guess."

Han came to put a hand on his shoulder. "Dash, old buddy, there are just some things you can't do anything about. This is one of them. We don't know who took the container. We don't know where it is. We don't know where *she* is."

Dash didn't comment that he *did* know that much. He'd seen her as they crossed the landing bay. She'd been standing, unfettered, beside a petite, dark-haired woman, looking down on them from a high, glassed-in gallery that ran partway around the upper latitudes of the dome. The body language between the two women hadn't been that of prisoner and captor, which gave Dash some reason for hope that Javul had things under control. That, and the fact that Han had been right about the soldiers on duty here—every one of them was a member of Bail Organa's elite guard. And Bail Organa, he knew, was not often a friend of Imperial policy. He had been outspoken in his opposition to the Emperor's more draconian measures— such as the infamous order to hunt down and annihilate the Jedi.

"C'mon," Han said, heading for the cockpit. "Let's go."

Dash followed. "Yeah. Sure. Where's Leebo?"

"Dunno. They sent him back to the ship, so he's gotta be here somewhere."

Dash activated his comlink. "Hey, Leebo—where are you?"

There was no answer. He tried again.

"Leebo? Leebo! Where are you, tin man?"

Still no answer.

He entered the cockpit in Han's wake and slid into the copilot's seat, reaching forward to activate the ship's intercom system.

"What's up?" Han was already doing his preflight prep, checking systems one by one.

"Can't raise Leebo. Maybe his comlink is down. Leebo, this is Dash. Get your tin can up to the cockpit."

Still nothing. Dash felt a tickle of apprehension. "They'd better not have confiscated him." He opened a channel to the facility control even as the dome rolled back overhead. "Docking Control, this is Dash Rendar in Docking Bay Alpha Nine. Did you remove my droid from the ship?"

"Sir?" The controller sounded startled.

"My droid. A modified LE-BO2D9 model. I can't locate him. Did your guys remove him from the ship?"

"I don't know, sir. Let me check."

The channel went dormant. Dash turned to Han. "Why're they being so polite?"

"Don't knock it."

When the connection went live again, the female controller was back, her voice crisp and businesslike. "Specialist Rand says you were asking about your droid. What seems to be the problem?"

"The problem is I can't *find* my droid. What did you do with him?"

"The droid unit was returned to your ship."

"You didn't impound him or something?"

"The whole ship was impounded, Captain, with your LE unit aboard. No one saw it leave." Now she sounded faintly amused.

"He might have snuck out while your guys were offloading the cargo."

"Why? Is your droid prone to wandering off without orders?"

"Not normally," Dash fibbed. "Did your guys turn him off?"

"That I can't tell you. I suppose they may have. Are you ready to launch?"

"Not without my droid!"

"I assure you, Captain, the unit is aboard somewhere. If by some wild fluke it's not, we'll find it and return it to you. Right now I need you and your friend to get off the planet. Please."

"Uh, Control?" said Han. "This is his friend. We're getting." He turned to Dash. "Go look for your droid. He's gotta be here somewhere."

"Right." Dash pulled himself out of the copilot's chair and went in search of Leebo.

THIRTY-TWO

DASH MADE HIS WAY AFT, PORT-SIDE FIRST, POKING INTO every compartment . . . again. He saw nothing amiss, but also no Leebo. He called out. He tried the comlink several more times. He even looked in the storage lockers in the crew's quarters, checked the engine room, the weapons batteries, the galley.

No Leebo.

Frustrated and worried, he made his way back around to the starboard side, thinking that just maybe the droid had hidden himself in one of the secret cargo holds. While Han had peeked into them to make sure the cargo was intact, neither of them had gone below to check them thoroughly.

Dash started with the aftmost compartment, kneeling to depress the near-invisible locking mechanism on the first deck plate. It glided upward on its hydraulic pistons, revealing cargo and nothing else. He poked his head into the opening, pulling out a glowlight and playing it about the interior.

Negative. He closed that deck plate and moved to the next. More nothing. He knelt to activate the next plate. His fingers had no sooner released the lock than it opened suddenly beneath him, flinging him from his feet. The hydraulics gave a whine of protest. Dash tumbled back and sideways, slamming his left shoulder against the hatch frame of the starboard docking ring and landing on his back across the threshold of the access corridor.

Breath knocked from his body, he looked down between his knees—and saw the impossible. Edge—battered, torn, but still alive—was rising out of the cargo compartment like an avenging demon, his body armor holed and awry. He wielded a cortosis staff in one hand and a darkstick in the other. Dash saw immediately that the Anomid assassin had not made the same mistake twice—the end of the darkstick's horrific claw dripped with a red liquid Dash knew was lethal.

He pushed himself farther up the access and scrabbled for his laser pistol, only to recall as it met his hand that the Alderaanians had removed its power cell and he hadn't yet reloaded.

No time for that now. The big Anomid already loomed over him, one knee on the edge of the cargo compartment. Without warning the assassin swept the cortosis staff toward Dash's midsection, its plasma blade spitting fire. Dash lashed out with booted feet. His heel connected with Edge's left hand. The staff spun from his grip, searing across the top of Dash's left thigh. He gasped in pain and kicked again, knocking the staff away, but Edge had the darkstick raised, ready to strike.

Dash met the strange orange eyes. They had been cold before—implacable, emotionless. Now they were filled with fire. This had obviously become personal. Edge probably wasn't used to having his prey skitter to safety or unseat him not once, but twice.

Dash felt a supreme sense of betrayal in the frozen moment before the darkstick began its downward descent toward his heart. Not his own betrayal, but Eaden's. He was angry. Angry that the Universe—or the Force or the Deity or whatever—had allowed Eaden to die and this death machine to survive. The injustice was galling and Dash roared aloud with it.

From out of nowhere, Leebo's pet MSE droid shot through from one side of the corridor to the other. The sudden, unexpected movement distracted Edge—only momentarily, but that was all that was needed. Two pulses of light flashed from behind the Anomid. One energy bolt hit his shoulder where the armor had been shot away. The other caught him with pinpoint accuracy in the back of the neck where the body armor met his helm. He jerked upright, his knees slipping from the rim of the compartment.

Han! Dash felt a surge of relief . . . until Edge toppled forward, the darkstick continuing its downward plunge.

Dash rolled half on his left side and the weapon's tip buried itself in the deck plating, roughly where his right lung would have been. He looked down the length of his body. The Anomid was laid out with his head between Dash's feet, his long, muscular arm stretched upward, his hand still clutching the weapon. His body was smoking where the energy bolts had caught him. Dash gagged on the smell of burned flesh.

The big sentient quivered, not yet done, and tried to push himself up.

"Oh, blast it!" said a voice from the main corridor. Two more energy bolts took out the hydraulic assists on the cargo compartment's hatch.

The heavy durasteel deck plate dropped shut, crushing the Anomid's lower body. He made a horrible, strangled bleat of rage and pain and looked up at Dash through those burning eyes. With a last, tremendous effort, Edge pulled the tip of the darkstick out of the decking, its tip dripping venom. He lifted it high, preparing to swing it at Dash—

And died.

Dash saw the light go out of his eyes, draining away like water from a broken bowl, and was glad he hadn't witnessed that moment with Eaden. The thought of it would haunt him anyway.

Edge went limp, his hand releasing the darkstick, which clattered to the deck. His body released its last breath.

Dash carefully moved the darkstick away from his body. Then he scrambled to his feet, wincing a little, and stepped cautiously around the corpse into the main corridor.

"Han, you are a—"

But it wasn't Han standing hip-deep in the next-door cargo compartment. It was Leebo. Mousie was by his side.

Dash gaped. "Leebo? But . . ." He glanced at the dead Anomid. "You can't . . . you're not supposed to . . . What *happened*?"

The droid gave as close to a shrug as Dash had ever seen. "I missed."

"You . . . missed."

"Is there an echo in here? I missed with the first two shots. I was aiming for the hydraulics. Got 'em the third time, though."

"You missed."

"That's what I said." Leebo glanced at the MSE unit. "Had some help, though."

Dash laughed and shook his head, his heart struggling to return to a normal rhythm. "You're something else."

"I'm a souped-up LE-BO2D9 Cybot Galactica repair droid. I am *not* something else."

"Hey!" Han appeared in the hatchway that led to the cockpit. "What are you two doing down here, throwing a party?"

Once Han recovered from finding a dead, armor-plated assassin in his secret cargo compartments, they confirmed his demise, stripped him of his weaponry, and put him in a contraband stasis pod that Han had added to his equipage. Dash had wanted to flush the Anomid out an air lock, but Han was insistent that there surely must be a bounty on him somewhere that could bring them some "serious credits."

Dash wasn't sure how he felt about making money from Edge's death, but he supposed there was a certain poetic justice to it. Maybe he could find Eaden's cousin or sister, give some of the bounty to them.

He was more intrigued by the alleged glitch that Leebo blamed for the assassin's destruction. The droid said he didn't want to talk about it—said it was humiliating to a mechanism of his capacity to have so badly missed a target. He was perfectly willing, though, to describe how he'd been alone aboard the *Millennium Falcon*—or rather how he *should* have been alone aboard the *Millennium Falcon*—when he realized there was another presence on the vessel. He'd seen Edge move from concealment in the aft hold and had hidden himself in the compartment beneath the deck plating.

"It didn't occur to you to call me?"

"It *did* occur to me to call you, but I figured that if I did that while you were chatting with the nice soldiers it might cause problems for you. So I decided to wait until you came back aboard."

"Which we did," noted Dash, "but you *still* didn't call me."

"Well, you see, I ran into a bit of a problem. I was hiding in the secret compartment there, when this big ugly guy moved in right next door. If I'd made a peep . . ."

Dash nodded. "Yeah, he'd have scragged you."

"Precisely. So, I waited him out. When he popped out of hiding, I figured to drop the lid on him, so to speak."

"And missed."

"And missed. Much to my dismay, of course. It was a humbling experience."

"You've got a BlasTech sighting mechanism built into

your optics," Dash reminded the droid. "Practically brand new. You trying to tell me it's faulty?"

"Must've gotten misaligned somehow," Leebo said blandly. "I ran a diagnostic, so it should be aces now."

"Aces."

"There's that echo again. You on some sort of repeat loop, boss?"

"Don't change the subject. That's a helluva glitch to result in the death of a sentient, don't you think?"

Leebo was silent for a moment, then said, "He was not a pleasant sentient. Initially, you seemed pleased that I . . . neutralized him."

Leebo, Dash had come to know, tended to retreat to a more droidlike way of self-expression when cornered. Right now, he sounded almost like Oto. "I can't say I was unhappy about it, no. If you hadn't shot him—"

"I didn't shoot him. I shot the hydraulics and missed."

"Okay. If you hadn't missed the hydraulics, we probably wouldn't be having this conversation and you'd belong to Han."

"Force forbid," said Leebo with a metallic shudder.

"You don't like Han?"

"He treats me like a machine."

"You *are* a machine."

"There, you see? His attitudes are rubbing off on you. I'll be pleased to return to Tatooine."

They did that—uneventfully, thank the stars—some ten standard days later, moving at flank speed and making only one stop for fuel at a little outpost off the beaten track. In Mos Eisley, they discovered—much to Han's glee—that he'd been right about Edge. There was a bounty on his masked and helmeted head. Dead or alive. It seemed that in executing some of his Black Sun contracts, he had assassinated a rogue Vigo who happened to be the favorite nephew of the Mandalore, himself. The ruling council of the New Mandalorian tribes had therefore put a bounty on him.

Han was altogether too tickled by the idea that he had done what Boba Fett had not.

"*You* didn't do anything, Han, old buddy," Dash reminded him as he, Han, and Leebo left the Mandalorian "embassy"—a suite of rooms in the Dowager Queen Hotel. "In fact, *I* didn't do anything except almost get myself staked to the decking with a darkstick. Leebo killed the assassin."

"I did not," Leebo objected. "And I'll thank you to stop saying that I did. Last thing I want is to get a reputation as a rogue droid. I simply missed my target. It was a glitch in my software, which I have fixed. I was merely trying to disable him or slow him down so you could deal with him."

"There, you see? Even Leebo says he didn't do it," argued Han. "He can't spend the bounty anyway. He's just a machine."

Leebo's head swiveled toward Dash. "See what I mean?"

"Oh, can it, tin pot," growled Han. "Look, Dash, d'you feel a fifty–fifty split is unfair?"

Dash shook his head. They'd had this argument all the way back from Alderaan. Dash maintained that since he'd nearly been killed by the assassin three times and his droid had "neutralized" him he might be entitled to 60 percent. Han argued that since *he* had rescued Dash from the first attempted assassination and helped Javul Charn complete her mission *and* the kill had taken place aboard the *Millennium Falcon,* he'd easily earned a full half—if not more. Dash had agreed to the fifty–fifty split mostly because he was tired of listening to Han go on about it.

"It's fine. Really. I've got enough to bail *Outrider* out

of Kerlew's dock. In fact, I think Leebo and I will just drop over there right now and pay him off."

"You sure? I was gonna suggest we pop in to Chalmun's for a glass of ale. My treat. Supposed to meet Chewie there today. I hope he's got something lined up—that bounty money'll just about cover most of my existing debts."

They'd reached the turning at Kerner Plaza from which they could see the façade of the cantina. Dash gazed up the street. "Tempting, but no. I really want to get back to *Outrider*. Been away too long. I miss her. And besides," he added frowning, "there's too many stormtroopers around today. Makes me nervous."

There were indeed a number of the white-armored soldiers roaming about, some congregated right in front of Chalmun's.

Han shrugged. "Have it your way. See you later, then?"

"Maybe. Say hello to Chewie for me."

"Will do." Han held out his hand, and the two men clasped forearms in a gesture of friendly solidarity.

"It wasn't a bad adventure," Han said. "Lucrative, anyway. Sorry about your girlfriend turning out to be a Rebel and all that. I know . . . that's gotta sting."

Dash met Han's eyes. They were uncharacteristically solemn. "Yeah, well. I'll get over it. Smooth spacing."

"Same to you." Han turned on his heel and whistled as he strode toward Chalmun's.

Dash and Leebo started across the plaza, Dash noticing once again, somewhat uneasily, the large numbers of stormtroopers. They continued on to Spacers' Row and the docking facility. Dash was relieved to note that his passcode still activated the security lock on the street access for Docking Bay 92. That meant Javul had been as good as her word and had paid all the repair and docking fees. Otherwise, Kerlew would have most likely changed the code.

"It'll be real good to get back aboard the old girl," he told Leebo as they entered the bay. "I missed having my own command."

The lights came on as the motion sensors picked up their presence and Dash stared blankly at what they revealed—an empty bay. The *Outrider* was gone.

"Huh," said Leebo. "Looks like you'll have to miss it a bit longer."

THIRTY-THREE

"I COMPLETED THE REPAIRS ABOUT FIVE DAYS AFTER you and Han lifted off," Kerlew told Dash as they sat in his preternaturally neat office-*cum*-workshop. "Would've been done a day earlier but we had to recable the auxiliary power bus to the port hyperdrive."

Dash sat forward in his formchair. "Ker, where's my ship?"

"I'm getting to that. About ten days later, I got a message from Charn's road manager telling me they were going to need to move the ship for security reasons. About a week ago, a pilot and crew came and paid off all the repairs and docking fees and added a fat bonus to lie to anyone other than you who asked after her whereabouts. They took her."

Dash felt a chill glide down his spine. "*Did* anyone else ask after her whereabouts?"

Kerlew nodded, looking grimmer than Dash had ever seen him. "Imperials. An Imperial colonel and a six-pack of stormtroopers. Dash, what the hell were you *doing*?"

"He was saving the galaxy," said Leebo drily.

Dash glared at him. "I was guarding a celebrity with stalker problems. They just turned out to be bigger problems than I was led to believe."

"Imperial stalkers?" Ker shook his head. "That's pretty big."

"You have no idea." Dash tried to relax, to lean back

in his chair and look unflustered. "Okay. So, where did they take her?"

"I don't know. They didn't say. They only left this." *This* was a data wafer, which Kerlew extracted from his vest pocket and handed over to Dash. "It's passcoded," he added.

Dash glanced up from the wafer. "What's the code?"

"Two ships. They said you'd understand."

He didn't understand at first, but it came to him pretty quickly. So after they'd checked their credit balance and gotten a comfortable room in a hotel somewhat less up-scale than the Dowager Queen, he slid the data wafer into the computer terminal in their room and entered the phrase *Nova's Heart Deep Core*. That didn't work. Frustrated, he tried a few more permutations on the theme and finally cracked the lock with *Nova's Deep Core Heart*.

The message was simple. It was an address. In Tatooine's planetary capital, Bestine. And another passcode. The passcode was followed by a phrase of three words: *Buy new clothes*.

Dash was puzzled. Why in the world would Javul send him to the seat of Imperial power on Tatooine? He knew a moment of apprehension that maybe, just maybe, she was setting him up. Getting rid of him by sending him where he'd be arrested.

But no, that made no sense. What made sense was that she was leading him precisely where no one would look for him. He could only hope that the *Outrider* was at the end of this wild chase.

"Your girlfriend has a quirky sense of humor," Leebo told him, sounding enough like Han to be irritating.

"She's not my girlfriend," Dash said testily.

"You only wish she was, I guess . . . yeah, yeah, I know: shut up, tin man."

Dash did as Javul suggested. He bought new clothes—nice clothes, clothes that made him look more like a successful merchant than a scruffy smuggler. He shaved. He bought a high-end travel bag to keep his new and old clothes in and even made sure Leebo was transformed into a well-oiled, shiny droid.

They took the regular shuttle to Bestine first thing in the morning, debarking at the central terminus and stepping out into the gleaming streets of the capital city. Bestine was the most cosmopolitan and largest settlement on Tatooine, a city of sculpted, graceful stone buildings the same color as the desert and ruddy mountains that ringed it.

They took a speeder cab to the address they'd been given. The route took them past the capitol building, a beautiful, domed structure—the tallest in Bestine. It was now guarded by Imperial stormtroopers, who looked incongruously out of place there. Their white body armor was blinding in the light of Tatooine's two suns.

The address turned out to be an inn. The data wafer directed them to the "Bright Sun" suite, and the second passcode admitted them to a suite of rooms that was, without any exaggeration, the most luxurious residence Dash had been in since he was a boy. He hadn't even imagined a place like this existed on Tatooine, but of course, it must. The wealthy, the celebrated, and the diplomatically important must be lodged somewhere. He was none of those things, and felt conspicuous because of it. But oddly, none of the staff or residents of the inn seemed to find him of the least interest. He was just one more well-heeled resident.

In the suite's opulent study was a HoloNet terminal to which Dash went immediately upon their arrival. Behind him in the living room, Leebo uttered a metallic sigh and dropped the travel bag. His heart rate rising, Dash activated the terminal and saw that there was a message on it.

"Play message," he told it.

"Voice recognition necessary," said the terminal in a prissy female voice. "Please repeat this phrase: *Bantha flop.*"

"What?"

"Inappropriate response. Please repeat: *Bantha flop.*"

"*Bantha flop.*" Leebo was right—his girlfriend did have a quirky sense of humor.

And of course, it was Javul. She shimmered into existence, looking achingly lovely and equally unattainable. She was dressed in traditional Alderaanian style—a floor-length gown of deep blue with a sash of woven gold and silver that matched her hair, which was done up in elaborate braids. He thought her smile was wistful. Or maybe he only hoped it was.

"My cousin got the present you sent," she said brightly. "It was everything she hoped for. We can't thank you enough—no, really—we can't. I hope someday I get to thank you in person. But in the meantime, I've arranged a little surprise for you. A token of my appreciation and affection. It's in slip 4134A at the Bestine Port Authority. You can pick it up whenever you like."

He sagged back into the chair, relief flooding him. The *Outrider* was safe. Safe and repaired and waiting for him a stone's throw away. He took a deep breath and let it out. Just for the moment, then, he did belong here. He gazed up into Javul's holographic face.

As if she were reading his mind across time and space, she said: "I hope you'll stay and enjoy the other part of my gift awhile. At least until things calm down a bit in the outside world. You deserve it. I've made sure both your room and board—not to mention bar tab—are open-ended." She hesitated, and now there was no doubt about the wistfulness in her eyes and her smile. "I wish I could see you again. It's not fair, you know, because you can see me anytime you want."

That much was true, Dash reflected as he reached out his hand to freeze the image. She gazed down at him through those amazing silver eyes, smiling. He could see Javul Charn just about anytime he wanted merely by firing up the HoloNet and watching one of her shows.

He just wasn't sure whether that was a good thing or a bad thing. But it was definitely a true thing.

He reached out again and unfroze the image. An instant after he did so, the holo changed to a wider angle, showing two women side by side. One was Javul—the other was the dark-haired beauty she'd been with back on Alderaan. This time he recognized her. He blinked in astonishment.

Princess Leia Organa?

Javul's *cousin*?

Couldn't be . . .

"Well," he heard Leebo murmur from behind him, "she *did* say she had friends in high places . . ."

Dash didn't respond. He was thinking about what it must be like to have climbed up from rags to not just riches, but royalty . . . to be able to indulge a friend in one of the classiest hotels in this section of the Rim for an indefinite time . . . to be able to do all that and yet be willing to sacrifice it all—to risk political prison and very possibly execution—to attempt to free a galaxy.

Javul Charn was quite a woman.

"So," Leebo said, "y'gonna enlist after all, boss?"

Dash was quiet for some time. Then he grinned and shook his head. "Tell you what," he said. "When Han Solo joins the revolution—*that's* when I'll join."

"From what I've seen of Han Solo," Leebo said, "and based upon what I hope is an unbiased and unsentimental view of sentient behavior, I think you're pretty safe, then. Because Solo would have to be frozen in carbonite before he'd hold still for that."

"Exactly," Dash said. "No worries, then." He stood, stretched, and looked about. "Didn't I see a carafe of Corellian brandy somewhere around here?"

Read on for an excerpt from *Red Harvest*
by Joe Schreiber

Available now in print format

3/DEEP-DOWN TRAUMA HOUNDS

NICKTER AWOKE IN THE CAGE.

He had no memory of how he'd gotten here, or how long he'd been inside. The last thing he remembered was sitting in the infirmary, waiting for Arljack to come back and check the wound on the back of his neck. And in fact, for one disoriented moment, he thought he was still there. *It's cold in here,* he'd started to say. *Hey, Arl, you mind turning up the heat a little bit?*

But this was not the infirmary.

He tried to sit up and slammed his head against the metal bars above him hard enough to make him let out an angry moan of pain. Just exactly what was going on here? The cage was small, forcing him to remain hunched forward, either on his hands and knees or in a slouch-shouldered sitting position. The top part of his tunic had been ripped away, leaving him naked from the waist up. His back hurt, *really* hurt, from the base of his skull all the way down to the bottom of his spine—a low, steady throb that made his molars ache.

As if to mock his immediate claustrophobic situation, the room outside the cage was very large, and very dark. From inside, Nickter could see almost all of it. It was a circular space, perhaps fifty meters across, illuminated by an irregular assemblage of flashing monitor equipment, candles, and torchlight. Laboratory equipment crowded every available surface and corner. Pipes and wires were draped from tables and desks, connecting odd piles of disjointed equipment, condensers, flasks, beakers, and burners. The walls were glass, and although he couldn't see anything out there but darkness, Nickter had the vague feeling that he was very high up.

Sudden realization blindsided him.

He was at the top of the tower.

"You're awake," a voice said.

Nickter jerked upright at the sound of the voice and very nearly screamed.

Standing outside the cage, staring down at him, was a tall, broad-shouldered, black-robed figure that blended almost imperceptibly into the shadows. Nickter already knew exactly who it was, even before the flickering torchlight of the room revealed the man's face—a long sculpture of bone and half-lidded eyes, the famous curvature of the peaked upper lip, how it always seemed to be smiling slightly at some secret thought. A fresh spasm of apprehension leapt through him, raising hackles across his back. The eyes were the worst part, he thought: how almost silver they were, how they seemed to glitter with a feverish accumulation of ambition and indifference.

"Lord Scabrous," he said, or tried to say. His mouth felt parched, and his lungs couldn't seem to get enough air. "What am I doing here?"

The Sith Lord didn't answer. But the eyes kept staring down at him . . . past him, somehow, as if there was something else inside the cage with him.

He could smell himself, the stale cheap grease of panic and perspiration seeping through his skin. The pain in his back had intensified from a throb to a sharp stabbing agony that shot down his ribs and up into his neck. It was getting worse by the second, like the sting of sweat in an open wound. Whatever injury had been inflicted upon him, it was deep, and whole packs of nerve receptors—those obedient trauma hounds—were circling back and forth, busily delivering the bad news.

Groping around behind him, Nickter felt something cold and smooth and hard sticking out of his skin just above the base of his spine. He looked around and saw what Scabrous had been looking at—it was some kind of tube, implanted directly into a vertebra. The sticky ring of exposed flesh around the wound site felt raw and hot, swollen, and it burned when he touched it. Sliding his hand upward, he felt another tube above it, and another, coming out of his back, all the way up to his neck. There were at least six of them protruding out of him, as big around as his finger. He realized that he could feel them pulsating inside his spinal canal—that was the source of the gnawing pain.

"What . . . what is this?" he asked, aware of how different his voice sounded already, high-pitched and wobbly. "What did you do to me?"

Scabrous still didn't answer. He wasn't even looking at Nickter anymore. He had walked around behind the cage now, where the tubes ran between the wire bars into what looked like some kind of mechanized pump with a wide flask mounted on top.

Rattling around inside the cage, Nickter stared at it. The flask was full of murky reddish yellow liquid. Next to the pump sat a small black pyramid covered in lines of engraved text—what he realized, through his pain and fear, had to be a Sith Holocron. They'd learned about it at the academy, but he'd never actually seen one before.

And then he saw other things, dozens of them, in glass bottles lined up across the wide platform next to the pump.

Flowers.

All black.

All different.

All dead.

Nickter squirmed in the cage. None of this made any sense, and the irrationality only intensified his mounting terror. He was sweating profusely now—it was *dripping* off him in big, oozing droplets. The urge to beg, to grovel, to bargain for his

life, or at least for an end to the pain, was almost irresist-
ible. The only thing that stopped him was the suspicion, based
on everything he'd heard about Scabrous, that the Sith Lord
wouldn't even listen. Scabrous stood behind the cage, alter-
nating his attention between the flowers and the Holocron.
Finally he selected a flower, opened the glass chamber on top
of the pump, and dropped it inside.

"What is that?" Nickter asked. "What are you doing?"

Scabrous glanced at him, as if hearing him for the first time.
When he finally spoke, his voice was low and resonant, deeper
than Nickter remembered. There was an awful intimacy to it,
as though the Sith Lord were whispering directly in his ear.

"You were humiliated today at the temple, Wim Nickter—
humiliated *badly*. You have shown yourself to be weak and
easily defeated."

"It was Lussk!" Nickter burst out. "He used the Force on
me, he—"

Scabrous lifted his hand. "There is still one way in which
you may yet prove useful. That is the offer I make to you, one
of redemption."

Then he pressed a button on the pump.

Staring at it, Nickter saw the black flower swirling in the
reddish yellow fluid, its petals shredding as it dissolved. The
pump let out a faint whining noise, like half a dozen odd vacuum parts called into dubious service. At first he felt nothing
except for the odd vibration of the tubes in his back.

Then the pain he'd been enduring up till now became
abruptly, horribly worse. It slammed through his body, goug-
ing through every millimeter of his nerve endings, turning
them white-hot.

Nickter arched forward and screamed. The pain owned him:
he surrendered to it utterly. It became a vast, all-encompassing
neutron star, and as it sucked him forward he saw Scabrous
watching him through the cage.

The last thing Nickter saw before he blacked out was Scabrous turning away from him, swinging his arm across the

long counter above the pump, sending the flowers and their vessels crashing to floor.

4/DRANOK

PERGUS FRODE DIDN'T MIND HIS MAINTENANCE DUTIES AT the academy's landing pad. It meant he got the first look at the new arrivals, often a pretty sorry lot, and he was privy to some sensitive information even before some of the Sith Masters found out about it. Not a bad gig for a pilot-turned-grease-monkey whose last job had been wiping down engines at the Kuat Drive Yards.

Tonight, for instance—when the Corellian cruiser banked and began descending into the snow-strewn landing lights— Frode knew exactly who it was. He would have known even if Darth Scabrous's HK droid hadn't been standing right next to him, whirring softly to itself in anticipation. Frode didn't mind droids—most of the time he actually preferred them to organic life-forms, especially on Odacer-Faustin.

"Statement: I shall alert Lord Scabrous, sir," the HK said, "that his guests have arrived."

"Sure, good," Frode said, watching as the cruiser extended its landing gear, feeling the decks absorb its settling tonnage. A moment later the main hatchway whooshed open, and the landing ramp dropped down with an unceremonious *clank*.

Coming forward to meet it, Frode watched as the two bounty hunters stepped down—*swaggered* down was more like it. The first, a tall, stocky, bald man with a permanent sneer in green-tinted goggles, stopped at the bottom of the ramp and looked around disdainfully as if he wasn't at all sure he even wanted to stay. He was carrying a metal case under one arm, linked to his wrist with a thin chain.

"What do you think, Skarl?" the bald man asked. "Cold enough for you?"

The flight-suited Nelvaanian standing next to him wrinkled

his snout and gave a brief snarl, revealing a row of sharp, inward-pointing upper teeth. Then he and the man both turned and glared at Frode, who had already taken a step back.

"Where's Scabrous?" the man demanded, lifting the metal case. "We brought his package. He's supposed to meet us here."

"I will take you to Lord Scabrous, sir," the HK said, gesturing back in the direction of the academy's main grounds. "He is my master, and I have been dispatched to escort you to the Tower. You and your"—the droid glanced uncertainly at the Nelvaanian—"copilot?"

"Skarl's my partner," the man said. "My name's Dranok. Anything that's worth having in this galaxy, you can get through us." He made no move to follow the HK. "Speaking of which, your boss better have the rest of the credits he owes me for this little beauty. It wasn't exactly easy to procure."

The HK responded promptly. "Answer: Payment has been arranged in full, sir. Rest assured that you will receive it shortly."

Dranok nodded, the surly expression never quite leaving his lips as he glanced around the snowy terrain surrounding the landing pad. "What a pit." Glancing at Frode, he jerked one thumb back in the direction of the ship. "Keep her hot, Ace. We're not staying on this rock one second longer than we have to. And refuel her while you're at it—think you can handle that?"

"Sure," Frode said, "no problem." He'd already decided he didn't care for the man or his partner, but he was careful not to let it show in his voice. "It'll be ready when you get back."

Ignoring him, the bounty hunter turned and followed the droid with the Nelvaanian easily keeping pace to his right, paws crunching in the snow.

By the time they reached the tower, Dranok had already decided how he was going to handle this.

Right up to the moment they'd landed, he hadn't been entirely sure about his course of action. It was nothing personal:

he and Skarl had always worked together well enough. The Nelvaanian was a superior tracker, and always good in a fight. Plus he was loyal, a trait that Dranok obviously didn't share. But money-wise, things hadn't been going so well lately—their last few jobs weren't paying as much as he'd hoped, and Dranok was tired of splitting everything down the middle.

So it was settled, then. Once Scabrous paid the balance of what he owed them—

"Statement: It's through here, sir," the HK said, gesturing up at the tower. "Right this way."

Dranok paused in his tracks and looked up. He'd seen some weird architecture in his time, but the Sith Lord's tower was unsettling in a different way. It was imposing, yes, and much taller than it had looked from the air, but there was another quality to it, an indefinable sense of wrongness, as if it had been built at some unnatural angle so that it seemed to curl down on top of him like an immense black claw. He'd once overheard talk in some spaceport about the Sith, how they'd learned to manipulate spatial geometry itself, creating buildings that were, in themselves, detached from physical reality. The guy telling the story had claimed you could get lost inside a Sith labyrinth and never escape. Dranok had dismissed it as a lot of drunken superstition, but looking at the tower now, he wasn't sure. He didn't like standing in front of it, and liked even less the idea of going inside.

But that was where the payment was.

And that settled it.

"All right." He turned to Skarl. "You better wait out here, just in case something goes wrong."

The Nelvaanian looked at him and gave an uneasy growl. *This isn't how we normally do things,* that growl said. *This isn't standard operating procedure.*

"Hey," Dranok said, with all the brusque, hail-fellow-well-met heartiness that he could muster, "trust me, will ya? We're both safer if you're out here watching the door. I'll settle up with Scabrous and bring the money out."

And before Skarl had a chance to argue, he followed the droid inside.

Even though they were out of the wind, Dranok felt the temperature drop sharply. It was dark enough that his first few steps were guided mainly by the pale blue lightspill from the HK's dorsal processor array. A second or two later, his eyes began to adjust and he could make out the wide, circular space around them, supported by pillars and massive stone arches that made up the tower's lowest level. The air smelled wet and dirty, and there was an unpleasantly musty human component to it that reminded him of the bathhouses on some of the Inner Rim planets he'd visited.

"Statement: Follow me," the HK's voice said from up ahead, gesturing to a waiting turbolift. Dranok ducked inside, and as the door sealed shut behind him, he realized that the droid had not followed.

He was alone.

The turbolift shot upward fast enough to leave his stomach behind. Dranok felt the first prickle of unease down the small of his back. The lift was still rising. Was it taking him all the way to the top?

Finally it halted, and the doors opened.

"Lord Scabrous?" Dranok called out, loud enough to make himself heard. "Your droid sent me up." He realized that he was holding the metal case in front of him like a shield. "I brought your package."

Silence. It was a big circular room—to his eyes, it looked like a laboratory furnished by somebody with a serious fetish for the arcane. Dranok had heard that some of these Sith Lords could be decidedly peculiar, mixing technology with the ancient ways of their people, preserving the old ways whenever possible. This proved it.

Tall arching windows made up the surrounding walls, with sconces, candles, and torches protruding above them, along with pulsing panels and banks of lights. Machinery hummed with a low, irregular drone that made the air it-self seem to vibrate in Dranok's nostrils and the pit of his throat. He made his way past the piles and tables of scientific equipment, not particularly liking the way the torches made his shadow leap and twitch across the bare stone floor behind him, as if there was someone following on his heels. A smell hung in the air, thick and familiar but as yet indefinable—chemicals? No, it was sweeter than that, almost cloying, like a cooking smell.

He walked over to the window and glanced down through the falling snow at the academy below. From here it looked like a ruin, abandoned and forgotten. The occasional faint glimmers of light that burned in the windows of one of the buildings—some kind of dorm, he assumed—only made it look more hollow somehow, a place that had fallen into the possession of ghosts.

You're getting jumpy, he scolded himself. *Cut it out.*

He turned and walked back toward a stack of machinery half buried in shadow. Something crunched under his boot, and he paused to look at it.

Flowers.

Squatting, the bounty hunter set the metal case aside—it was still cuffed to his wrist—and reached into his pocket for a glow rod. He switched it on, shining it down in front of him. The crunching had come from broken glass, test tubes or vessels that Dranok guessed had held the different species, before they'd all been dumped or thrown unceremoniously across the floor.

He opened the metal case and looked at his own flower, the alleged Murakami orchid itself, comparing it with all of those scattered over the cobblestones. The black-market spice dealer who'd sold it to him had guaranteed that it was a genuine article, the rarest in the galaxy, stolen from a secret Republic bio-lab on Endor. The dealer had even provided him documented proof, complex chemical and gas spectroscopy equations that Dranok had pretended to understand.

But now, looking at these other flowers on the floor—rejects all—Dranok found at least two that looked exactly like it.

His breath caught in his throat.

He'd been duped, and now—

"Dranok."

The bounty hunter froze at the sound of his own name, the voice turning his breath to dry ice in his lungs. Up ahead, standing between him and the exit, a tall, dark-cloaked figure gazed back at him from the other side of a long stone table. Dranok realized that he was looking into the face of a man with long, refined features, the aquiline nose, raked brow, and prominent cheekbones stretched out until they were almost a caricature of arrogance. Thick gray hair, a strange silvery blue color, swept back away from his forehead. The figure extended one long-fingered hand, gesturing him forward, and at the same moment Dranok saw the man's eyes flicker and pulse as if reflecting the burst of some far-off explosion.

"Lord Scabrous."

"Did you bring the orchid?"

"I—"

"Where is it?"

A bluff, then—the bounty hunter realized that it was his only way out. He had bluffed his way out of tight spots before. This would be no different.

"This is it," he said with manufactured brusqueness, holding up the open case to show its contents. "The Murakami orchid, as you requested."

When Darth Scabrous didn't move to take it—in fact, he didn't seem to move at all—Dranok unlocked the chain from his wrist, set the case down in front of the Sith Lord, and stepped back. Still, Scabrous made no indication of coming around to examine the flower. His eyes remained locked on Dranok.

"Did you come alone?"

"My associate is waiting outside," Dranok said. "Just in case."

"Your associate."

"That's right."

"And you have brought no one else with you?"

Dranok scowled a little. "Who else would I have brought?"

Scabrous apparently didn't judge the question worthy of reply. The bounty hunter frowned, genuinely flummoxed now,
his confusion only tightening the clenched fist of anxiety in his
guts. "Enough questions," he shot back, hoping the tone of
impatience might help mask the fear. "I delivered the orchid as
we agreed. Now where's my money?"

Scabrous still didn't make any move to respond. The moment stretched, and in the pursuant silence Dranok realized
that he smelled something else gathering around him, growing
more potent, stronger than the reek of dead flowers: an aroma
of roasting meat that had slowly begun to fill the air. Despite
the tension, he felt his mouth beginning to water. It had been a
while since he'd eaten. His stomach gave a noisy growl.

"You have failed me," Scabrous said.

"What?"

"That is not the Murakami orchid."

"How can you tell? You haven't even looked at it!"

Scabrous lifted his head slowly. His entire body appeared
to stiffen, to grow taller somehow—an illusion, certainly, but
Dranok still felt himself taking a step back, like an unruly
child being taken to task, spreading his hands out in supplica-
tion. "Now, wait a second—"

"Sit down."

Dranok felt his knees buckle involuntarily, and he dropped
down hard on the stone bench that he hadn't realized was
there.

"Despite your failure, your payment awaits you." Scabrous
gestured behind him, to an arched doorway that Dranok
hadn't noticed before, and the HK droid stepped out pushing
a cart with a huge silver tray on top. The droid wheeled the
cart to the table and set down a plate and utensils in front of
Dranok, along with a cup and a pitcher. "Help yourself."

Dranok shook his head. Whatever was underneath the lid of

the silver tray, he wanted no part of it. And he realized now, with the merciless clarity of hindsight, how everything he'd done—taking the job, trusting the shady fence who had sold him the orchid, coming back up here alone—had all been links in some colossally ill-advised chain of disaster leading up to this penultimate moment of reckoning. Yet he could not stop his hand from stretching forward toward the platter.

And reaching out, he lifted the lid.

He stared at what lay underneath, sudden horror piling up inside his throat like a clogged siphon. It took less than a second to realize that the shaggy thing in front of him was the severed, stewed head of his partner, Skarl. The Nelvaanian's mouth had been pried open wide enough to accommodate the ripe red jaquira fruit that had been thrust between its jaws. Dead, boiled eyes gaped up at him with what almost looked like accusation.

"What's wrong?" Scabrous's voice intoned, from what sounded like very far away. "You fully intended to betray him, did you not? I simply saved you the trouble." And then, leaning forward: "A traitor and an incompetent. One wonders how either one of you managed to survive this long."

Dranok tried to stand up and discovered that he couldn't lift his weight from the chair. Suddenly every part of him seemed to weigh a ton.

"Let me go."

"Every traitor makes a meal of his allies." Scabrous held up a knife and fork in front of the bounty hunter's face. "This is your last meal, Dranok, and you must eat it, every morsel. That is the offer I present to you. If you can do that, I will allow you to walk out of here alive."

Dranok recoiled, struggling harder to pull himself free. But the only part of his body that he could move was his right hand, the one that Scabrous was allowing him to lift in the direction of the dining utensils. Jaw clenched, he grasped the knife from the Sith Lord's hand—and then thrust it forward, as hard as he could.

The knife didn't even get close to its intended target. Scabrous flicked his own hand in the bounty hunter's direction, a simple, almost offhand gesture, an act of disinterested dismissal, and Dranok felt his throat pinch shut, his windpipe siphoning down to a pinhole. A sharp and immediate weight seemed to have clamped down over his lungs. Tears of panic flooded his eyes, and his heart started pounding as he thrashed frantically in the seat, blackness already closing in around the edges of his vision. All at once everything seemed to be happening from a great distance away.

As Scabrous released him, allowing him to slump down from the seat to the floor, the last thing Dranok heard was the sound of some kind of creature shuffling and breathing and making a noise that sounded oddly like laughter.

Star Wars: Knight Errant
John Jackson Miller

A thousand years before Luke Skywalker, a generation before Darth Bane, in a galaxy far, far away . . .

The Republic is in crisis. The Sith roam unchecked, vying with one another to dominate the galaxy. But one lone Jedi, Kerra Holt, is determined to take down the Dark Lords. Her enemies are strange and many: Lord Daiman, who imagines himself the creator of the universe; Lord Odion, who intends to be its destroyer; the curious siblings Quillan and Dromika; the enigmatic Arkadia. So many warring Sith weaving a patchwork of brutality – with only Kerra Holt to defend the innocents caught underfoot.

Sensing a sinister pattern in the chaos, Kerra embarks on a journey that will take her into fierce battles against even fiercer enemies. With one against so many, her only chance of success lies with forging alliances among those who serve her enemies – including a mysterious Sith spy and a clever mercenary general. But will they be her adversaries or her salvation?

'Beautifully written, this title is one that will really satisfy the reader' **** *Emotionally Fourteen*

'[a] well-written set-up for what promises to be an exciting new action adventure series'
www.starwarsaficionado.com

arrow books

STAR WARS
THE OLD REPUBLIC

IN A GALAXY DIVIDED
YOU MUST CHOOSE A SIDE

CREATE YOUR OWN EPIC STORY

IN THIS HIGHLY ANTICIPATED

MULTI-PLAYER ONLINE VIDEOGAME

YOUR SAGA BEGINS AT
WWW.STARWARSTHEOLDREPUBLIC.COM